WESTWARD

FORGE BOOKS BY DALE L. WALKER

Legends and Lies
The Boys of '98: Theodore Roosevelt and the Rough Riders
Bear Flag Rising: The Conquest of California, 1846
Pacific Destiny: The Three-Century Journey to the Oregon Country
Eldorado: The California Gold Rush
Westward: A Fictional History of the American West

WESTWARD

A Fictional History
of the American West

28 Original Stories Celebrating
the 50th Anniversary of Western Writers of America

EDITED BY

DALE L. WALKER

A Tom Doherty Associates Book
New York

WESTWARD: A FICTIONAL HISTORY OF THE AMERICAN WEST

Introduction and Notes copyright © 2003 by Dale L. Walker

A Forge Book
Published by Tom Doherty Associates, LLC
175 Fifth Avenue
New York, NY 10010

www.tor.com

Forge® is a registered trademark of Tom Doherty Associates, LLC.

Library of Congress Cataloging-in-Publication Data

Westward : a fictional history of the American West : 28 original stories celebrating the 50th anniversary of Western Writers of America / edited by Dale L. Walker.—1st ed.
    p.   cm.
"A Tom Doherty Associates book."
ISBN 0-765-30451-1
1. Western stories. 2. Historical fiction, American. I. Walker, Dale L. II. Western Writers of America.

PS648.W4W479   2003
813'.0810878—dc21

2002045481

First Edition: June 2003

Printed in the United States of America

0 9 8 7 6 5 4 3 2 1

Copyright Acknowledgments

*

Eastward I go only by force; but westward I go free. . . .
And that way the nation is progressing. . . .
—Henry David Thoreau (1817–1862)

Contents

INTRODUCTION

In the 180 years of the life of the Western story, that only unique American literary form, every Western writer has paid a debt to the historical record.

James Fenimore Cooper's Leatherstocking saga (*The Deerslayer, The Last of the Mohicans, The Pathfinder, The Pioneers,* and *The Prairie*), written between 1823 and 1841, not only gave us Natty Bumppo and Chingachgook, two of the enduring characters of Western literature, but presented with great accuracy their pre–Revolutionary War milieu.

In a thirty-year span, Zane Grey produced something like sixty-five Western novels and six or eight story collections. He traveled, explored, and hunted in the lands he wrote about and studied their histories assiduously. (Imagine evoking the Utah country in the days of Mormon dominion better than he in *Riders of the Purple Sage,* or a historically truer fictional treatment of the transcontinental railroad than *The U.P. Trail,* or a better treatment of reservation Indians than in *The Vanishing American.*)

Louis L'Amour (a longtime WWA member) wrote 108 books, most of them Westerns, between 1950 and his death in 1988, and researched his stories in his travels and from a vast home library of historical books. In 1981, at the Santa Rosa, California, Western Writers conference at which he received the Saddleman Award, he told the audience that his favorite reading materials were pioneer diaries. (*Hondo,* the novel that made him famous, with John Wayne's movie version assistance, was a gritty, historically sound evocation of the Apache campaigns in the Southwest; *Sitka* had the Alaska purchase as its backdrop; the Sackett family saga of seventeen novels was meticulously researched, from the family's origins in Elizabethan England to their adventures in the Carolinas, Tennessee, the Southwest, California, and Mexico. The Talon and Chantry sagas were also solidly "historical.")

Even the old dime novelist and pulp writer usually* knew something about the sidearm his hero wore and the horse he rode in on, and set his story in a place at least dimly familiar as the Old West. Many of the founding members of Western Writers of America, virtually all of them graduates of the College of the Pulps, discovered when they began writing for the "slicks"—the *Saturday Evening Post, Liberty, Collier's,* and the like—that historical accuracy in their tales was demanded by editors and expected by sophisticated readers.

The modern Western writer has a keener fidelity to history than any of his predecessors, whether in writing the "traditional" Western story—usually imaginary events in an imaginary setting—or what has become known as the "historical," in which events, places, and often the characters are rooted in the historical record. The old-style Western story still has an audience, predictions of its imminent demise notwithstanding, but is growing more historical, with more authentic backdrops and more realistic plots and characters. The true Western "historical," often deriving from some actual event—the Oregon Trail, the Alamo, the Little Bighorn battle—and the real characters participating in such events, requires greater discipline, more research and historical knowledge, more invention. But the result, when the writer combines his narrative gift with the unimprovable drama of the *real* American West—its humor, horror, romance, and sheer poetry, its cast of characters beyond human invention—is a greater story.

IN *WESTWARD* THE SAGA OF THE OLD AMERICAN WEST UNFOLDS in twenty-eight stories, from the sighting by an Indian of a weird elk-dog creature—a horse—in Kansas in 1541, to a gunbattle in a Utah copper mine in 1913. Between these are tales of the Lewis and Clark expedition, mountain men, the Alamo, the California gold rush, the massacres at Mountain Meadows and Sand Creek and on the Bozeman Trail, battles on the Rosebud and Little Bighorn and at Adobe Walls, the Civil War in the West, the Apache campaigns, and the Texas Rangers. Here too are stories of fevers, blizzards, droughts, and lone-

---

*But certainly not always, as proven in Bill Pronzini's hilarious 1997 book, *Six-Gun in Cheek,* an "Affectionate Guide to the Worst in Western Fiction."

liness; of Indians, homesteaders, cowboys and cattlemen, lawmen and outlaws, hunters, miners, and soldiers. Here, living again, are Crazy Horse, Jedediah Smith, Tom Fitzpatrick, and Jim Bridger of the Shining Mountains; Rip Ford and Leander McNelly of the Texas Rangers; Doc Holliday, Libbie Custer, Belle Starr, Billy Dixon, John Chivington, Charlie Russell, King Fisher, John Wesley Hardin, Dan DeQuille of Virginia City; a black slave who crossed the continent with Lewis and Clark; and somebody who looks suspiciously like Buffalo Bill Cody.

Westward is a collection of new stories that tell the history of the Old West; it is a testimonial to the power of the historical Western and its ability to teach and entertain simultaneously; and it is a showcase for the wondrous talent to be found in Western Writers of America, which, in 2003, celebrates the fiftieth anniversary of its founding.

Some of the writers in *Westward* are familiar names, veterans of the Western story, and some are newcomers, a few presenting their first story in print. The beauty of this mixture of old and new, and evidence of the durability of the Western, is that it is difficult to tell who is the veteran and who is the newcomer.

TO THE READER OF *WESTWARD:* THIS IS A JOURNEY THROUGH THE life and times of the Old West. The stories, all of them new and written specifically for this book, are arranged chronologically. Most anthologies can be dipped into anywhere (as can this one), but here, front to back, is an opportunity to take a journey westward through time and place with twenty-eight of the best Western writers as your guide.

Dale L. Walker
El Paso, Texas
August 3, 2002

First Horse

DON COLDSMITH

In 1979, Don Coldsmith had a chat with a Doubleday editor and mentioned an ancient Spanish horse bit that had been found on the Central Plains. "If that bit could talk," Coldsmith said, "we'd have a story." The editor responded instantly, "Write me that story."

In 1980 Doubleday published Coldsmith's *Trail of the Spanish Bit* (now past twenty printings in English plus translations into German and French) and the rest is history—historical fiction of the highest order by one of the preeminent Western writers of all time.

Don Coldsmith is the author of 40 books, 150 magazine articles, and 1,600 newspaper columns. There are more than six million copies of his novels in print.

Born in Iola, Kansas, Coldsmith served as a combat medic in the Pacific in World War Two and earned a doctorate in medicine in 1958. He served thirty years as a family practice physician (delivering more than 3,000 babies!) before closing his office in 1988 to devote his time to writing.

Coldsmith is past president of Western Writers of America, Inc., a Spur Award winner, and an inductee into the Writers Hall of Fame of America.

DREAMER, THE BOY WAS CALLED.
It had never been his real name. When he was born, smooth, soft, and healthy, his family had called him Possum, because of the comical way his hair stuck out in all directions, like that of the namesake animal.

According to the custom of the People, he would wear such a name until his First Dance, in the autumn of his second year. At that time, his grandfather would bestow a name upon him. Usually it would be the grandfather's own name. It was forbidden to speak the name of the dead, so a person must give away his name before he "crossed over." Otherwise, the words that formed that name might be lost from the language of the People. It had happened once, the elders had related at the story fires.

That was not a problem in the case of this child. The grandfather's name was Wolf, and there were others with that name. Any name would be acceptable, but in the end the name bestowed was Little Wolf.

That name too was short-lived. This child, from his birth, had borne a facial expression that made others smile. He had arrived in the world wide-eyed, looking around his mother's lodge with great curiosity. He had the appearance of *understanding* what he saw.

"The spirit of this one is old and wise," said the old woman who had helped with the labor and delivery.

BY THE TIME HE HAD FOUR WINTERS BEHIND HIM, THE BOY HAD established a reputation for puzzling questions.

"Why is grass green?"

"Where do the stars go when they go out?"

"How do the geese know when winter is coming?"

Such a child is both a joy and a frustration for parents.

"Because that is the way it is, Little Wolf," his father would say.

He would spend long periods of time sitting, watching the breeze ripple the grass of the prairie, or the clouds as they drifted overhead. Sometimes his soulful eyes seemed fixed on something at a great distance. He could watch an anthill for half an afternoon, seeming to comprehend their strange ways. A dung beetle, rolling a ball larger than herself, could occupy his attention for half an afternoon.

His parents spoke of these things to the holy man, Sees Beyond.

Sees Beyond studied the child, watched him for part of a day, and spoke to the concerned parents. Yes, he agreed, a special child, one born with the understanding and experience of the ages.

"You can see this in his eyes," he said. "I am made to think that his wisdom will be a great help to the People."

"He will be a leader?" suggested Long Bow, the child's father. "A great hunter?"

Sees Beyond shook his head.

"Not in that way . . . Nor as a warrior. This one is a dreamer. He may already see things not seen by others. See how his eyes are looking into the distance, beyond the hills, maybe beyond earth's edge?"

"This is good, Uncle?" asked the concerned mother, using the term of respect used to address any adult male of the People.

The holy man smiled.

"Of course, Mother. If he uses the gift well."

"And if he does not?"

"Then he will lose the power that such a gift carries. Of course, he must use it for good."

"What do you mean by this?" the boy's father asked. "What 'power'?"

"That of his spirit gift." The holy man was becoming a bit impatient. "This child can see things which will benefit the People. If he does not use the gift, it will disappear. Or, if he uses it against others, it will turn and hurt *him*."

"*Aiee,* all this makes my head hurt!" exclaimed Dove Woman. "How will we know how to teach him?"

Sees Beyond smiled.

"You have an older child, no?"

"That is true. A girl."

"It is good. You know how to raise a child. Now, you treat this one as you would any other. Answer his questions, teach him truth and respect. When he is a bit older . . . But, this one is wise. Maybe he is ready now. Let him come to my lodge sometimes. I will watch and teach him, if you wish."

"It is good," said Long Bow. "Should he go to the Rabbit Society also?"

"Of course! He must learn, as any other child, the ways of the People. His spirit-gift is an extra responsibility."

He paused.

"He could refuse the gift, you know . . . That would avoid the responsibility but he would lose the power. But he is the one to decide. The look in his eyes tells me that he will accept both."

"THE BOY IS THIRSTY FOR LEARNING," SEES BEYOND REPORTED A few days later. Little Wolf had visited the lodge of the holy man and his wife each afternoon. "He is already beginning to see some visions."

"Dreams?" asked Long Bow.

"He is a dreamer. And, he learns quickly. This one is important."

It was not long until some began to refer to the youngster as the Dreamer. He had friends among the young people, but he still spent much time by himself, watching the ways of the prairie. While he enjoyed the games and contests, he also treasured the time spent alone. And he grew, in wisdom and stature.

HE WAS NOW IN HIS TWELFTH SUMMER. SOME OF THE GIRLS OF the same age were beginning to change in bodily shape. Sharp childish angles were giving way to softly rounded curves. This did not go unnoticed by Dreamer, but he was somewhat shy, and felt inadequate to compete with older warriors for female attention.

It is often so. Young women come of age a season or two before their male counterparts. Thus they are sought for wives by men with a little more experience. Those girls who had been Dreamer's friends in the Rabbit Society moved on, some into the lodges of respected warriors. He had mixed feelings about this, but did not let it trouble him. His time would come.

He continued to ponder and to learn, but seldom demonstrated his knowledge and understanding to others, except for his mentor, Sees Beyond.

"SHOULD I TAKE MY VISION QUEST THIS SEASON, UNCLE?"

Sees Beyond studied the young man. The years had flown, almost beyond the holy man's comprehension. His pupil must be in his sixteenth summer now, approaching manhood.

"Maybe. Why do you ask now? Are you made to think so?"

"How would I know?"

"A thing of the spirit. You have much understanding. If you feel the call, go ahead. Only you can tell."

FOR THE PAST SEVERAL SEASONS DREAMER HAD GAZED AT A mound-shaped prominence on the distant prairie. It seemed taller than other hills and ridges, and in a way he did not understand, it seemed to attract his attention. It was probably a full day's journey to the west of the area where the People usually made their summer camp. Since he could first remember, this place had seemed to call out to him. There was a feeling that from the top of that mound, one could see the very rim, where earth meets sky.

Sees Beyond had told him what to expect from fasting. He carried a waterskin, and a few strips of dried meat with which to break his fast when the quest was finished.

"At about the third day," the holy man explained, "your senses will all be sharper. You will find it easier to see, to hear . . . Ah, never mind. It cannot be described. You must *experience* it. You will know . . ."

IT WAS A FULL DAY'S TRAVEL, AND THEN A HARD, STEEP CLIMB TO the crest of the rolling hill. His stomach protested audibly, but became quiet as he gazed to the west, where Sun Boy painted himself with unbelievable brilliance before disappearing for the night. It was the most thrilling time of his life.

The voices of the day creatures quieted, replaced by the voices of the night: a coyote's chuckling call and her mate's answer, creating the impression of at least six or seven animals; the hollow call of *Kookooskoos,* the great hunting owl; the chirp of crickets in the prairie grasses; a whippoorwill in the oaks along a distant stream . . .

At even greater distance, he could make out the bellow of a buffalo bull searching for female companionship, and the song of the gray wolf who constantly circled the herds, waiting, watching for the weak, lame, or sick to fall behind.

Dreamer was hungry, of course. He built a small fire with sticks he had carried. It was not needed for warmth or to cook, but as a signal to whatever spirits might dwell here. *Here, I intend to camp.* He tossed a pinch of tobacco into his fire to gain the goodwill of the spirits, who are known to appreciate its fragrant incense. Then, he lay down on his buffalo robe to watch the stars circle overhead. The Seven Hunters began their nightly circuit of exploration around their camp at the Real-star, in the northern sky, which never moves and always marks the way. Just for amusement, he verified that he could still identify the Hunter's Dog, a smaller star at the heels of the second Hunter in the line. He sipped a little water from his waterskin and waited, anticipating whatever events might come.

Nothing did. He slept only a short while and awoke, disappointed, to face the second day, a little bit discouraged. He recalled with distaste a remark of the holy man, who had cautioned: *Sometimes nothing happens.* The second day was uncomfortable and frustrating. He had seldom experienced boredom. There was always something to observe, to cause wonder, or appreciation, or to arouse his curiosity. These were not things to expect, but to enjoy when they happened. Now, he began to realize that he had expected too much. His heart was very heavy. Besides, he was hungry.

On the third day, he awoke with the startling clarity of thought and senses that Sees Beyond had described. *Ah! Now it comes!* he told himself. But again, there were only the sounds of the prairie. This day, too, passed. He prepared to depart when daylight came, and rolled into his robe for the night, deeply disappointed. Had he done something wrong, he wondered, to cause the quest to fail? He was never sure, afterward, whether the vision came as a dream or if he wakened to experience it, but it was daylight. He was looking across the rolling prairie, watching the grazing animals at a distance . . . buffalo, antelope, and elk. The elk bulls wore antlers, with the soft fuzzy appearance that told of summer growth, not yet polished for the mating rituals and combat ahead. Nothing unusual.

Suddenly he noticed an elk with no antlers, apart from the others, circling a small band of buffalo. It carried something on its back, as one of the dogs of the People might carry a pack when they moved. He focused on this strange beast, and moved closer for a better look. He could not explain, later, *how* he moved closer, except to say there was a sensation of floating, high, overlooking the scene from *above*. This marked the experience as a dream, or . . . Could this be his *vision*?

That which had appeared to be a pack was now seen to be a *man,* sitting on the elk-dog creature. He wore a shiny garment, and carried a long spear, also shiny. The man appeared to control the animal with thongs or ropes around its head, pulling on something which the creature held in its mouth.

Now the strange pair approached a young buffalo cow, and with some sort of signal from the rider, it seemed, the elk-dog charged forward. The cow bolted, but had not gone far when the man thrust his long spear into the animal's left side. It fell, kicking feebly, and he dismounted to begin to butcher.

Dreamer awoke or returned from his highly improbable vision, puzzled as to its meaning. Maybe Sees Beyond could help interpret.

"A DOG AS BIG AS AN ELK, ON WHICH A MAN RODE?" THE HOLY man asked, puzzled. "I don't know, Dreamer. It must have meaning, to be shown to you later, maybe. Anything else you remember?"

"No . . . Well, maybe. It seemed to me that somehow, this elk-dog wore a turtle on each foot."

"A turtle? Well, when the time is right, you will be shown. Maybe. And the man killed a buffalo? Such an animal would be an easy way to hunt buffalo, no?"

The two chuckled together. It was often difficult to approach buffalo, to draw near enough to use the bow or spear. The most effective way to acquire meat for the People was to drive a herd toward the "buffalo jump" and over the cliff's edge. This jump had been used for more generations than anyone knew. Maybe since Creation, when the People first crawled through a hollow log into the world of sunshine, and began to hunt in the open grassland.

Sometimes such a drive failed, and there would be much hunger in the lodges of the People during the Moon of Snows and the Moon of Hunger.

IT WAS THREE SEASONS LATER THAT DREAMER AND HIS BOYHOOD friend Badger were scouting a small band of buffalo. Sometimes it would take several days to maneuver the animals into position to even attempt the drive that would stampede the herd over the jump.

They were watching a band of about thirty, mostly cows and calves, when Dreamer noticed another creature grazing quietly nearby. Were his eyes deceiving him? How could this be? He found himself looking at the creature of his vision quest, a dog as big as an elk, with something on its back. A flat object, with dangling straps. His head whirled in confusion.

"*Aiee!*" said his friend Badger. "What is that?"

It was several bowshots away, and it was grazing quietly.

Ah! thought Dreamer. *It grazes on grass, like an elk. But does the elk-dog eat meat also?*

The flat pack was there, but no man or spear could be seen. Dreamer noticed another thing immediately. The beast in his dream had been dark gray-blue in color. This one was reddish, and its coat appeared smooth and shiny. It struck him that these are two of the four colors of the ceremonial color cycle. An odd thought fluttered through his mind. Could there also be such elk-dogs which are yellow or white, to complete the sacred cycle of night, morning, day, and sunset? That would provide very strong medicine.

Such thoughts were interrupted by Badger.

"Do you suppose it is good to eat?"

Dreamer stifled his indignation. "I am made to think, Badger, that it has better purposes."

"What could be better than eating?"

Dreamer had never told anyone but Sees Beyond about the dream creature. Now, he must.

"Badger," he said, "I have seen this animal before."

"How? Where?"

Dreamer waved the question aside.

"My vision quest . . . I told only Sees Beyond."

"This is your *totem*? Your *guide*?"

"I don't know. Maybe. But when I saw it, a man was sitting on it. He had a long spear, and he killed a buffalo by chasing it, sitting on this elk-dog."

"You are serious?"

"Of course."

"Then where is he?"

"I don't know. Lost, or dead, maybe. He wore a shiny shirt and hat."

"Dreamer, you have been too long in the sun!"

"No, it is true. Look! He sat on that flat bundle, and his feet were in those straps that hang down."

"He was *tied* on?"

"No, it did not seem so. Just sitting. He was controlling the animal with some thongs. See, hanging below its head when it looks up? I must get closer."

The buffalo shuffled away, not really alarmed, as he made his way down the hillside. Badger watched from above.

The elk-dog saw him coming, raised its head and made a thundering noise. It was a startling sound, and Dreamer hesitated, then stopped to consider it. But a dog barks a welcome, does it not? Maybe an elk-dog does, also. There seemed no threat here, and had he not seen a man *sit* on one of these creatures?

He watched a little longer, and then moved slowly ahead. The elk-dog did not seem alarmed. It must be accustomed to people. He spoke softly to it, and it turned to look at him, its eyes large, dark, and liquid. There was wisdom in such eyes, and he saw no danger.

"My brother," he whispered to the animal, "I mean you no harm."

The elk-dog watched him without alarm, curious. He approached, a little nearer, and continued to talk softly. The animal took a step toward him. The straps and thongs on its head were familiar, as in his dream. One long thin strap was broken, and another dragged on the ground. He surmised that this must be a way to control the animal's movements.

The spirit of the creature reached out to him strongly. For some reason, Dreamer thought of the apology which the People addressed to the first buffalo kill of the season: "We are sorry to kill you, my brother, but upon your flesh our lives depend." Maybe a similar communication . . .

"My brother," he began, "we do not know each other, but I am made to think that our spirits mix well without harm to either. Let us learn . . ."

There was a soft snuffling noise from the elk-dog as it stared into his face at close range, unafraid.

He remembered now, from his vision quest, the mystery of the turtle on each foot of the elk-dog. He looked down. Yes, it was true. There, on each foot . . . It was as he bent to examine more closely that he heard a low moan from the tall grass beyond, and jumped back.

Almost hidden in the grass was a man. He lay on his back, his face drawn with pain, eyes squinting against the sun. The lower parts of his cheeks were covered with dark brown fur. His head was shiny and round, and . . . No, that was a hat of some sort. The man rolled partially over and tried to sit up, which induced vomiting. Dreamer watched, fascinated but unmoving. At least, this man must be that . . . A *man*. He did not think that a spirit-creature would vomit.

The fallen warrior wore the shining metal garment that now seemed familiar to Dreamer. Beside him lay the long spear, the shaft broken.

Now the man tugged at the shiny round hat, and lifted it from his shoulders, revealing curly hair, matted with blood.

Badger, who had followed his companion unnoticed, watched in wonder.

"He can take his head off?"

The stranger slumped to the ground, exhausted, barely aware of their presence. Blood trickled down his cheek.

"Shall we kill him?" suggested Badger.

"No, he is badly hurt," Dreamer said. "There is much here that we do not know, but his medicine is strong. I have seen it. It helps this one to ride the elk-dog, and to hunt the buffalo. Badger, go, tell Sees Beyond of this . . . *No one else*. Bring him back. I will stay with this one."

DREAMER WATCHED HIS DEPARTING FRIEND CROSSING THE VALley toward the camp of the People, then turned back toward the injured man.

The eyes were open . . . *Blue* eyes . . . *How can he see with such eyes?* Dreamer wondered. They appeared to him like those of the old and blind. The eyes tried to focus on his face, and Dreamer smiled, to reassure the other. A head injury such as this could be fatal, but the man seemed strong and healthy. Sees Beyond would know more about the possibilities. This stranger's medicine must be powerful.

Already he felt that though the medicine of this stranger was vastly different, it was possible that it could blend with his own, and with that of the elk-dog. He could almost imagine the sensation of sitting astride the elk-dog's back, bracing the long spear for the thrust. The spirit of the animal had already spoken to his own, and they mingled well. If the fallen warrior survived, he could teach the People much. If not, there was still the elk-dog. Maybe there were other elk-dogs. This man would know of such things, if he lived.

He turned his attention to the injured man, trying to appear reassuring. He couldn't tell whether the warrior was completely aware of his surroundings, but there seemed to be a certain consciousness in his eyes now. A look of concern, not alarm, exactly. There was a certain confidence in the man's demeanor, though his head must ache powerfully, with such an injury. If only they could talk. Maybe later, he could find some way to communicate. Maybe the stranger would know hand signs. If not, perhaps Sees Beyond would be able to help with that.

Of one thing Dreamer was sure. From this day, the world would never be the same again, for either himself, or the hair-faced stranger.

Or, for the People.

Encounter on Horse-Killed Creek

BILL GULICK

The Lewis and Clark expedition of 1804–1806 is the first marker on the long trail of the history of the American West.

Here, in the fall of 1805, during the crossing of the Bitterroot Mountains, a young apprentice hunter with the expedition has a momentous, potentially dangerous, encounter and a punishment he could never have anticipated.

Bill Gulick of Walla Walla, Washington, is among the most honored members of Western Writers of America. He was a regular contributor of Western fiction to *Liberty,* the *Saturday Evening Post, Esquire,* and *Collier's;* he is the author of twenty-seven novels (several of which—*Bend of the River, Road to Denver,* and *Hallelujah Trail*—were turned into memorable movies), two hundred short stories, countless magazine and newspaper works, and such prize-winning nonfiction books as *Snake River Country,* now in its fifth printing.

For many years, Gulick worked with the Nez Perce, Umatilla, Walla Walla, Cayuse, and Yakima tribes on projects to bring about a better understanding of Indian lands, water, fishing, and sovereignty rights.

Among many awards for his literary work are the Western Heritage Award from the National Cowboy Hall of Fame and the Saddleman Award from Western Writers of America.

of the stalk, neither man had spoken, not even in whispers, communicating by signs as they always did when hunting meat to fill hungry bellies. Two steps ahead, George Drewyer, the best hunter in the Lewis and Clark party, sank down on his right knee, froze, and peered intently through the glistening wet bushes and dangling evergreen tree limbs toward the animal grazing in the clearing. Identifying it, he turned, using his hands swiftly and graphically to tell the younger, less experienced hunter, Matt Crane, the nature of the animal he had seen and how he meant to approach and kill it.

Not a deer, his hands said. Not an elk. Just a stray Indian horse — with no Indians in sight. Matt signed that he understood. Turning back toward the clearing, George Drewyer began his final stalk.

Underfoot, the leaf mold and fallen pine needles formed a yielding carpet beneath the scattered clumps of bushes and thick stands of pine, which here on the western slope of the Bitterroot Mountains were broader in girth and taller than the skinny lodgepole and larch found on the higher reaches of the Lolo Trail. Half a day's travel behind, the other thirty-two members of the party were still struggling in foot-deep snow over slick rocks, steep slides, and tangles of downed timber treacherous as logjams, as they sought the headwaters of the Columbia and the final segment of their journey to the Pacific Ocean.

With September half gone, winter had already come to the seven-thousand-foot-high backbone of the continent a week's travel behind. All the game that the old Shoshone guide, Toby, had told them usually was to be found in the high meadows at this time of year had moved down to lower levels. Desperate for food, Captain William Clark had sent George Drewyer and Matt Crane scouting ahead for meat, judging that two men traveling afoot and unencumbered would stand a much better chance of finding game than the main party with its thirty-odd men and twenty-nine heavily laden horses. As he usually did, Drewyer had found game of a sort, weighed the risk of rousing the hostility of its Indian owner against the need of the party for food, and decided that hunger recognized no property rights.

Twenty paces from the horse, which still was grazing placidly, George Drewyer stopped, knelt behind a fallen tree, rested the barrel of his long rifle on its trunk, and took careful aim. Two steps to his right, Matt Crane did the same. After what seemed an agonizingly long period of time, during which Matt held his breath, Drewyer's rifle barked. Without movement or sound, the paint horse sank to the ground, dead—Matt was sure—before its body touched the sodden earth.

"Watch it," Drewyer murmured, swiftly reversing his rifle, swabbing out its barrel with the ramrod, expertly reloading it with patched and greased lead ball, then opening the pan and pouring in a carefully measured charge while he protected it from the drizzle with the tree trunk and his body.

Keeping his own rifle sighted on the fallen horse, Matt held his position without moving or speaking, as George Drewyer had taught him to do, until the swarthy, dark-eyed hunter had reloaded his weapon and risen to one knee. Peering first at the still animal, then moving his searching gaze around the clearing, Drewyer tested the immediate environment with all his senses—sight, sound, smell, and his innate hunter's instinct—for a full minute before he at last nodded in satisfaction.

"A bunch-quitter, likely. Least there's no herd nor herders around. Think you can skin it, preacher boy?"

"Sure. You want it quartered, with the innards saved in the hide?"

"Just like you'd do with an elk. Save everything but the hoofs and whinny. Get at it, while I snoop around for Injun sign. The Nez Perces will be friendly, the captains say, but I'd as soon not meet the Injun who owned that horse till its head and hide are out of sight."

While George Drewyer circled the clearing and prowled through the timber beyond, Matt Crane went to the dead horse, unsheathed his butcher knife, skillfully made the cuts needed to strip off the hide, gutted and dissected the animal. Returning from his scout, Drewyer hunkered down beside him, quickly boned out as large a packet of choice cuts as he could carry, wrapped them in a piece of hide, and loaded the still-warm meat into the empty canvas backpack he had brought along for that purpose.

"It ain't likely the men'll get this far by dark," he said, "so I'll take 'em a taste to ease their bellies for the night. Can you make out alone till tomorrow noon?"

"Yes."

"Cut the meat up into pieces you can spit and broil, then build a fire and start it cooking. If the smoke and smell brings Injun company, give 'em the peace sign, invite 'em to sit and eat, and tell 'em a big party of white men will be coming down the trail tomorrow. You got all that, preacher boy?"

"Yes, sir, I have."

"Good! Give me a hand with this pack and I'll be on my way." Slipping his arms through the carrying straps and securing the pad that transferred a portion of the weight to his forehead, Drewyer got to his feet while Crane eased the load. Grinning, Drewyer squeezed his shoulder. "Remind me to quit calling you preacher boy, will you, Matt? You've learned a lot since you left your pa and home."

"I've had a good teacher."

"That you have. Take care."

Left alone in the whispering silence of the forest and the cold, mistlike rain, Matt dragged the severed head and hide into a clump of nearby bushes. Taking his hatchet, he searched for and found enough resinous wood, bark, and dry duff to catch the spark from his flint and steel. As the fire grew in the narrow trench he had dug for it, he cut forked sticks, placed pieces of green aspen limbs horizontally across them, sliced the meat into strips, and started them to broiling. The smell of juice dripping into the fire made his belly churn with hunger, tempting him to do what Toussaint Charbonneau, the party's French-Canadian interpreter, did when fresh-killed game was brought into camp—seize a hunk and gobble it down hot, raw, and bloody. But he did not, preferring to endure the piercing hunger pangs just a little longer in exchange for the greater pleasure of savoring his first bite of well-cooked meat.

Cutting more wood for the fire, he hoped Drewyer would stop calling him preacher boy. Since at twenty he was one of the youngest members of the party and his father, the Reverend Peter Crane, was a Presbyterian minister in St. Louis, it had been natural enough for the older men to call him the preacher's boy at first.

Why Drewyer—who'd been raised a Catholic, could barely read and write, and had no peers as an outdoorsman—should have made Matt his protégé, Matt himself could not guess. Maybe because he listened more than he talked. Or maybe because he was having the adventure of his life and showed it. Whatever the reason, their relationship was good. It would get even better, Matt mused, if Drewyer would drop the "preacher boy" thing and simply call him by name.

While butchering the horse, Matt noticed that it had been gelded. According to Drewyer, the Nez Perce were one of the few Western tribes that practiced selective breeding, thus the high quality of their horses. From the way Chief Cameahwait had acted, a state of war existed between the Shoshone and the Nez Perce, so the first contact between the Lewis and Clark party—which had passed through Shoshone country—and the Nez Perce was going to be fraught with danger. Aware of the fact that he might make the first contact, Matt felt both uneasy and proud. Leaving him alone in this area showed the confidence Drewyer had in him. But his aloneness made him feel a little spooky.

With the afternoon only half gone and nothing to do but tend the fire, Matt stashed his blanket roll under a tree out of the wet, picked up his rifle, and curiously studied the surrounding forest. There was no discernible wind, but vagrant currents of air stirred, bringing to his nostrils the smell of wood smoke, of crushed pine needles, of damp leaf mold, of burnt black powder. As he moved across the clearing toward a three-foot-wide stream gurgling down the slope, he scowled, suddenly realizing that the burnt black powder smell could not have lingered behind this long. Nor would it have gotten stronger, as this smell was doing the nearer he came to the stream. Now he identified it beyond question.

Sulfur! There must be a mineral-impregnated hot spring nearby, similar to the hot springs near Traveler's Rest at the eastern foot of Lolo Pass, where the cold, weary members of the party had eased their aches and pains in warm, soothing pools. What he wouldn't give for a hot bath right now!

Visually checking the meat broiling over the fire, he judged it could do without tending for an hour or so. Thick though the forest cover was along the sides of the stream, he would run no risk of getting lost, for following the stream downhill would bring him back to the clearing. Time enough then to cut limbs for a lean-to and rig a shelter for the night.

Sometimes wading in the increasingly warm waters of the stream, sometimes on its brush-bordered bank, he followed its windings uphill for half a mile before he found what he was looking for: a pool ten feet long and half as wide, eroded in the smooth basalt, ranging in depth from one to four feet. Testing the temperature of its water, he found it just right—hot but not unbearably so, the sulfur smell strong but not unpleasant. Leaning his rifle against a tree trunk, he took off his limp, shapeless red felt hat, pulled his thin moccasins off his bruised and swollen feet, waded into the pool, and gasped with sensual pleasure as the heat of the water spread upward.

Since his fringed buckskin jacket and woolen trousers already were soaking wet from the cold rain, he kept them on as he first sank to a sitting position, then stretched out full length on his back, with only his head above water. After a time, he roused himself long enough to strip the jacket off over his head and pull the trousers down over his ankles. Tossing them into the clump of bushes near his rifle, jacket, and moccasins, he lay back in the soothing water, naked, warm, and comfortable for the first time since Traveler's Rest.

Drowsily, his eyes closed. He slept . . .

THE SOUND THAT AWAKENED HIM SOME TIME LATER COULD HAVE been made by a deer moving down to drink from the pool just upstream from where he lay. It could have been made by a beaver searching for a choice willow sapling to cut down. It could have been made by a bobcat, a bear, or a cougar. But as consciousness returned to him, as he heard the sound and attempted to identify it, his intelligence rejected each possibility that occurred to him the moment it crossed his mind—for one lucid reason.

Animals did not sing. And whatever this intruder into his state of tranquility might be, it was singing.

Though the words were not recognizable, they had an Indian sound, unmistakably conveying the message that the singer was at peace with the world, not self-conscious, and about to indulge in a very enjoyable act. Turning over on his belly, Matt crawled to the upper end of the pool, peering through the screening bushes in the direction from which the singing sound was coming. The light was poor. Even so, it was good enough for him to make out the figure of a girl, standing in profile not ten feet away, reaching down to the hem of her buckskin skirt, lifting it, and pulling it up over her head.

As she tossed the garment aside, she turned, momentarily facing him. His first thought was: *My God, she's beautiful!* His second: *She's naked!* His third: *How can I get away from here without being seen?*

She would be around sixteen years old, he judged, her skin a light copper color, her mouth wide and generous, with dimples indenting both cheeks. Her breasts were full but not heavy; her waist was slim, her stomach softly rounded, her hips beginning to broaden with maturity, her legs long and graceful. Watching her sink slowly into the water until only the tips of her breasts and her head were exposed, Matt felt no guilt for continuing to stare at her. Instead, he mused: *So that's what a naked woman looks like! Why should I be ashamed to admire such beauty?*

He began breathing again, careful to make no sound. Since the two pools were no more than a dozen feet apart, separated by a thin screen of bushes and a short length of stream, which here made only a faint gurgling noise, he knew that getting out of the water, retrieving his clothes and rifle, and then withdrawing from the vicinity without revealing his presence would require utmost caution. But the attempt must be made, for if one young Indian woman knew of this bathing spot, others must know of it, too, and in all likelihood soon would be coming here to join her.

He could well imagine his treatment at their hands, if found. Time and again recently the two captains had warned members of the party that Western Indians such as the Shoshone, Flathead, and Nez Perce had a far higher standard of morality than did the Mandan, with whom the party had wintered, who would gladly sell the favors of wives and daughters for a handful of beads, a piece of bright cloth, or a cheap trade knife, then cheerfully provide shelter and bed for the act.

Moving with infinite care, he half floated, half crawled to the lower right-hand edge of the pool, where he had left his rifle and clothes. The Indian girl still was singing. The bank was steep and slick. Standing up, he took hold of a sturdy-feeling, thumb-thick sapling rooted near the edge of the bank, cautiously tested it, and judged it secure. Pulling himself out of the pool, he started to take a step, slipped, and tried to save himself by grabbing the sapling with both hands.

The full weight of his body proved too much for its root system. Torn out of the earth, it no longer supported him. As he fell backward into the pool, he gave an involuntary cry of disgust.

"Oh, shit!"

Underwater, his mouth, nose, and eyes filled as he struggled to turn over and regain his footing. When he did so, he immediately became aware of the fact that the girl had stopped singing. Choking, coughing up water, half-blinded and completely disoriented, he floundered out of the pool toward where he thought his clothes and rifle were. Seeing a garment draped over a bush, he grabbed it, realized it was not his, hastily turned away, and blundered squarely into a wet, naked body.

To save themselves from falling, both he and the Indian girl clung to each other momentarily. She began screaming. Hastily he let her go. Still screaming and staring at him with terror-stricken eyes, she snatched her dress off the bush and held it so that it covered her. Finding his own clothes, he held them in front of his body, trying to calm the girl by making the sign for "friend," "white man," and "peace," while urgently saying:

"*Ta-ba-bone,* you understand? *Suyapo!* I went to sleep, you see, and had no idea you were around . . ."

Suddenly her screaming stopped. Not because of his words or hand signs but because of the appearance of an Indian man who had pushed through the bushes and now stood beside her. He was dressed in beaded, fringed buckskins, was stocky, slightly bowlegged, a few inches shorter than Matt but more muscular, a man in his middle twenties, with high cheekbones and a firm jawline. He shot a guttural question at the girl, to which she replied in a rapid babble of words. His dark brown eyes blazed with anger. Drawing a glittering knife out of its sheath, he motioned the girl to step aside, and moved toward Matt menacingly.

Backing away, Matt thought frantically: *Captain Clark is not going to like this at all. And if that Indian does what it looks like he means to do with that knife, I'm not going to like it, either.*

Knowing George Drewyer to be the best linguist in the party, Matt had spent a good deal of time with him during the party's journey up the Missouri River and across the Shining Mountains, endeavoring to acquire a knowledge of Indian words helpful in communicating with the various tribes. *Ta-ba-bone* meant "white man" in the Shoshone tongue, Drewyer said, while *Suyapo* meant "crowned ones" in Nez Perce, the "crowned" signifying the hats worn by white men. Of course, it always was wise to use hand signs as well as words, Drewyer said, for though local dialects might vary widely, sign language was clear, graphic, and universally understood among the plains and mountain tribes that used it.

Trouble was, Matt thought desperately as he backed away from the knife and tried to cover his nakedness by putting on his soaking-wet trousers, the lessons given him by George Drewyer so far had not taught him how to clasp his hands together in front of his chest in the sign for "peace" while those same hands were busy at knee level pulling up his pants.

More nimble-fingered than he, the Indian girl already had slipped her buckskin dress over her head, put her hands through the armholes, and pulled its hem down below her knees. As Matt worked his trousers up to his waist, she spoke sharply to the Indian man. Halting his advance, he answered without removing his gaze from Matt's face. He asked her a question. She answered hysterically. He asked another. Her answer this time was more composed. Deciding that he had done all he could to convince them that he was peaceable and friendly, Matt stopped trying to communicate by word and sign, put on his jacket, moccasins, and hat, but was careful to make no move toward his rifle, which was leaning against a nearby tree.

Shaking her head in reply to another question, the Indian girl giggled. Pointing a finger first at Matt, then at herself, she burst into a torrent of words, broken by *"Eeyahs!"* and *"Aayahs!"*, illustrated with expressive hand gestures that appeared to be describing what had happened.

Even though he could not understand her words, the movement of her hands, the mimicry of her facial muscles, and the lights and shadows that came and went in her eyes made her meaning perfectly clear to Matt.

Going through the motions of undressing, she touched her lips and opened her mouth as if singing, then gestured toward Matt and touched her ears to show how he had become aware of her presence. With remarkable insight, she pantomimed his surprise and alarm, then made tiptoeing gestures with the first two fingers of her right hand to indicate how he had tried to slip away undiscovered. Listening to her intently, the Indian man let the knife arm fall to his side. The anger left his eyes, replaced by a glint of amusement.

Again doing the foot-shuffling and arm-swinging act in mimicry of a white man, the girl reached up and out, stiffened, appeared to slip, threw her arms wide as if falling, then gave an accurate imitation of his disgusted cry.

"Ohh-shee! Ohh-shee!"

At this the Indian man hooted with laughter. Sheathing his knife, he bent over, hugged himself and exclaimed, *"Ahh taats! Ahh taats!"*

Needing no interpreter to translate the expression as "Very good! Very good!", Matt sheepishly wondered if the Indian girl and man knew what *his* exclamation had meant.

Smiling broadly now, the Indian man linked his index fingers in the sign for "friend." Matt responded in kind. Raising his open right hand to shoulder level, palm toward Matt to show that it held no weapon, the Indian man shook it from side to side, querying, "Who are you?"

"Suyapo—white man." Matt returned the query. "Who are you?"

"Nimipu," the Indian said, passing the index finger of his right hand just under his nose as if thrusting a skewer of dentalium through the septum. "Nez Perce."

Most Western Indian tribes called themselves by one name, Drewyer said, their neighbors called them by another, while the French-Canadian explorers who had first made contact with them fifty years ago identified them with casually applied names that were more rough translations of their visual tribal identification signs than accurate descriptions of their appearance or character traits. Never mind that the Blackfeet's feet were red, that the Gros Ventre's bellies were no bigger than any other Indians, that the Flathead had normal craniums, and that the Nez Perce seldom if ever pierced their noses—the French Canadians had named them, and that was that.

Again the Nez Perce made the querying gesture, following it with a more specific question, tapping Matt's chest, asking him his name.

"Crane," Matt said. "Matt Crane." Finding no way to translate his first name into sign language, he attempted to signify his last name by making the sign for a pair of very long legs wading in water, then flapping his arms slowly to signify a large bird flying. "Crane," he repeated. "Matt Crane."

"*Ah!*" the Indian said, his dark eyes glowing with sudden understanding. "*Moki!*" Repeating the long-legged, wading mime, then the slow-flying act in much more realistic fashion than Matt had managed, he made it clear that he was well acquainted with the bird after whom Matt's family was named. "*Moki Hih-Hih.*"

Tapping the Indian's chest, Matt queried him as to his name.

"*We-wu-kye Ilp-ilp,*" the Indian said. Placing his hands beside his ears with the fingers extended upward to resemble a large rack of horns, he lowered his head and pawed the ground in a perfect imitation of a bull elk. A few more gestures and hand signs made Matt understand that the man's name was Red Elk, that the girl was his sister, *Hattia Isemtuks,* which translated into the lovely name Moon Wind, and that he himself now was *Moki Hih-hih,* which translated into White Crane.

Now that it had been established that they were meeting as friends, the exchange of information went with surprising speed and clarity. A large band of his people was camped not far away, Red Elk said, digging and cooking camas bulbs in a marshy area called Weippe Prairie. The Nez Perce had heard that a party of white men was on its way up the Big Muddy and across the Bitterroot Mountains and were prepared to welcome the Crowned Ones with open hearts. If Matt Crane would come with Red Elk and Moon Wind to their father's lodge, he would be given food, drink, warmth, and shelter.

Later he would be pleased to accept their hospitality, Matt said, but for now he must decline. Explaining that the main body of the Lewis and Clark party was a day's travel behind, he related their sufferings from cold and hunger, told how he and another man had been sent ahead to find game, and described the type of animal they had found and killed. Only the fact that the men were desperate for meat had induced them to kill the horse, Matt said, and as soon as the two captains met the Nez Perce leaders they would pay the owner of the horse a fair price for it.

A small matter, Red Elk said. The Nez Perce had many horses. He would send Moon Wind to the Nez Perce camp, where she would tell her father that a party of white men would meet with the bands led by Twisted Hair and *Tetoharsky* tomorrow afternoon. Meanwhile, he would return with his new friend to the clearing where the meat was being cooked and would remain with him there to make sure no harm came to him. As soon as Moon Wind had delivered her message she would fill a parfleche with cooked camas and salmon and bring it to the clearing.

Signing that she understood, the Indian girl gave Matt a shy smile, then was gone . . .

DURING THE TWENTY-FOUR HOURS THAT PASSED BETWEEN THE time George Drewyer shot the horse and the main body of the Lewis and Clark party came straggling down the trail, Matt basked in anticipation of the praise he would be given by Captain William Clark for the way he had conducted himself. Had he not made the first contact with the Nez Perce? Had he not kept it peaceful under trying circumstances?

Indeed he had. But because of a slight error in judgment, he was in no condition to greet the party when it arrived shortly after noon, next day. Instead, he was squatting in a clump of bushes off to one side of the trail with his trousers down, groaning in agony as his bowels reacted violently to last night's supper of steamed camas and dried salmon.

His error in judgment, he now realized, had been his politeness in abstaining from eating horse meat when he learned that Red Elk would not touch it. By signs, the Nez Perce made it clear that his people had a taboo against eating horses because the animals served them so well in traveling, hunting, and war.

"This is a Nez Perce tribal custom," he said. "But the Crowned Ones live by different rules. Eat the horse meat if you like. I will not be offended."

"I cannot eat while you go hungry."

"I will not be hungry long," Red Elk said with a laugh. "Moon Wind will bring food."

"Then I will wait."

"Good!" Red Elk said, looking pleased. "When she comes, we will eat together."

Since the sweet-tasting, mushy camas was the first fresh vegetable Matt had eaten for a long while, he partook of several helpings. Soaked in boiling water to moisten it, the dried salmon tasted delicious, too, and he made up for all the solid food he had missed the past few days by eating until his stomach was comfortably full.

Feeling drowsy a couple of hours after darkness fell, he said good night to Red Elk and Moon Wind, pulled up his blanket, and went to sleep, lulled by the warmth of the fire Moon Wind was carefully tending, and soothed by the patter of raindrops on the small waterproof skin tepee, which was much cozier than any shelter he could have improvised.

At first, he slept well. Then his stomach began to growl, he began to toss and turn in discomfort, and he wakened to find his abdomen so swollen and tight he could hardly breathe. Sitting up, he groaned and clutched his stomach. Why hadn't he eaten the horse meat instead of the unaccustomed foods? Why had he wolfed down that third bowl of camas? Why had he let Moon Wind give him that fourth piece of fish? Oh, dear God, why didn't his belly just burst like an overinflated balloon and give him relief from this cramping pain?

Mumbling an apology to Red Elk and Moon Wind for disturbing their rest, he crawled out of the tepee on his hands and knees, staggered a few steps, lowered his trousers barely in time, squatted, and voided his bowels in an explosive liquid movement. Somewhat relieved, he returned to the tepee, lay down, and tried to sleep. Within minutes, the stuffed feeling returned, followed by cramps and another overpowering urge to evacuate. Again he stumbled out into the cold, rainy dark. For the rest of the night and well into the next morning the flux continued, draining him of strength. Since neither

Red Elk nor Moon Wind, who had eaten the same food, was affected, his ailment had to be caused by the change in diet, he knew — but knowing brought little comfort or cure.

In mid-morning the rain stopped, the sky cleared, and sunshine warmed the clearing. Well aware of his condition, Red Elk rebuilt the fire under the strips of horse meat, which the rain had extinguished during the night, filled a bowl with water from the creek, and told him to drink. Moon Wind disappeared for a time, then returned carrying a pouch full of dark-colored bark. Heating several small stones in the fire, she put some of the bark and water into a bowl, picked up the stones with two pieces of wood, dropped them into the water, and brewed a concoction that looked like tea.

"Eat," Red Elk said, handing Matt a small piece of broiled horse meat.

"Drink," Moon Wind said, steadying the bowl for him as she raised it to his lips.

He tried. But one bite of meat and two sips of the bitter-tasting tea were all that were required to set off another rebellion in his tortured digestive tract.

He groaned, rose, and headed for the bushes.

By noon, the acute attacks of cramps had eased off, but he was so weak he could barely stand. A dozen or so Nez Perce curious to meet the Crowned Ones had come to the clearing from their nearby camp, among them an older couple whom Red Elk introduced as his father and mother. Rubbing her stomach and grimacing, the mother made it clear that she was familiar with his complaint and sympathized with his pains. When Moon Wind showed her the concoction she had brewed, the mother tasted it, nodded, and indicated that if he continued taking his medicine he would soon feel much better.

Less frequent though his trips into the bushes had become, he again was on one when he heard horses moving down the trail, followed by George Drewyer's hearty greeting.

"Hey, Matt! Where are you?"

Staggering weakly out into the clearing, Matt muttered, "Here, George," then sagged to the ground.

"My God, boy! What happened?"

"I ate some food that didn't agree with me."

Nodding to Red Elk and Moon Wind, Drewyer helped them

ease Matt to a supine position, with the Indian girl putting a folded blanket under his head.

Drewyer called, "Captain Clark!"

"Yes?"

"Got a real sick man here. Can you take a look at him?"

Before leaving the East, Meriwether Lewis had studied for six weeks with the most renowned physician in the country, Benjamin Rush of Philadelphia, learning the skills he would need during the journey across the continent. As a matter of course, he had passed on this acquired knowledge to the man destined to share the command of the expedition, William Clark. More suited by nature to diagnose ailments and administer remedies than the quick-tempered, impatient Lewis, the practical-minded, self-contained Clark soon was doing most of the doctoring for the party's members.

It was Dr. Rush's firm belief that diseases were caused by morbid elements invading the body. If in the circulatory system, these morbidities could be drained and the patient cured by bleeding. If in the digestive tract, they could be cleansed by dosing and purging.

Summoning all the strength he could muster, Matt tried to sit up and tell Captain Clark all the interesting things he had learned about the Nez Perce. Brusquely, the captain silenced him.

"Lie down, son. You're looking poorly."

"It was the food, sir—"

Taking his pulse with one hand, then feeling his forehead for temperature with the other, Captain Clark grunted:

"I know! I know! Too much fresh horse meat eaten on an empty stomach was bound to give you the colic. Fetch me my medical kit, George. Matt here needs a dose of Dr. Rush's Bilious Pills. Nothing like calomel, jalap, and Glauber's salt to flush out the system!"

York's Story

DALE L. WALKER

The Indians much asstonished at my Black Servant and Call him big medison, this nation never Saw a black man before . . ."

"(yorked Danced for the Inds)".

"Sergt. Floyd was taken violently bad with the Beliose Cholick and is dangerously ill . . . every man is attentive to him (york prlly [principally])".

"Here my Servant York Swam to the Sand bar to geather greens for our Dinner . . ."

Such were the references William Clark made to his slave York (whom he called a "servant") during the Lewis and Clark expedition of 1804–1806. These brief, sporadic mentionings of York, and a few sadder details Clark supplied in letters to Meriwether Lewis and others after the expedition, comprise the sparse historical record on this man. (Everything else that is known or can be guessed about York can be found in the amazing 1985 book, *In Search of York,* by Robert B. Betts.)

Dale L. Walker is past president of Western Writers of America, Inc., and recipient of four

Spur Awards and the Owen Wister Award for lifetime contributions to the history and literature of the West. He is author of such Forge books as *Legends and Lies, The Boys of '98, Bear Flag Rising, Pacific Destiny,* and most recently *Eldorado: The California Gold Rush.*

CERTAINLY, I UNDERSTAND YOUR
question. I have been asked it before. I was asked it by Sergeant
Floyd when he was dying of the cholick and I was attending him
with sips of water and cool cloths and drops of camphor that summer
day when we were outward bound. He called me "Captain Clark's
nigger" and supposed me to be bitter.

The Book says I am cursed by the sin of Ham but Sergeant Floyd
died and I lived and Captain Clark took me to the Western Sea where
I saw things no man of my color before me saw.

How, I ask, could I be bitter?

MY PEOPLE CROSSED THE MIDDLE PASSAGE EIGHTY OR MORE
years ago and by God's insistence survived the voyage and fetched a
good sum on a slave block in the Carolinas. My mother, called Rose,
became a house servant for the Clarks on their lands in Virginia and
Kentucky; my father was a field worker, then, after he was found to
have a way with horses and mules, he became a plowman and a
teamster. He was named York, after the river that flowed between
the Rappahannock and the James, and called Old York after I was
born and also named York.

John Clark was partial to my father. Many times I saw them
talking and nodding and pointing out across the plantation lands,
and once I saw Mister John slap my father on the back and laugh at
something Old York, who was grinning and looking at his feet, had
said. My mother was much in favor, too, serving Miz Ann, matriarch
of the family, who had borne ten children and was often vaporish.
When I was brought in from the tobacco fields to be her son William's body servant, and began spending my waking hours in the big
house, I often heard Miz Ann call out, "Rose? I need you, Rose."

Master William was runty in those days, a skinny, pink-skinned, red-haired boy, much given to maundering and arranging toy soldiers for battle. His father little heeded him, and Miz Ann, that sad, kindly, woman, tended to "hover over him" too much, her husband liked to say. Of William's five brothers only the oldest, named George, a great fighting man in the Ohio country, paid him mind. It was George who brought the toy soldiers home and who would teach William to shoot, dress game, read a map, make a trail, and abide in the forest.

I came inside the Clark home in the woods of Caroline County, Virginia, in the year of 1784. I was robust then, lean but muscled from field work, and "smart," or so Mister John said of me. He gave me no instructions about serving his son but Old York said that Mister John wanted me to do more than tote the boy's bathwater and empty his slop jar and lay out his clothes. Mister John was fond of the Poor Richard proverb "Up, sluggard, and waste not life; in the grave will be sleeping enough," and had his daughter Frances sew a sampler of it to hang on the wall above William's bed. He told Old York that he wanted William to "get out in the daylight" and "show more vigor."

We became companions, Master William and I. We rolled hoops, ran races, swung on ropes, clambered, explored, wrestled, built breastworks of dirt and fought Indians with guns we shaped from tree limbs. And once we dug for treasure.

THE DIGGING OCCUPIED US TWO WEEKS IN MAY OF THE YEAR after an old vagabond with wild eyes, a dirty white beard, and a long black coat over his ragged garments, rode his mule onto the plantation and approached the house where he found us drawing water at the well. He waved his stick toward some hillocks in the distance and babbled some words we did not comprehend, so we ran to the house and found Mister John, who came forth, musket in hand, and we trailing behind, and asked the nomad's business. "A tinker," the ancient said, "a master of the whetstone, and foremost, a servant of the Lord and an exhorter for the Lord." For water and a piece of bread for himself and some water and feed for his animal, he said he would mend and sharpen and pray with us.

Miz Ann heard the commotion and hastened out to the dog run and beckoned to us to bring the man forward. She questioned him closely, then bade him sit on the stoop and had Rose bring him bread, salt meat, and a dipper of water.

Master William and I hurriedly tended the mendicant's mule, and upon returning watched him as he noisily finished his meal. He then stood and threw his arms wide, rolled his eyes back and uttered some words in a gargling tongue that threw him into a fit of coughing that decorated his beard with crumbs and spit. He trembled in silence for a moment, then shot his eyes open and peered at each of us, lingering on Miz Ann's face as he began a long raspy prayer animated with much flinging of arms and thumping of chest. I did not know enough of the Book to understand much of his hortatory but it seemed to please Miz Ann, who thanked him for his blessings, said she did not require his other services, and that he had paid for his meal with his message. She had Rose put some corncakes and another piece of meat in a bag for him.

We shadowed Mister John as he led the tinker to his mule and stood off while they talked. Again the man shook his stick toward the hills off to the west of the house and we heard him say something like "Tum-you-lie, sir," and the word "gold." Then he mounted his mule and soon vanished over the rise.

Mister John was much amused by the encounter for when he walked with us back to the house he spoke with a broad smile on his face. "Our tinker-preacher is a learned lunatic, a harmless candidate for Bedlam. Among his talents is that of a scryer. For a coin he offered to reveal what he saw in a dirty piece of green glass he carried in a hide sack around his neck."

"Did you give him a coin, Father?" William said.

"No. 'No coin,' I told him, and I reminded him of our hospitality. He then offered his findings gratis. He says there is likely a treasure of gold in those hills yonder."

William looked at me wide-eyed, then at his father. "Can we dig, sir? York and I? Vigor and exercise, out in the daylight?"

"A fool's errand," the father said, but the next day he tired of his son's nagging and without a word handed him a pickhead and a well-worn hoe.

With an adze we fashioned a rude haft for the pick and some shims to seat it in the iron head and set out afoot for one of the mounds the scryer had identified. It was a narrow hillock covered with weeds, wildflowers, and sharp rocks, about fifteen rods in length, no more than two high, surrounded by a verdant dale.

We threw our shirts off, rolled our trousers, and swung pick and hoe with a will, splintering the pick handle in an hour and taking turns with the hoe until it, too, snapped.

"Tomorrow," William said, "at daybreak. We'll take a horse, some bread, a jug of water, and save time. Meantime, we rehaft our tools."

Oh, how we dug! For two weeks we hacked at the hillock. We wore out the hoe. We broke the pick handle thrice. We blistered and bled our hands in freeing boulders, and swatted biting flies. We poured sweat and stank and dug and dug. The pocks we made on that mound were many but we sank few more than two or three feet before we decided that place would not yield treasure and moved to a fresh spot.

Mister John rode out to watch us on several occasions, bringing a fresh jug of water and a sack of food. He'd hand the jug and sack to us and say with a big grin, "A barter, now don't forget. These provisions for half the gold you find!" Another time he said, "I suspect a Virginia Ophir may be under that hill! Don't forget our pact!"

He knew there was no gold there, of course, and soon enough we knew as well.

On what turned out to be our last day of digging, Master William uncovered a long bone with knobs on each end, and when I relieved him in the hole I found a human jawbone with five teeth adjoined, and a few minutes later, the rest of the skull with a long clump of black hair trailing behind, some rib bones and three pieces of rotted deerskin. We placed these artifacts in our food bag, and when we reached the house, I laid them out on the stoop while William went in to collect his people.

"An Indian," Mister John declared as he examined the skull and jawbone. "Killed in battle, beyond doubt. Brained. See the hole here?" He stuck his finger in a jagged crack on top of the skull.

Miz Ann emerged at that moment, peered at the display on the stoop and stood transfixed, her hand quivering over her mouth.

"William, York," she said, "take them back and bury them where you found them. You will do no more digging. Even a heathen burial ground is a sacred place."

We did as we were told. We covered up all the other pocks we'd dug on that hillock as well, then, at his mother's instruction, William read some verses of Scripture.

Those weeks of digging for gold amongst the sacred tumuli would pale to a dim memory when we set out across the continent many years later and experienced a hundred greater adventures. But we were boys then, and in sharing the experience became somewhat of friends.

MISTER JOHN TOLD MY FATHER HE WAS MUCH PLEASED WITH HIS son's vigor and "progress toward manhood" and credited me. "Your boy has been a help," he told Old York.

After some months of sport and adventure on the Clark plantation, we were permitted to take horses and ride over the hills to tidewater. There we fished the Rappahannock for alewives or anything else that would swallow a worm, sailed bark-wood boats, flailed around in the shallows, and taught ourselves to swim.

We knew our separate places. Old York made certain that I, especially, knew mine. When William and I wrestled, I was careful not to hurt him. When we raced I was pleased to reach the goal on his heels. When we dug, I dug longer and deeper. When we swam or climbed or swung I was alert to his welfare. When he talked, I listened and nodded and smiled and offered nothing unless asked, and even then, offered little.

You realize, sir, that being a body servant was an honor? Yes, and I was careful not to fail at it. I enjoyed privileges few others had. I ate my meals with Master William, rode horseback with him, and learned things from him, some of the things forbidden by custom and law.

Miz Ann taught him the alphabet, and to read and write, and he tried to teach these things to me. I grasped some of it but was better at remembering, very good at remembering words, and when I didn't understand one I would ask him and if he didn't know, he would ask his mother, who always knew.

There were nine of us (the family never called us slaves or niggers—Miz Ann would not stand for it) on the Clark lands in Virginia in those times and we had regular prayer meetings, always on the

Sabbath and sometimes during the week, at twilight. Miz Ann's life was piloted by the Book and she made certain that we learned some Scripture and much of the life of Jesus. Most often she would conduct the meetings but on occasion one of her married daughters who came visiting would read from the Book. I recall but twice when we were subjected to an itinerant preacher with a hectoring voice, louder than the tinker-scryer of our May adventure. The meanness of manner of these gospeling tramps made us wonder if Jesus, so gentle a man, judging from his words and the words of those who knew him, countenanced the hellfire threats and red-faced anger of such agents borrowing on His name.

Miz Ann read from the Book to my mother and me after William joined the Kentucky militia and left me behind. I remember from these readings the tenth chapter of Genesis, about Ham, the youngest son of Noah and one of but eight people to survive the Flood. Miz Ann said Ham became the "father of the dark races" and had sons named Cush, Mizraim, Phut, and Canaan.

I dreamed of myself as Nimrod, Cush's son, who was a "mighty hunter before the Lord."

She read us the chapter of Revelations where it is told of the awful judgment against the mighty city of Babylon and how the merchants there had no one to buy their gold and precious stones, their spices and wines, "and beasts, and sheep, and horses, and chariots, and slaves, and souls of men." She explained to us there were slaves even in those olden days when the Book was written. However, she said, she preferred the word "servants."

And she read from Jeremiah and told us he was a Hebrew prophet. We did not know what a Hebrew was until she told us they were a tribe of people who lived in Africa. (I knew of Africa, the land of Rose's and Old York's birth.)

One verse in Jeremiah, in the thirteenth chapter, "Can the Ethiopian change his skin, or the leopard his spots? Then may ye also do good, that are accustomed to do evil," puzzled me all my life.

OUR PEOPLE WERE FORBIDDEN BY CUSTOM AND LAW TO KNOW about weapons, yet I came not only to know about weapons, but how to use them.

This came to pass after Captain George Rogers Clark, the eldest son and the eminent soldier of the family, came home the last autumn the family resided in Virginia. He was a great oak of a man, brown as an acorn, weathered and shaggy from his years in the wilderness, and William could scarcely contain his excitement the day he told me his brother was taking us into the woods for lessons in weaponry. "He says we need to know how to shoot. We might be attacked by Indians someday, maybe like those buried in that hillock yonder."

We went to the woods every day for two weeks until Captain George had to return to the army, and what William learned of shooting and the operation of weapons, I learned as well.

One morning Captain George brought down a deer with his rifle, cut its throat and butchered the animal with a great skinning knife he carried in a scabbard on his belt, and a keen hatchet that was slung from a loop of rope beside his packsaddle. He talked all the while, showing us how to do the work, cook the meat, and save the hide, made supple by scraping it clean to thinness, rubbing it with the animal's fat and brains, and stretching it over a frame made from a sapling.

We learned to load and fire a musket he had taken from a dead redcoat, a heavy and awkward weapon with a hurtful recoil that he called Brown Bess. We fired as well a fine flintlock, one of a pair Captain George had had made by Efraim House, a celebrated Pennsylvania gunsmith. These were things of beauty with their stocks of polished tiger-stripe maple, blue-black iron barrel, rifled bores, and cunning mechanisms. Captain George spoke of them as affectionately as if they were his offspring. He showed us their every portion and device and spoke sternly of caring for them, of cleaning the wood and particularly the metal parts—the hammer jaws that clamped on a square of sharp flint, the tiny oval pan alongside the lock with its pinhole to carry the priming charge into the breech; the frizzen, the springs, the iron post that created the sparks from the flint striker.

We loaded and fired and cleaned. We made pads for our bruised shoulders. We laughed at the reflections of our powder-blacked faces in the stream. We shot at targets Captain George set up. We shot at squirrels and rabbits and roosting buzzards, and loaded and fired and cleaned.

After a few days Captain George retired his beloved Pennsylvanias and brought us two others, rather more worn and not so sleek but still excellent weapons.

By the end of those two weeks he pronounced us "able marksmen," and during the family's removal to Kentucky, William and I were responsible for bringing game meat to the household table and thus did I become the Nimrod of my dreams, a mighty hunter before the Lord.

WILLIAM WAS FOURTEEN AND I ABOUT TWO YEARS OLDER WHEN the family gathered its belongings and animals and crossed the Alleghenies and floated its wagons down the Ohio River to its new home, called Mulberry Hill, in that part of Virginia called Kentucky. Captain George had helped build a fort near the Falls of the Ohio some years earlier to protect the settlement that came to be named Louisville, and selected the land for his family. It was a fine and fertile tract of three hundred acres on which was built a six-room log house and outbuildings.

The journey there was no lark, as William and I had expected. What vigor we had gained from our games and adventures on the Virginia plantation was tenfold increased by the work assigned us, which was no less than was expected of every man in our party. We dug rocks from the trail, laid our backs against mired wagons, chopped firewood, stood as vedettes, felled trees for rafts, fed and cared for the animals, foraged for roots and berries, and hunted.

We were five years at Mulberry Hill before William departed to serve as a militiaman on the Ohio frontier. He was now tall, deep-chested, strong and durable, and had aspired to soldier from childhood. In the years of his service he returned home twice a year or when permitted, and in our rides across the Clark lands he told me of his adventures and battles. One particularly savage fight he described occurred in the Ohio country against Indians who made their stand behind a barricade of trees uprooted in a violent windstorm. In this battle he fought alongside another Virginian from Albemarle County, a somewhat younger man named Meriwether Lewis. They became comrades-in-arms and fast friends and their destinies—as you and all the Republic well know, sir—were thereafter to be knotted.

In Captain Clark's absence I married a servant girl named Belinda who came to us from the Farquahar plantation to the south of the Clark lands. She bore me a pretty baby but died in the bearing, and the girl-child survived but a day.

Nor was Death yet done with me. God, in his inexplicable wisdom, was poised to send his minion to strike me again, and William as well.

Captain Clark, as I called him by then, resigned the army and returned home in 1796 and we had two untroubled years together at Mulberry Hill and the other Clark plantation at Shelbyville. He took me with him on a journey down the Ohio and Mississippi to New Orleans where he conducted some business, and upon our return in the spring, Miz Farquahar, old friend of the Clarks, had grievous news awaiting us. Two months past a fever had swept westward from Chesapeake Bay and assailed many Kentucky settlements, including Frankfort and Shelbyville and Louisville. Among those it carried away were Miz Ann, Rose, Old York, and three field workers.

Miz Farquahar had suffered as well, had buried her husband and two of her young children, and no amount of ministering to any of them, no cold cloths or rubbing of limbs or clysters or teas from bitter roots or reading from the Book over their sweat-soaked beds, could stave off Death.

Mister John Clark was spared, but only briefly. He was weakened by the fever and died before the new century dawned.

I found the mounds where the survivors buried my people, and on a day darkened by thunderheads placed marking stakes upon them while Captain Clark read about the Everlasting Life they would all have in God's Kingdom.

As we stood there, the wind whipping the pages of the Book, I thought of those other mounds, the hillocks we had torn asunder as boys searching for gold. At some time in the distance, I wondered, might some other eager boys dig here and find these bones and would there be a Miz Ann to warn them of the sanctity of the place and insist they disturb it no more?

THE CORPS OF DISCOVERY! AH, SIR, WHAT CAN I TELL OF IT THAT has not already been told? That is was a glorious enterprise? That it succeeded beyond Mister Jefferson's wildest dreams? Who does not know these things?

I have little to offer except to say that I was there, beginning to end, and was both blessed and cursed by the experience.

IN THE SUMMER OF 1803 CAPTAIN CLARK TOOK ME WITH HIM TO the Falls of the Ohio where we were joined by Captain Lewis, his comrade at the Fallen Timbers. There, with a number of army men and volunteers, we boarded a keelboat bound for St. Louis where the commanders of our expedition had much planning to do. Not until the spring of the year following did we depart with the keelboat and two smaller vessels, forty men, and Captain Lewis's big, lovable dog Scannon, up the Missouri River toward our wintering place among the Mandan people.

Now, dressed in buckskins, a jaunty tricorn on my head, my flintlock on my shoulder, I was a stalwart member of the Corps of Discovery and prepared to do my part—no, *more* than was expected of me—as we ventured out toward the Western Sea.

I remained Captain Clark's body servant but that work, never demanding in our youth, had diminished the more as we grew to manhood. I was called Clark's slave by Captain Lewis and Clark's nigger by others on the expedition, but Captain Clark never used such words (Miz Ann, living or dead, would not stand for it) nor did he call upon me for his personal needs. He shaved himself, bathed himself, even mended his own clothing. What of the taskmaster he had in him was directed toward others for, as in every gathering of men, we had layabouts in our company. He knew he did not have to hand me a weapon if we were in need of meat nor an ax if there was chopping to be done.

So, I helped build Fort Mandan, our winter quarters, and Fort Clatsop, on the mighty river that emptied into the Western Sea. I was among the Nimrods of the expedition, killing buffalo, deer, elk, bear, wild turkeys, sage hens, geese, and brant—whatever I could find—and I cooked the meat and fish I caught.

I gathered herbs and those which Captain Lewis pronounced edible I stirred in a stewpot with chunks of meat, including once the rancid flesh I carved from a leviathan that washed upon the shore near Fort Clatsop. And while I did not prepare it, I ate roast dog among the Pierced Nose people and stewed dog, boiled with wild leeks, rhubarb, and other herbs, among the Flatheads. (My friend Scannon, Captain Lewis's faithful dog, stayed close to his master's side when we were amongst the dog-eaters and thus survived the journey.)

I stood the watch and joined scouting parties; poled, and pulled at the oars and cordelles, until my body grieved and I lay awake on my pallet through the night, as if frozen solid, staring at the stars. Like many others, I nearly died of the labor of the struggle across the Bitterroots, nearly drowned in the rivers when our boats over-turned in rapids or were snagged on sawyers and rendered fixed in the current until we hacked them free.

I learned the rudiments of medicine from Captain Lewis who had learned them from an eminent physician of Philadelphia, and I often attended the sick and injured. The Snake girl Captain Clark called Janey was with child during our winter with the Mandan peo-ple and being but a child herself suffered great pain and difficulty in the birthing. Captain Lewis administered to her a foul potion made of a crushed rattle from a snake which gagged her and caused her to vomit but which seemed to hasten her labor. When her boy-child was freed from her belly, I gave her an herb tea, and stewed berries, and broth from the cookpot, and I stayed by her side until she re-cruited her strength. Since her husband, a feckless Frenchman called Charbonneau, neglected her, I fashioned a cradle board from willow wood, elk hide and sinew, and a piece of fishnet, so that she could carry the boy (named Jean Baptiste but called Pomp by Captain Clark) on her back as we pushed on.

YES, IT IS TRUE: THE CAST OF MY SKIN WAS OF INTEREST, EVEN awe, among the aborigines we encountered. During that first winter of our journey a Minataree chief came to our camp with an entou-rage, and while I was feeding the fire this ugly, one-eyed, fur-clad figure approached me, his retainers at his side. I stood and we stared at one another. The captains and several of our men saw us and gathered behind me while the chief, called Le Borgne, smiled, made hand signs, and uttered some words to his confederates. George

Droulliard, our translator, said, "He wants to touch you, York. He thinks you have black warpaint on, or mud, or got scorched in a fire. He's never seen a nigger before."

I smiled at Le Borgne and stepped up to him. He wet his finger and rubbed it on my cheek then looked at his finger and my cheek, and turned and laughed, holding his finger out for them to see.

Thus did I discover my special usefulness among the savages as we wandered west. The incident with Le Borgne was to be repeated many times, among the Osage, Ree, Absaroka, Snake, Nez Perce, Flathead, Clatsop, and numerous tribes and bands whose names I never knew. In one region after another I was examined by savage eyes, felt of, and asked to dance, to which I complied at the captains' urging. I would throw my head back, shuffle my feet, hold my arms out and turn in a circle while my audience nodded, laughed and clapped and chattered at one another. This tableau cannot have been much different than what Old York and Rose experienced on the Carolina slave block except that, despite many efforts among the Indians to purchase me, I was not for sale.

Only once was I angered at one of these inspections and entertainments, this when a tribal elder felt my body too personally and with too much insistence. In that instance I drew my skinning knife when I failed to extract myself from his clutching, and he withdrew while the others of his people laughed and the captains blanched and pulled me away. Captain Lewis was furious with me and upbraided his partner for my conduct but Captain Clark took me aside and said, "I do not blame you, York. Were I you I'd have used the knife on that heathen."

You may prefer not to make a record of this, sir, but, truth be told, the uniqueness of my color served me as well as it served our expedition. The Ree women, among others, found me as comely as I found them, and I, whom they called Raven's Son, was invited into their lodges at night more than once, most often with the blessings of their mates. In this I followed the example of many men of the expedition, including Captain Lewis. My master did not indulge — be quite clear about this, sir: He was much in love with a Virginia girl and faithful to her — and he said nothing to me about my venturings except to warn me that many Indian women had been poxed by French trappers.

But enough of my "role," as you call it, in the Corps of Discovery. It was insignificant except in that it instilled in me a fateful sense of independence from which nothing good thereafter flowed.

In September 1806, we gained St. Louis, our journey's end as it had been the beginning, and soon after traveled on to the Shelbyville lands where I spent the last carefree months of my life.

While Captain Clark was away on a mission to Washington, and with his beforehand blessing, I remarried. She was a girl of about fourteen years called Belle, a house servant with the Dinwiddie family of Shelbyville, who also consented to our marriage. We were a happy pair, my tiny, shy Belle and I, in those months before Captain Clark came home and instructed me to pack his trunks and prepare for our return to St. Louis.

Thus, my heart broken, I left Belle behind as the Captain and I journeyed to Fort Pickering, thence across the river to that steamy, teeming, stinking town where the only life I had known came to a sad conclusion.

I had labored three years with the Corps of Discovery, had "been a help," as John Clark said of me many years past, and had tasted independence. I rarely had orders to follow, was trusted to do my part, and did my part, and more than my part. Then, I filled my days; now, in St. Louis, I discovered more travail than any I encountered with the expedition.

I blame myself. I continued to serve Captain Clark, whom I now addressed as "General," befitting his new eminence as Brigadier of Militia and Indian Agent for Louisiana Territory. But in the big house in which he was now ensconced with Miz Julia, his wife, I had little to do and grew restless, even "fractious," as I overheard him report of me to Captain Lewis, now governor of the territory, who often came visiting.

My miseries, which I ought not to have outwardly expressed, were that I missed my wife, was homesick for Kentucky, had grown tired of idle confinement, and began to think myself too pridefully as more of a man than an accessory to another man.

General Clark tried to assuage me. In the year 1810 he directed dispatches to Washington and allowed me to accompany the courier as far as Louisville so that I might have a reunion with Belle. I returned with the courier and his escort and showed my gratitude with insolence, asking that I be freed from his service.

The general was capable of ire and I saw it that day and hung my head but did not apologize for affronting him.

The following year he manumitted me and all his servants and arranged for those who wished to return to Kentucky to be hired to work on the Clark lands. Some stayed with him in St. Louis as employees.

He took me aside the day I departed and said he had not forgotten my service to him and to the expedition. "Of late you have sorely tried my patience," he said, "but I measure that as a mere inconvenience in the scheme of our many years together."

With that, he read a letter to me that he was sending his brother Jonathan in Louisville ordering that I be given a dray and four strong horses and "encouragement for employment."

He told me I could earn a decent living in the drayage business and reminded me that Old York had a way with horses and so might I. At the end, he said, "Mind this, friend York: You are a free man now. You have no one to direct your days but yourself. Do not permit your freedom to be a burden."

Of course it *was* a burden; how could it not have been?

You ask if I am bitter as if you expect me to be.

Do you recognize the admonition "Let all bitterness, and wrath, and anger, and clamour, and evil speaking, be put away from you, with all malice"? Miz Ann Clark taught us that and never was wiser advice writ. I have tried to abide by it. I have tried *not* to follow Isaiah's example when he said, "I shall go softly all my years in the bitterness of my soul."

I never expected a sack of gold coins and an allotment of land, the rewards the others received, for my service in the Corps of Discovery. I have had, after all, a life of rewards. I was General Clark's servant and friend from our childhood and have spoken of the privileges those honors bestowed. I learned to utter these words you are writing down, learned many other things forbidden to my people by custom and law, and eventually I was accorded the greatest gift of all—my freedom—to a joy that you, who have always been free, cannot imagine.

I have rue. I regret my insolence toward General Clark and trying his patience; I rue my station in life in which I remain, even though a free man and sole author of my failures as well as my successes, awkward in my freedom and confused as to how I can make it less a burden.

But bitter? I am a man cursed by the sin of Ham, the Ethiopian who cannot change his skin any more than the leopard his spots, but one who journeyed to the Western Sea and saw things no man of my color before me saw.

How could I be bitter?

Melodies the Song Dogs Sing

WIN BLEVINS

Greatest of all the mountain men and one of the most compelling figures of the Old West was Jedediah Smith (1799–1831), born in Bainbridge, New York. He came to the Rocky Mountains in 1822, accomplished all that is told in the story that follows, and died at the hands of Comanches in a buffalo wallow on the Cimarron River nine years after he came to the wilderness.

Thomas Fitzpatrick (1799–1854) of County Caven, Ireland, stands second only to Smith among the trapper-explorers of the Rockies. Called Broken Hand after he crippled a hand in a firearms accident, Fitzpatrick also served as a guide for the army and Oregon Trail pioneers, and served as an Indian agent.

Novelist Win Blevins is an authority on the Plains Indians and fur-trade era of the West. His rollicking tribute to the mountain man, *Give Your Heart to the Hawks,* remains in print thirty years after its first publication; his novel of Crazy Horse, *Stone Song,* earned several prestigious literary prizes; and such novels as *Charbonneau, Rock Child, RavenShadow,* and most recently, *So Wild a Dream* (first of the "Rendezvous" series of novels of the Rocky Mountain fur-trade era) have established him as among the best writers of the West.

"YOU DON'T UNDERSTAND ONE damn thing about Jedediah Smith," I said softly at the bunch of them.

I know what the men say about me: Every damn thing he feels shows on his face, and sometimes his tongue lashes it out. All right, this time I sounded grumpy as a griz. What I felt, though . . . Hard to talk about. Call it the biggest ache of my thirty-something years. Can't say more yet.

I glared across the table at all four of them.

"How about a game?" Pegleg called from across the cantina. Three of the men got up and shambled that way. I noticed that they'd rather play euchre, or that new game, poker, or any pathetic game, than listen to me moan and groan.

What if you are Tom Fitzpatrick? You're miserable company.

Understandable.

Only Antoine, the Frenchy breed, stayed. Though he's an old *compañero* I sent hard thoughts at him: The cantina's full of tables. Why don't you go find a better drinking partner?

I sipped at the booze and coughed at its roughness. Maybe Antoine liked drinking my liquor. A jug of *aguardiente,* what the Mexicans call brandy. I hadn't had a good brandy, much less whiskey, since I left Ireland. In America and Mexico we drink whatever rotgut anyone brewed up yesterday. I felt like cussing the New World liquor and New World ways and everything else about this misbegotten continent. Other times, I feel like it's really a New World, a chance for human beings to start fresh. The tides of my feelings are big.

I poured another drink for Antoine, then myself.

Antoine was the one who'd come to find me this afternoon. Him and me and the whole outfit just rode into Santa Fe three days ago. The two of us, we've ridden together since I first came to the mountains, 1823. What would that be, eight years and three months ago?

71

Today four Mexicans came to town to trade, and among the stuff was a bear claw necklace, two fine percussion pistols, and a rifle. Antoine for sure recognized the weapons, but he just told me there was something I should take a look at.

Jedediah's. Even if I hadn't known the guns, I'd never have missed the silver chain with the griz claws he wore hidden under his shirt.

Goddamn every wicked-hearted son of a bitch . . .

"From Comanches we them traded," said this young Mexican. "You like?" Mexicans speak English funny, but at least it has melody, not that flat, American accent.

I asked how the Comanches got them, and he told me their story. I'd have to tell Sublette and the others.

"For why did he come on this trip?" Antoine asked me, knowing perfectly well. "He quit. What you call it? Retired."

Well, he tried to.

"I never understand this man anyhow. I like him, but no understand him."

Nobody did.

All past now. Jedediah Smith was dead.

"Maybe you talk about him?" said Antoine. Probably thinking not to help himself, but me.

THE FIRST TIME I LEARNED ANYTHING ABOUT JEDEDIAH SMITH was on that beach below the lower Ree village. Diah had come down from the junction of the Missouri and Yellowstone, three hundred miles upriver, bringing a message from Major Henry to General Ashley. He came alone, in a canoe, traveling through Indian country at night and caching during the day. Right quick the rest of us, even greener on the mountains and plains than him, thought of all the Indians eager to pop the scalp off a lone white traveler and said to ourselves, "That hoss is *some*."

Still, we didn't warm to him. He didn't have much to say, seemed to prefer his own company, and did something queer: I'd never seen anyone but a priest do it. He read a worn copy of the Bible.

We'd traded for some horses and needed to hold them somewhere. The beach below the village was as good as any other choice, but still indefensible. Diah volunteered to head up twenty men who would mind the new horses. The Rees claimed they had good hearts. We weren't so sure. I think every man on the beach that night went sleepless. The next night too.

When the Indians opened fire at first light, shooting down from behind pickets, half our men and most of the horses fell in the first volley. Those of us left alive squeezed behind dead horseflesh and returned fire, when we could get up the gumption to stick our heads up. Shooting at enemies behind pickets was pissing into the wind.

Ashley and the bulk of the men were in mid-river on the two keelboats. He sent two rowboats for us, and some of our lot made it to the boats alive. Others jumped into the river, and some of those never came up. The rest of us gave them what covering fire we could.

Before long we fools still on the beach saw the Rees advancing from upriver, intending to finish the job. Diah hollered at me, Tom Eddie, and Jim Clyman to run like hell. He gave us cover, and with mountain luck we made the water and swam. Diah was the last man off that beach.

Then everybody knew he was *some*. And we felt things for him we didn't talk about.

The next day, after we floated downriver, we buried the bodies of the two wounded who didn't survive. Diah came up with another of his surprises. He preached a powerful and sonorous prayer, the first time I'd ever heard American Protestant preaching. Though such a sermon could never convert a fallen-away, priest-hating Catholic like me, it gave my mind a twist, and more than that. Probably none of us remembered the exact words later, something about having seen God's sternness and needing now to see His compassion. What we couldn't get out of our minds was the strange and remarkable man who was our comrade.

Of course, the prayer made some snicker. Ignoramuses are everywhere.

As things fell out, Ashley assigned me to the first brigade Diah ever led. It was also the first to go to the mountains overland. On the way he got mauled by the griz—everybody knows that story. While the rest of us quaked at the sight of all that blood from his head, Diah coolly instructed Clyman how to sew up his scalp and his ear.

Sometimes I've wondered if that's when it began to happen.

• • •

IT WAS THE DREAMS, THE DREAMS THAT WOULDN'T GO AWAY. He lay in his blankets with his scalp blood-gullied and his ear screaming out pain and squirmed and rolled and flailed with fever and dreamed . . . of going into a bear's mouth.

Later, as his companions told it, he found out how the griz knocked him down and took his head in its great maw. That's how he got those scars, which he would carry to his grave.

The dreams, though, were not horrors. They were ceremonious. Jedediah would enter a great room, the way he imagined maybe a novice came into the cathedral where mysteries would be performed. Then a priest would emerge, a representative of God on earth, or of the Roman Pope. Coming in, Jedediah felt like a supplicant. The sleeping, feverish man rebelled. As a good Methodist he despised Rome and all its trappings and falsehoods. Yet the supplicant marched on to the front of the room. There he knelt— the supplicant could not see what he bowed down to, and was frightened. The supplicant rose, bowed again, and walked forward mechanically into the huge mouth of a great, gilded statue of a grizzly bear.

That was as far as the dream went, ever. Jedediah would wake up, shake himself violently, and throw off his childish fears. The moment he slept again, the dream returned, the same dream, it seemed like, forever and ever.

After a few days he was well enough to pay attention when Fitzpatrick and Clyman told him how he got hurt. That made the dream a little less strange, but no less disturbing.

The moment he could sit in his saddle, he led the men on west. Work kept the dream at bay.

He told himself the dream was a peculiar version of Jonah going whole into the belly of the whale. Yet he still didn't know what to make of it. In his prayers at night he laid it before his God. But God seemed silent on this subject. Perhaps He was even far away, away in the settlements.

Diah said nothing of the dream to any man.

In the Crow village that winter a medicine man presented Jedediah with a strange gift, a trio of grizzly bear claws.

Some of the more superstitious trappers believed the Indian medicine man had supernatural powers. As a Christian and a modern American, Jedediah emphatically believed not.

He told himself that the claws were nothing but a symbol of his survival of the attack of the bear, something to be proud of.

He strung them on a rawhide thong and wore them under his shirt, so no one would think him superstitious, or maybe so no one would know he worshiped the bear in his dreams.

Later, in California, he bought a silver chain and strung them on that. Always, for the rest of his life, he wore them. In bad moments he thought of them as the mark of the beast, but he never took them off. He couldn't have said why.

I TOOK A SIP AND THOUGHT A MOMENT.

Antoine, you weren't in that first brigade. We could hardly believe Captain Smith, as we called him then, was ready to ride just ten days after that griz worked him over. Nor did we easily believe the things we saw him do over the next year. Jedediah Smith showed himself a special man, a cut above, a statement I don't make lightly. In February, though we should have sat out the winter for another month, he got us going and after some hard times—really hard—we found the Southern Pass to the Siskadee. We knew right off it was the mother lode of beaver country. So he had fulfilled one of his big ambitions, finding a fur fortune.

The man had a bigger ambition, though, much bigger. He wanted to fill in all the blank spaces on the maps of the western half of the New World. When he started, almost all of it was terra incognita. Everywhere he went he kept a journal of what he saw and did, and drew careful, exact maps of the country he traveled. Consider: Between 1825 and 1829 he rode (or often walked) from St. Louis across the Great Plains and Rocky Mountains to the Great Salt Lake, across the deserts to San Bernardino, California, across the Sierra Nevada and back to the Salt Lake, then back to California, up the coast to the Columbia River, and back to the Yellowstone country. Gives me saddle sores just to say it all.

On those journeys he consistently took the hardest jobs, accepted the biggest risks, and looked after the welfare of every man as best anyone could. He taught the men who followed him what it is to be a hero.

Which might give us second thoughts about becoming one.

Sometime, I don't know when, the troubles started for him. I mean the deep-inside-the-mind troubles, the ones a man can never ride far enough or fast enough to get away from.

THE DREAMS GOT WORSE. AT NIGHT HE TURNED INTO ANIMALS. At first this seemed in its way civilized, ceremonial. He was a grizzly, and as a grizzly would walk down the central aisle of a cathedral he could never really see. He knew there were pews, and statues along the side, and stained-glass windows bringing holy light into the nave. It all had a kind of Catholic feeling, which made his Methodist spirit shudder. But he knew it was worse than Catholic—it was pagan. He could never see what kinds of statues were there, or what order of priest presided, or worst of all what demon of Satan or Mammon commanded the nave, and there was worshiped.

His journeys down that central aisle were odd. First he would be a grizzly, then an elk, then a moose, and then a wolf. The order of his incarnations seemed inflexible and somehow important. And he felt the heart of each animal, for it was his own heart. The grizzly was bold and bloody, ready to seize salmon from a rushing river or run down deer and devour them. The moose was still, watchful, bovine of mind, superior to all other creatures. The elk was tenderhearted, jittery, pleased to graze but eager to run. The wolf was cunning, sly, ready to pounce upon the weak, the defenseless.

What the creatures shared, though, horrified both the dreaming and the waking Diah. They had no words, no thoughts, no consciousness above the primitive, no souls. They were cut off forever from God. They were, he trembled to think, mere beasts of nature.

In the mornings, after these splendid dream pageants, he woke in cold sweats. He thought of his comrades, who he sometimes thought were becoming Indians. He thought of the Indians, who were as placidly natural as beasts, unaware of their exile from God. He thought of the beasts, denizens of the darkness.

He thought many mornings what he never permitted himself to say: I am losing my soul.

.   .   .

His second trip to California, seemed like, was devil-tormented. Every possible disaster grabbed him.

I have always thought that Diah made those trips, well, not for the reasons he said. His official reason was to find new trapping grounds—see if there was beaver southwest of the Great Salt Lake, especially, and maybe find out if California was beaver country. After all, he was main partner of the new company Smith, Jackson, & Sublette, and finding fur was their business.

He never said a word about what really pushed him. First part of it was to fill in that map he was always working on, get a picture of the whole big West in his mind and then on paper, and publish it. Second part was, Diah had a hunger to see new country like no man I ever knew. Much as he wanted to go to heaven, he was in love with the earth—the shoulders of hills, the saddles between mountains, the stretchings and dippings of deserts, the curves of creeks.

It was this hunger and this love that bound me to him. Where everyone respected and admired him, I loved him.

Sometimes I wonder if he condemned himself for this love of wild places. Maybe he saw it as another form of worldliness, devotion to the things of time, another barrier between him and the eternal.

Regardless. Halfway back to California, he visited the Mojave Indians again (as we call them now), there on the Colorado River. Hospitable as they were in 1826, he expected no trouble, and divided his men into two groups to raft across the river. While the first bunch was in midstream, the Mojaves fell on the nine men left and rubbed them out right quick, and all the horses too. The survivors had to fight the Indians off on the other side, slip away into the Mojave Desert, and walk across it to San Bernardino, finding water along the way. Only a brigade led by Diah would have lived through it.

That may have been when he met the priest he talked so much about, Father José, the head of San Gabriel Mission. Strange that a papist could mean so much to Jedediah.

Making a long story short, he met up with the men he left there the year before and they all headed for Oregon. Along the way, he went out one morning to scout ahead, leaving strict instructions for the men to let no Indians into camp. As you've heard, they did the opposite, and the combined brigades were massacred. Only Diah and three others survived.

We gave him up for lost. After another year, when he'd recovered his furs, he limped into rendezvous and gladdened every heart.

Yet the two massacres, and all the men he led to their deaths, maybe they weren't the worst of that trip. Diah told me something I don't think he talked about to anyone else. I'll tell you, but I don't know if I believe it, quite. Cursed little incident as he was riding into a Paiute village . . .

THE WORLD SWAM THROUGH JEDEDIAH'S EYES. HE HAD PERMISsion to ride into the village, making signs first with the lookout and then the leader. They seemed skittish. He suspected, since they were down near the Grand Canyon of the Colorado, that these people had never seen a white man before, and seldom seen a horse. Still, they said go ahead, we want to trade.

But the world swayed. Heat waves undulated up from the sand and made his mind rock like a boat. Otherwise he would have paid sharper attention to the little girl.

She suddenly stood up from her play in the creek. She stared down like she was seeing water monsters. Then she looked up straight at Diah, eyes wide with horror, mouth open in a silent scream.

And she keeled over.

Diah was quick off his mount to lift her slight body in his strong arms and hold her like he would his own child.

The girl's nose and mouth hadn't even been under water, but . . .

Villagers came screeching out, their fear of strangers overcome by alarm for the girl. Jedediah handed her to the woman who acted like her mother. Then he turned toward the men of the brigade, who still sat their horses, looking unconcerned and maybe a little tickled.

Diah kneeled to put himself at the girl's height and made himself see what she saw. He looked at the brigade reflected in the still water of the creek, rippling and flickering mysteriously. Then he looked up at it directly. American horses, giants compared to the Spanish ponies she might have seen in that country, if she'd ever seen horses at all. Men with faces of white, a ghostly color. Hair of colors that hair can't be—sun-bleached yel-

low, red, and brown. And wild, impossible hair, covering men's faces, making them . . .

Have we become monsters? cried the soul of Jedediah Smith.

For the little Paiute girl, as he'd instantly known, was dead of fright.

He told me more than once, as we passed the time around campfires, that not only were Indians dangerous to white men, wilderness itself was. Not to their physical lives, but to their souls. Instead of bringing civilization to the wilds, or Christianity to the heathen, the beaver men were themselves becoming wild creatures.

One time I joked at him, "At least you're not."

He gave me the most stricken look I've ever seen from a human being. "You don't know," he said, in a voice like the moaning wind.

I started to say I damn well did know. We all could see he didn't drink. He read Scripture while the rest of us were seducing whatever women were willing. If there was a dangerous job, he was quick to take it. He treated everyone, white, black, or red, with respect. If the Bible spells out righteous correctly, I've never known a man so righteous.

But I held my tongue. I could see my friend was suffering.

"I feel the need of a Christian church," he said.

I had to admit: I couldn't tell what was going on, in the dark of night, in the heart of Jedediah Smith.

I wanted to help him. But I myself am an unbeliever. I do not credit these imaginings of divinity, these shadow plays of morality . . .

Oh, never mind. I could not help my friend. God forgive me my unbelief.

In Monterey he went to a priest and confessed. Him, a devout Methodist. He couldn't believe it, not when he first thought of it, not when he entered the church, not when he was at the confessional. He offered himself one flimsy excuse. Father José had been such a good man, such a good Christian, maybe . . .

Jedediah Smith was determined, regardless of whether the priest in that confessional box was good or bad, to bare his soul. He told about his terrible mistakes, leading two brigades of three dozen men and getting nearly every one killed. He told of his usurping the right the Lord God reserved to himself, vengeance—for Jedediah Smith had sometimes lusted for blood, had taken sneaky pleasure in the sad necessity of killing Indians. He spoke frankly of the lust in his heart: He had left home originally because he wanted the woman who married his older brother Ralph, and he wanted her still today. He was a vicious hypocrite: He left the drunken and lecherous carousings of his men to go to his tent and in private, in fantasy, covet his brother's wife.

He told of being a murderer. He had become such a monster, he confessed, that the mere sight of him had killed an innocent Paiute child.

He saved the most important and the most difficult for last. He dreamt continually of becoming an animal. In these dreams he was a bear, a moose, an elk, or a wolf, usually all four, in a ritualistic procession that mocked Christian ceremony. He feared that he was making himself from a human being, a physical chalice carrying a sacred spirit, into a mere animal, a body without a soul. He feared that he had snuffed out, in his own heart, the divine spark.

Here he let his voice rise and sound out. "This is the one unforgivable sin," he cried. "I am the killer of God. I have killed him within myself."

He fell silent, self-condemned, beyond hope.

The priest murmured something about never doubting the power of God to redeem, but Jedediah hardly listened and didn't understand. Then the priest assigned him foolish outward acts to perform, saying "Hail, Mary" so many times, counting his rosary beads so many times, as though he would soil his hands with such papist perversion.

He stumbled from the dark confessional to the shadowed church and into the bright, sunstruck streets of Monterey in a rage. Accused, found guilty, and sentenced to death. He wanted to bawl out to a forgiving God for mercy. But this God was dead, murdered by Jedediah Smith.

DURING THE LAST TWO YEARS HE WAS REMOTE, BOTHERED. WE did big beaver hunts, marching through Blackfoot country where no one had trapped before, to speak of, because Bug's Boys are so dangerous. We went in numbers, Jedediah led coolly, and we came away with no blood lost and a harvest of peltries that would satiate the avarice of a Midas.

Everything looked so good, you remember, that I went in with Jim Bridger and some others and bought the whole shebang from Smith, Jackson, & Sublette. Now we were the big power in the mountains, and we wanted to do as they had done, pluck a fortune out of the creeks.

Jedediah? He'd decided to retire. That's what he said—retire. Go to St. Louis and live the life of a gentleman. He could afford a grand house and servants. He could put his money to work, instead of going hungry and thirsty and cold and risking his hide for it. He could escape the wild life. He could return to civilization, his beloved church, and a community of Christians.

WINTER CAMP ON THE WIND RIVER, CHRISTMAS EVE, *1829. A courier was about to leave for St. Louis, to make the dreadful trip across the bitter, snowy, windy plains to take care of essential fur business. Jedediah sent along a letter, an "unworthy son" addressing his "Mutch Slighted Parents." He assured them that his business was nearly completed, and "I will endeavor, by the assistance of Divine Providence, to come home as soon as possible, the greatest pleasure I could enjoy, would be . . . to be in company with my friends."*

On the same day he wrote his brother Ralph, "I find myself one of the most ungrateful, unthankful, Creatures imaginable. Oh when Shall I be under the care of a Christian Church? I have need of your prayers, I wish our Society to bear me up before a Throne of grace."

When he finished one more profitable hunt among the Blackfeet, Jedediah did close his business, selling out to his friends Tom Fitzpatrick, Jim Bridger, and three others. Then he turned his face toward the settlements, and in October reached that fur capital with a great load of peltries. The newspapers sang praises of his career in the mountains, his great accomplishments under the most arduous conditions, and his well-earned wealth.

He bought that big house and retained servants. Now he would have time to finish that map, far more complete than any yet published, and write that book about his adventures. Best of all, two of his younger brothers joined him in St. Louis.

At last he had everything he wanted. Didn't he?

. . .

I got to St. Louis late. The deal was, my partners and I would send word to St. Louis to let Smith and Jackson know whether our hunts were good and we wanted a wagon train to supply us for another year in the mountains. You remember, Antoine, I found all of you near the kickoff point, Lexington, Missouri, heading west. Instead of March I'd arrived in May. The first surprise was that you weren't headed for our rendezvous but for Santa Fe. The second was, the leaders were Bill Sublette and none other than Jedediah Smith.

Right quick we agreed that I would go along with your outfit to Santa Fe, and there, somehow, Smith and Sublette would outfit me.

I was glad to be with Diah. But I couldn't ask the questions I wanted to ask. My friend, you foreswore the mountains. You feared they were turning you into a heathen. You wanted preachers, not medicine men. You sought hymns, not the howls of wolves in the lonely night. You wanted good, God-fearing people around you, not this ragtag bunch of Kentucky backwoodsmen, French-Canadian half-breeds, Spaniards, and Indians.

Why, Jedediah, why are you going back to the wilds?

He commented in an offhand way that the Santa Fe trade would be profitable. Maybe after Santa Fe he would go into Mexico and see some new country.

I looked into his eyes for the truth. Though I couldn't be sure, and he would have denied it, I thought Jedediah had become like me. He no longer found his sense of the divine in the crucifix, or at the altar of a Christian church. He found it on the mountaintop, in the sunset across a waterless desert, the croak of the raven, the harmony of the coyotes. Funny, Diah and I used to like to sit quiet, when everyone else was asleep, and listen to the coyotes sing. Some called them prairie wolves, and others called them song dogs. I liked that name song dog. Their yips, heard individually at first, didn't quite make music. But then they would begin to answer each other—yes, I'm here, yes, I want to mate, yes—and the many cries melded into a magical music. The music of my heart, I told Diah. Too wild a heart, Diah answered.

But if Diah was changed, I couldn't bring myself to speak to him about it. He was too private a man for that.

For a good while it was an uneventful trip. We followed the usual trail as far as the Cimarron crossing. There we had a choice. Stick with the Arkansas, the long way, or cut over to the Cimarron. Trouble was, the Cimarron River lay forty or fifty miles south, and it was a dry drive. Plus, when you got there, you might have a hard time finding water. That river has a way of disappearing and popping back up.

We took the shortcut. Time was important, especially for me, as I was going to miss rendezvous. Three days later, when all the water we could carry was gone, we got desperate.

Jedediah and I went ahead to find water. It felt good, the sort of task we'd done together many times, the risk we'd run over and over and laughed about. Just like you and I have, Antoine.

Before long we came to a hollow that showed signs of water but was dry. I stayed there to dig, to see if I could get a little help for man and beast.

Jedediah rode off in the direction of the river, and none of us ever saw him again.

You remember how we eventually found some watery holes in that damned river, and eventually got to Santa Fe.

I kept hoping he would turn up.

Until today, when you spotted his necklace and weapons.

After you went off, I grilled those Mexicans for every detail they'd got from the Comanches. Seems it went down like this:

He found water and rode right up to it, since his horse was suffering from thirst.

The Comanches were hiding, waiting for a buffalo to come to water.

They surrounded him. He tried to make palaver with them, but it didn't work. Someone shot him.

Knowing his fate, Jedediah raised his rifle and blew the leader to kingdom come.

The rest of the Comanches riddled him with bullets and arrows.

They took what he owned, and probably his scalp too. They left his body, I'm sure, but we wouldn't find it in a month of looking.

He belongs to the ravens now, and the coyotes. The sun will parch his flesh and bleach his bones. Sooner or later the wind will blow his dust wherever it goes, wherever it goes.

You know what?

I think he died where he wanted to, and maybe when. I think his casket of sand is a good one, and the murmurings of the river waters as good as hymns.

He couldn't bear his conflict any longer.

Jedediah, your mind read Scriptures. Your heart sang the melodies of the song dogs.

Gabe and the Doctor

RICHARD C. HOUSE

Virginian Jim Bridger (1804–1881) spent nearly fifty years in the Rocky Mountains as explorer, trapper, and guide, surviving countless Indian skirmishes and battles against the trackless and remorseless wilderness.

Among his many memorable traits, Bridger was the maestro of the "windy," the tall tale told to his mountain-man mates around a campfire on the trail or at the annual fur-trade fair called rendezvous.

The story told here is no windy—at least insofar as the encounter Bridger had with Dr. Marcus Whitman at the Green River rendezvous of 1835. The rest of it, masterfully told by R. C. House, sounds authentic as well.

Richard C. House is a past president and the only member of WWA (or any other writers' organization) to have an asteriod named after him. The honor came as a result of his twenty-three-year career as an editor for the NASA Jet Propulsion Laboratory in California.

He is the author of twelve novels, many stories and nonfiction works, and appears reg-

ularly in audiobooks and anthologies. Under
the penname Beau Jacques he has written extensively in gun publications and is recognized
as a guru in the blackpowder-muzzleloader fraternity.

While we continued in this place, Dr. Whitman was called upon to perform some very important surgical operations. He extracted an arrow point, three inches long, from the back of Captain Bridger, which was received in a skirmish three years before with the Blackfeet Indians. It was a difficult operation because the arrow was hooked at the point by striking a large bone and the cartilaginous substance had grown around it. The doctor pursued the operation with great self-possession and perseverance; and the patient manifested equal firmness.
—Samuel Parker, *Journal of an Exploring Tour Beyond the Rocky Mountains* (Ithaca, New York, 1838.)

BRIDGER SHOOED THREE WOOZY
celebrants away from the small campfire. With grim determination he hustled Marcus Whitman to it by the arm, looking anxiously over his shoulder to make sure they wouldn't be disturbed.

Dr. Whitman, new to the dusty, smoky, and noisy sprawl of the 1835 rendezvous, was amused by, and humoring, the crusty, insistent man in frayed buckskins blackened by smoke and varnished by hand-wipings of old meat grease. Forcing down a grin, he consented to being led like a roped goat.

Broken-Hand Tom Fitzpatrick, Whitman's guide on the long journey west, had assured him that the legendary Bridger could be of considerable value to the doctor-missionary's plans to minister to the Indians in Oregon; thus Whitman was delighted to meet the fabled pathfinder.

Bridger crouched, motioning Whitman to get close to the fire on the seat-logs near him. When the doctor hunkered down, the mountain man hitched himself annoyingly close.

Bridger abruptly reached out a hand, rudely catching the back of Whitman's head and jerking it closer to him. Whitman complied and bent, still amused over the eccentric behavior of the peculiar Western trapper, guide, and legendary tale-spinner.

"Doc," Bridger began in apologetic, hushed tones. "I got some-thin' I got a desperate need to take up with you. I ain't seen a real sawbones in I don't know when."

His voice and his eyes pleaded; something odd, Whitman thought, for a man of Jim Bridger's reputation for being bold and aggressive.

Here was a man, he knew, who had faced death in a hundred ways, had fought, lived with Indians and romped with their women, battled man-killing beasts of the wilds, at times nearly starved or died of thirst. And foremost, this formidable man had traced the land-marks, the rivers, and the trails around and over the frowning, for-bidding mountains and across the bleak unending plains in the hunt for beaver, and for sustaining meat. Here was a man who truly matched the mountains, who knew this mighty land intimately.

"At your service, sir. Want to tell me of your problem?" He half expected Bridger to unburden himself about a case of the piles, or a dose of the pox caught from an unhealthy squaw.

"It's a arra, Doc," Bridger said, cocking his shaggy head and grimacing self-consciously.

"A what?"

Bridger glared impatiently now, his voice gruff. "A arrahead! Three year ago it were, in a scrape with the Blackfeet. I taken a arra into my person. For a fact, two of 'em, but one of 'em's out and gives me no more miseries. The other'n—the head—stayed stuck yonder where I sit down. My nether regions."

"I understand. Pray continue, Mr. Bridger. Be assured your se-crets are safe with me. My professional oath."

Bridger relaxed a bit. He looked around him; no one was close. "You can call me Gabe. Or Jim. Rest do. Whatsomever, a boy in our mess was a young thickheaded German, name of Riehl. Well, after we settled with the Blackfeet that time, Virginny, like we called him—he's long since been killed and skulped by the Pawnee—set about to yank them arras outten my backside. Lord, he was rough! You know them bullheaded Germans when it comes to finishin' a job of work once started. Them arras seemed stuck there for good and all. But one wun't too far under the hide and slid out slicker'n calf slobber after only a mite of bindin' agin the tender meat because of the barbs. He twisted and turned 'er a bit and I jerked and squirmed a fair amount, and out she come."

Whitman shuddered at Bridger's graphic revelation, still beguiled by the old raconteur's yarn. In these entrancing moments, Whitman's major cares and concerns briefly vanished: his dreams of a God-sent medical mission among the heathen Oregon Indians; his love for and visions of marriage and a worship-filled future in the West with his intended bride, the comely Narcissa Prentiss; his current traveling companion, the peevish Reverend Samuel Parker, and all the other joys and travails of this often maddening quest to serve the Lord in a country ignorant of or oblivious to His great and merciful power.

Instead, Whitman hung on the next revelation of the rugged myth-man next to him at the dwindling rendezvous fire. Bridger's eyes narrowed.

"Trouble is, Doc, the other arra slipped its moorings. Naught but shaft and sinew wrappin's come out. Virginny still went at 'er like a duck on a June bug with his skinnin' knife. Even lanced my hide and hams for a better look. That arrahead was cached outten his reach. Lord, it pains me to recall. After he'd dug in my meat for a lifetime of misery, it took considerable persuasion, but I got him to call off his expedition. I figured when I got back down to the states, I'd see a right regular sawbones and git 'er treated proper. Say this: it never festered."

"It's still in there?"

"Right smart."

"Three years?"

"Yassir."

"The pain must be excruciating."

His prospective patient warmed to his tale.

"Gets so I don't pay it particular mind most of the time, Doc. Sometimes she gives me the miseries of the damned. Like too long on a plug hoss and I commence to relive Virginny's cuttin' and pokin' and proddin' and pryin' with every jolt."

Bridger edged away, propped elbows on knees and continued.

"Cain't sleep on my backside neither er I'll forget and roll over and she'll twist in there and send me six feet straight up with a whoop in the middle of the night!"

"I'll have a look at it, but there's little I can do out here, Jim," Whitman said. "I have the instruments, but nothing to dull the pain of such a major procedure. From what you tell me, it's buried deep, probably in bone. Laudanum simply isn't enough to help in a surgical invasion so major. They'll hear you scream all over this camp."

"Doc, you don't know me. Ner do you know this kentry and how it can prove a man! I'll stand it, 'y God, never you mind. You're the first chance I've had to get 'er outten there clean and proper. I mayn't ever get another chance. I'll pay whatever it takes."

"Money is no object, Jim. Though it offends me to the core, I could deaden you with whiskey."

Bridger stiffened. "Never you mind, Doc. I take whiskey for my shinin' times. This here ain't one of 'em. I wun't abide laudanum neither. That rot's for pilgrims, greenhorns, and other such lily-livers and pork-eater trash. Permit me to take 'er like a standin'-up, 'y God, plews-and-parfleche hivernant! I'll not scream, you can take my word. That's somethin' this coon's never gone back on. Just that you have to do your cuttin' and diggin' in my lodge so's these nosy ol' coons wun't have to know."

"Why all the secrecy?"

Bridger looked Whitman in the eye. "Doc, you're new to this kentry. I respect your grit for comin' here. And why. But they's two things a hivernant cain't abide. That's never to retreat from a fair fight, ner get snuck up on from behind."

"Those wounds were in a fair fight, even with the odds against you, I'm sure. You didn't retreat, and they sure didn't sneak up on your blind side.

"I've told some bodacious windies around the night fires," Bridger went on. "Of where I been, what I done, and what I seen. Them coons know what I tell 'em is stretched a mite if not pulled plumb outta j'int. This one's for a fact and they'd no-how figure it was true. I'd be hee-hawed."

"I still don't understand," Whitman said.

"That's what I been trying to tell ya about, you being a pilgrim that don't understand this kentry, ner us hivernant mountain men. Don't you see? Them arras was stuck in my hind end! How're them coons yonder s'posed to know I wun't skedaddlin' er let myself get booshwhacked from my backtrail? Any of 'em's a sign of stupidity or cowardice."

Whitman brightened with inspiration. Bridger had revealed that a great deal more than pride was involved; his legend, too, was at stake.

"Cowardice!" he exclaimed. "You've carried that arrowhead inside you and suffered the agonies for three years and that's cowardice? From what you tell me, you and Virginia and others were surrounded. That you're here is testament that you fought your way out against a superior force."

"Was in a surround, 'y God!"

"No dishonor in that."

"Nary a whit, Whitman." Bridger's usually grim-set mouth twisted into a small grin with his pun.

"What's this 'hivernant' you speak of?"

"Why, Doc, that's a pork-eater that ain't et but hog, hominy, and hoccakes down on the farm before comin' out here to trap. If he lives long enough to get to his second ronnyvoo—or he wintered over, you might say—he can call himself a hivernant, a hibernator, like a griz."

Mulling all that, Whitman decided on a brazen gamble. Fitzpatrick told him he'd have to earn the esteem of these men of the Shining Mountains. Here was the chance to win Jim Bridger's eternal gratitude and for himself to become the talk of the rendezvous encampment.

"Jim, if you say you could stand my opening the old wound to probe for the arrowhead without a peep, why not show the world— and your cronies—once and for all what Gabe Bridger's really made of? They'd forget to ask how you got the arrow. Have me do it before the whole camp. Wouldn't you be about the greatest hivernant of all?"

Bridger blinked as he regarded Whitman soberly.

"Doc, I'd have to drop my britches. Out here we may have rough manners, but we're particular about showin' off our privates or our bare backsides."

"I'll put a cloak of some sort over you with a hole to expose only the area I work on. No one has to see more than that."

The trapper's doubting eyes suddenly turned bright. "Done, by beaver! Give these ronnyvooin' coons somethin' to chew on over the night fires for years to come!"

Whitman exulted. He was well on his way to creating his own legend.

Within an hour after Bridger broke the news to his old friend, the genial Joe Meek, word of the upcoming surgery—as Old Gabe predicted—became the talk of the rendezvous, a refreshing surge of campfire chatter and celebration among the rough-and-tough-as-hell rustics calling themselves mountain men. Fresh jugs of Taos Lightnin', a staple at the annual trappers' fair, put dispositions in a merry mood to await the morrow's main event.

Marcus Whitman, strolling the darkening camp alone, absorbed the strange and fascinating experiences and sensations among this untamed, raucous breed. The lateness of the American Fur Company caravan of trade goods, coupled with talk of the dreary market for beaver pelts, had dampened the usual no-holds-barred revelry of the rendezvous. Now a new, vigorous spirit burst forth to swell the roar of celebration.

Typical of the frolic, wild wagering and nightfire auguring sessions began in deadly earnest. The betting stakes between the Bridger loyalists and the surgery skeptics were measured in beaver plews. In many cases, the results of a year's suffering and labor were laid on the line. Forget the much-needed trade goods. "Hell, this hyar's ronnyvoo!" was the inebriant's cry. "Hyar goes hoss and beaver!"

All asked the question, Would Old Gabe endure the ordeal stoic or screaming? Self-styled soothsayers lurked beside every fire. The odds quickly favored him howling his fool head off. Nobody could take that kind of punishment, regardless of the stakes. Betting was rampant.

The object of the furor, who held the decision in the grip of his jaw, was the heaviest investor in his own behalf. Jim Bridger intended to clean up in side bets.

Promptly at nine in the morning in the valley of New Fork of the Green River, deep in the celebrated Shining Mountains country, Jim Bridger stepped out of his lodge with great flourish to confront crowds of cheering—some drunkenly jeering—mountaineers, and stoic, stone-faced, but inquisitive Indians, watching silently in ranks opposite the trappers.

The Indians had heard that the first true white medicine man they'd ever seen or heard of was this morning to perform what they considered a miracle on Blanket Chief Bridger, a man many of their people respected, and an even greater number feared.

As he regally emerged into the sunlight, momentarily and theatrically appraising and bowing to the throng surrounding him, Bridger—living up to that Indian name—was cloaked from neck to hock in a brand-new, thick crimson Hudson's Bay blanket with broad and rich black edging. Near his right flank a four-inch-diameter hole had been cut to facilitate the surgeon's work. The blanket was gathered and clutched to his chest; his feet were encased in gorgeous new fully beaded moccasins of colorful Sioux design and manufacture.

He had bathed and groomed himself, and glowed with cleanliness, and the posture of magnificent strength.

Around him the noisy throng formed a great thirty-foot-round space in respect to patient and surgeon, pressing together in ranks three, four, and five deep. The gathering of Indians opposite the trappers adjusted themselves about the same.

Ominous as a waiting guillotine, a jury-rigged operating table stood stark in its simplicity, and coldly sinister in function. Broad and thick oak planks, supported by fat, waist-high whiskey barrels, that had served as a trading table had been lent by the traders. Commerce had wisely adjourned for the surgical ceremony occupying nearly everyone's attention. The table had been spread with another new blanket.

Taking his place beside him as Bridger popped out of his lodge, Joe Meek, like a dueler's second, fell into step as his friend marched resolutely toward the waiting torture rack. In addition to the debonair Meek's colorfully beaded but begrimed buckskins, he was gaily caparisoned in a thick red wool voyageur's cap, its long, tapering top and knot rakishly dangling over one ear. A matching scarlet wool sash with yellow yarn accents was knotted at the side of his waist, the streamers and fluff-ends dangling to his knee.

Ceremoniously holding it aloft for all to see, Meek waved a two-inch-wide, six-inch-long parfleche strap, dense rawhide cured to near iron hardness. It was Bridger's only concession to the coming agony. He'd clench it in his teeth as Whitman applied his scalpel and probes.

The onlookers gave way as a bareheaded Dr. Whitman, like a duelist, in crisp white shirt open at the throat, rolled sleeves, and tight-fitting buckskin trousers, appeared. With him strode the Crow Indian subchief, Walking Feather, a particular Bridger favorite, and his way of acknowledging his many Indian friends. Whitman had asked for an assistant, and Walking Feather came to Old Gabe's mind.

The Crow chief, who had struggled to gain fluency with English, was a frequent interpreter in the rendezvous camps and was accepted warmly by the trapping fraternity. Now, beside Whitman, in his best Indian finery, he proudly carried the doctor's leather-bound surgical chest under his arm like cased pistols.

In the spread of warm morning sunlight, the principals and their seconds met at opposite sides of the rude table.

"Mr. Bridger," Whitman greeted his patient.

"Dr. Whitman, good mornin' to ya, sir."

"And to you, sir. If you please, my assistant, Chief Walking Feather."

"We're acquainted," Bridger said, and with that made hand signs of peace and brotherhood.

The gathered Indians nodded at each other silently and grinned and felt good. They, too, had wagered.

Bridger spoke up. "Gentlemen, my associate, Mr. Joseph Lafayette Meek."

Meek's eyes sparkled, relishing the mock formalities. He shook hands all around.

"Mr. Bridger," Whitman said. "Shall we proceed?"

"At your will, Doctor!" Bridger answered loudly, jubilantly waving at the crowd and hoisting his rump to the table and rolling onto it. In an ungainly hands-and-knees pose on the table, the crimson blanket draped like a tent, he again spoke up. "Unless the doctor wants to ask me somethin', them's my final words till the doc takes his last stitch. Then I'll beller all I damned please."

"We'll howl with ye, Jim!" someone yelled out of the mostly silent crowd; a ripple of approving laughter followed.

The hush returned; not a breath stirred; the mild air was heavy with unaccustomed silence.

Bridger flopped prone, resting the side of his head on crossed arms. Whitman adjusted and tucked the blanket gently so its prearranged hole exposed the ugly scar of earlier, clumsy efforts.

Joe Meek stood close to his friend's head with his ready slab of parfleche. Walking Feather waited beside Whitman with abundant pads of white surgical lint to stanch the flow of blood as required.

"Now or never," Whitman muttered, poising the scalpel, guessing at his proximity to the "arrahead." He began, laying a quick and bloody incision along the scar. Bridger trembled and rammed his head hard into the crossed arms.

The wound was deep and Gabe's whole body convulsed as the probe sought contact with the buried object.

Bridger at last beckoned for the parfleche strap and gripped it hard between his jaws. Whitman motioned to Walking Feather for more pads and dabbed at the flowing blood.

Whitman sweated now. His once well-brushed hair dangled down his forehead in wet tendrils; his shirt back was stained with sweat.

Deeper he went with the probe to make contact with the foreign object and Bridger jerked violently, but silently. A massive sigh rolled over the onlookers.

The physician straightened up. "I've found it," he murmured in relief to Walking Feather and Meek. He turned back to his work, peering intently into the raw wound, probing his way. "Dear God!" he was heard to gasp.

He leaned near Bridger's head, swollen and purple with the immense strain of the jaw-grip on the mangled parfleche strap. Tears glistened on his cheeks.

"I've found it, Jim. Something I hadn't expected. It's embedded deep in the bone . . ."

"Get it outta there, Doc," Bridger grunted around the rawhide bit. "I cain't hold out much longer."

Whitman's voice cracked with emotion. "It's buried. It's a thin metal arrowhead and when the shaft was yanked on, it was bent like a fish hook. I don't have the tools. I think—"

"Damn you!" Bridger growled. "Get it out of there! If it takes goin' in with a hammer and chisel, finish your work, man!"

Meek looked across at Walking Feather whose dark eyes betrayed fears for his old friend. Meek nodded in understanding; in many ways, each of them shared a place on Bridger's bed of torture. Old Gabe was that kind of friend.

Whitman motioned to the Indian. "Those large forceps, if you please, sir. Best I've got." He looked hopelessly at Meek. "It's fused in there with cartilage. I'm sure it won't budge."

With a wad of the surgical lint, Whitman dabbed at his streaming forehead and looked quickly at the hushed, expectant crowd. Forceps in hand, he sent another glance at the cloudless sky. "Give me strength, Lord," he muttered. "Give me the steadfast courage of this man."

With that he urged the forceps into the wound; Bridger's body set up a violent convulsion that rattled the oak-plank tabletop.

"I've got it," Whitman growled through gritted teeth. "Now, Jim, get a good bite on your leather. She's coming out! I have to push down hard to release the hook and break it free. Take a grip!"

Bridger tensed for the final agony. Whitman pushed against the instrument, his own arm trembling with the strain. "It's loosening," he grunted hoarsely after long seconds of prying and forcing. "I can feel it wiggle."

Bridger's head now thumped hollowly and involuntarily against the planking, his face bloated and dark with blood, his eyes, when he opened them, a bloodshot crimson.

"It's coming, I can feel it. Just a few more wiggles. Any second now." Whitman twisted the forceps. "Here it comes. Agh!" His arm jerked and out of the wound came the dripping forceps clamped on the disfigured arrowhead. He tossed the mess on the table and signaled to Walking Feather for his suturing needle and thread, already prepared.

"You won't notice this hardly at all, Jim, after what you've been through," he said, wiping blood from the incision. His patient was silent.

"Jim?" Whitman sought again. Bridger lay unmoving. Whitman checked his pulse and pressed his ear to his heaving lungs. "Jim? He must've passed out."

"I'm here!" Bridger snapped. "Get the gawdam job done!"

Relieved and smiling despite the profanity, Whitman turned to the work of stitching up his incision and preparing a dressing.

"We're through, Jim. You can howl now."

"Hain't got the stren'th," came the muffled voice of the man with his head lolling on the table. "You boys gonna have to help me."

Walking Feather strode around the table as Meek tried to support his shaky friend at the edge. Together they helped stand him up. His features pale and drawn, Bridger stood weakly, surveying the crowd.

"Well, boys," he said, his voice trembling, "I done 'er, by beaver. I won!"

A cheer went up that rattled the lodgepole tips of Bridger's nearby tepee. Everybody was jubilant; even the losing bettors felt they'd gotten their money's worth.

An unstable and drained Marcus Whitman was also quickly at Jim's side, watching his patient's face and eyes for aftereffects and checking his pulse and heart rate. "Want that arrowhead for a souvenir, Jim?"

"Nah, throw the dratted thing away. I lived with it three years and, like a spiteful woman, I want it outta my sight!"

"I just don't know, my friend," Whitman said, "how you lived with it. Don't know why infection didn't kill you."

Bridger mustered his first grin since climbing up on the table.

"Doc, there's somethin' else you gotta learn out here. The air in this kentry is so pure, meat just don't never spoil!"

A Man Alone

JOHN V. BREEN

We still remember the Alamo 167 years after the little mission church in San Antonio and its 150 defenders fell to a Mexican force of two thousand men commanded by General Antonio López de Santa Anna.

The heroes of the Alamo—Crockett, Bowie, Travis, Bonham, Dickinson, in particular—form a Texas Valhalla, and the ninety-minute fight has given birth to great legends.

"A Man Alone" is a superb story about two of the legends—the "line in the sand" Colonel William Barrett Travis supposedly drew with his sword, and the one man who did not cross the line and who thus survived while all the others died.

John V. Breen of Lancashire, England, was drawn to the American West through the movies and television he saw growing up in a small farming community. "I was especially captivated by the pictorial splendors placed on film by John Ford," he says, and at a young age began reading the classic Western writers, beginning with Will Henry's 1950 Custer novel, *No Survivors*.

Among Breen's short stories are "The Last Detail," about the arrest and death of Sitting Bull as seen through the viewpoint of a Lakota policeman; and "Ghost Shirt," a part historical, part ghost tale that switches between a Scottish museum and the battlefield at Wounded Knee.

THE DAMNED SOUL KNOCKED
on the door of my San Felipe boardinghouse as the windows of
taverns and town houses turned yellow with lampglow.

The light from the porch lantern revealed him as six feet of gaunt
and smoke-dark flesh that suggested Creole blood in his veins. Beneath a black slouch hat, his homespun jacket and leggings were
threadbare and decorated with a thin patina of dust from some wilderness trail. He was lightly equipped, his only baggage a ragged
blanket roll and a Kentucky long rifle in better shape than its owner.

"Evening, ma'am." Age-old weatherboard creaked under the
weight of down-at-heel boots as he stepped forward a pace. He came
garlanded with a smell of woodsmoke and black powder, stale tobacco and staler sweat.

He removed the hat and exposed a tangle of silver hair. His eyes
were sunken and bloodshot, mirrored the ocean deeps in their dark
and fathomless gaze. "A man up the street said you run an orderly
house. I need a room and a square meal. Come morning I'll be
aboard a wagon bound for Corpus Christi."

I wrapped myself in the shawl I'd draped around my shoulders,
the cool April evening beginning to seep into sixty-year-old bones.
"I prefer permanent boarders—those in the professions. You could
try the hotels."

He stood the rifle upright on the porch. "They won't take me
in. I've only a few dollars to my name, and need them to pay the
wagon man. It's a rough road I'm going down. I'd appreciate a bite
to eat before I go—and a dab of food to take with me. Charity ain't
my game. I'm carrying something of value you could later trade for
money. Ma'am, I ain't et hot food in four days, and can't rightly
remember when I was last under a roof."

I started to close the door, then hesitated. My late husband's
hardware business had prospered and we along with it. I was com-

fortable in my gray years, and as thrifty at sixty as when a young schoolteacher in Richmond, Virginia. I didn't need his passing trade; yet in my ease I wasn't without compassion or unmoved by the gaunt look.

"You'd best come in, then." I beckoned him inside. He shut the door behind him and followed me down the dimly lit hall and into the parlor, passing below the delicate work several absent spiders had carried out in nooks and crannies I was now too stiff and stout to reach.

I sat beside a fire the late hour had almost robbed of its flame. I gestured at a hickory chair opposite. He propped rifle and blanket roll against the fireplace and sat down. I folded my hands and inspected the dust on him. "You've traveled some."

His eyes roamed around the room, briefly alighting on treasure and curio, fixture and imperfection: a bone china tea set and porcelain figurine, grizzly bear rug, and heavy oak furniture. A pair of fine lace curtains, suspended from a window whose sash and sill were in need of fresh paint was a daily reminder of how I missed the man who'd wooed and wed me, missed him near as much for his labors as for the sweet love he'd once freely given.

He rested the slouch hat in his lap. "Traveling's been my life these last ten years. I'm a stranger to parlors."

One of the absent spiders emerged from a dark corner. It paused beside hickory and then scuttled beyond lamplight again. "There's been bad men visited this town. Some are still here. But you don't have that look, so I'll chance the law isn't on your trail. What you need to know is there's rules I won't bend for king or queen. They involve liquor and tobacco—I won't tolerate either one. If you can't go a night without partaking of them there's no bed here for you."

His fathoms-deep gaze remained unblinking for a moment. "I'm out of tobacco. I confess to sampling every kind of demon brew, but it ain't drink that's brought me this low."

I nodded. "What is it you wish to give for payment?"

He reached into his jacket pocket. The silver fob watch he handed over was scratched and tarnished. In its pristine glory it would have graced the silk vest of an officer and a gentleman. Indeed, it once had. One of my former boarders, no less.

I examined the watch and the engraved initials as though both were unknown to me. The man behind the initials was now bones in the ground, and had since passed into legend. Dead or alive, I doubted he would have bequeathed the watch to anyone other than a close and stalwart friend. But somehow I wasn't yet convinced the parlor harbored a thief.

I looked up. "You must have seen better days to be owning this."

"It ain't mine by rights. The man who gave it me feared it might end up a souvenir, and south of the Rio Grande. It's dulled from having been down a hundred and one trails with me. It ain't worth much on its own. But there's plenty would pay cash money for it once they knew who the initials stand for. If I wasn't so down on my luck, I wouldn't part with it. But lady luck went missing once I was clear of the north wall and what was waiting on the other side."

"The north wall?"

His dark eyes widened. "Of the Alamo . . ."

I raised an eyebrow. "You were there?"

"Was and then left. The night before the Mexicans broke in."

In the ten years since the battle, I'd overheard many a discussion where one or another of the participants claimed to be a bona fide survivor. Some of the speakers were harmlessly deluded. Others pathological liars. Yet one story lived on.

I reclined in the wing chair. "It's said one man slipped away."

The dark eyes studied me intensely, seemed to look into my very soul.

I rested my hands on the chair arms. "I've heard every sin and woe under God's heaven. Those who confided in me were sound judges—I don't possess a loose tongue. I'll go to my grave harboring a hundred torments and a thousand secrets."

The sigh he gave was as surf over sand. "Hell, you ain't no barroom crowd. And I'm a long time tired of living under an alias. I daresay you've heard of me—I'm Louis Rose."

The name was a legend in its own right—but a blighted one. Disparaged throughout Texas. Gutted and quartered by tongues as sharp and vicious as the bayonets so many of the Alamo's hallowed defenders were hung up on. Sometimes not even a barbed comment greeted its utterance. Merely phlegm and tobacco juice, aimed deliberately at the nearest cuspidor, or into the dust of a rutted street or sun-scorched plaza. The name Louis Rose was an appellation no one in the West would wish to covet. But one man was burdened with it.

"You have a cross to bear."

He sighed again. "I haven't given my real name to another soul since the Alamo fell. That's when I first heard it cussed over in a tavern—right here in San Felipe. If those who cussed me had known I was in their midst, I would have looked upon being tarred and feathered as a reprieve. Texans don't take kindly to cowards and deserters. Not that I've been either one."

He gripped the slouch hat's dusty brim. "Now that you know me, I wouldn't hold it against you if there ain't no longer a room to rent. I'd like to lie on feathers again, but if you consider me bad company, I'll go sleep under the stars."

There are times in a man's life when it may prove useful for him to disown his given name, so long as it can just as easily be reclaimed. But, through fear, to always have to hide it from the world was surely worse than being born a bastard whelp and lacking a father's signature. I did not envy Louis Rose his secret years.

I offered reassurance. "I don't judge others by what I hear. There's evil walks this earth. But most of us are neither in league with the devil or entirely free of sin. We are merely flesh and blood."

He pointed at the watch. "It belonged to Colonel Travis."

"You knew him well?"

"As a friend as well as a commandant. Fact is, I still know him."

"How is that?"

"I see him."

"His ghost?"

"Not just his . . . though it's his I see most clearly. All the rest are present too. All those I left behind. Bowie, Crockett, Almeron Dickinson, Jim Bonham. They all come visit me."

"How do they come?"

"In a dream I keep having. One that begins and ends in the same fashion. Has me out in prairie country, like I was the night I slipped through the Mexican lines. It's the quietest stretch of prairie I ever encountered. No coyotes yapping, no crickets chirring. No wind on the rise. Just me and the darkness. Then they come walking out of the brush, in one long column, and all of a piece. None of them lacking a limb or displaying a wound. Nor any one of them blood-stained. Yet I know by instinct they have crossed over to the other side. For I don't hear no marching feet, or leather boots creaking. Or the sound of any breathing."

He lowered and shook his head. "That's how they step past the fire I'm sat around. One by one and without a word spoken. Travis is the last of them. When they've gone a dozen yards beyond the fire, they halt as one, and the Colonel turns and stares at me. There's a moon out, and I see him clearly. Watch him beckon me. When I don't stir, I see his look turn sad. Then I don't see his face at all. Just the back of him as he turns away and the line goes marching on."

He raised his head. "It's how it's been these last ten years. There ain't many nights when they don't march past. It never seems to matter where I lay my body down—they always come calling."

Louis Rose wasn't the first occupant of the hickory chair to have his sleep invaded by visions of the dead. Other lost souls spoke of being plagued by shades from their past. Some suffered blood dreams. A soldier or two, and more than one Texas Ranger. Men routinely required to bear arms and frequently resort to them. Yet, to the best of my knowledge, none were haunted by so many for so long.

I fingered the locket at my throat. "Might be you could leave them behind if Texas was no longer your stomping ground."

He shook his head. "I've been gone from Texas the best part of five years. Been as far west as a man can go. Then rode north and east. Even spent me a year down in the Florida country, sharing space with skeeters and gators, and what's left of the Seminoles. It's made no difference. I believe I could go to China, and they would still come visit me. Follow me down the Silk Road. Ghosts don't need no ticket to travel."

Beside me on the mantel the soft chimes of a domed and gilded Swiss clock disrupted the evening hush. I listened to the chimes toll time passed by and reflected on the prospect of the ghost army following Louis Rose onto foreign soil. I found his assumption impossible to counter. Dreams knew no boundaries. Same as ghosts couldn't be corralled.

I broke the silence that followed. "Why do you think they haunt you so?"

"Because their ranks are incomplete without me. I should rightly be with them. Only the ladies who remained at the Alamo should have survived to see the sunrise. It's not what I thought the night I went over the wall—but I do now."

"Those you left behind—do you believe they condemned you?"

"I condemn myself. When I left, nary a one of them gave me a black look or spoke ill of me. They knew me well enough."

"That you were no coward?"

He nodded. "Will Travis knew it too. It's why he gave every man there the choice to stay or go. He knew none of us lacked backbone."

I recalled my husband's somber report on the Alamo's fall. He was in Gonzales when the widow of Almeron Dickinson arrived with news of the blood sacrifice inside the mission's walls. It was Susannah Dickinson who reported on Louis Rose's refusal to stand. Forever sullied his name in Texas eyes. The widow spun another tale too. One still subject to fierce debate.

"Mrs. Dickinson spoke of your going. Said you were the only man not to cross the line Colonel Travis drew in the sand."

Louis Rose remained a solemn study. "I've heard that story. Hell, I'm still hearing it."

He looked past me, his eyes suddenly unfocused, a man peering into his own dark history. Momentarily engulfed by a deep and abiding memory of a fateful night and an equally fateful decision. One that left him branded and despised.

His eyes regained their focus. He turned the slouch hat full circle, as though it were a ship's wheel. "Will Travis had words in him none of the rest of us could spell. But he wasn't given to theatrics."

His hands became still, the hat becalmed. "There was no line."

His softly spoken revelation exposed as fiction what many considered a cast-iron fact. He removed from the tapestry of the Alamo's shining legend its most enduring pictograph.

Wise after the fact, I nodded sagely. "But you were alone in your desire to leave?"

He returned the hat to his lap. "I'd been to war before I ever set foot in Texas. Sailed against the British—in Napoleon's navy. It's where I learned the tactic of an orderly retreat when the odds favored the other side. No captain I ever served under stayed put when an enemy ship of the line sailed into view sporting more cannon than our own vessel. It's why I told Will he was wrong, and that I'd rather take my chances on the outside than sit and wait for death to come get me."

He raised a hand and rubbed the back of his neck. "I was wrong. History shows Will Travis bought Texas precious time it sorely needed. Was likely the difference between winning and losing. What I did left me bedeviled by the dead and cursed by the living. I wish now I'd stayed and joined the rest of them in walking the streets of Glory."

He shifted slightly in his chair. The same chair once occupied by the man who gave him the choice to stay or go.

The Alamo's first and last commandant had boarded with me only briefly, yet the impression he made proved indelible. It would be fair to say that Will Travis had something of the dandy about him in the shape of his white hat and red pantaloons, and could charm the ladies like no other. But it was his resolute manner I most recalled. A characteristic I deemed would have others eager to rally to his cause.

I confessed the knowledge I'd earlier kept hidden. "I was once acquainted with Colonel Travis. He struck me as a man loath to condemn another if he thought them a straight arrow."

Louis Rose nodded. "He knew I was that. It's why he argued for me to stay. But when he saw I was determined to take my chances, he shook my hand and gave me his blessing. If I got through, my aim was to link up with Sam Houston and the force he was gathering. I never reached the General. When I came within range of him I already knew I was branded. It made me fear I wouldn't get past saying my name without one or another of his army would club me, or else shoot me stone dead in my boots."

He ran a hand through his unruly hair. For a moment I saw him elsewhere. Not sitting in a hickory chair but scaling a high wall and then advancing into a darkness crowded with danger. Slipping through the Mexican ranks, and so close to some of their number as to hear the prayers more than a few of them would surely have recited as they waited for trumpets to sound.

It was no mean feat to steal past so vast an armed camp, and one in a state of high alert. In different circumstances it would have been lauded. Instead, Louis Rose ended up damned in speech and print.

I offered a note of overdue sympathy. "I doubt a messenger from God would have persuaded Colonel Travis to change tack once the thought was in him to defend the ground he was on."

"Will Travis was stubborn," Louis Rose agreed. "But, by God, he respected those who came under his banner, he never saw himself as better than any man there. I should have been with him when he fell."

I sensed in his tone a quiet regret, upon his countenance an agony but half-hidden. One reminiscent of the anguish expressed by a friend of the family as he told of visiting the battleground shortly after the victors departed.

He found the Alamo in ruins, the shattered remnants of its walls and barracks a monument to blood and fury. Worse still was the patch of scorched and blackened earth he came upon. The site where the bodies of Travis and the rest of the sons of Texas were piled and then burnt. A cremation transacted with neither honor nor dignity. Proof enough that, even in death, the defeated experienced no quarter.

I brushed a loose gray hair from my blouse and stood up. "What's waiting for you in Corpus Christi?"

"A scrap, I reckon. Mexican government's turned hot-blooded again. Politicians this side of the border fear an incursion. General Zachary Taylor is down there, recruiting volunteers. I aim to be one of them."

I came and stood at his elbow. I lightly rested a hand on a gaunt shoulder. "You're aged some to still be a fighting man."

He glanced at the Kentucky rifle. "Where I'm concerned war's an old story. There's nothing I ain't been privy to. Whether I live or die don't rightly matter—it's redemption I'm seeking."

I allowed him supper in the parlor. Whether the night he spent under my roof was peaceful or disturbed by Texas ghosts, I never knew. He'd confessed enough, and prying wasn't in my nature. When he rose an hour before first light, I was in the kitchen and waiting with a hearty breakfast and the provisions he'd requested. Afterward, I attempted to give back a dead man's treasure. "Here, take this watch. I don't need the cash money it might raise. Life's sometimes a hard road. Every one of us travels it deserves a charitable act along the way."

He reached out and folded my hand around silver. "Keep it, for your kindness. My bones tell me I'm heading into a bloodbath. If it comes to a fight down there, I won't be scaling no wall. This time I'll stand fast. If I don't pull through, Will's watch might yet go astray. I reckon he'd be happy if it was safe in Texan hands."

He let go my hand and reached inside his jacket. The folded sheet of paper he handed me was yellow and brittle with age. "It's something else the Colonel gave me. I never showed it to anyone, for fear they wouldn't believe he wrote it. Might be you'll recognize his hand or mark, or sense him in what's written. If you do, I'd be obliged if you show it to who you know. If I ever reach heaven's gates, it would ease my passage through them if I knew there's some in Texas no longer thought ill of me."

He went out into a cold blue light and a town shone down upon by a bright lone star. A little less gaunt, but smoke-dark as he ever was. I took the sheet he'd given me into the parlor. Seated in the hickory chair, and donning spectacles, I read a dozen or so lines of faded ink.

The Alamo, March 5, 1836
I wish it to be known that on this day I gave all here the chance to stand with me or attempt to make their escape. Louis Rose has chosen the latter course. I do not condemn him for his actions and neither does any man here. He has proved a stalwart defender of the flag of freedom, and lacks nothing in the way of grit. He merely does what he thinks best.

I'd rather he stayed. Our fate here is sealed, but at least we will meet it together. Whatever fate awaits Louis Rose outside of these walls, it is one he must face alone. And there may be no more harrowing experience known to humankind than the approach of an unknown and lonely fate.

If by some miracle he is able to slip away, I trust he will spread the news of what those he left behind are about to do for Texas. Of the stand we have taken here at the Alamo.
William Barret Travis

I finished peering at the script. For a moment I sat and remembered momentous times in Texas, and an individual both charming and resolute. Then went and opened a drawer in a chiffonier. The file I retrieved was home to a compendium of letters and mementos from bygone years, some recent, others relating to days of flaxen hair and dewy eyes. Another country now.

The sheet of paper I returned with to the hickory chair was as aged as the one Louis Rose left behind. Its contents proved to be as I remembered them. A collection of pleasantries rounded off with an appreciative word regarding the hospitality extended to the writer during his brief residence.

I dispensed with the spectacles and stared naked eyed at the two signatures confronting me. Then returned the sheets to their original folded state.

I placed them together inside the file. It was only right they should rest in proximity to each other, for their sentences were composed by the same hand. One sheet of no importance to anyone but a widow, long on memories. The other a note from history. A truth. One I determined I would bring to the attention of editors and others of known influence the length and breadth of Texas.

In order that I might gain absolution for the man from the Alamo.

Jonas Crag

JOHN JAKES

Until Fort Sumter, no event of the nineteenth century could surpass the California gold rush for the sheer clamor created among the American people. Thousands fled the comforts of hearth and home to find a way to the "diggings" where newspaper reports insisted that all that was needed to get rich was a jackknife, a pick, and a pan, to extract gold from the hills around the American River and the boomtown of Sacramento City.

Most arrived too late at rainbow's end to find little more than a "wage"—a few dollars a day. Some came late but didn't care: They had missions other than mining gold.

Internationally celebrated for his historical novels, John Jakes began writing Western stories in the 1950s and in the first sixteen years as a freelancer published forty books and two hundred stories. Even before his "Kent Family Chronicles," those eight "Bicentennial" novels published between 1974 and 1980 that sold 40 million copies, he had a devoted following for his science fiction, Western, and historical works. Following the Kent Family series, his fame was assured in his "North and South" trilogy on the Civil War, his *California Gold* in 1989, the "Crown Family Saga" (*Homeland*, *American Dreams*), set in Jakes's hometown of Chicago, and such recent historicals as *On Secret Service* and *Charleston*.

THE WEARY STRANGER WALKED
uphill into Lost Camp at sundown. Orange light tipped the Sierra
peaks but the canyon was a chilly purple hue. Lost Creek rushed
along with a colder, noisier sound than at noon, and through the
gloaming drifted the first flick-flick of decks being shuffled, the first
laughter of homely whores tuning up for the night.

No one paid much mind to the weary stranger. One look and
you knew: another argonaut arriving too late. He was maybe twenty-
three, going on forty after crossing half the continent. Holes in his
moccasins showed his grimy feet. His beard reached to his navel. His
ragged shirt and pants had seen so much hard traveling, pelting rain,
frying sun, desert dust, their original colors were undetectable. His
shoulder-length hair already showed strings of white, but what really
gave him away was his face. An ordinary face, neither handsome nor
ugly; instead call it plain, rather long, burnt as dark as the hull of an
Ohio buckeye, the skin wrinkled and dry, the eyes with that familiar
look of suffering. Make that twenty-three going on sixty.

The stranger paused in front of one of the larger mercantile tents
along the slope of the gulch masquerading as a street. The pause was
unwise: A piss pot sailed out of nowhere, trailing its effluvia and
narrowly missing him. Then someone shot two holes in it in midair,
unleashing a veritable Niagara.

The stranger stayed put and gazed thoughtfully at the gaudy
wooden sign over the big tent's entrance.

MONTMORENCE ESSENTIALS & EDIBLES.
Generous Credit.

For the first time, the stranger's face revealed some sort of emotion. It appeared to be a near-smile; a musing satisfaction. That
would be Mr. Morley Montmorence, late of Cincinnati, the duly

elected captain of the Ohio Rushers, chosen because he stated flatly that the others in the twelve-man mess should elect a businessman. No matter that they were crossing a couple of thousand miles of savage and largely unmapped land, elect a businessman, he knew how to organize things, get things done.

He surely did that, thought the stranger, his face returning to its marblelike passivity. His name was Jonas Crag and he was dog tired this October night in 1851. He went in search of a place to lay his head, content in knowing he'd found the captain and could deal with him at leisure.

BECAUSE HIS LATE MOTHER HAD OPERATED A SMALL, BUSY INN ON the Lebanon–Dayton coach road, an inn that served hearty meals to travelers, Jonas Crag had learned to cook standing beside the widow Crag at her stove. Therefore he'd been elected to cook for the Ohio Rusher mess, twelve argonauts from the southwest corner of the state who knew each other slightly if at all. Jonas had joined the company after his mother went to her reward. He gave her church most of the proceeds of the sale of the inn, keeping only a small sum to outfit himself for the trek west.

The vote to elect a cook would have been unanimous except that Jonas modestly refrained from raising his hand. The Rushers pooled some of their funds for groceries, which Jonas laid in before their wagon train rolled out of Independence in the early spring of 1850. Already the prairie was crowded with stampeders heading for California.

The first days of the journey were almost pleasant: ever-changing vistas of flower-dotted flatlands; glimpses of a buffalo herd, vast as a brown sea; and Jonas found that his morning coffee, eggs, and flapjacks were well received, as were his evening soups and ragouts. Well received, that is, by all except Morley Montmorence, the elected captain. For no reason that Jonas could identify unless it was his youth—he was the youngest of the company by six months—Montmorence liked picking on him.

The first time it happened, Montmorence opened with a question. "Did you have education?"

"One-room school. When I was eleven I had to quit. Ma needed me to help at the inn after Pa died."

"Pity. I had two years at Miami in Oxford. Don't believe there's another college man among us except for our lawyer. It's amazing how an education—Latin, Greek, rhetoric—puts you above the mob."

Barring this kind of exchange, and occasional unwarranted references to "the dummy" uttered behind Jonas's back—but loudly enough so that he heard them, which perhaps was the intent—things went well until they were out of Independence three weeks, and Jonas wandered away from the train at midday in search of wild onions.

JONAS RESISTED THE LURE OF VARIOUS TENTS AND SHANTIES CAtering to the after-dark appetites of miners, and settled for a place identified as—wouldn't you know?

MONTMORENCE'S HOTEL.
Flop $2, Water & Towel $1.

He wasn't surprised to find Montmorence involved in such widespread commercialism; the captain had lectured the rest of them during the short time Jonas was with the company:

"Boys, I know you're going for the placer gold but not me; I'm a businessman, and as such, it's my firm conviction that the man who will make the money in the mines is the man supplying the miners with what they need. I look forward to your patronage if our paths cross," he said with a merry smile.

Montmorence usually smiled. He was a bland, ordinary chap, no more than thirty, with dimples and sharp little eyes, quite friendly and jolly most of the time. You wouldn't know from looking at him that he was an evil businessman. Back in Ohio, Jonas had heard that Montmorence had driven more than one struggling farmer to the wall, seizing the victim's land without so much as a blink. Maybe that's how an evil businessman succeeded, by not looking evil, but just like the hymn-singing fellow next to you in the pew, then striking suddenly.

Jonas spent the night on a cot in the large tent, amid a constant coming and going of miners who snored, coughed, passed buzz-saw farts, called out plaintively for Sally or Susannah or Mother—one even had the audacity to start to relieve himself between the cots until someone told him to go outside or he'd get a bullet in his ass.

The following day, somewhat but not fully refreshed, Jonas wandered through the camp, watching the miners busily panning or operating their rockers at their claims along the cold-looking creek. Jonas had no plans to join them. The only thing on which he agreed with Montmorence was the formula for success; Montmorence's little homilies on the trail from Independence had opened Jonas's mind to new possibilities in California. He didn't feel he owed Montmorence anything for those insights, since Montmorence had damn near killed him.

As the sun inevitably set again, Jonas strolled to the Montmorence retail store and eating place. He now wore his revolver stuck in his deerskin belt, the muzzle touching his left hip, which, like his right one, had virtually no spare flesh on it. He'd wintered in Salt Lake with the peculiar Mormons, friendly enough except in matters of commerce, where they were Scrooges of the first rank. Even working at odd jobs and eating half decently, he didn't gain weight; he'd lost too much in the terrible ordeal to which Montmorence had condemned him.

TRADE WAS LIGHT IN THE EATING TENT. TWO YOUNG MINERS— so far Jonas hadn't seen a single *old* miner—sat joshing and playing cards while swigging from a whiskey bottle. A large scarlet-faced man with an immense chest read a Sacramento newspaper behind the makeshift bar, lumber laid across barrels.

Jonas took a chair, raked his fingers through his bird's-nest beard in an attempt to look more presentable. The man from the counter came over, snapping his bar towel.

"Hello, pilgrim. New around here?"

"Yes, I am."

"Want to drink or feed your face?"

"The latter," said Jonas, a reply whose slightly literary quality gave the red-faced man pause. The man introduced himself as Brown,

Beef for short. Jonas said, "Pleased to meet you. I'd like some stew if you have it. Rabbit, elk, anything's fine, as long as it's seasoned with a little garlic."

"We don't serve nothing with garlic. The boss, he hates garlic. It makes him puke."

"Could I speak with the gentleman?"

"He ain't here yet."

"Then I insist on waiting."

"Insist?" said the other, leaning over so that his shadow fell on Jonas, who gracefully slid the revolver from his belt, laid it on the table alongside the small deerskin pouch he'd brought along.

"Yes, insist," Jonas said. The heavy man squinted as he thought that over and decided against a ruckus with the armed customer. He returned to the bar and his paper.

Jonas sat quietly, patiently, for nearly an hour. Several more miners came in, ordering drinks and eats and increasing the general level of jollity in the tent. About half past six, Montmorence strolled in, smiling and waving to the patrons. He saw Jonas. He gaped.

"Jonah?" he cried. "I mean Jonas?"

"You can call me either one, like you did before you threw me out of the mess."

"Shit in the morning, I can't get over this." Montmorence slapped his hat on his leg and pulled up a chair. "You little son of a gun. You made it. Beef, a bottle of our best for this customer." The astonished pug was slow to realize his employer meant it. He rummaged around the bar while Montmorence smiled his biggest smile. "You made it. You made it."

"No thanks to you. You left me in those cottonwoods and I know you thought I'd die."

"But you didn't," Montmorence exclaimed.

"No, by Jesus," Jonas said, his gaze very hard. "I'm a mild-tempered fellow, but what you did was unconscionable and un-Christian. I'm here to settle the account."

OUT PAST PRIMITIVE FORT KEARNY, ON THE SOUTH BANK OF THE wide brown Platte, no better than mud moving slow as lava, Jonas cooked his fatal rabbit ragout, which he'd seasoned with cut-up wild onions pulled fresh from the prairie that day. Montmorence sniffed his tin plate.

"What the devil's in this, Cookie?"

Jonas despised the term "Cookie," which Montmorence therefore delighted in using along with "dummy," but he kept his temper. "Why, I suppose you mean the wild onions I dug up this morning."

"Wild onions. I thought so. Back in Ohio we called them meadow garlic. I hate garlic."

"Whatever you call it, it makes a good seasoning."

"I'd go along with that," said a young man with silky yellow mandarin mustaches down to his chin. This was their lawyer, as Montmorence called him: Cedric Slipper, Esquire, from Dayton. His practice hadn't been too good, so he'd kissed his wife and infant son and lit out with the Rushers, promising that he'd soon pan enough gold to give them a new start in California. Slipper was Jonas's one friend in the mess. They often discussed, speculated on, Montmorence's murky past—his reasons for leaving Ohio. They were no more informed when they finished than when they started.

"Well, you can just go to hell," Montmorence declared. "Garlic makes me puke." He stuck out his tongue with a horrendous gagging noise that disgusted the others. He sailed his plate high and wide; bits of the ragout flew across the setting sun, a picturesque effect.

"No more damn garlic."

"I'm the damn cook," Jonas said.

"You idiot, I'm the captain."

"Then *you* can go to hell."

Thus the enmity began.

Jonas didn't purposely antagonize Montmorence, or cause strain within the mess by preparing any more dishes with wild onion, also known as meadow garlic. He did dig up some for himself, stashing away the bulbs and chewing on the tender green tops. One time as Jonas was doing this, Montmorence passed by. He stopped and sniffed; Jonas's breath was strong. Montmorence pierced Jonas with a furious look before stalking on.

One day soon after, as Jonas was taking his turn at the reins of the plodding oxen, he felt a sudden, violent disturbance in his lower regions. He leaned to the left just in time and vomited. Five minutes later, he scrambled down and ran into some brush with his britches around his ankles. He barely made it before his bowels exploded.

Later, burning up, Jonas lay under a thin blanket as the stars came out. He heard a member of the company named Pfellows declare, "It's the Asia cholera, boys. Running rampant out here, they say." Pfellows was a sometime apothecary, the closest thing to a physician in their company.

"The cholera," Montmorence repeated in a dark way. "Liable to kill every one of us."

They carried Jonas in the wagon for two days while he alternately burned and froze. Twice his uncontrolled bowels let go before he could escape the wagon, and the mess and stink brought down curses from his traveling companions. Pfellows complained that he was beginning to feel touchy in his middle. At the campfire that night, Montmorence announced a decision.

"Jonas, we're leaving you."

"Wh—what?" Jonas mumbled from where he lay under the blanket, two feet from the fire and still freezing.

"It's a hard decision but I'm the captain and this is a matter of business. You'll either die or recover, there's nothing we can do about it either way, but before that happens you're liable to infect the rest of us. We can't allow it. So we're leaving you tomorrow morning in that grove over by the river."

Cedric Slipper said, "I object. He's one of us, he signed the articles as we all did. We can't simply abandon him."

"Oh yes we can, if we want to get to the diggings." Montmorence set his lips in a firm line. "Do you know your Bible? The sailors abandoned Jonah when he caused a big storm. They put him overboard. If it's okay for the Israelites, it's okay for us."

"Jonah. Jonas. Jonah. Say, that fits, don't it?" said Pfellows, who was always a bit slow to catch on. Jonas was too weak and sick to protest; could hardly summon so much as a silent curse directed at Montmorence.

"If I carried a gun I'd do something about this," Cedric Slipper said.

"Well, you don't, so you can't," Montmorence said. "Just shut up and pray you don't get sick too."

In the morning, the Rushers lingered as the rest of the wagons in the train set out ahead of them. Hidden from their fellow travelers by clouds of prairie dust, Montmorence and Pfellows lugged the enfeebled Jonas to the hot shade of the cottonwood grove. They propped him against a tree together with a wooden canteen of water and a packet of beef jerky, neither of which he could possibly swallow or keep down. Montmorence held his hat against his vest as though speaking over a bier at a funeral.

"Goodbye, old pal. No hard feelings. We had to do it for the sake of the majority. Get well soon."

Off they went, down the slight rise, in the direction of the dust cloud. One of the Rushers whipped the oxen to catch up with the rest of the train.

At least he didn't call me a dummy, Jonas thought.

"SO YOU DID GET WELL," MONTMORENCE EXCLAIMED, BEAMING. "Did nature take its course? Did you just throw it off, come out of it?"

"Not exactly." Jonas toyed with the revolver lying near the deer-skin pouch. "Five days after you left—I was near starved to death by then—two more wagons came along. Four priests and two lay brothers from the college of Notre Dame in Indiana."

"You're joshing me," Montmorence said, continuing to beam in an effort to inject some levity into the somewhat tense situation.

"No, sir. Brothers of the Order of the Holy Cross, sent to California to pan for gold because the college is nearly broke. They took me in. They risked the cholera to care for me. Brother Anselm did get sick but he pulled through. They took me to Salt Lake, where I wintered. They were decent Christian men," Jonas finished in a pointed way.

"Look, I know you must feel some resentment, but it was a necessary business decision."

"I made one myself." Jonas undid the string on the pouch. "To find you and make you a proposition." He threw back the flap of the pouch. Montmorence recoiled from the aroma.

"Phew. Is that what I think it is in there?"

"Yes, sir, a large bulb of Mexican garlic. The real goods, not the wild onion kind. Here's the proposition. Eat the garlic, one clove at a time, or pick up this pistol and kill me."

Montmorence grew wild-eyed, his gaze roving around the crowded tent where miners slapped down cards and slopped down watered drinks. Beef was so busy at the improvised bar, he failed to notice his employer's frantic looks. Montmorence laughed, more like a cough. "That's your deal? Your proposition? You're an imbecile."

"Call me what you want, I think you'll swallow the garlic because I don't think you'd care to shoot me. Bad for business. There's a penalty for murder."

Montmorence's glistening face twisted, his vain attempt at mirth. "You're even stupider than I thought. There's no law in Lost Camp."

"There is in San Francisco, where Cedric Slipper hung his shingle. He knows I'm here, and why. He expects me back. He doesn't like you any better than I do. Anything happens to me, he'll have lawmen on your trail."

Montmorence slapped the table with both hands, loudly enough to turn the heads of a couple of toil-weary miners. One took note of Jonas's revolver and nudged his partner but the man was more interested in drinking his whiskey and sorting his cards.

"Let me tell you this, and get it through your dumb skull—Jonah," Montmorence said. "I won't shoot you and neither will I eat your fucking garlic."

Jonas sighed. "Then I have to walk out of here. If I do, then some night when you don't expect it, I'll sneak back and set fire to this place. Your hotel too. I'll follow you wherever you go. Burn down anything you build. I tracked you here, didn't I? Took seven months, camp after camp, but I found you. I'll find you anywhere, and burn you out. So it's kill me or eat the garlic."

Montmorence's face lost every trace of smarmy confidence and took on a pallor which Jonas swore was decidedly green. "What if I buy you off? How much do you want?"

"Nothing. No deal."

"You don't know how sick I get on garlic. I have some kind of aversion, a reaction, down here in my belly. I'll die."

"Like I almost did when you left me behind? I doubt it. Now come on, I haven't got all night. Which is it, the gun or the garlic?"

Montmorence swiveled his head in an even wilder manner but attracted little attention; a painted lady of large proportions had entered the tent and was breezing among the miners, tickling them with her pink boa and whispering things. Montmorence spoke in a strangled way.

"The garlic, you little son of a bitch."

"Fine."

Jonas quickly slid the revolver off the table into his lap, where it couldn't be easily grabbed. He opened the pouch and withdrew the cloves of garlic which he'd already separated. Montmorence grimaced and turned his head and gagged.

Jonas raised his hand. "Oh, Beef?" Beef took notice. "Would you bring your boss some water or whiskey or whatever he wants?" To Montmorence he said, "You may need to wash it down. I'm not completely heartless."

"Fuck yourself, you insane ninny. Give me the garlic." Montmorence snatched several cloves, shoved them in his mouth and chewed frantically.

His eyes bulged. His cheeks purpled. He seized his throat with both hands and fell sideways out of his chair, landing hard on the dirt floor. Beef came running with a bung starter. Seeing his victim on the floor strangling to death, Jonas realized he'd made a terrible mistake.

"So I got down on my knees and pounded him on the back until he spit it out," Jonas said to the gravestone. The gravestone stood on a windswept plot of ground on one of San Francisco's highest hills. Clouds flew across the sun, throwing beautiful patterns of light and shadow on the rippling bay.

"I guess I'd already had enough of a victory by then, and he might have died. I never meant to do to him what he did to me, just scare him out of his pants. Right away, Beef the barkeep shook my hand and said, 'You saved his life.' Which I did. But you saved my life, Cedric. I guess it was a damn-fool scheme, but I got away with it because he thought you were waiting for me, ready to bring the law down on him. I'll always be grateful, Cedric."

Cedric Slipper of course could not hear him, lying under the marble slab which his widow had provided after Jonas wrote her. Unsuccessful in the diggings after a few months, Cedric had indeed established a practice in San Francisco but it, too, was short-lived, as

Jonas discovered when he looked up his friend after journeying from Salt Lake. The landlord of Cedric's office block said Cedric had been shot to death as an innocent bystander in a street brawl. Last April it was; he hadn't been waiting for Jonas at all, as Jonas told Montmorence. But his presence in Lost Camp had been real, and Jonas would indeed be forever grateful.

Jonas said a prayer, put on his hat, and walked down the windy hill in the sunshine.

IN 1880, JONAS CRAG LIVED IN A THIRTY-ROOM MANSION WITH his wife and nine children. The house overlooked booming San Francisco from another of its highest hills. Newspapers referred to Jonas as the Hotel King. He owned fourteen thriving and well-regarded establishments throughout the state and displayed his name proudly on each. All were noted for their cleanliness and cuisine, traditions inherited from Jonas's innkeeper mother.

In each hotel, Jonas employed the best chef he could find. He insisted that every chef plant a private garden to grow herbs, onions, and Mexican garlic, which the dining room offered in soups, ragouts, and other dishes.

Jonas Crag was one of those fortunate argonauts who endured terrible hardship on the trek to California, found no gold but discovered a satisfying and profitable life anyway. It was from Morley Montmorence that he'd learned the lesson: The man who would profit from the great rush for gold was not the man who froze in the mountain streams but the man who sold the freezers what they needed. As he grew older, Jonas again supposed he should thank Morley Montmorence for that unwitting counsel, but he never saw or heard of him again after leaving Lost Camp, walking out the same way he walked in.

Montmorence adhered to his own business plan by following the gold stampeders who went hither and yon chasing the latest rumors of a strike. He followed them in their search for a mysterious lake of gold in the Sierras, never found. He followed them to the Fraser River in Canada, then Pike's Peak. Eighteen sixty-four found him in Virginia City, Montana, and the late 1870s in Deadwood Gulch in the Black Hills. There the trail darkened. Jonas of course knew none of this, his path crossing that of Montmorence only once more, in 1881, when it became clear that Montmorence had ultimately been unable to follow his own advice successfully.

A telegraph interrupted Jonas's breakfast one morning in San Francisco. "Ye gods," he exclaimed as he read the dire news. He kissed his wife and children, packed a valise, and hopped a southbound Southern Pacific.

On the main street of Bakersfield, at the base of the broad sunbaked central valley, he confronted the remains of his local hotel. Nothing was left but blackened timbers, iron bedsteads melted into grotesque shapes, remnants of gilded picture frames from the barroom, and similar residue.

"Arson," declared the deputy sheriff, brooking no argument.

Jonas scuffed through the ashes, saying nothing. Ironically, only one object had escaped the blaze—the wide and gaudy sign which formerly had hung above the entrance.

CRAG'S BAKERSFIELD HOTEL
J. Crag, Esq., Innkeeper & Publican

"Got the bodies at the funeral parlor," the deputy informed him. "Want to see them?"

" 'Specially the firebug."

In the windowless room smelling of nameless foul chemicals, Jonas said to the undertaker's assistant, "Where were they found?"

The deputy horned in. "Alley, back of the hotel. Otherwise they might be cinders." One guest had died in the fire. All others, and the night staff, had escaped.

The assistant lifted a sheet. Jonas grimaced as he gazed at the chalky face of Beef Brown. Old Beef and Montmorence had fallen out somewhere along the line and Beef had sunk deep into poverty and drink. When he turned up in Bakersfield, asking the hotel manager for a loan, he insisted he was an old friend of Mr. Crag's. Jonas sternly refused the plea sent by telegraph but by return telegraph offered Beef a post as a porter. Beef did not turn it down.

"The firebug plugged him?" Jonas said.

"Yep. After Beef surprised him lighting some oily rags in a pile of wood scraps in the alley. Beef lived long enough to tell the tale.

When the other fellow shot him, Beef pulled his knife and stabbed him twice in the belly."

"Can't imagine why someone would want to burn down one of my hotels," Jonas mused. "I make it a practice not to make enemies. Let's see this fellow."

The assistant raised another sheet. Jonas grew nearly as pale as the corpse.

"I know him."

The deputy was astonished, and a casual stranger would have felt the same considering the victim's appearance: long, ratty hair, skin tinged with dirt, a rancid smell of poverty lingering on him, a stigma death had not yet obliterated.

"He smells as bad as I did when I walked into Lost Camp." Jonas's remark was met by bewildered expressions. "I stampeded with him thirty years ago, all the way from Ohio. We went through a bad patch together. We weren't friends when we parted."

"You suppose he saw your name outside and decided to do you dirt?"

"Must be so. Maybe there was nothing much left in his life but wanting to get even. Those were strange times, the stampede years. Men were sure they were going to get rich one way or another. This fellow was positive but I guess he didn't. I didn't either, not in the diggings. Poor Montmorence, that was his name, he had a lot of brass. All I had was"—Jonas gave a last lingering look before the sheet fell—"what most of us had, some hope. Montmorence was certain."

"Dead certain. Haw, haw."

Jonas didn't bother to answer the deputy. Feeling sad, he went out into the afternoon light that fell on California with the brightness of gold nuggets.

Inquest in Zion

IVON B. BLUM

Mountain Meadows: such a poetic name until the word "massacre" is added to it.

The butchery that took place there in the grasslands of southern Utah in September 1857 yet stands as the West's single greatest monument to hatred and violence.

At Mountain Meadows, a band of fifty Mormon elders and some three hundred Paiute Indians laid siege to a wagon train and forced the entire company to surrender. Then, as the emigrants trudged along a trail, the "Saints" and their Indian confederates fell on them, killing 120 men, women, and older children with gunfire, club, knife, and ax.

Those named in "Inquest in Zion" are the real culprits.

Ivon B. Blum is a retired Los Angeles attorney with over thirty-five years in private civil practice. He is the author of many stories and eight books, most recently *River of Souls: A Novel of the American Myth,* about a boy struggling to manhood during the Taos revolt in New Mexico.

As a youth Blum worked on a cattle ranch and panned for gold in Nome, Alaska. A believer in research for his fiction, Blum has traveled the Santa Fe Trail, visited Paris and Quintana Roo, Mexico, and fished and walked much of the High Sierra country.

Mountain Meadows, Southern Utah Territory,
September 1857

Meadow silent except wind, wind, wind.

No Indian yells. No gunshots.

I smell our unburied dead.

Outside our wagon fort, a fierce-jawed man waves a dirty, white shirt. He and the one I hear called John D. Lee ride toward us.

Our men shake fists and wave rifles.

Loud men talkin' quiet. Prayers, maybe. Lee cryin' now.

Before the Indians came, we kids played hide-and-seek in tall grass. Now I think, *Ollie, ollie, oxen, free, free, free.*

Rough hands load me into a wagon with the little children. A strange white man climbs up.

Mama says, "Sarah, sit with these babes. Pretend you're only seven. Keep still!"

She hugs me too hard and I'm afraid.

Wagon starts up. I wave at Mama. Wind plucks our tears.

Strange men with gray-white faces walk beside Daddy and our men, unarmed now, strung out behind the women and older children.

Rifles glint cold in the sun.

A bearded stranger, like a statue, sits a black horse.

"Do Your Duty!" he shouts.

There's Daddy. The white stranger next to him points his rifle. The rifle puffs smoke. Daddy falls down. It's a game.

Sudden smoke-puffs in firecracker flashes along the marching line. Thunder in my ears.

Ashes, ashes, all fall down.

Mr. Lee is behind our wagon.

He shoots no one.

My ears can't hear. Winds are silent.

Burnt powder. Eyes stinging. Painted Indians run from brush. There! Mama stumbles. An Indian strikes Mama with his ax. Mama falls down. Why's Mama flopping in the grass?

I see Nancy, Lucy, Susa.

Run! Run!

Painted Indians with wide open mouths.

Nancy, Lucy, Susa, runnin', runnin'.

I clap hands. *Ollie, ollie, oxen . . .*

Knives, axes, bloody cuts . . . oh, bloody . . .

Wagon over hill. Can't see no more.

"Charlie! Charlie Fancher!" I can't hear my own scream.

Charlie! Painted Indian! Knife flashin' in sunlight.

John D. Lee throws Charlie up into our wagon, saves him.

Plink! Plink!

Something hits me hard.

Cedar City, Southern Utah Territory, May 1876

Sarah "Wingy" Dunlap stood in the middle of the trail. She faced Young Lee. She didn't want a fight; only it was time he knew.

He toed a dirt hole and looked miserable.

"Why'd you come back to Utah?" he said.

"I come for an eye and a tooth, for . . . my dead."

"You was . . . ?"

"At that massacre. I saw it all till the wagon gone over the hill."

"But only nits was saved, too young to remember."

"I was small for my age."

"Revenge? Missouri revenge against Mormons? You?"

"Aint no Missouri about it. I come to see all of them hang what done it to me and mine."

"My pa?"

"John D. Lee? Him most of all. But not him alone. I come to find all of them what done it. I'll testify against them at your pa's trial."

She gently brushed his shoulder with her good hand.

"Seems like," she said, "you'd want to help me put the blame where it rightly belongs. For your own sake and for your family."

"It's dangerous," he said.

"I saw them. Your pa. Three or four others close up. I remember their faces."

"How you must hate us!"

She sagged into his chest and put her arms around his waist.

"I did till you brought me, near dead, out of the desert, your ma nursin' me, your pa layin' his hands on me and prayin'; and I lived to be courted by you, to come here."

She hugged him hard. The frozen bend in her left elbow fit well in the small of his back.

"Lord save me," he whispered.

"What?"

"I can't help it . . ."

He choked up for a moment then whispered against howling wind, "Still love you."

Wind snatched the last from her hearing.

"I guess you can't."

Young Lee pushed her away, as if forever. He climbed aboard his red horse and looked down at her. She saw despair in teary eyes.

"Just get the hell away from me," he said.

She knew there was nothing more to say and mounted her dapple horse. She stopped at the turnoff to her cabin on the old Irontown road. Looking back she saw only empty heat waves.

Mama would have known. All the woman things. That lonely, urgent feelin'. Love of a man? Need? Or just heifer love? Damn!

"Young Lee!" she shouted. "I can't help it either . . . a-hatin your pa . . . and a-lovin you."

With a jerk, the dapple horse started toward her new home in southern Zion.

SARAH BEGAN HER SEARCH AMONG FOLKS AT WILKINS'S DRY-goods store.

"This here is Abel Knight," Wilkins said. "Abel, Miss Sarah is visiting us from Arkansas."

Sarah had bumped into the young man while backing away from

the canned-goods shelf where she had dropped a can of peaches.

"Howdy," Sarah said.

She bent down to retrieve her peaches.

Abel Knight made no move to help.

Sarah stood up. Abel fixed his stare on her frozen left arm.

This man is snake-eyes, she thought.

He reached a hand toward the Colt pistol at her hip.

Her hand was there first.

"Can you shoot that big pistol, ma'am? I mean hit something you aim at?"

"Damn betcha, Mr. Knight. Excuse me."

Sarah put the cans on the counter with the rest of her purchases. The door slammed behind.

"Sorry, ma'am," said Wilkins. "His pa, Sam Knight, whole family, have been here since the beginning."

A deep woman's voice chimed in.

"Samuel Knight was with the militia in 1857 when the army invaded Utah to bring down the Mormon church. Hard times make hard men."

"This here's Mrs. Ann Doty," said Wilkins, "Cedar City's schoolmarm. She knows some about that massacre you was asking after. Some think she knows too much."

Ann Doty's hazel eyes smiled at Sarah from a pixie face beyond the prime but still inviting girlish sharing.

"I'd like to talk to you sometime," said Sarah.

Ann smiled like a conspirator.

"Next Tuesday. Stay for supper. The Doty School on Main just across from the saloon." Ann laughed. "It gets real interesting some nights."

She called out, "Brother Wilkins, I'm taking two yards of the yellow print. Please set it down to my account."

Then she went out, not slamming the door.

"A real nice woman," Wilkins said, tallying Sarah's purchases. "Was I you, though, I'd fight shy of that schoolteacher's tales."

"Now that John D. Lee is goin' to trial again, I'd think . . ."

"Folks hereabouts know all they want from what they've heard; and what some seen."

"Seen?"

"Some fifty men or more from Iron County went to the meadows," he cupped a hand to his mouth, *the day after the massacre. More'n a hundred bodies put under that day.*"

It was in her visions: wind and fierce-jawed wolves tugging victims' bones from shallow graves.

Could this man Wilkins have helped bury Mama, Daddy, sisters?

"You saw how Abel Knight can act," Wilkins whispered.

"I saw."

SARAH RODE DAPPLE DOWN MAIN STREET FOR HER FIRST MEETing with Ann Doty.

She smelled the evening rise of fresh droppings cooling in the dust of day's end. Sheer mountainsides echoed a coyote's call. Nearby, a privy door slammed.

The saloon, just opposite the Doty house below Center Street, spilled sounds of bored men laughing and dreary piano noise.

Ann smiled Sarah into her parlor, whitewashed by a Tiffany lamp's cheery glow.

She took Sarah's buckskin jacket and hat. Sarah shook out long, red hair.

Ann reached for Sarah's gun belt.

"Back home," Sarah said, "I hauled my tobacco from town to town. Mr. Colt was the only thing kept the wolf from the campfire, so to speak. It's become part of me, I guess."

"But in here? Well, suit yourself."

Ann pointed to the stuffed chairs and danced for the kitchen, shunning Sarah's offer to help.

I believe, Sarah thought, this's the nicest room I've ever been in. Flowers. Lace. A woman's room. And me in men's pants, smellin' of horse and backwoods, totin' a gun and not knowin' the difference till now.

They ate in the warm glow of candle-dance.

Sarah told Ann of cabin life in Arkansas. Years of growing and selling her own tobacco. No mother or father, no other women, just an old, know-nothing uncle.

Sarah felt the warmth of home in the telling and in this woman's eyes; and didn't hear the gush of her own motherless years spilling across old lace.

After dinner they moved into the parlor. The table between the chairs held fat ledgers and a pile of brown newspaper clippings.

"When I first came to Cedar City," Ann said, "folks made me welcome. I started with more than forty pupils. I have only twenty-seven now."

"How come?"

"It seems I have rubbed open an old wound."

"The massacre?"

"Yes. I didn't realize. To me it was local history; but mysterious. Two years ago, Lee's first trial—mistrial I call it; for that's how it ended—brought it all bubbling up again after seventeen years. For many hereabouts, that history's alive in their families and they want the story kept hidden. Now, just when folks thought it might be over, they've decided to try Lee again."

"This time he'll hang."

"What?"

"That's what the papers back home say."

Sarah gripped her left elbow. There I go again. She thought of Young Lee. Sayin' too much . . . too soon.

"If my Aaron were alive, he'd have seen and shut me up."

Sarah nodded toward a gilt-framed photograph of a lean, bearded man standing beside a yoke of oxen, two small girls in hand.

"Is . . . was that him . . . your family?"

"Yes. Aaron was called on to follow the new prophet, Brigham Young, from Kirtland in Ohio. We went from one Zion to the next, always seeking the sun. We were full of zeal for our religion as we marched over prairies and high desert mountains."

She looked up at her long-ago family.

"Zeal, then, and later? After all the songs, my man, my babes, Katy and little Ellen, died, one by one. Cholera. A raw land. Hard winters. And hard men . . . asking me to join their . . . harems. For me, Zion's had its sorrow."

Ann was quiet for a time.

"Funny thing," Sarah said. "No dirty diapers or crying, no tobacco spitting, or cholera, in my memories."

• • •

AWKWARD SILENCE. EACH REMEMBERING THEIR OWN DYING songs. Sipping coffee until faint sounds like far-off wind rustling high grasses cleared memories.

"*Sheeee-deee-viiil! Shee-dee-vil!*"

It came on them like a squall.

"She-devil! Bitch! Diggin' intah ol' bones."

Sarah jumped to the open front window.

"*Biiii . . . tch.*"

She saw a man silhouetted in the doorway of the saloon.

"C'mon, Abel," she heard. "Leave her be . . ."

Ann smiled like she was shot and didn't quite know it yet.

SARAH TOLD ANN OF THE LEES AT LONELY DELL. AT MENTION OF Young Lee, her voice thickened.

"You like that boy, do you?"

Sarah said nothing.

"Is it that bad? Hum. Yes, I can see it is."

If this woman knows me, Sarah thought, and such things right off, what else do women know . . . that I ain't learned?

"The son of John D. Lee," Ann said. "That's serious with the trial coming up.

"It's said Lee's raped young girls, slit the throats of helpless women; not just at the massacre but later. And often."

Ann stopped as if thinking it over.

"I believe the massacre; but the rest? The rest is legend."

"I know it is," said Sarah, remembering the care Lee'd shown for his family, his rough hands quelling her desperate fever, praying over her . . . and Young Lee a-kissin her on the thousand-mile log.

THEY SPENT THE REST OF THE EVENING PORING OVER OLD NEWS clippings and reports.

Sarah shuddered when she found herself described in Indian Agent Forney's report.

"Only a little girl," said Ann, looking over at Sarah. "No name.

141

Says a bullet shattered her arm. Six or seven. That would make her, let's see . . ."

Sarah said it quick and a little loud. "I'm near thirty."

Ashes, ashes, all fall down; the shattering noise of gunshots and Indian yells; blood like colored raindrops in a dream. Blood . . .

"Where's this man Higbee?" Sarah saw in her vision his command to *Do Your Duty!* mixed now with the question in Ann Doty's eyes.

"Hidden out for years. Probably dead by now."

"I bought my dapple horse from Issac Haight," Sarah said. His name was in the old papers. He was Stake president back then but Sarah hadn't seen him at the massacre.

"Of the leaders who might stand trial with Lee," she said, "only Haight's still around."

"There's William H. Dame. Big commander of the Iron County Militia. All took orders from him. Lives at Parowan."

Ann yawned.

"If I'm to have any pupils left to teach, I'd better get some sleep . . . and teach some other history."

They undressed in the dark. Each took a side in Ann's feather bed.

"Ann. In the morning, I'll ride on up to Parowan to see Mr. Dame."

"Mind, Sarah. Dame's cut from the same cloth as Abel Knight's father."

"Old-timer?"

"Afraid of truth."

A PLUMP WILLIAM H. DAME GREETED SARAH WITH A WAN SMILE. He seated her in a small office in the new temple building at Parowan.

"I seek counsel," she lied.

The small clock on the wall struck ten. Above it hung a framed document, dated at Parowan, August 12, 1858, a short handwritten paragraph followed by many signatures.

"Never too busy," Dame said. "Miss, eh, hmm."

"Dunlap. I'm new to this country and have been courted by a son of John D. Lee."

"I was once Lee's commander as lieutenant colonel of the Iron County Militia. In '57 and '58 when we were at war with the United States."

"What I need counsel on . . ."

"Oh, yes. If I can."

"Well, anyway, the son, name of Young Lee, is a Mormon; and I'm not. He wants to marry."

"That counsel's easy. Such marriage is forbidden by the church. You must convert."

"What bothers me most, Colonel Dame, is Young's father. Young says his pa was just obeyin' orders of his superior officers in the militia."

Sarah hesitated a moment.

"As Mr. Lee's commander . . ."

"I've been cleared by the church of that whole disgraceful business," he said, pointing to the document on the wall.

Sarah began to read but Dame interrupted.

" 'We have carefully and patiently,' " he recited without reading, " 'investigated the complaints against President William H. Dame . . . and are fully satisfied that the complaints . . . are without foundation . . .' "

"I see John M. Higbee signed," she said. "Did Issac Haight?"

"Yes. There. And Indian scout Nephi Johnson, Apostle George A. Smith."

He gave the paper a thoughtful look.

"I bought a horse off of Issac Haight. We got to talkin'. He says you ordered the massacre." She lied in a strong, even voice. "What do you say?"

"What? It was Haight . . ."

It's in his face, Sarah thought. Dame let Haight or Higbee . . . or Lee give the order to slaughter us. But Dame was for it! I've got my answer but I can't hang a man I didn't see on the ground that day; and that church clearance. Ain't he the clever one.

• • •

On her way back, Sarah headed for Issac Haight's ranch.

She shuddered at thought of him but she needed to know the whole of it.

Haight sat astride the corral fence. He looked around as Sarah rode up.

"From the lather on him," said Haight, "I'd say you've come a ways this morning."

"Yes, sir. We been to see Colonel Dame."

Sarah smiled at the gaunt old man.

"For counsel," she added.

"Sound. Every woman needs counsel, time to time."

"We talked some," Sarah said, "about the old days down here and him and you and Lee."

"Lee? You talked about John D. Lee?"

Sarah pointed. "This gray horse. I came to thank you . . ."

Haight waved a hand at her.

"They was good old times . . . creating Deseret."

"Dame said he ordered Lee to save the emigrants at all hazard."

"Lee was a major in the legion. Took his own counsel."

"Dame said most likely you ordered it . . . what was done."

Sarah sensed the same menace as before; saw something like death in his eyes. The fatal truth of all these men, Dame, Abel Knight, Lee, and this old Saint, suddenly struck her. She wished she'd rode on by it all.

"Me? No. I gave no orders but that those poor emigrants must be saved."

Haight's eyes deepened to match the blue of the sky.

"Why do you ask, missy, about events . . . best forgotten?"

"My interest is in Young Lee and the burden he bears on account of his father."

"A father's sins . . ."

Piety joined the fierce look. She saw he was judging her.

"I'll tell you a little something of that day . . . For the boy's sake . . . and yours."

He wagged a finger up at her.

"And mind; if need be, I'll deny I ever spoke of it."

Sarah wondered why he'd care about her or Young Lee . . . or truth. Maybe she'd goaded him good with what Dame said.

Haight pointed southwest toward Mountain Meadows.

"Colonel Dame and me come to Hamblin's ranch late Friday night. The deed was done that day. Mind you, for a whole, long week, it was Indians. Indians . . . alone . . . did it."

There's Daddy. The white stranger next to him points his rifle at Daddy. The rifle puffs smoke. Daddy falls down. It's a game.

Sarah shivered in the saddle and put a hand down as if to say, Stop all the lies.

"Just listen," Haight said. "Maybe fifteen, eighteen small children was laid out by the fire. A little girl whimpered and cried, bloody arm broke above the elbow."

Sarah tucked her wingy arm close in.

"The next morning, after a sad breakfast, we went out to the meadows. A blue mist hung low over the brush. In that mist, we saw men like ghosts with necks and limbs bent and stiff. Children entwined with mothers. Sisters holding hands. You could see surprise, panic, terror, frozen in their dead faces."

Crack! Crack! Crack!

Sarah thought she heard wolf jaws snapping old family bones.

"With the sun, the bodies came alive with flies. The boys worked fast to get them under. With the sun full up, we gathered at the spring and washed away the death that was on us. Dame, Higbee, Lee, and me, we swore upon the blood of our Prophet never to talk of what had happened there to anyone.

"Colonel Dame was some sissified by the spectacle. He cried at sight of it."

Haight's voice suddenly jumped like a preacher's does to end the sermon.

"Leave God to judge our actions in the light of our loyalty to His cause and the establishment of His kingdom here on earth."

Pride blushed the old man's face.

Dapple pawed the sand in the silence.

"You gave the oath?" she asked.

"They took it. All but one has kept it, even Lee. And now Dame accuses . . . me?"

"You signed Dame's clearance."

"Orders. And that Covenant of Silence. Orders."

Haight gripped her with iron fingers.

"What I told you was counsel."

For an instant his face deadpanned and sky-color drained from his eye sockets.

"Whether people think it was Dame or Lee or me or someone else don't matter. Lee will hang and that will end it . . . for all of us."

"Lee won't name you or the others? To save himself?"

"Lee is chosen. A lifetime of loyal, steadfast devotion. The best among us, perhaps."

Haight's empty eyes turned sky-blue again.

"Goodbye, missy."

He turned and walked toward the corral.

Sarah pulled Dapple's head around, applied a heel to the ribs.

She heard Haight call after her.

"To break counsel is dangerous. Heed it!"

SHE THOUGHT ABOUT HAIGHT'S THREAT; BUT, AT SUPPER, SHE told Ann, anyway, of her day's interviews: how Dame put it on Haight and Haight sayin' it was only Indians; how they gave the orders, lettin' others do the killin'; and how Lee'd been given up as scapegoat.

She couldn't speak about all the twisted bodies.

"Now you're part of the covenant," Sarah said, laughing to cover the sickness she still felt.

Ann didn't laugh.

Barroom babble from the saloon filtered through open front windows.

"Boys are kind of whooping it up over there."

"When I rode up, they called me 'she-devil' and 'bitch,'" said Sarah.

"They meant me."

"Oh, Ann. Do you take them—"

"Seriously? I lost three more pupils today. I'll tell the Bishop tomorrow that I've been mistaken to search into history. I'm through. I repent. It's the Mormon way. The Bishop'll get the word around."

"You're quittin' the truth?"

146

"I can't *live* here and *tell* the truth. Be best for you too, Sarah."

"Not me, Ann. I can't quit."

Suddenly, Ann's plump lips and hazel eyes bloomed with a knowing smile like a rose opening to a new dawn.

"Well, I guess you can't, at that."

Sarah reached out a hand.

Both of them were alone and female and treated as outsiders in a man's Kingdom of God. Childless widow imagined a grown daughter to mother. Motherless young woman soaked up female wisdom so long denied her.

"The Lee boy?" asked Ann. "He still hasn't been to see you?"

"I guess he's quit me for good."

Sarah saw a glow in Ann's eyes, sunny and teary at the same time.

"Dear Sarah," she whispered. "Remember. You got to *make* a man see you fit in the arms of his soul."

"But how?"

"He can't do much 'fitting' if you're here and he's yonder."

"I can't make him come."

"No. But you can go . . . to him."

Sarah laughed an embarrassed laugh.

"I just couldn't."

"Of course you can. Go and make him see you."

She saw Ann catch her breath, put a quivering hand to her breast as if fighting a mother's cry. After a moment, Ann reached for Sarah's wingy arm, gripped it gently.

"Well," she said, her voice steady. "A man thinks he does the courting; but that isn't the half of it. Sparking's what that boy needs. Honest-to-God female sparking."

"Do you really think I should . . . ?"

"Go to him? I know it, Sarah!"

She wanted to hug Ann; saw that her own need to cling hard to a woman was Ann's need too. They embraced at first, then held each other a long time like mother and daughter at final parting and wept a little.

• • •

IN THE SALOON, ABEL KNIGHT SWIPED THE WHISKEY GLASS AWAY
and turned the bottle up to his lips. He sat and drank as table noise
of cards, coins, and men's talk swirled around him.

Bob Hammond played solitaire nearby.

Suddenly, Abel Knight lurched up, knocking the chair over. He
pulled the Remington from his belt and opened the gate to check
rounds. He pushed the pistol back in his belt. Without a word, he
went to the door and braced himself.

Hammond looked up from his cards.

"Hey! Abel? Where the hell you a-goin?"

When Knight kept on, Hammond tossed down the cards and
jumped to the door.

"Damn it, Abel. Slow up."

He saw Abel weaving in the street. Hammond caught up.

"You hear? C'mon back."

Abel pushed him into the dirt and stumbled toward Ann Doty's
front door.

SARAH WALKED SLOWLY FROM THE KITCHEN WHERE SHE HAD JUST
refilled the coffee cups.

"I must be getting old," said Ann. "I had to go back over the
old newspaper stories; but I found it."

The rose of her knowing smile was full open.

"Found what?"

"The names of the children in the Fancher party who survived."

Sarah smiled.

Ann pouted. "I'd so hoped you'd trust me . . ."

"One was a Sarah Dunlap," said Sarah. "A girl with a shattered
arm."

Their eyes met and held for a long moment. Consent and for-
giveness passed between them.

"The stories you can tell," whispered Ann.

"It's been time you knew," Sarah said.

Ann glanced over her shoulder at the sound of spurs and boot
steps and heavy breathing just beyond her door.

Sarah felt the air around her tighten.

. . .

THE FRONT DOOR SLAMMED WIDE OPEN. ABEL KNIGHT, HUNCHED and weaving, stood full in the light spilling from the Tiffany lamp.

Ann jumped up to face the intruder.

Sarah saw another man come into the light behind Abel. He grabbed Abel's shoulder.

"Abel Knight," said Ann Doty.

She put hands on hips and squared up to him.

"Look at my door; and you owing me for the whole of the last school year. You're drunk."

Hammond tried to pull Abel back. Abel shook him off.

Abel wrestled the pistol from his belt.

Frozen-eyed, Sarah hung suspended over the tunnel of that gun. Smoke erupted from it. Thunder pounded her ears. She felt the sucking shock of it; and saw the Tiffany lamp go dark.

New shock shattered tight air. Her own fisted Colt bucked and pain ran up her arm.

Through the smoke, surprise painted Abel's face flat white.

Men ran from the saloon and crowded around the doorway.

"Looky," said one. "It's Abel . . . and the schoolmarm."

THE MEN WERE GONE, SOME TO TELL SAMUEL KNIGHT HIS SON shot the schoolmarm and was himself shot dead by Sarah in self-defense.

The house was dark and cold. Sarah dressed Ann for the grave.

She looked down at Ann's face, milky in the surprise of morning, all the pixie in it flushed by pale dying.

Reflection brought feeling with coming light. She whispered as if the bats might hear.

"You and Young, all I've ever loved, are gone from me. Until tonight, that boy I shot was innocent as Young Lee for all their fathers done to mine so long a time ago. Well, tonight I killed Knight's boy for my own daddy."

She waited for the exhilaration of triumph, felt a welling need to cry. She shouted at the empty dawn.

"I've give some back! I have entered the Promised Land of my vengeance. I am . . . fulfilled."

Tears refused her still.

"Why don't I feel it?"

Cedar City, Southern Utah Territory, June 1876

Sarah'd seen Ann buried a month ago. She'd met Knight at the cemetery. Only daggered looks passed between them. In her visions he'd driven the hindmost wagon at the massacre with their wounded until he and others killed them.

Now it was night. She sat alone in her cabin on the old Irontown road reading Ann's papers, bucking her resolve soon to bear witness against John D. Lee and to bring in Dame, Haight, and Knight.

Suddenly, she heard Dapple trumpet from the corral. Another horse answered.

Have them Knights come for me? Sarah grabbed up the Colt.

A saddle creaked and knuckles barked on the door.

"Who's there?" she said, voice sounding steady in spite of her pounding heart. She eared the hammer back.

"I'm hungrier'n a Gentile's wife out here."

"Young Lee? That you?"

"It ain't Brigham."

She yanked open the door. Lamplight spilled onto Young's backside as he led the red horse toward the corral.

Sarah followed, the pistol forgotten in trembling fingers.

"Make him see you fit in the arms of his soul," she heard Ann say. He come all this way. Ain't that some seein' and fittin'?

Young opened the gate still not looking at her.

Her words just came.

"Don't put your back to me, Young Lee. Don't shame me this-a-way . . . like it shames some folks I know to say what they're a-feelin'."

He turned then. She saw starlight swimming in teary eyes, heard his throat rattle a laugh.

She heard Ann's voice: *"What that boy needs — honest-to-God female sparking."*

She tossed the Colt aside and jumped to the top rail of the corral. He reached up for her. Off she flew into the dark of his arms. Next thing, she was lying on her back in dust and dung and straw. She kicked and twisted and bucked; but he held her.

He kissed her hard. She kissed him back. They panted and kissed and cried in a universe of two.

Dead Man's Hollow

JAMES REASONER

A young orphan-farmer in South Texas gets a chance to serve with the Confederate Cavalry of the West under Rip Ford in '64?

It just doesn't get much better than that and no writer can improve on James Reasoner's handling of the situation.

John Salmon Ford (1815–1897), was a South Carolinian who reached Texas in June 1836, served in the Republic of Texas army as a lieutenant, and during the war with Mexico earned his nickname for the death notices he sent to the families of casualties in his unit, ending each letter, "R.I.P."

Juan Cortina was a cattle rustler–freebooter in the Brownsville area of Texas in the late 1850s and 60s who later became governor of Tamaulipas.

Texan James Reasoner has been writing professionally for twenty-five years. His novels *Cossack Three Ponies* (coauthored with his wife L. J. Washburn, the award-winning mystery novelist) and *Under Outlaw Flags* were nominated for Spur Awards by Western Writers of America, Inc.

Reasoner is currently writing The Last Good War series of World War Two novels for Forge Books, as well as Civil War Battles, a series of historical novels.

THEY WEREN'T DEVILS, MIND
you. They were Yankees. In South Texas, in the summer of 1864,
there wasn't much difference betwixt the two. I leave it to you to
decide which was worse.

When they first came out of the early morning mist, I didn't
know who they were. Just man-shapes with rifles in their hands,
that's all I saw. Then one of them came closer and pointed his rifle
at me and hollered, "Don't move, boy!" and I saw the blue uniform.

I had a hard-used Walker Colt on my hip, but the blamed thing
weighed so much it took a while to get it into play. So I didn't even
try, knowing that the Yankees would shoot me to doll rags before I
could get a shot off. I felt bad about it, figuring that it was my
bounden duty as a good Confederate to die right then and there for
the cause, but when it came right down to the nub, I wanted to go
on living. I lifted my hands and said, "Don't shoot."

The soldiers closed in around me. "All we want's the cows," said
the fella who had told me not to move.

I had just stepped out of my cabin, on the way to do the milking,
when the Yankees popped up out of the brush. I had an old bull and
three cows in the pen, along with a calf that had been born a few
weeks earlier. "Leave me the calf, anyway," I said.

The soldier frowned like he was thinking it over. "We're a for-
aging party," he said after a while. "Our orders was to forage. We're
supposed to bring in all the cows and pigs and chickens we can find.
We're on short rations down at the fort."

That was Fort Brown, down at Brownsville, he was talking
about. I'd heard that Federal troops were there again. They'd been
in and out of Brownsville a few times since the war started. They
would occupy the town, then leave, then do it all over again, I guess
depending on the whims of some general who was way off in Washington City or someplace like that. I didn't much care one way or

the other as long as they didn't bother me. But like this soldier said, they were running short of supplies, and I'd heard that they were scouring the countryside for anything they could get their hands on. Looked like there was some truth to the rumors.

I counted. There were eight of them. I couldn't fight them, so I shrugged and said, "All right. Take what you got to take. But that ol' bull's stringy as hell and wouldn't make good eatin', and if you leave me him and the calf, I might could start over."

The soldier who was doing the talking looked at me squinty-eyed. "You alone here?"

"Yep. This is my place now. Folks're dead."

"How come you ain't in the Reb army, big strappin' boy like you?"

"Last summer, my pa and two brothers fell in Devil's Den, up yonder at Gettysburg. I figure that's enough of a price for one family to pay, especially seein' as I'm the last one left."

The Yankee nodded. "Could be you're right." He looked around at the other soldiers. "We'll leave the bull and the calf. All right?"

They didn't argue with him, and I was starting to feel a mite grateful even though they were going to go ahead and steal three out of the five cattle I had to my name, when I heard hoofbeats in the chaparral and a high-pitched yell ripped out.

I knew what that meant. Bullets were about to commence flying. I turned tail and ran like hell for the dogtrot.

The riders swept around the corner of the cabin and drove right over those Yankees. Guns banged and roared and lead whined around like mosquitoes. I ducked down behind the butter churn and hauled out that big Colt, but there was nothing to shoot at. The horsebackers were right amongst the Yankees, and I couldn't shoot at one without taking a chance on hitting the other. So I just kept my head down and watched the battle, what there was of it.

The Yankees didn't stand much of a chance. They were afoot, fighting mounted men, and outnumbered to boot. They had single-shot rifles too, and the riders were using Colonel Colt's revolvers. A lot of powder was burned in a brief while, and when it was over, a couple of the riders had minor wounds and all the Yankees were dead.

So were my cows.

I couldn't believe my eyes as I walked out of the dogtrot and looked at the pen. Every single one of those cows was on the ground, even the calf. I didn't know whether to bawl or cuss, so I did a little of both. "You killed 'em!" I yelled at the man who seemed to be in charge of the group of horsebackers. He was giving orders, telling a couple of the other men to ride out through the brush and make sure there weren't any more Yankees skulking around.

The leader turned in the saddle to look at me. He was a young fella, only a few years older than me, and well set up. He said, "You mean the Yankees? Yeah, we killed 'em, all right. Been trackin' that bunch since yesterday."

I pointed at the pen. "I mean my cows!"

He turned his head and looked. "Sorry. When that much lead gets to flyin' around, there's no telling where some of it will go."

I was a little sad about the dead Federal soldiers too, believe it or not. "You didn't have to ride in shootin' like that," I said.

The young fella's face got sort of hard and grim, and he said, "You wouldn't feel like that if you'd seen what those Yankees did yesterday afternoon over at the Jefferson place."

Ed and Ab Jefferson were neighbors of mine, redheaded terrors who were about ten years older than me. Both had been in the war but had been mustered out the previous year.

"What are you talkin' about? What happened to Ed and Ab?"

"Dead, the both of 'em. They tried to stop those Yankees from drivin' off their pigs."

Ed and Ab dead. I couldn't hardly believe it. The Yankees had seemed nicer than that to me. Of course, I'd been willing to let them take my stock without a fight. I supposed I didn't feel quite as bad about them getting killed. I sure did hate to lose those cows, though.

"What in blazes am I gonna do now?"

"Anything holding you here?" the young fella asked.

I looked at the dead cows. "Not now."

"Come along with us, then. We're goin' to Brownsville to drive the Yankees clean out into the Gulf of Mexico."

I couldn't see anything better to do, so I said that was fine with me.

．　．　．

THAT WAS HOW I CAME TO MEET CAP'N MATT NOLAN AND JOINED up with the Cavalry of the West, called by some the Rio Grande Expeditionary Force and led by old Rip Ford, the famous Texas Ranger. He wasn't a Ranger anymore, though. He was a colonel. Not in the Confederate Army, not officially, but everybody called him Colonel anyway and he was damned sure in charge, no doubt about that. Even General John Bankhead Magruder, the boss of the Confederacy's whole Trans-Mississippi Department that included Texas, agreed that Old Rip was running the show for the Rebs in South Texas that year.

Ford was as distinguished-looking a gent as you'd ever want to see, tall and slender with plenty of white hair and a white beard that he kept trimmed pretty close. His eyes were a little deeper set than some folks, but not so much that it looked like he was peering out at you from a cave. He had a voice that rolled like a preacher's, but he could cuss better than most preachers I've known. He had been a doctor at one time in his life and had ridden with the Rangers. He had fought outlaws and Indians and Mexican *bandidos,* and now he was fighting the Yankees. He had been away from the action for a while, serving as director of conscription for the army in San Antonio, and as soon as I saw him, I could tell he was itching for a good fight.

Cap'n Nolan's troop had been patrolling west and south of Corpus Christi, but they had received orders to rendezvous with the main body of the Cavalry of the West as it headed south toward the Rio Grande Valley. They had been on their way there when they found the bodies of Ed and Ab Jefferson and took a side trip to track the sons o' bitches responsible for those killings. And found me in the process. Once I'd agreed to join up, we rode south as hard and fast as we could. My old saddle mare was game, but I began to worry that she couldn't hold to that pace. Nobody wanted to miss out on the fun, though, and Matt said Colonel Ford wouldn't wait for us if we were late.

"We got to get the Yankees out of the valley," he explained to me as we rode. "What with the Federal blockade along the East Coast, the only way to get any European trade in and out of the Confederacy is through the Gulf of Mexico. That trade had been going through Matamoros and Brownsville, straight across the Rio. Now with the Yankees squattin' there at Fort Brown, trade goods have to be hauled all the way up to Laredo before they can get across the river. That sure has played hob with everything."

"Why's it so important?" I asked him. I'd never given much thought to matters economic, other than how much I could get for the stingy little crops I raised.

Matt looked over at me and said, "From what I hear, the Confederacy's in bad shape and gettin' worse by the day. It's got to have some money if it's goin' to have a chance to survive, and that means trade. Cotton out, money and guns in. It's as simple as that."

I nodded. Even I could understand that, simple farm boy that I was.

We rode hard and met up with Ford at a little wide place in the road called Banquete. Matt swung down from his horse and went over to a tall old man with a white beard and saluted, then shook the old man's hand. Then they sort of slapped each other on the back a couple of times, and I knew the old man was Rip Ford. Matt had known him since the early days of the war and ridden many a trail with him. I could tell the colonel was a fighting man just by looking at him, a Texian through and through.

Matt waved a hand at me when I'd got off my horse. "This is Andy Parkhurst, Colonel. He'd admire to join up with us."

Ford looked at me and said, "Are you ready to fight some damn Yankees, Private Parkhurst?"

From the way he called me Private Parkhurst, I reckoned that enlisting in this particular army wasn't an overly complicated affair. I nodded and told him, "Yes, sir, Colonel, I am."

"Welcome to the Rio Grande Expeditionary Force." Old Rip shook my hand. It was an honor I've never forgotten.

WHILE IN CAMP AT BANQUETE, COLONEL FORD RECEIVED WORD that the Yankees had made an attack on Laredo. The Confederate forces there under the command of Colonel Santos Benavides had driven off the Federals, with considerable help from the citizens of the town. We were waiting for some more men that Colonel Dan

Showalter was supposed to be bringing us, but news of the fight at Laredo made Old Rip sort of antsy. He decided not to wait anymore, and we rode out bound for Laredo.

Matt Nolan's bunch, including me, did most of the scouting on the trip, so I spent a lot of long hours in the saddle. This must have been what it was like to be a Ranger back in the old days of the Republic, I thought, ranging over a harsh, mostly empty land, always on the lookout for enemies. Of course, back then the enemies were Comanch', rather than Yankees. There wasn't much difference, in the eyes of most folks in that border country. The Indians were more bloodthirsty, but they were more honorable too.

Those Confederate units led by Colonel Showalter were made up of Arizona boys. They finally came in about the time we got to San Fernando Creek, four days after leaving Banquete. That gave us a pretty sizable force, and it would be even bigger once we got to Laredo and hooked up with Colonel Benavides.

When we rode into that border town, it was the most impressive settlement I'd ever seen. San Antonio was bigger, but I'd never been there. Across the river was Nuevo Laredo, also a good-sized town, and quite a bit of political intrigue was going on over there. From what I gathered, the Mexican government had about as many factions as a dog has fleas, and they were all fussing with each other. Some of them supported the Confederacy, some of them supported the Union, and some didn't give a hang and were just out to grab as much power as they could. Right then, the fella in charge in that part of Mexico was General Juan Cortina. Now, Cortina and Rip Ford were enemies from way back, but they respected each other, and Cortina was never one to let old grudges get in the way of backing what he saw as a winner. So he was sort of on our side for the time being and even arranged safe passage with the Yankees for Colonel Ford's wife and daughter to visit Mrs. Ford's sister in Brownsville. Old Rip and Cortina might've fought tooth and nail in the past, but they weren't the sort of men to make war on each other's women and children and didn't believe in anybody else doing so neither.

So there we were in Laredo, two hundred miles upriver from Brownsville, and Ford wasn't of a mind to just sit there. The Cavalry of the West took to the saddle again, heading down the Rio toward the Gulf.

The Yankees must have heard we were coming, because every time we came to a settlement we found that Federal troops had been there but had pulled out in a hurry in recent days. We passed Rio Grande City and Edinburg, then got held up for a while waiting for our supply train to catch up with us. Word came that the Yankees had withdrawn all the way to Brownsville and were concentrating there at Fort Brown. Wanting to see if that was right, Old Rip sent out what the soldiers call a reconnaissance-in-force, bound for the Las Rucias Ranch, about twenty-five miles upriver from the fort.

Most of the time, summer in the valley is hot and dry. But that day, it rained fit to beat the band. The skies were gray as we set out, and they opened up before we got there. It was a real toad-strangler. And if that wasn't bad enough, a bunch of Yankee cavalry was waiting for us at Las Rucias.

There were a hundred of them and about sixty of us, and I reckon each side was a little surprised to see the other. The Yankees started the ball by opening fire on us. I heard the shots before I could see anything. The rain was pouring off the floppy brim of the old hat I wore, so it was like I had a waterfall a couple of inches in front of my face. I took off the hat and crammed it in my shirt, figuring it was better to get my head wet than be blind in a gunfight. My Walker was wrapped up in oilcloth and stuck in my saddlebags and wouldn't have worked too well in that downpour anyway. But I had a carbine I'd been issued when I joined up, and when I spotted muzzle flashes ahead of us, I dismounted and used the saddle to steady the gun while I aimed over the mare's back. That mare was too old and tired to be very skittish, so she stood there pretty still while I shot off a few rounds in the general direction of the Yankees. Then somebody yelled for us to mount up and charge, so I did that.

Looking back on it, I was scared, sure, but since I couldn't see very well, I didn't get that awful worried. And no matter what the weather, if a bullet got me I wouldn't see it coming, so what was the point of brooding about it? They tell me this is a good attitude for a soldier to have, but I don't know about that. It's just the way I was.

The thunder rolled and lightning tore holes in the sky and the rain came down, and we fought hot and heavy with those Yanks for a little while before they turned tail and ran back to the ranch head-quarters. The ranch house at Las Rucias was made of brick that had been freighted up the river. The Federal troops forted up in it for a while, until the rest of the column caught up to those of us who'd been in front. Then, facing several hundred men, the Yankees ran again, taking off into some canefields across the river. We scooped up most of them, taking them prisoner. Only a few got away.

I had burned a lot of powder that day but didn't know if I'd actually killed anybody or not. Twenty of the Yankees were dead, so it was possible. The thought that I might have ended another man's life didn't make me happy, but I had signed on to fight, and the sooner the Yankees were out of the valley, the sooner we could all quit killing each other.

Now there was nothing much in the way of opposition between us and Brownsville, but we were still having supply problems. Not only that, but more men were coming in all the time, and Colonel Ford wanted the biggest force he could get when he moved on the city. So we pulled back a ways and waited a while longer, until things had settled down a little. During that time, I rode on many a patrol, scouting the river road just in case the Yankees decided to come to us.

They didn't.

Our bunch swelled to some fifteen hundred men, most of them hard-riding, hard-fighting Texians. But Showalter's Arizona territo-rials were pretty tough too, tough enough so that when we started on the march toward Brownsville, Old Rip put them right up front, at the head of the column.

Not all the Yankees were at Fort Brown. We ran into some of their cavalry at the Ebonal Ranch, where there had been a skirmish between some Texians and old Juan Cortina back in the days of the border wars. Matt told me about it later, having heard the story from Colonel Ford. There wasn't time for much talking while we were swapping shots with the Yankees.

This time it wasn't raining and I could see what I was shooting at. The Yankees put up a fight for a little while, and then some of us charged them, including me. The enemy was close enough this time for me to use that old Colt of mine. That thumb-buster weighed over four and a half pounds and was hell to aim and fire one-handed, but it packed a lot of punch. I only hit one Yankee, but the bullet knocked him clear out of his saddle. When I rode by later, after they had broken before our charge and lit out for Brownsville, I saw that the fella was dead and got a hollow feeling in my guts. Well, now I had killed a man, and that was for certain sure.

OLD RIP MOVED US SO FAST OUR SUPPLIES NEVER COULD KEEP UP with us. That was a problem the whole way. We kept having to stop and wait for the wagons. I've heard it said that an army can live off the fat of the land, but not in the South Texas brush country. That land's just not fat enough for that.

We started hearing rumors that General Herron, the Federal commander at Fort Brown, was going to evacuate Brownsville and pull back to Brazos Santiago, an island in the Gulf off the mouth of the Rio Grande. If that was the general's intention, though, he didn't get in any hurry about it, because after a couple of weeks passed, the Yankees were still squatting at Fort Brown and in the town of Brownsville itself. They had even established a defensive line west of town, which made it look like they didn't plan on going anywhere any time soon.

One evening, I rode out with Colonel Ford, Cap'n Nolan, and several other men to take a look at the Federal position. Old Rip studied on it through a spyglass for a while, then said, "By God, enough is enough! I'm tired of waiting for those bastards to move, so we're going to move them!"

The next morning, that's what we set out to do. This was not to be a cavalry fight. We were dismounted, moving forward on foot. I had that carbine clutched tight in my hands when we set off. As usual, the Yankees got off the first shots, but then we loosed a volley at them and ran forward, yelling at the tops of our lungs. I don't know why it helps to holler when you're going into a fight, but it does, no doubt about it.

Those Federals put up a good fight. More than once as we charged, I heard the whine of lead past my ears. Men were hit and fell, and some of them got up and kept on and some didn't. I fired and reloaded, fired and reloaded, until we came to a long, narrow low place in the ground and flung ourselves down there to take advantage of the cover. I asked one of the fellas next to me if this place had a name, and he told me it was called Dead Man's Hollow.

Knowing that didn't make me feel a whole lot better.

I'd been in the two fights before, but they had been fast and furious and not like this one at all. This time the Yankees didn't break and run. They stayed where they were, hunkered down behind whatever cover they could find, and we did the same. From there we shot at each other, and shot at each other, and shot at each other some more. You hear about famous battles and they're all flash and fire, armies sweeping here and there, circling and feinting, and generally going about it like the whole thing was some sort of fancy dance with bullets and artillery. I'm here to tell you it's not always that way. Sometimes war is nothing more than lying on some hot, rocky ground and keeping your head down as much as you can and every so often sticking it up just long enough to let off a shot toward the enemy, who's more than likely doing about the same thing you are. If not for all the racket and the fact that you might die at any time, it would be so boring you might just doze off.

And then after a while you get thirsty, and you make the water in your canteen last as long as you can and when it runs out you suck on pebbles to try to work up a little spit. You get hungry too, but you don't have anything to eat except a little jerky and you know if you gnaw on it, it'll just make you thirstier, so your belly gnaws on you instead. You can't get up to take a piss either, because if you do, some damn Yankee sharpshooter will likely put a ball through your head. All you can do is hold it and wait for night to fall so you can move around safely again. Worse comes to worst, you can piss your pants, but you don't want to do that because, hell, you're a soldier and soldiers don't do such things.

And between worrying about all that, you shoot some more. Burn that powder, throw that lead.

War, as they say, is hell. It's also downright unpleasant.

Dead Man's Hollow was as close as we could get to Brownsville, because if we advanced any farther, we would be within range of the artillery the Yankees had in the town. We had the Yankees bottled up, however, and they couldn't go anywhere, either, except to retreat.

So we lay there and took potshots at each other for several days, until finally somebody realized there weren't any shots coming from the Federal positions anymore.

Ford sent a mixed force of Texians and Arizona boys under Colonel Showalter to take a look around the town. I made sure I was one of the Texians. After being stuck in Dead Man's Hollow for all that time, I was chomping at the bit to be up and moving around again. The hollow lived up to its name. Several of our men had been killed there. I was mighty glad I hadn't been one of them.

The scouts circled around on horseback and made a fast run into Brownsville. We were ready to gallop back if the Yankees gave us a warm welcome. But nobody welcomed us at first. The streets were empty, like Brownsville had become a ghost town. Then some of the civilians began to pop their heads out of doors, and we found out pretty quick that the Yankees had pulled up stakes earlier that day. Fort Brown was east of the settlement, and when we rode out there, we discovered that the Federal troops were gone from there too.

I was one of the boys who galloped back to Colonel Ford with the news. He had a look of satisfaction on his fierce old face, but he said, "Don't just sit there, damn it! Ride on downriver and see how far those blue-bellied bastards have gone!"

I swapped horses, since my mare was played out, and so did the rest of the scouts. Then we took off for the tall and uncut, following the river road past Fort Brown. We caught up to a few Yankee stragglers, but they didn't do any more than throw a few wild shots at us before they lit out. As a rear guard, which we figured they were supposed to be, they weren't much count. We followed them all the way to where the land ran out and the waters of the Gulf began, and we saw the heavy-loaded boats taking men and horses and cannons out to Brazos Santiago. Since there was nothing else we could do short of swimming our horses after them, we turned and rode back to Brownsville.

When we got to Fort Brown, the Confederate flag was flying from the flagpole on the parade ground. I reined in and looked at it, and a good feeling came up inside me. I'm not much sold on the idea of war, but if I've got to be in one, I'd sure as hell rather that my side win than the other side.

Of course, in the end, the Confederacy didn't win. But in the

Rio Grande Valley, in the summer of 1864, Old Rip Ford and the Cavalry of the West damned sure didn't lose. Nor did we the next year, at the Battle of Palmito Ranch, the very last battle of the whole blamed war. That's something, anyway, and I never forgot it, or the men I rode with in those long-ago days.

The Hundred Day Men

MICHELLE BLACK

At daybreak on November 29, 1864, the Third Colorado Volunteer Cavalry squadron, commanded by Colonel John Chivington, attacked a sleeping Cheyenne village on Sand Creek in the eastern edge of the territory. Carbine- and cannonfire, and the relentless hunting down and murder of innocents—women and children—resulted in at least two hundred Indian dead, despite the fact that the Cheyenne chief Black Kettle flew a white flag of surrender.

The massacre resulted in congressional inquiries and a military fact-finding tribunal which convened in Denver in February 1865. No military action was ever taken against Chivington.

Michelle Black was born on the Kansas prairie and graduated from the University of Kansas law school with honors.

After practicing law in both private and public sectors, she and her husband (also an attorney) moved to Colorado where, in 1993, she began concentrating on fiction writing.

Her first novels, *Never Come Down* and *Lightning in a Drought Year*, won regional and national awards, and her Forge novel *An Uncommon Enemy,* about the aftermath of Custer's 1868 battle of the Washita, earned generous critical praise. A mystery-sequel, *Solomon Spring,* was published by Forge in 2002.

"Silas Soule's wedding was the first I ever attended that required an armed escort for the groom. I mean, I've heard of bridegrooms being escorted to the altar with a shotgun aimed at their *backs,* but never aimed elsewhere for his own protection." I did not intend to make a joke, but several of the fellows could not help but chuckle at the sad humor of it.

Others in the room frowned at the ones who laughed for failing to respect the gravity of the day. We sat in Si's own house on Curtis Street after all. His lovely bride might have overheard us. I glanced into the next room where the women congregated, my own wife among them. Young Mrs. Soule insisted on pouring tea, though a phalanx of black-clad ladies hovered about to wait upon her.

The irony weighed heavily on everyone. A bride for only three weeks.

Sitting in the darkened parlor with the heavy velvet drapes drawn tight at midday, stifling the room with the late April warmth, it was hard enough to shake off the gloom, yet I felt the need to defend my good-humored friends. "Si would have laughed too."

Everyone nodded at the truth of this. Everyone except a boy in the corner whom no one seemed to know. He looked barely eighteen and showed a manner of being farm-bred. How did he know Silas? Had he served with him in the army as most of the rest of us in the room had? He did not wear a uniform and I did not remember him. Perhaps he was a member of the wife's family.

Si's wedding had been the only bright spot in an otherwise grim and terrible year. Only he would have been tempted to do something as hopelessly optimistic as commit matrimony in the midst of all the roiling turmoil that was now Denver City. After steadfastly refusing to join in the carnage at Sand Creek in November, after being threatened with court-martial, even hanging, for this refusal, after braving two credible death threats attempting to dissuade him from testifying about the truth of that dark day, his response was to get married.

He had looked as calm as a choirboy the very day he was called before the military inquest on Sand Creek. I was not so sublimely composed. I feared for his safety as did all those who cared about him.

I saw the tear in the eye of his lovely fiancée, then still Miss Coberly, as she kissed him goodbye in her father's carriage before he set to the task of telling the board—and the world—about what really happened on November 29, 1864.

"Ho, Ned, good to see you," Soule had called as he alighted from the rig. "You remember Ned Wynkoop, don't you, dear?"

"Of course, I do." She smiled through her tears and extended her hand.

I shook it as I removed my hat and nodded to her parents.

"Please give Mrs. Wynkoop my regards," she said. Then she added as she pressed my hand more tightly, "Look out for him."

I knew just what she meant.

Silas would have none of this. "Don't be silly, darling."

She let a worried sigh slip out as the carriage jerked into motion and bore her and her concerned family away.

She had good reason for her fretfulness. Soule was exposed to enough danger as the new provost Marshal of Denver, but that was nothing compared to the threats he had garnered from those who did not wish him to testify.

"Ready for today?" I asked as we mounted the steps to the temporary military headquarters.

"Ready and eager," said Soule with his usual smile. "Let Chivington's men do their worst."

I COULD NOT SIT IN THAT COURTROOM UNDER THE HATEFUL, burning gaze of John Chivington, my one-time commander and a man I had once considered a friend, without thinking back on the events that had brought us all to this sorry affair. My own testimony would involve the months leading up to that day on the shore of Big Sandy Creek.

The war still ground on in the East, North against South, yet all we Westerners could think of was the Indian peril last year. I certainly thought of little else. As the commander of Fort Lyon in the eastern part of the Colorado Territory, I had my prescribed duties, of course, but I also had my family to worry about. My wife and infant son had just joined me in that barren place when news of the shocking fate of the Hungate family reached us. I received the standard information through the usual channels. My wife's parents, however, sent us more personal news from the scene.

The Hungates were a farm family living on the high eastern plains. A marauding band of Indians killed them and mutilated their poor bodies. Their shocking remains were displayed to the citizens of Denver City, inciting a panic.

Governor Evans prudently requested funds from Washington to raise a state militia. A call went out for volunteers to enlist for a service of one hundred days to fight the Indians. Seven hundred Colorado men answered and were outfitted as the Colorado Third Cavalry. John Chivington was placed in their command.

One hundred days.

I ROSE AND STEPPED INTO THE HALL AFTER CATCHING MY WIFE'S eye. She struggled to smother the rustling of her stiff, dark skirts as she left the second parlor and joined me. She had abandoned her fashionable hoops in deference to the somber event, as had many of the ladies present.

"How's Mrs. Soule holding up?" I said.

She shrugged. "I think she's still in shock. She talks only about the most trivial things. Seems to be avoiding the obvious."

"Does she blame me for what happened?"

"Good heavens, no. Why would she do that?"

"I might have talked him out of testifying. He might be alive today if I had."

"You knew him as well as anyone and you know that no one could have stopped him."

"I suppose you're right."

Si was not one to shrink from a challenge. He never flinched at danger when a moral principle was at stake. He was a mere boy, still in his teens, when his father brought him out to the Kansas Territory to set up a "station" on the Underground Railroad. Together they smuggled slaves to freedom. He joined the Jayhawkers and even went to Harper's Ferry to rescue old John Brown. The stubborn abolitionist, however, longed to die a martyr's death and refused Si's attempted deliverance.

I found all this out from talking to mutual friends. Si would rather tell a joke or sing a song than recite his daring deeds. Now it was his turn to die a martyr's death. Despair for my lost friend weighed heavily on me.

I rejoined the men in the parlor after refilling my glass with brandy. Normally, I would not indulge in strong drink so early in the day, but this was scarcely a normal day.

"There are those who say that Chiv was afraid of being laughed at. Maybe that's what drove him to it." George Price made this observation about the motives behind the attack on Black Kettle's village. The village of a noble man whom I had come to admire and respect. Whose safety *I* had personally guaranteed. A man who had relied on my word and the integrity of the United States Government. A man who had ultimately watched his people slaughtered for his trust.

"Both he and Evans were running for Congress, don't forget." I asserted this boldly, unable to disguise my bitterness. Last fall, Colorado had decided to vote to join the Union. Evans wanted to go to Washington as the state's first senator and Chivington longed to join him as a member of the House of Representatives. The political plans of both men were nullified when the statehood initiative was defeated in the fall election.

I was not at Fort Lyon that fateful day in November. If I had been, the butchery would never have occurred. I can say this with absolute confidence and resolve. I also sense with an awful certainty that persons now the subject of the inquest knew this and thus engineered my absence, but I cannot prove it.

"Killing Indians was the best way to win votes in the Colorado Territory last autumn," I went on.

Several men nodded. How embarrassing for the leader of the Colorado Third, which soon came to be known as the "Bloodless Third," because they wandered around the plains of the territory for three months, never locating a single Indian warrior upon which to wreak vengeance and secure their place in the annals of Colorado glory.

"Chiv had to have been feeling a lot of pressure to deliver some kind of victory. His Hundred Day Volunteers had scarcely a week left of their enlistment period."

"Tick, tick, tick," said Bob Merrill with a snicker. All chuckled at the biting quip. All except one.

"Colonel Chivington is a great man!" said the boy in the corner who had been so noticeably quiet. The passion in his voice jolted everyone from their melancholy dullness.

"*Was* a great man, I'd say." This from Fred Crantz.

"We all served with Colonel Chivington at Glorieta," I said to the boy. "He was a great man there. He distinguished himself. He was truly a hero."

"We were all heroes at Glorieta," said Bob Merrill.

"Here, here," said George Price. "To Glorieta Pass!"

We raised our glasses and drank a toast to our shared victory over the Rebel forces in New Mexico two years before.

"We just wanted to be heroes too," said the boy. "With the war to save the Union near played out, boys my age all missed our chance."

The sorrowful tone in the young man's voice caused us older fellows to chill with apprehension. I say "older" yet not a man in the room was above the age of thirty. That did not stop us from *feeling* old.

The boy looked at the wondering faces that surrounded him and said in a deliberate voice, "I was one of Colonel Chivington's Hundred Daysers."

Price's reaction was outrage. "How the devil can you sit in Silas Soule's's parlor and pretend to mourn him?"

We all prickled at the growing tension in the air.

"I'm his wife's cousin. I have as much right to be here as any of you. My mother and hers are sisters."

"Do you know the coward who shot him?" Price demanded.

"I didn't have nothing to do with that. What do you take me for?"

"I'm not sure," said Price.

Soule's testimony had been devastating to the glowing reputation of Chivington's Hundred Day Men. He had detailed how the former Methodist minister and his officers had been fully informed of the peacefulness of the Cheyenne village, yet had insisted upon attacking it anyway. Soule had called the plan murder and declared that any man who would take part in the slaughter was a "cowardly son of a bitch." Si seldom minced words.

Chivington's response had been to threaten Soule with hanging. Still he would not back down. He refused to allow any of the men in his company to raise a weapon that day. He even tried to place some of them between the Hundred Daysers and the betrayed Cheyennes.

But all of his courage and pluck could not stop the terrible determination of John Chivington.

I hate to envision the look on the face of the stunned Black Kettle. Si said he flew a white flag of surrender above his tepee, as I had instructed him to do. He also hoisted an American flag given to him by the Commissioner of Indian Affairs himself. But neither stopped the bullets.

The repugnant aftermath of the "battle" heightened the charges against Chivington. Soule sat on the witness stand for two full days describing the "unnatural outrages"—as the commission delicately referred to them—that the soldiers of the Third, no longer called Bloodless after that day, were accused of perpetrating on the bodies of the dead and dying.

"THERE'S NOTHING THAT SAYS THOSE INDIANS DOWN THERE weren't the ones who murdered the Hungates," said the young man, a defiant edge creeping into his voice. "Nobody told plain soldiers like me that the tribe was peaceful or surrendered or nothing."

For an instant, I felt pity for the boy. I am quite certain he knew nothing of the true situation when he was ordered to attack.

"Exactly what *were* you told?" I said.

"My captain said we finally found 'em and now was the time to fight. Now was the time to seek glory and vengeance."

Glory and vengeance. More misery and horror were perpetrated in servitude to those two words than any others in the English language, I'm convinced. No wonder the killing goes on and on down the countless centuries. Men always seem to find good reasons to annihilate each other. Chivington's militia was no different. Nor were our red-skinned brothers. If what I understand of their culture is correct, they live for the fight as much as any other breed of men.

But not Black Kettle. He had long since tired of the fight. He sadly recognized who would ultimately prevail, a bitter truth few of his nation yet wished to acknowledge.

"I'll assume for the sake of the argument, boy, that you had no notion the village was peaceful when they ordered you to open fire," said Crantz. "But what possessed good, civilized Christian men—or so you all claim to be—what possessed you to desecrate those bodies like you did?"

"I didn't see none of that," said the boy.

"You must have seen *something*," said Price. He folded his arms across his chest and waited. He loved Soule like a brother. We all did. Price had been with Soule in Central City a few weeks ago and had witnessed one of the attempts on Si's life. Shots were fired from ambush but failed their mark.

Price said Si had told him that he expected to be killed for his testimony. He said he did not fear death, but only that his name would be blackened were he not there to defend it. How true that was becoming. Chivington's attorneys were already busily entering into the inquest record bogus statements that Soule was a known drunkard. Such detestable actions made my blood boil. That John Chivington would stoop to this level—a man who had been a close friend of Si's—sickened me.

"They say there was some scalpings," the young man admitted. "But what's the harm? They was dead. They'd do the same to us if they could. I suppose the boys just wanted souvenirs."

"Souvenirs?" I said. "Cutting off men's and women's private parts? Cutting off fingers to steal the rings? Cutting a baby out of a mother's belly and then scalping it? Putting a live baby in a feed box and toting it around only to throw it out on the ground when you'd lost interest in it?"

"I never saw no baby in a feedbox," said the boy, his anger growing. "That's all a damned lie if you ask me."

My wife appeared at the door of the parlor. She whispered, "Gentlemen, please lower your voices. We can hear you in the next room."

All fell silent for a moment after this delicate reprimand, but the emotions in the parlor still floated upon a seething current.

"Everyone called us heroes when we marched back into Denver

City," said the boy. "They gave us a big parade. The newspaper called us all glorious and brave."

"I would not trust the *Rocky Mountain News* to report on yesterday's weather correctly," said Merrill. "What's your name, boy?"

"Tom."

"Well, Tom, are you so certain of your actions as to justify the cold-blooded murder of Silas Soule, the man we all came to bury today?"

Three days previous, a trap was laid on the streets of Denver for its provost marshal. Si and his wife had just returned to their home when they heard the sound of gunfire. He grabbed his gun and dashed down Lawrence Street toward the blast.

A man named Squires waited for him with gun drawn. Soule and Squires raised their weapons and fired them in a dead heat. Soule caught a bullet in the cheek and was killed instantly. His assassin was hit in his arm and ran away into the night leaving a trail of his own blood.

"Captain Soule was killed because he was slandering the good name of the Third," said the boy. "All those stories he told at the hearing had to be lies."

"How do you know what he testified about?" asked Price. "The proceedings have been secret."

The boy did not answer this.

"But I guess you would not know this, since you 'didn't see anything,'" Price persisted. "If nothing wrong happened, your reputation is secure."

Young Tom rose from his seat and declared, "I don't have to justify myself or any of the Hundred Daysers to you! Who are you all anyway?"

"Just the dead man's closest friends," said Price.

Tom stomped out of the room.

I excused myself soon after and stepped out upon the small back porch. A fresh breeze, scented with new spring growth, cleared my head. Then I realized I was not alone.

Young Tom stood in the yard, oblivious to my presence. I could not see his face. He leaned against a small tree, hunched over, his head hanging. From the slight jerking flexes of his back, I guessed him to be crying—a potent reminder of just how young he was, too young yet to master his emotions.

His bravado in the parlor had been a show. For an instant, I pitied him. His bid for glory with the Hundred Daysers was not unfolding quite like he had planned. I yearned to know his mind. I had my own opinion on the motives of his commander, whom I knew so well, or thought I did.

But what of Chivington's men? What brought them to that terrible day? Had they no conscience at all? This young man's tears seemed to hint otherwise.

I cleared my throat to announce my presence. He started at the sound and quickly wiped his face on his shirtsleeve.

He turned and glanced at me cautiously. I tendered him a cheroot, a peace offering of sorts. He declined, but I lit up.

"Those men in there are taking this pretty hard, you know."

He said nothing, but came over and sat next to me on the cold stone step.

"Emotions are raw after what happened," I added.

"I reckon that's to be expected," said Tom. "I'm sorry he died. Really, I am."

"He was a good man. We all loved him. Men who fight a war together tend to form a kind of bond as close as blood itself. You can understand our grief, I'm sure."

"I met him at his wedding to my cousin Heresa. He seemed a fair sort. Jolly. A nice singing voice."

"Do you really think he lied about Sand Creek?"

He shifted uneasily. "Colonel Chivington said it was right and honorable to use any means under God's heaven to kill Indians and that he damned any man who would be in sympathy with them."

"Well, I guess I'm damned, and Si too."

"I didn't mean that the way it came out." He sighed. "Sometimes, when ideas get turned into the real thing, it's not how you thought it would be. At Sand Creek . . ."

"I get the feeling you saw *something* that day."

He seemed to mull over whether to talk, how much to say. He stared at the alleyway, clogged with the carriages of the mourners inside.

"In the afternoon, most of the shooting was over. The day was cold but nobody seemed to care 'cause we was all so happy and proud of the battle and all." He swallowed hard. "I saw a little redskin boy. Just a youngster, maybe three. A little younger than my baby brother. He was running in the sand, stark naked and crying. A fellow next to me raised his rifle and took a shot at the kid. He missed and muttered an oath I won't repeat. Then a second fellow yelled, 'I'll take him!' and he had his shot but missed as well. A third man laughed at the other two. He climbed down off his horse and aimed his rifle. He said, 'I'll show you how this is done, farmboys!'

"His bullet found its target. The little fellow hit the sand while all these men around me clapped and cheered." The catch in Tom's voice hinted he hovered near tears again. "It made me feel kinda sick. I said, 'What'd you do that for? He was just a little kid.' And they accused me of being an Indian lover and I said, 'The hell I am,' and I damned any man who dared to call me that. But . . . I can't stop thinking about it. Especially since Captain Soule was shot and all. Before that, I was ashamed to say we was relations, but after . . . I don't know. It was wrong that they shot him."

"Who? Silas or the little child?"

"Both, I guess." He hung his bewildered head. "I told my minister about it. All's he would say was, 'Everything happens for a purpose.' But he didn't tell me what the purpose was. I've been puzzling it over in my mind ever since."

"Life tends to throw out a lot more questions than answers."

"Lord, that be the truth." His sad, helpless smile made him look even younger.

"If the commission called you to testify and you told them that story about the little boy, do you suppose the good men of the Third would shoot you too?"

The young man's anger flared. He turned to me with a furious glare and no doubt a planned retort . . . then stopped himself just as abruptly. He ducked his head and said nothing. He hugged his chest and rocked back and forth on the porch step as I finished my smoke.

I rose to reenter the house, but he did not join me. His troubled gaze was fixed on the carriages in the alleyway, but I think he was trying to see something else entirely.

Leaving Paradise

LENORE CARROLL

Margaret Irvin Sullivant Carrington, whose voice is perfectly captured by Lenore Carroll in "Leaving Paradise," was the wife of Colonel Henry Beebe Carrington (1824–1912), a Yale graduate and lawyer who served with the 18th U.S. Infantry in the Civil War. In 1866 he was assigned to Indian duty in Nebraska and established Fort Phil Kearney on the Bozeman Trail that year. The trail penetrated Sioux and Cheyenne tribal lands and the fort immediately became the focus of Indian hostilities. These culminated in the massacre of December 21, 1866, in which an eighty-man command, led by Captain William J. Fetterman, sent out by Carrington to punish the hostiles, was annihilated.

Margaret Carrington was author of the classic frontier memoir, *Ah-sa-ra-ka, Home of the Crows; or, the Experiences of an Officer's Wife on the Plains* (1868).

Lenore Carroll is the author of five novels, most recently *One Hundred Girls' Mother*, and more than a score of published stories. She teaches writing in the Kansas City area, is a member of the Great Alkali Plainsmen (a Sherlock Holmes scion society), and the Kansas City Posse of Westerners International.

I HAVE JUST READ FANNIE'S memoir, a moving account of our departure from Fort Phil Kearney in the blizzard. I shall never forget that bone-freezing journey from the Big Horns to Fort Caspar. Fannie was seven months pregnant and we accompanied her husband's corpse—a frozen cortege.

Her memoirs reveal the hardships we faced on the frontier— unfortunate like the lack of fresh vegetables, inconvenient like living in tents, or exasperating like doing without servants; some huge and tragic like losing a husband. The obverse of the coin was the beauty of the West which we were privileged to see in its untouched state.

So much happened in those few months. We left Fort Laramie in early summer. The Platte River ran full and muddy and the days were already hot. On the trail, living with two small boys in an army ambulance filled my days as we moved over untouched landscape of remarkable and subtle beauty. At first I missed the lush green of my Eastern home, but soon I came to love the long Western vistas, rolling grasslands, and clear skies with their austere beauty. Major Jim Bridger, the mountain man, led us hundreds of miles westward. He was one of the few white men who knew these lands as well as their Indian occupants. He disappeared each day to scout ahead and returned to confer with the colonel, my husband, as to the route we should take and where to site the fort.

We arrived in the foothills of the Big Horns early in July, and the first day the mule-drawn mowing machines cut the grass where the plaza would be. Soon our tents stood in straight lines around the pa- rade ground, imparting comeliness and system to the whole. The second day brought our first sight of Indians, who watched us from a distance, then magically evaporated like mist. The third day, Indians crept inside the picket, starting the bell mare so that the company horses followed.

The people, the place, the trials are still vivid in my memory after these many years.

My husband's orders required him to establish a fort to guard the Bozeman Trail, and that is what he did. He organized the sawmills, directed the construction of the buildings and the discipline of the men.

The men set up the two steam sawmills in the mountains where the tall Douglas firs stood and began cutting trees for the barracks, warehouses, stables, and laundress quarters. The wagons of the wood train transported lumber down to the fort. The quartermaster's yard accommodated teamsters, wagon makers, carpenters and mechanics, the blacksmith, and armorers. Soon the officers' and men's quarters, guardhouse, magazine, hospital, sutler's stores, and band building arose from the pounding and sawing. And of course, the stockade fence surrounded all.

We found ourselves in an earthly Eden, Absaraka, as the Indians called it. In every direction, natural beauty ministered to my hunger for space and light and furnished such choice intercourse with nature that I was consoled for the separation from my family. At first, we women reveled in the freedom of the untouched landscape. We cantered to Big Piney Creek for a picnic, with the children in a wagon. The grass and wild oats grew so dense that a horse could hardly be forced to a trot. We gathered delicate wildflowers along the cold creek running through the foothills, where our children played. Sagelike incense scented our fire. Dark-feathered birds of unfamiliar species sang over our picnic. We brought extract and sugar to make lemonade to the children's delight. Snow-topped Cloud Peak seemed to look down upon us with a cheerful face, sunlight making his features glisten. We gathered chokecherries and wild plums for pie and stained our hands with juice.

Then a small party of Indians, dressed in their beads and feathers, stormed down upon us, whooping and threatening. We gathered the children and hurried back to the fort before they could make another foray. The driver fired a shot into the air, to let them know we were armed. They could have killed us all, but did not.

After that, the ladies gave up their gallops. We played croquet within the gates, or played Authors, or had a quiet quadrille in the evening, with good music and conversation.

One evening that summer, when we sat outside, Major Bridger came to my house carrying a thick book. He greeted my husband, the colonel, with a half-salute, then nodded to Dr. and Mrs. Reid and sat beside gentle Lieutenant Bingham, a manly young officer.

"Evening, Miz Carrington, Colonel Carrington."

"Beautiful night, Major Bridger," I said. "We were commenting that we see more stars here than back East."

"The air is clearer and you're closer to 'em in these mountains."

I thought he was in his forties, but learned he was closer to sixty—rawboned, thin, and agile, with blue eyes and auburn hair faded with gray. I told him my eyes were the same blanched shade as his and he said the clear Western light bothered us more than it did brown-eyed people. He wore the same old blue army overcoat and slouch hat he had worn on the scout. I thought of him as our guardian angel because he knew so much about the West and his head held maps of hundreds of places. He had had his own silver mining company and owned a trading post, but had little intuition about business. When my husband received orders from General Philip St. George Cook, living in Omaha, to discharge Major Bridger, the colonel wrote "Impossible of execution" on the back of the order and retained the guide on full duty. Major Bridger's ability to parley in the Indian tongue or sign in their universal language made him invaluable. I heard rumors that he was a drunkard, but I never saw him so. He seemed exceedingly alert, a condition we gradually came to share.

I invited him to sit with us and he told my sons a fanciful tale about a mountain lion that chased and chased him up a high mountain. When he paused, Harry asked, "Then what happened?"

"Why, he ate me!" he said. And we all laughed.

After the children were put to bed, Mrs. Reid left and the rest of us went inside and Major Bridger laid the book on my parlor table. "Would you read a bit?" he asked.

"You want me to read a play of Shakespeare?"

"Yes, ma'am. I cain't read and I hunger for the music of his words. And he told some good stories."

"We can take turns," said Lieutenant Bingham. I could see boyish enthusiasm in his comely young face, so I found *Hamlet* and began. Lieutenant Bingham sat beside me and read Hamlet's part while I read the others. We had a good lamp which cast a mellow amber glow over the pages. The house was crude, with the constant wind whistling through the gaps, but we had real windows and a good cookstove. We stopped after one act but we enjoyed it so much we promised to continue the next night.

"Thankee, ma'am." Major Bridger took the volume and looked at me. His eyes told me his gratitude. He had begun to lose his sight and mightn't have been able to see well enough to read even if he could. After that, we read most nights, and other women and men joined the group, except those nights in August when we stayed outside to watch the aurora borealis's merry dances and vaulting streamers. We gazed transfixed at the unreal tints of the gorgeous coronas unfolding across the night sky.

MAYBE IT WAS THE SOUND OF MACHINERY THE INDIANS HATED. The sawmills rent the air with their shrieking whistles. The blades of the mowing machine clattered as it leveled the grass of the plaza. Inside the fort, the pounding of hammers and the scrape of saws never ceased.

My husband, the colonel, tried to shield me from the knowledge of marauding Indians, but when he slept in his clothes with his pistol at his side, I knew the seriousness of our situation.

Each loss was fierce and painful. We caught glimpses of Indians, then another body would be found. Major Bridger warned, "Better not go fur. There's Injuns enough lying under wolfskins, or skulking on them cliffs, I warrant. They follow you always. They've seen ye, every day." We heard wolves calling at night and I wondered if they were truly four-footed, or clever two-footed imitators.

Poor Mrs. Grummond arrived pregnant in September, so we coddled her as we would a younger sister. Fannie was flighty and couldn't seem to learn to cook, so we invited her and her lieutenant husband to mess with us. She seemed scarcely older than my son Jimmy, and they both doted on Mrs. Horton's pet antelope. Her husband was as hotheaded as Captain Fetterman, who said two days after he arrived that a company of regulars could whip a thousand Indians and a regiment could whip the whole array of tribes. I watched Major Bridger's face when this was repeated. He snorted, but said nothing.

Even I could see that the Sioux and Cheyenne light cavalry were better adapted to the hills and valleys of that Eden than our mounted infantry, with its cumbersome howitzers.

From the second day after our arrival the Indians raided, stealing horses and cattle until we scarcely had milk or butter. They attacked timber details and wood trains, even harassed water parties at nearby creeks. Men were killed and injured. Every work party had guards, but stealing and scalping bands constantly troubled our men, showing themselves splendid in ambush and decoy, perfect in horsemanship, cunning in strategy, careful and wary in battle, and fiendish in vengeance.

Each building in turn became our Sabbath sanctuary, as no chapel was planned. The string band accompanied our voices raised to the Almighty. Our splendid forty-piece band played at guard-mounting in the morning and at dress parade at sunset. Their afternoon drills and evening entertainments contrasted strangely with the solemn conditions constantly suggestive of war.

All major buildings were finished by October 31, when we celebrated a Muster-for-Pay holiday, with a flag-raising and speeches in the afternoon and an evening levee at our house where officers in full dress and ladies of the garrison enjoyed music, social dancing, and other entertainment. I treasure a copy of the speech Colonel Carrington delivered on that occasion. He acknowledged the bravery of the men and their hard work, and marked the deaths of officers and soldiers. I watched Old Glory rise. It was the first time the American flag had flown between the Platte River and Montana Territory. The simultaneous snap of presented arms rang out in salute. The long roll of the combined drum corps was followed by the full band playing "The Star-spangled Banner." The cannon opened fire and our magnificent flag slowly rose to masthead and was broken out in one glorious flame of red, white, and blue.

WE LIVED FOR DAYS, WEEKS, AND MONTHS OF CONSTANTLY RE-curring opportunities, seeing Indians in small and large parties dashing at pickets, driving in wood parties, badgering water details, and with dancing and yelling, challenging the garrison to pursuit. It is war when one, two, or more casualties mark the issues of a day and give evidence of the cunning barbarity and numbers of the foe; when night alarms are common, and three men are shot within thirty yards of the gates; and when the stockade becomes a prison wall. The Indians did not forage in trains or on pack mules; their campaigns were not extensively advertised in advance, nor did they move by regular stages or established routes, but even a woman could see that the Indians were daring and watchful, estimating our strength. They were too fond of their hunting grounds to yield possession to the stranger. The officers at headquarters in Omaha never understood that we were in a war zone and they never sent enough replacements to fight a war.

ONE BRILLIANT NOVEMBER DAY A SLIGHT FALL OF SNOW HALF-covered the earth. A timber train went out, a water party worked at the larger creek, and details labored on a ditch near the fort. In the mountains, the sawmills were busy. The band was just marching from the guard parade when an alarm was given.

Jimmy and Harry ran home immediately, as they had been taught.

A party of seven Indians dashed through thick cottonwoods and made boldly for the picket on Pilot Hill. Instantly, relief for the mounted picket, always saddled and ready, were out of the east gate on a run, but no one could be in time. The despised howitzers were brought and a case shot was sent as a swifter messenger. The shell from the "gun that shoots twice" exploded over the Indians' heads. A second shell and they all took cover. In the meantime, only about seven hundred yards from the front gate, fifty Indians made a dash for the horses of Major Bailey's mining party. Another howitzer shell scattered this group, and a larger Indian detachment was sent toward them, but flashing mirrors passed a quick signal from the summit of the Lodge Trail Ridge. Plans had been foiled and these Indians disappeared. Private Patrick Smith was shot many times not half a mile outside the gates. He broke the shafts off the arrowheads and crawled into the fort where Dr. Reid went to his aid, but Smith died within twenty-four hours.

Later that day, a working party felling trees was attacked by Indians who broke through the woods and killed two of the detail who were separated from their comrades. About two in the afternoon, another alarm was given. Fifteen Indians were galloping between the fort and the mountain, to capture the picket, but Captain Fetterman and Lieutenant Bingham went in hot pursuit and scattered the Indians.

In their pursuit, Bingham's cavalry left the main body. I think of his last minutes racing through the grassy swales, the wind and sun in his face, his horse's mane flying. He was ever keen to do his duty. He heard the hoofbeats of the Indian ponies he was chasing, and saw their prints in the snow. Perhaps he heard a mule deer bound away into the trees when a tree branch dropped its cap of snow.

Captain Fetterman searched for Bingham's party, but came across Grummond's party first, who were besieged by the Indians, and he saved them. A few minutes later, he found Bingham's body. Sergeant Bowers was lying nearby, still living although his skull was cleft through with a hatchet.

The next morning I wept as the long-held notes of taps floated over the parade ground. We buried Lieutenant Bingham and Sergeant Bowers while a light fall of snow, blown by a chill wind from the Big Horns, powdered the graveyard.

Major Bridger stood nearby, then helped Mrs. Grummond home over the rough ground.

"We cannot stop them. They keep coming no matter what," I said to him.

"This is their home, ma'am. They won't give it up without a fight."

Thus our cemetery filled up with the victims of violence. Everything in nature is so beautiful, that one could look upon such frontier life with something like complacency were it not for these savages. Sometimes it seemed as if nobody cared if we had help or not.

ON DECEMBER 21, JUST A FEW MORE TRAINS OF SAW-LOGS WOULD furnish ample lumber to complete the office building and a fifth company quarters. Although snow covered the mountains, the morning was quite pleasant. The children ran in about eleven o'clock, shouting "Indians!" and the pickets on Pilot Hill could be distinctly seen giving the signal of "many Indians," on the line of the wood road. The wood train was in corral only a short distance from the garrison. We soon were watching for other demonstrations, while a detail was organized to relieve the train. Captain Fetterman asked and obtained permission to go with the detachment. Lieutenant Grummond, Captain Brown, and citizens Wheatley and Fisher also joined the party. The colonel gave orders and obliged Lieutenant Wands to repeat them. As if anticipating some rashness, the colonel halted the mounted party at the gate and gave additional orders. Because of his wife's health, Grummond was urged to be prudent and avoid all rash movements that would draw them over Lodge Trail Ridge.

The world now knows what ensued that bitter day. After dark Captain Ten Eyck returned with forty-nine bodies, and made the terrible announcement that all were killed.

I received the widowed Mrs. Grummond as a sister into my house. She bore her lot with Christian fortitude. The next day, in spite of continuing danger, the colonel promised Mrs. Grummond "not to let the Indians have the conviction that the dead could not be rescued." He set the fuses and adjusted the ammunition so that the application of a single match would destroy all and gave orders that the women and children were to be put in the magazine with water, bread, crackers and other supplies, in the event of a last desperate struggle, to be destroyed all together, rather than have any captured alive.

The colonel went in person, with Captain Ten Eyck, Lieutenant Matson, and Dr. Ould in the party. Long after dark, the wagons and command returned with the remaining dead, slowly passing to the hospital and other buildings made ready for their reception. Grummond's body was found and eventually accompanied us on our midwinter march back over the plains. All the bodies lay along or near a narrow divide over which the road ran, and to which no doubt the assailed party had retreated when overwhelming numbers bore down upon them. Captain Fetterman and Lieutenant Brown were at the point nearest the fort, each with a revolver shot in the left temple, and so scorched with powder as to leave no doubt that they shot each other when hope had fled. So ended lives that were full of pride and confidence that morning.

A long line of pine coffins, duly numbered, was arranged by companies along the officers' street, near the hospital. The detail to dig the huge grave was well armed and accompanied by a guard. So intense was the cold that constant relays were required. Over the great pit, fifty feet long and seven feet deep, a mound was raised, and the dead were buried with a sad and solemn stillness that is with me yet.

As if Nature herself were shocked, that very night winter descended with unmitigated severity. Guards were changed at least half-hourly and officers, ladies, and men sought their beaver, buffalo, or wolfskin coats for protection. The uniform caps were useless. Men had permission to suit themselves. Mittens ended at the shoulder. Buffalo boots and leggings rose to the thigh. Hats with bushy wolf tails pendant, tippets, comforts, coats and vests of skins made an odd style of uniform. Keeping warm was the principal work of all who had no part in hauling water, cutting wood, taking care of stock or issuing supplies.

The holidays were as sad as they were cold. The only bright moments were my boys' pleasure at their Christmas toys; they knew but didn't understand what had happened. Charades, tableaux, Shakespearean readings, the usual muster evening levee at the colonel's and all the social reunions were dropped as unseasonable and almost unholy. Sedate but genial sympathy brought a closer fraternity. The guard was constant. A stranger might have thought we were besieged.

A few days after New Years' Day General Wessels arrived with two companies of cavalry and four companies of infantry, which had waded through knee-deep and hip-deep snow with the mercury ranging from twenty-five to forty degrees below causing frostbitten hands and feet. The order to remove headquarters to Fort Caspar had to be obeyed regardless of weather conditions. The quartermaster fitted up army wagons with small sheet-iron stoves for the women and children.

That day I embraced Major Bridger, doubting I should ever see him again. His shrewd eyes met mine. His hand lingered on my shoulder.

We left Fort Philip Kearney on January 23, 1867, at one P.M. Although the snow had again begun its fantastic drifting and plentiful resupply, the march had to be made.

Wives of band musicians in wagons with their future trumpeters, flutists, and drummers shrank into their clothing as closely as possible. The thermometer hanging inside our wagon lingered at thirteen degrees below zero. Stalking in front, guide Bailey led us to Clear Fork where we ate.

Of course, for a while there was a keen watch for Indians. We plowed, dug, and plodded on. Before night we formed a corral at Crazy Woman's Fork. Wood was abundant, but the moisture that rolled from the logs refroze and soon each fire was girt about by a constantly thickening circle of ice. Cooking was out of the question. Hatchets broke our bread, and water was warmed. Thanks to the little stoves in each wagon, the ladies prepared warm coffee and chunks of the last of the Fort Phil Kearney turkey softened over the fires. After supper, we closed ourselves up in our wagons. My Jimmy and Harry and Bobby Wands cried of the cold. They looked like a pile of furs heaped together next to the stove. Lieutenant Wands was everywhere, encouraging drivers, cheering soldiers, and keeping himself alive. Sometimes a desperate man would throw himself down, determined to have a sleep even if he froze to death. With chattering teeth and aching limbs and benumbed feet, the men resorted to general stamping to keep up circulation. After eight hours, we waited for the rising moon to let us progress over the low lands beyond. Few were able to sleep.

Mrs. Wands and Mrs. Grummond kept up the fire. At three, the mercury, which had registered thirteen below, settled in the bulb and froze. The night dragged. By four o'clock, the men began harnessing with frozen hands. Many teamsters and half the escort were more or less frozen, with hands already black. At five A.M. we were in motion. The sky cleared, the stars were brilliant, and the aurora borealis streamed farewell.

Although I had demanded the driver of our wagon be relieved regularly, he said his feet "went to sleep." He was well cared for, but did not survive the amputation of both limbs two days later at Fort Reno. The men did not want to get up the next morning. They were freezing and did not know it. The colonel ordered their legs lashed to start the circulation and bring them to their feet.

The day was still and clear. The glare of the sun was blinding, requiring goggles. Buffalo kept us company until we were within a few miles of our destination. We arrived at Fort Reno, where the stricken men were attended to and we were welcomed.

I am grateful we left in a blizzard, not able to see more than a few feet because of the wind-blown snow, the gravedigger snow which tried to bury us as we had buried our fallen. It would have been intolerable if the sun had shone, if the birds had called, if the grass had undulated like swelling waves, if Cloud Peak had given a shimmering farewell. I'm glad the snow shrouded the beauty that had welcomed us to Paradise.

The Indian read the book of fate. When garrisons were established in Absaraka they were forced to abandon their homes, and fight or yield. They saw the last retreat of the buffalo, elk, and deer invaded by a permanent intruder.

With all this, and the recurring feelings of bitterness which prompted us to exterminate this foe, now comes, after all these years, the inevitable sentiment of pity and even of sympathy with the bold warrior in his great struggle. A dash over the plains or breathing the pure air of the mountains contrasts with the machinery and formalities of what is called civilized life. It seems but natural that the red man in his pride and strength should bear aloft his spear point, and resolve to fight his way through to the Spirit-Land.

Miss Libbie Tells All

SUSAN K. SALZER

No army wife of the years of the Indian Wars was more celebrated than "Miss Libbie," Elizabeth Bacon Custer (1844–1933), who married her beloved "Autie," George Armstrong Custer, in 1864. She followed him faithfully all their twelve years together and was a formidable "keeper of the flame" for the fifty-seven years she survived him. She lectured brilliantly and like Margaret Carrington wrote a classic memoir of army life—in fact, three of them: *Boots and Saddles, or, Life with General Custer in Dakota* (1885); *Tenting on the Plains* (1887); and *Following the Guidon* (1890).

While she and Custer (she also called him Armstrong) were devoted to each other, Elizabeth was fully aware of her husband's occasional unfaithfulness during his absences on campaign. The encounter with the famed soldier on the train described here actually happened and the rest might well have.

Susan Salzer is a newspaper reporter, feature writer, and editor. Her first published story appeared in *Northwoods Journal* and won first prize for short fiction at the Ozark Creative Writers Conference in 2000.

She writes between the hours of her free-lance work and maintaining a home for her physician husband and four children.

THE ACHE OF HER NEURITIS
woke her before sunrise, as it often did these days. She remained in
her bed, watching through her window as day broke and remembering other dawns, when the days began with reveille instead of
pain and each was full of promise.

After a time she heard Margaret in the kitchen. Gingerly, the old
woman climbed from her bed and reached for a cane hanging over
the footboard. Even a trip down the hallway was difficult without it.
But despite her age and infirmity, she could not bear to spend an
entire day indoors. Today, as every Thursday, she would walk three
blocks to the Cosmopolitan Club to lunch with the ladies. Often, on
the return to her Park Avenue apartment, she went a bit out of her
way to pass the prestigious Doral Hotel, where the doorman knew
her and called her to the attention of prosperous guests. He knew
this pleased her. Sometimes she was asked to sign an autograph.

From the bathroom she heard Margaret passing with her breakfast tray and called to her.

"Set out the lavender silk, dear, and the hat with the dotted veil."
She relied on veils now to disguise the years, but once she had been
the belle of the garrison. Sunbeam, her husband called her.

Her spirits sank when she reentered the bedroom. The usually
cheerful Margaret appeared distraught; she had been weeping. There
was a time when the old woman would have only pretended concern
for a maid's unhappiness, but age and loneliness had changed her.
She loved this girl almost like a daughter. She wanted to know her
trouble, to help if she could.

"It came yesterday," Margaret said, withdrawing a piece of paper
from her apron pocket. "I didn't read it till this morning, after he
left for work." It was a letter, vulgar and unsigned, telling in graphic
detail of her husband, Patrick's, infidelity. The old woman was very
fond of the handsome Irishman. The athletic set of his hips and

shoulders reminded her of her own husband, dead now for more than half a century.

"I don't know what to do, Miss Elizabeth," Margaret said, her voice breaking. "Things haven't been as good with us as I've let on. I've even thought about leaving him. There's another man, someone I knew before we married. I've wondered if his offer's still good."

Elizabeth's heart began to race, as if she had taken a fast-acting medicine.

"The club can wait this morning," she said, laying a hand on the girl's arm. "Bring the coffee to the parlor, dear. We'll sit a spell."

She walked to the drawing room, to her favorite chair by a window that overlooked the East River. She unfolded a Mexican serape that lay over the chair's arm and spread it across her legs. Its bright colors, made by Indians from a dye made from prickly pear juice, were as bold today as the day she bought it. It had seen her through Texas "northers," Kansas sandstorms, the ferocious cold of the Dakotas.

Margaret came from the kitchen carrying a tray. She placed it on a low table before the chair, then walked to the window.

"He's all I ever wanted, Miss Elizabeth," she said in a soft voice, looking down at the Manhattan streets nine floors below. "He's only a deliveryman, not famous like your general. No one will ever write any books about my Patrick—he couldn't read them if they did—but I've loved him since the day we met."

Looking at the slender, young wife, the old woman saw another much like her, alone in a tent on a warm spring afternoon. This was an unwelcome apparition, one she held at bay during her conscious hours, though it sometimes stole into her dreams.

"Margaret," she said quietly, "our marriage wasn't always the 'unbroken sea of pleasure' I said it was. In fact, I considered leaving the general. Like you, I wondered about a previous offer."

"Miss Elizabeth!" Margaret looked with disbelief at the aged widow, whose face still retained traces of the porcelain prettiness so widely admired when she was young. Her devotion to her soldier husband was legendary.

The other nodded. "I've never spoken of it, not to anyone. You understand that what I'm about to tell you must never be repeated."

She looked directly at the girl, who realized she was being entrusted with a life's work. "It won't be," Margaret said.

Closing her eyes, the old woman followed the drumbeats of her past back to another time and place, where the world was all endless prairie and sky and they felt that they would live forever. She was unsure where to begin. Should it be with her discovery, just two years after their marriage, of the playful and intimate letter signed "Gloria" which planted the first seedlings of doubt? Or the October day they arrived at Fort Riley, thrilled by the wide-open country and eager for a fresh start? As if it were yesterday, she recalled General William T. Sherman's words to her as she stepped down from the ambulance: "Child," he said, offering her his hand, "you'll find the air of the plains is like champagne."

She drew a deep breath.

"It happened in Kansas, we'd been there less than a year. Things were going well for us again. We were both so glad to leave the South; Texas was too hot and the people so behind the times, you'd think the war had never ended. And Autie was delighted with his new regiment. That spring he was called into the field; it was his first campaign against the Indians. I stayed behind, at Fort Riley. I missed him dreadfully."

She was not permitted to accompany him on campaign, but she would have if allowed. Though she pretended to be a coward, because the men liked it and cowardice was expected of a woman, the only things she ever truly feared were boredom and losing the man she loved. His amorous letters to her only heightened the pain of separation. He wrote of his hunger for her, complained that he had been too long without that certain something that only she could provide. "So long," he wrote, "as to almost forget how it tastes."

"After about a month, he asked that I be allowed to meet him at Fort Hays. General Sherman not only agreed, but offered to deliver me himself as far as Fort Harker. My colored woman, Eliza, and another friend came with me. We traveled by rail, in his palace car. We'd only met a few times, General Sherman and I, but he was quite charming. He entertained us with amusing stories about the social scene in Washington and St. Louis, about Little Phil Sheridan's latest misadventures on the dance floor. He was a great favorite with the wives, General Sherman was, they always made a big to-do when he visited the garrison."

Margaret was surprised. She knew Sherman only from his photographs, in which he appeared pitiless and predatory, and from stories her father told about soldiering with "Uncle Billy" during the war. His favorite was of the cold winter day in 1864 when he and the great general stood together in the frozen mud beside a South Carolina road and talked about cooking. "These Carolina beans will never equal our Yankee ones," Sherman said then, "but you can make money by cooking them an hour and a half." One of Margaret's earliest memories was of her father weeping the February day in 1891 when he learned of Sherman's death.

"Oh, yes," the old woman said, as if reading her thoughts. "He wasn't the hard, cold warrior the world thought he was."

ELIZABETH SAT BY A WINDOW, READING *THE GALAXY*, WHILE THE others dozed in their upholstered seats, lulled by the rhythmic clack of wheels on rails. A shadow fell across the page. She looked up to see General Sherman standing beside her.

"May I join you?" he asked, already taking a seat.

"Of course."

"Do you mind if I smoke?" His hand was poised over the inner pocket of his blue coat.

"Please do," she said. "I enjoy the aroma." This was untrue, but a lieutenant colonel's wife was in no position to deny General William Tecumseh Sherman, commander of the Division of the Missouri, the pleasure of his cigar.

She turned her face to the window. It was early May, the Kansas prairie was at its best, verdant and dotted with purple and yellow wildflowers. "My husband says this is fine country," she said. "All it needs is more water and good society."

Sherman gave a short laugh. "That's all hell needs."

She looked at him, eyebrows raised in mock surprise. "Why, General Sherman, who once told me the plains were intoxicating, the very air like champagne?"

He laughed again, this time more warmly. "You remember? And so it is. The Indian problem is a nuisance, though, and it'll only get hotter now we're into their swarming season. I'll tell you frankly, this campaign's been a fizzle so far. I didn't give General Hancock fourteen hundred men to host peace parleys and burn empty villages. Maybe I should turn that husband of yours loose on them. Maybe he and his boys will do the job for us."

"Well, have no concern on that account," she said with pride. "My husband is a fine soldier and a very brave man."

"So I'm told," he replied. "Brave even to rashness. Mind you, I'm not being critical. That's not a bad trait in a cavalry officer, Elizabeth. May I call you Elizabeth?"

"Of course." She smiled sweetly, sensing danger.

"Sheridan and Grant speak highly of him, Sheridan especially. God knows I need a cavalry man who's willing to act and ready to fight. Someone who'll do more than just stir the bucks up."

She nodded in agreement as he drew on his cigar.

"There's only one answer here," he continued. "I don't care what the Indian-lovers of the Interior Department say—sooner or later the poor Indian will have to go under. No amount of sentiment can save them. We'll have to wipe them out or make them stay where they're put. This will be an inglorious war, Elizabeth, not apt to add much to our personal fame or comfort. I hope your husband understands that."

He studied her through a haze of smoke.

"I'm sure he understands what needs to be done," she said, cautiously.

Sherman crossed his long legs and tilted his head to one side. "We'll see. I don't want to offend you, but I feel I must speak frankly. His men don't like him much, I'm told. Not like his Michigan boys during the war. And his judgment appears suspect. What did I hear a few weeks ago?" He paused, wrinkling his brow for effect. "Oh, yes. Bolted the column—alone—to chase an antelope, didn't he? Got lost? Shot his own horse? A stunt like that doesn't inspire much confidence. Not with the men, certainly; not with me either. And I don't like the way he plays up to the pygmies of the press. What is he, political?"

Elizabeth felt her heart pounding in her chest, a burning in her face and throat. It was inappropriate for an officer to speak to a subordinate's wife in this fashion. Her usual polish and mental quickness deserted her. She struggled for words.

"I don't know about those things, General Sherman," she said at last, "but I do know my husband. You can rely on him, sir. Surely he proved his worth during the war."

He smiled. "They tell me your husband is a lucky man. I didn't appreciate the truth of that until meeting you, Elizabeth." His pale gray eyes held hers, glinting like a flick-knife. "Do you remember that night last October, the night you arrived at Fort Riley?"

"Very clearly," she replied, heart pounding. "It was October twelfth, a Tuesday. Our quarters weren't finished, we all stayed with Major Gibbs and his wife, your brother John was there too. We had a lovely meal." She continued, hoping to take the conversation in a more manageable direction. "Chicken salad, a delightful turkey galantine—"

He interrupted her. "I didn't sleep a wink that entire night. I couldn't rest for thinking of you just a few feet away. Do you know that still, whenever I close my eyes, I see your face, your lovely face? Your smile, your hair. Everything about you is so fine, Elizabeth, so genteel, so . . . sweet."

She felt a burst of fear. This officer held her husband's future, and therefore her own, in the palm of his hand. Yet it was undeniably thrilling to hear such words from the man who had brought the South to its knees, from one whose place in history was guaranteed.

When she said nothing, he continued.

"I sometimes think the Mormons have it right. A man should be allowed to change his wife if he wants to. And God help me, I want to." He covered his eyes with his hand. Unlike her husband's, it was rough and ungroomed, the fingers thick as sausages. "Mrs. S. is an Irish Catholic who'd consider a man who gets drunk six times a week and mistreats his family—but keeps true faith and goes to church on Sunday—a higher form of manhood than a patriotic soldier at the head of a victorious army. The woman is tireless; she beats this Catholic drum of hers relentlessly. How I envy your husband the treasure he has in you, Elizabeth."

She was an accomplished flirt, adroit at deflecting advances with a witty remark or, when necessary, a withering one. But this was different, not only because of who he was, but because of what she felt for him. She wanted to touch him, to comfort him as she knew she could, but he was not a man to trifle with and what he asked of her was unthinkable.

"I'm sorry for your unhappiness," she said softly. "You deserve more. I don't know what else to say."

He lowered his eyes and nodded. "I suppose I would have been disappointed if you'd said otherwise." Raising his eyes again to hers, he added, "Just know this, Elizabeth. If he should ever disappoint you, if you ever find yourself alone, remember what this shabby old soldier said to you today. You can be sure he will."

"Miss Elizabeth?"

The old woman awakened, as if from a dream. "Oh, I'm sorry. Where was I?"

"On the train."

"Yes, well, on that journey General Sherman professed feelings for me. I was astonished. I had no idea how he felt. He also said some troubling things about my husband."

"Did you tell the general? Your husband, I mean?" Margaret walked from the window to a settee opposite the other's chair.

"No, I couldn't. He'd be distressed, naturally, and we had enough turmoil that summer. The Cheyenne and Sioux went on a rampage, raiding settlements, burning stage stations. No one knew how to fight them, not even my husband. Everyone was frustrated. Then in June, just a few weeks after our . . . exchange . . . on the train, General Sherman berated him for trying to negotiate a peace with the Indians. Accused him of meddling in politics." At the time she wondered at Sherman's vehemence, if her husband was being punished for circumstances beyond his control.

"Things went from bad to worse," she said. "A young lieutenant named Lyman Kidder and eleven men were butchered trying to deliver orders from General Sherman to my husband in the field. Armstrong found their bodies ten days after they were killed. The remains showed evidence of dreadful torture. The remainder of the campaign was unsuccessful. Then came the court-martial."

A letter started that trouble too. Elizabeth never knew for certain who sent it, though she suspected the snake Benteen. Of the two officers whose inaction on the battlefield doomed her husband some nine years later, Captain Frederick Benteen was the one she despised most, for he, unlike the other, was no coward.

"My husband received an anonymous letter alleging a dalliance between Captain Thomas Weir and me. It was untrue, but Autie went wild, riding a hundred fifty miles in just fifty-five hours to be by my side. He was charged with desertion, but, oh, how I rewarded him for it!"

Margaret was not well educated, she had not read Elizabeth's books or attended her lectures, but she knew of her "one long, perfect day" in the summer of 1867, a day of love, "for time and for eternity."

"I thought he did that because of the cholera outbreak," she said. "Because he was worried about you getting sick."

Elizabeth shook her head. "We told it that way, it made for a better story. We didn't mention that he beat the tar out of poor Tom Weir when he got to Fort Riley either." She did not care what made him do it, she loved him more for that desperate ride than anything he ever did, before or after.

She sipped her coffee and when she spoke again her voice had lost its softness. This next would require all her strength, like revisiting a familiar but abandoned place, haunted and malignant.

"That spring I started hearing rumors about an Indian woman captured at Washita. Sallie Ann, they called her. One afternoon, I rode with my husband to the stockade by Fort Hays, where they kept the Cheyenne prisoners. I needed to see her for myself."

The Indian girl stood apart from the others in the muddy yard, holding a baby wrapped in animal skins. Unlike the other women, her hair was braided and her face was free of the greasy red paint her sisters wore. She was young, no more than nineteen, and lovely when she smiled. She smiled only for him.

"It was true. I saw it at once." The old woman's voice cracked. "The emotion in those black eyes was unmistakable."

She fled back to the camp on Big Creek, urging her blooded colt to such a furious speed her escort could scarcely keep pace. Desperate to be alone, she ran to her tent and fell on her bed, a hospital cot, shaking with hurt and rage. The day was sunny and warm. An earthy-smelling breeze blew in through the window, her husband's hanging shaving glass tapped rhythmically against a tent pole. Men called to one another as they went about their work. With a sudden resolve, she pulled her work box from beneath the cot, laid her portfolio across her knees and began to write.

"I wrote to General Sherman in Washington," she told Margaret. "By then his star had risen even higher, Grant had named him General of the Army. I asked if he still had feelings for me. I don't know what I expected. Divorce was unheard of in those days, but I wasn't thinking logically. I simply said if he wanted me, I would come. Oh, it was sweet, the writing of that letter! I wanted to hurt Autie as badly as he had hurt me. Worse!" She reveled in the thought of his shock and humiliation. The glorious Boy General, forsaken for a bigger man! And by her, his Sunbeam, his Rosebud, his Darling Standby, his Libbie!

"It seemed only just, after what he'd done to me," she said. "To us."

Slowly she got to her feet and walked to the marble bust of her husband that stood on her writing desk. He wore the undress uniform of a major general, the way she loved him best.

"Of course, I didn't send it and I was right not to. Our best times were ahead of us." If she could relive any of her years, it would be those they spent at Fort Abraham Lincoln in the Dakotas. The philandering had stopped, they were surrounded by family and friends, their demons seemingly behind them. She reached out to touch the cold, stone face.

"I could never leave my Autie. Yes, he betrayed me." She did not mention her suspicions about her husband and the woman who sculpted the bust she now touched, or that the sculptress, Vinnie Ream, later became one of General Sherman's mistresses. She disliked the bohemian artist and believed her unworthy of either man. "Yes, he could be a preening horse's ass. I wasn't blind to his faults. But he was also a fearless soldier, a tender lover, a joyous companion. I never regretted my decision to stay. How could I? I was Mrs. George Armstrong Custer. Everything I am, I owe to him."

She stopped speaking, overcome by waves of warm and sweet relief. She had confronted it all, without the half-truths and self-delusion, and still it was true. It was as if she had ridden alone through Indian country in the midday sun and emerged unscathed.

"What about General Sherman?" Margaret asked. "Did he approach you again?"

Elizabeth shook her head. She heard that his last years were sad ones, that he became a philanderer, taking even his daughter's friends as lovers.

"No, not in that way, though we did communicate from time to time," she said. "Usually it was I who initiated the contact. I sought his help with my pension and for getting rid of that awful statue of my husband at West Point." She signed her letters to Sherman, "Desolate Me." He responded immediately, without fail. "He became my advocate, and I couldn't have had a better one."

But did he remember that May afternoon in 1867 and his words to her on the train to Fort Harker? Sometimes she thought he did. "Every man who is a man must respond to your appeal," he wrote in one letter. "I sympathize with every pulsation of your wounded heart" in another. Were these merely an officer's gallant words to the widow of a fallen comrade? She would never know.

"Why did you tell me these things, Miss Elizabeth?" Margaret asked. "Why, after keeping them to yourself all these years? Are you saying I should accept Patrick's infidelity?"

The old woman walked to her and took both of Margaret's hands in hers.

"Not necessarily, dear. Just trust what your heart tells you. Don't feel you're settling for crumbs if you stay, but know the difference between devotion and stupidity. I think you will." In a sudden surge of memory she recalled words that had once brought her comfort.

"If it helps, Margaret, some say that without betrayal, there can be no loyalty."

How I Happened to Put On the Blue

OTIS CARNEY

The Western Apache, also called the *Coyotero,* is the largest of the six distinct Apache tribes (the Lipan, Chiricahua, Mescalero, Jicarilla, and the Kiowa-Apache, are the others).

Beginning in 1863, when gold was discovered on their lands, the *Coyoteros* began a series of small-scale skirmishes with the army that culminated in the Camp Grant Massacre of 1871 in which about a hundred Apaches, given asylum in the Camp Grant vicinity, were slaughtered by a band of whites, Mexicans, and Papago Indians.

In "How I Happened to Put On the Blue," a trooper tells what it was like to live and die in *Coyotero* country.

Few non-Apaches know the Apache people and their history better than Otis Carney. The O-O Ranch he runs with Teddy, his wife of fifty-two years, covers fifty square miles of Arizona lands and lies on part of the old Camp Grant military reservation. Three miles below the O-O lies the remains of the town of Bonita "where Billy the Kid shot his first man," Carney says.

A Princeton graduate and Marine Corps captain who flew in the Pacific for twenty-two months during World War Two, Carney is a screenwriter and author of seventeen books including the best-selling *When the Bough Breaks, New Lease on Life,* and *Frontiers: The Diary of Patrick Kelly, 1876–1944.*

Excerpt of a speech by Jacob Enoch Hardesty to veterans of the Order of Indian Wars, Tucson, Arizona, July 4, 1922.

It was the eighth day of July 1873 in the Pinaleño Mountains of what was Arizona Territory then. That Pinaleño country, which is the Apache name for "deer people," is a rough bugger that lays over in eastern Arizona between Willcox and Safford in the center of Apache country. We homesteaded in there, my pa, ma, and brother Mikey in 1871.

There wasn't no name on our canyon then. It was just one more slash in the red rocks. Like all the other cuts that went through the range, it run high up into fierce granity cliffs a man couldn't scale even if he wanted to. Some winters, snow would come swirling around the piñons and banking up deep at the crests where the tall pines stood. Often as a boy I'd wanted to go up there to kill bears which was roaming all over the place, and lion too. But being thirteen at the time, I had years to wait for a gun, Pa said, weapons being so dear in the territory that a grown man couldn't hardly afford one, even to save his own life.

So that afternoon in July, I was just packing a slingshot. Down where our adobe house was, the canyon fell open and spread into the desert, which was a dusty grassland dotted here and there with agaves, prickly pears, and shin dagger cactus. Moseying along slow, I'd snapped a few pebbles at jackrabbits and hit a red-tailed hawk too but didn't bring him down. Anyhow, right then I wasn't supposed to be out skylarking or hunting nothing except the milk cow. The miserable old thing was hiding out someplace up the arroyo above the house.

Tracking her higher and higher, I passed under live oaks dripping tiny pearls. It had rained good that afternoon, hallelujah and God's glory, Pa had cried, and now the hot old devil sun was hatching mosquitoes and flies. With fresh green feed to gorge on, the cranky old cow wouldn't want to come home no way, so I figured I'd have to slingshot her to get her to trot down to the corral.

Fact of it, my ma was cranky herself these days, and had me to doing a world of chores, taking the drudging off her back. She was in a family way, swole up and bulging heavy with the new baby kicking up hell in her belly, and getting ready to come out any minute. Mikey, my older brother, had plumb grown out of being Ma's chore boy. Ever since Pa had given him a machete for chopping mesquite and a dagger knife too, he and Pa would light out at daybreak, building fence in the desert. Dreaming, Pa said, of that great someday when he'd have enough coin jingling in his jeans to buy himself a few beef cows.

With the soldiers camping in tents north along the Pinaleños, putting up a new fort they was calling Grant, in honor of the president, the army would be a right proper business for years to come, at least until they run out of Apaches to kill. And then, even better, once they'd corralled the murderous buggers on the San Carlos reservation, who was going to keep 'em from starving if it wasn't for beef men like Pa?

Ma said, though: "Husband, I don't hanker for you and Mikey being out in that desert if Injuns is loose." Pa just grinned. "The boy's got sharp eyes and pig stickers to use if some devil gets too close. Anyhow, there ain't danger no more with them blue bellies making horse tracks up and down this region every day."

Pa had drug the whole family of us out of the Low Country of South Carolina. He'd been fighting the Yankees till they like to shot his arm off and run him west on the two good legs he still had. They'd always be blue bellies to him.

Presently I found the old milk cow in the arroyo and drove her back to the house corral. I'd just got my milk pail out and started to strip her when it struck me strange that there wasn't no sounds from the house. No smoke neither. Ma usually had supper going by this time. Was the baby finally a-coming? But where was Pa and Mikey? They'd got home early from fencing. They'd been out under the ramada, splashing water from the wash barrel and Pa firing up his pipe. They'd been there, washing and chatting, when I'd lit out after the cow.

Hollering for 'em, I run over to the house. The heavy slab door was half-open. I slid it back. Something grabbed my throat and flung me into the wall, my head banging rock, my lights going stars and black. I was down on all fours like a dog, something barking in my ear. But it wasn't Nestor. Our old pointer was lying in a pool of blood, his throat cut. Long black hair was switching past me, naked skin, mean faces striped white across the cheekbones, devil mouths grinning, screaming.

They had me by the shoulders, gleaming skin stinking strange, foul breath in my nose. A knife flashed at me, I tried to twist away. Two more Apaches in breechclouts and headbands swirled in through the door. Outside, horses had galloped up. A tall Apache run past with Ma's washing in his arms, another was lugging Pa's big mantel clock out the door. They were jabbering at each other like coyotes; one of them rushing past me stopped and kicked me in the belly.

The horses were whinnying like they knew me and of course they did. They were our horses being torn away, Pa's roan, Ma's mare, Mikey's and my two buckskins. The last Apache out streaked his bloody hands on the front door. He seen me crawling toward him. He swung on me with a black revolver, the muzzle hole looking as big as my eye. I ducked, blast of smoke, the bullet missing, ripping up dirt. Then they were laughing, whirling the horses, jumping on, running and clattering away up the canyon.

I lay with my face in the dirt until the hoofbeats died far off. Then I raised up to look, begun to crawl, crawling, weeping, screaming. Mama lay on her back the baby bulge in her belly ripped open, white and blue flesh oozing out. Papa was half across her, a bubbling bleeding hole in the back of his neck. But brother Mikey? Mikey alive? He was standing, but his knees wasn't holding him. He was standing half-sagged against the big oak hearth. Mikey's machete was pinning him to the oak, and his dagger knife was rammed between his eyes.

I moaned and hunched into the dirt like a dog, scratching at it, digging a hole to get down into the bottom of the world.

They found me that way, the next horses that come. Big-legged men were stomping in, some in canvas pants, some in blue with faded yellow stripes on the legs. With his boot, one man rolled Pa offa Ma, and when a young blue belly seen her ghastly body, he puked on the dirt floor. The first one, with stripes on his sleeves, grunted, "I told the goddamn lieutenant, you follow that *diablito* of dust, mister, it ain't wind making it. And he says—mind you, he ain't a week out here yet on the border—he sez, 'Why that's impossible, Sergeant. We've been gone too long from the post now. The mounts are played out.' Mounts! If we'd a followed and been here just an hour sooner, half hour mebbe . . ."

Another said, "Git your shovels. Nobody's catching no hostile this late, long gone up the canyon, scatter like quail. Attend the kid, least he's still breathing."

I must have passed out then. All I remembered was them blue bellies putting me on a big leathery-smelling American horse. They lay me over and roped me like a sack behind the saddle and the blue butt of the man who rode me away.

I never come home again, not for years. Close as I was to it, I just couldn't look no more.

When I finally got up my nerve to go back, they'd put a name on it. Hardesty Canyon, with three headstones stuck into the red dirt on the hill above the adobe. By then, it had begun raining good in the country. Presently years of wind and storm and arroyo floods begun knocking the stones down, scattering them, wiping them clean of the names scratched on 'em until you couldn't hardly tell if anybody had been here at all. Least of all, why.

Ah, I'm blubbering, I guess. Got way more story to tell you old comrades. Just have to wait a spell. Why do old men cry? I never used to . . .

Cavalry Journal, Vol. XXXII, July 1923
My Part in the Bloody Cibicu
By Sgt. Jacob Hardesty, U.S.A. Ret'd.
(Editor's note: The following account was dictated by Sergeant Hardesty. At Army Headquarters, Washington, D.C., June 1923, he had been decorated with the Distinguished Service Medal, not only for his participation in the Apache War, but for his service with General George Crook in 1886 in the termination of that war, and in the General John J. Pershing Punitive Expedition against Pancho Villa in 1916. Sergeant Hardesty's vernacular is the jargon used by

many soldiers in the Indian Wars. It has not been edited for grammar, but allowed to remain in its original form as a historical record.)

All these years, people have been jabbering on about the Cibicu fight. Maybe you don't want to set the record straight, but to me it's mostly a pack of lies. Some of what I say here I swore to in the court-martial at Ft. Grant, Arizona Territory, 1882. But the high brass wasn't listening. They had to kill somebody to make up for their blunder. Spill the red blood of the red man, and let their women hack their hair and arms in mourning and wail their Apache tears.

In 1876 I joined the blue belly army out of revenge on the Apaches who had killed my whole family three years before. I was sixteen when I signed on, but big for my age. Had no birth certificate, nobody to tell how old I really was. The frontier army didn't care. Anybody who looked like he could fight was welcomed with open arms. Where they sent me, Troop D, 3rd Cavalry at Ft. Grant, desertion was high. It run someplace around thirty percent. You couldn't blame the fellers, stuck way off in them forlorn mountains, chasing Apaches you never could see and least of all catch. Puff of smoke. They'd rip you with a big hurtful ball, size of your thumb, some minié out of the Rebellion or even the Mexican war, whistling hunk of lead that would tumble in the air and blow an awful hole in human flesh. Shoot back, you say? Nothing there! The murderous buggers would duck behind a rock and let you die.

In face of such an enemy, our officers were wrangling with each other like cats in a sack. Had to do with rank, and getting promotions, and old grievances out of the Rebellion that festered like wounds. Some of the officers were bad drinkers, a few so sotted we had to haul them around in ambulances. At least two I served with, when their bottles were taken away, went plumb crazy and killed themselves.

The men that didn't desert mostly drank anything that poured. Just, I suppose, outa the pure despair at this war that wasn't winning nothing and didn't make no sense. By 1881, when I'd finally made sergeant at Grant, I was getting a little bottle-soaked myself. No excuse for it. Hell, down at my poppa's abandoned homestead, which is now Hardesty, Arizona, I'd growed up in the rocky sorry country and could smell Apaches a mile away. But still, just below Ft. Grant, out in a grove of cottonwoods, temptation lurked for the trooper. Two old adobes there was hog ranches, all the rotgut whiskey a man could pay for, and Mex and some white harridan whores in the back rooms. One night I was drinking my sorrows away there, in comes a young mutt, all six guns and swagger. Shoots a man right beside me, civilian teamster. We collared the bugger. Soldiers rushed down from the fort and threw him into the guardhouse. Day or two later, what do I hear but that he'd escaped. Swore that the man he shot in the Bonita hog ranch was the first he ever killed. When I heard of him later, he was notching his gun plenty over in New Mexico, mouthy murderer using the name Billy the Kid.

I mention that night because one of the troopers that helped us collar the thug was an Apache Scout sergeant we called Deadshot. Not a big man, but wiry and the wisest face I ever seen. When he spoke, you knew he was saying it right. True. I'd seen him around the post a bit. He was hell to shoot that 1874 trapdoor Springfield we all carried. We seen him knock a *zopilote*, vulture, clean out of the sky. The officers give him the handle Deadshot, though his tribal name was Tahzay.

I was a little in my cups that night, rattled up by the killing of that first man the Kid put down. Poor Mex teamster, his blood was still splattered on my army shirt. Deadshot come to me in his quiet way, put his hand on my shoulder like: this here is a white soldier headed for trouble. So he says, "Dan juda. (All bad.) U-ka-she! (Get out of here. Go!)" To my surprise, what does he do but load me on his horse and pack me home with him, sober me up and get my head back on straight.

Home was a little rock house he'd built at the mouth of Hog Canyon which lays about four miles south of Ft. Grant along the slope of the Sierra Bonita mountain. When I waked up the next morning, Deadshot's wife, name of Kai-ta, had brewed me some strong tea out of herbs or plants she'd gathered, and a baked heart of agave cactus, which is one of their delicacies. It struck me how kindly they were to me, and I was to taste their hospitality again and again during that summer. To be truthful about it, their daughter, Eski-dan, was about the prettiest little Injun I ever seen. Couldn't have been more than sixteen or seventeen. They don't count ages.

But she had lighter skin than most, and was round and ripe, ready for a man. The thing was, Deadshot was trying to make peace with the white man world. That's why, as an enlisted scout wearing the blue, he was willing to kill his own people to bring that peace to the country. His daughter had been taught to sew by one of the officers' wives at the post. The lady figured she'd civilize and Christianize the wild little heathen so she hung the name of Hannah on her. Smart as she was, she was already learning English pretty quick, and when I'd come down from the fort, she and I would set along the arroyo, holding hands, and practicing words.

By damn, I was in love with her. Don't that sound strange? Hired to kill 'em, yet doing my best to get her to lie with me. She was chaste, though, and taught me that the Apache, by and large, is a truly loving human being. Their whole tradition is so generous that if one of them killed a deer and you walked up, he'd give you half of it, hoping someday you'd do the same for him. Right then, with Hannah, I sure got to wondering what our war was all about. Couldn't we have just left the buggers be, and not blew away the gentle life they had, before we galloped it into the dust?

But it was too late, even by then. We'd already wrecked their old free life, and before us, the Mex and the Spaniards had slaughtered them. The Apache is a nomad. He lives by raiding and plundering. It's all he knows. So the war had been going on for hundreds of years, newcomers trying to exterminate these desert wolves and steal their ancestral lands. Couldn't blame the Apaches for fighting back, and when you go up against one, you're taking on the most sly, cruel, murderous animal on the face of the earth. That's what we come up against at the Cibicu. It was their last big cry for freedom.

I ain't fighting no battle again here. Grieves me to think about it, and too much has already been said. It come down to this. In the summer of 1881, an Apache medicine man, a tricky little wizard named Noch-ay-del-Kinne, got to dancing and dreaming about a world where all the white men were gone. Wiped out. He had a camp up on Cibicu creek, forty-six miles from Fort Apache. Hundreds of Apaches were flocking in to hear him howl and to do the sacred dances with him. He was already right famous among his people. President Grant had hauled him back to Washington and give him a big silver peace medal he wore around his skinny neck.

Then up in Santa Fe, the black robes, Catholic padres, had got their hooks in him and fed him as much of Christ's Resurrection as he could swallow. When he come home to Cibicu, he stirred it all into one big smoky pot that all of us knew was about to burst into flames.

My troop and two others were sent on a forced march up to the old log post of Fort Apache. Deadshot, Dandy Jim, Skippy, their first sergeant Mose and about twenty more enlisted scouts rode with us. Lt. Thomas Cruse, not long out of West Point, was commanding the scouts. A brave young man, and with good sense, too, if I do say so, because he chose me to ride with him, knowing that I could habla enough Apache maybe to get us out of some tight fix.

I couldn't, though. The die had been cast by old General Willcox, commanding our district. He was a Civil War vet, like many of them, and didn't have no patience or understanding of these dancing demon reds. What does he do but send a dispatch to our bearded old Colonel Carr, saying to the effect: If the medicine man won't quit his dancing and come into the post, go out after him and bring him in. If he won't come peaceful, kill him.

Colonel Carr didn't want no part of it, but because he and Willcox had been feuding for years now, he couldn't turn it down neither. Orders. Carry out the orders even at the risk of touching off a damn blundering war. August 28, 1881, sixty-eight white men of us, soldiers and packers together, rode into the medicine man's camp and hauled him out. I was as scared as I've ever been, before or since. Hundreds of Apache bucks, painted hideous and better armed than us, began crowding in around us. Noch-ay-del-Kinne's wife, like a little sparrow, come dancing in front of us, spraying some sacred herb outa her basket. One after another, wild-eyed bucks come rushing in at us, waving their lever action Springfields and screaming oaths. I says to Lieutenant Cruse: "This is getting scaly, sir." He nods and in his teeth murmurs, "Keep moving ahead, sergeant, don't look back." We finally got the medicine man and his wife down to Cibecu creek and set up camp just above the stream. The Apaches were on all sides of us by now. Deadshot come to me and kept saying "Dan juda!" Very bad. He was clinging to my arm, begging me to protect him from the soldiers' guns because he knew they'd be going off any minute now.

They did. The wild Apaches, not fifty feet away, begun blasting our camp. I don't know who started it, who shot first. It was pandemonium. I seen our men falling all around me. A good captain, big Hentig, was shot in the head and his striker beside him. I tried to hold onto my friend Deadshot, but in the confusion, with soldiers and scouts running every which way and shooting anything that moved, Deadshot got out of my sight and took cover in the willows beside the creek.

It's been figured that six hundred Apaches, ten times our number, surrounded us in that creek bottom. All I can say is that it was enough. Every pack saddle we was using as breastworks was riddled with Apache lead, as were many of our mules and horses. I fired off at least half of my hundred cartridges and had one Apache slug ventilate my hat. I hand it to Colonel Carr. He was a cool man in a fight. Had his thirteen-year-old son, Clarke, along with him, too. The gutty little lad had his own Marlin rifle and was shooting it hot. He later become an Army general. When the first fighting began, our sergeant, a big Irish veteran, carried out orders and blasted the medicine man into the happy hunting ground. Only he didn't die. When he started to crawl away, a trumpeter shot him through the mouth, and even then, when he was still trying to get away, a big Swede soldier split his head with an axe. His little dancing bird of a wife was running in to save him, so they shot her, too.

We marched out of Cibicu canyon that night. No talking, no lights, most of us shuffling on foot, so hungry and dragged out that I never thought we'd make it. Deadshot was still with us. He'd stop on the trail, warning the little bunch I was with. We'd listen, and the tall grass nearby would be rustling like quail was in it. Apaches, slipping away, hoping to catch us in a better place. If they'd had any kind of decent leader, not a one of us would have got out of there.

Sometime in the forty-mile walk, Deadshot and many of the other scouts slipped away. They were plumb terrified by what had happened. And in truth, if you've ever seen two dogs fighting, and more come in, pretty soon they all go blood-crazy and jump into a dozen different fights. I truly believe that's what happened in the blunder of Cibicu. The Apache scouts didn't know whether to be with us or against us. All of us knew we never should have been in there or tried to take their holy man out.

That needless fight touched off five years of Apache war that didn't end until General Crook and Miles in 1886 corralled Geron-imo and his bunch in the Sierra Madre of Mexico, and got them finally to quit.

By then, though, the one Apache I trusted and loved, was long gone. After the trial where the brass asked me to testify, but didn't listen, they set up a big scaffold at Ft. Grant. I hugged Deadshot goodbye, before they put the black hood over his head. Sprung the trap three times, Sergeant Dandy Jim, Sergeant Deadshot, and a comical little kid, Skippy, all dangled there to the tune of our bugle, blowing taps. Maybe they did desert and fire at the troops. I ain't never been sure to this day. But why them three? The other Apache scouts in the fight were sent to Alcatraz because nobody could ever pin down whether they was guilty. They got out after a few years, and two of them served loyally with us when I went with General Crook in '86 to bring in Geronimo.

It seemed to me that the Army had to kill somebody to clean its own skirts, and my friend was one of the ones who had to pay. Lt. Cruse said to me, "Deadshot was the wisest man in the scouts. We've lost our sage."

That night of the hanging, I rode down from the post to Dead-shot's little rock house in Hog Canyon. Hannah was kneeling, weeping beside a big cottonwood. She'd hacked off most of her hair. I looked up in the tree. Kai-ta, Deadshot's wife and Hannah's mother, had hung herself there. Going to join him, I suppose, for a war that had never been hers. I knelt and wept along with little Hannah. She didn't have no place to go. I stayed with her that night, and years of nights that followed. I buried that good woman at last, in the rocks of Hardesty Hill.

I left the Army soon after. Gone off to ranching in the desert, and only come back to the bluebelly service when they said they needed me as a scout and talker. Served out my time, I'm thinking, in the hope of saving more blood, red, white, and Mex, too, that didn't have to be shed. Nobody profits by war. Old men make them and young men die. We learned it at Cibicu, but ain't learned it good enough yet, I fear. Someday, maybe. Pray for that.

The Stand

MATT BRAUN

Of Billy Dixon (1850–1913), subject of "The Stand," Matt Braun writes: "He was a plainsman and buffalo hunter of remarkable courage. His exploits were recorded by Western journalists with something approaching awe. In July 1874, he survived the Battle of Adobe Walls, where twenty-eight buffalo hunters were attacked by seven hundred Comanches led by Quanah Parker. He fired the last shot of the fight with his Sharps, killing a warrior at a measured distance of 1,538 yards, just shy of a mile . . .

"Some poet of the later era wrote:

> *My books are the brooks, and my sermons*
> *the stones,*
> *My parson a wolf on a pulpit of bones.*

"For Billy Dixon and the men of his time, no better epitaph was ever penned."

Author of forty-eight books with 40 million of them in print worldwide, for thirty years Oklahoma-born Matt Braun has been among the best read and most honored of Western writers. Among his most popular novels are *The Savage Land, Cimarron Jordan, Buck Colter, The Kincaids, Lords of the Land, Tombstone, The Brannocks,* and *Black Fox,* the latter produced by CBS as a six-hour miniseries.

DIXON AND HIS CREW CROSSED the Brazos in early June. Two days later, along about sundown, they pulled into Fort Griffin. Their trek from Dodge City had consumed almost three weeks.

Fort Griffin was little more than a log outpost perched on a hill overlooking the river. Seven years ago, the summer of '67, it had been established as a deterrent to marauding Comanches. But the haughty Lords of the Plains were hardly intimidated by a handful of pony soldiers and a crude, weatherbeaten stockade. The western reaches of Texas were part of their ancestral hunting grounds, and a frontier outpost was easily skirted. They rode south to raid the settlements whenever it amused them.

Billy Dixon wasn't fretting about Comanches one way or the other. He had managed to keep his hair this long, and so far as he could recollect, the army hadn't had a damn thing to do with it. What interested him was the land—the vast, uninhabited stretch of plains sweeping west away from the cantonment. A new hunting ground.

On the hill, looking west by north, he could see that the valley of the Clear Fork was inviting buffalo country. Clean to the horizon the land was bounded by rolling prairies of lush grass, wooded hills, and swift-running streams. There was plenty of graze, hardly ever a scarcity of water, and lots of sheltered hollows to break the icy winds of winter. Unless he was wide of the mark, there were more shaggies roaming around out there than anybody had ever heard tell of.

After giving the fort a cursory inspection, Dixon and his men rode down to have a look at what passed for a town. The Flats, as it was called, was a squalid, ramshackle affair sprung to life on the level plain below the fort. Even to a buffalo hunter, the place looked to be nothing but a grungy pesthole. The only street consisted of three saloons, a log trading post, and a tent hostelry that advertised cots for two bits a night. This latter establishment provided a year's supply of cooties at no extra charge.

Closer to the river, where a grove of pecan trees towered overhead, there was a dingy collection of one-room shanties. Among the townspeople it was known as Naucheville, a local metaphor for the world's oldest profession. The ladies operating these one-woman brothels were advocates of the free enterprise system; they had something to suit the demands of any man. Whatever his tastes.

There were Indian breeds, whites, blacks, one high yellow, and a pink eyed albino dubbed White Lightning. They were as scruffy a bunch as a man could hope to find outside a kennel, but that was scarcely an obstacle to love for sale. On the distant plains, lust tended to cloud a man's eyesight.

A stranger to town might have been mystified by such a thriving industry in soiled doves. But it soon became apparent that the Flats was a regular anthill of commerce—albeit one of a most unconventional variety. The soldiers from the fort made up only a small part of the trade, squandering their paltry wages in a binge that generally lasted no more than a couple of nights. Freighters, bullwhackers, and an occasional drifter upped the take slightly, but not enough to make any lasting impression. By far the bulk of trade came from two distinct, yet oddly similar, factions.

Long before Fort Griffin became a frontier waystation, it had served as a hideout for assorted desperadoes and badmen. The Clear Fork of the Brazos was an isolated chunk of wilderness, remote from any railhead, settlement, or trade route. This backwoods solitude made it a perfect haven for men riding the owlhoot trail. On any given night, the Flats was crawling with renegades whose chief aim in life was to put distance between themselves and the law. Gunmen, bandits, cardsharps, common murderers, they all came seeking sanctuary—a fraternity of rogues gathered on common ground.

Then there were the cowhands. Throughout spring and summer great herds of longhorns were driven north from the Pecos valley, then wheeled east at Fort Griffin for an eventual linkup with the Chisholm Trail. Cattlemen frequently camped on the banks of the Clear Fork, and it wasn't uncommon to see upward of a dozen herds scattered about the countryside. Even on slow nights there were as many as fifty trailhands carousing through the Flats, most of them congregated around the local watering holes. The rest could be found standing in line waiting their turn down in Naucheville.

Though the cowhands were generally law-abiding, they had never been accused of being peaceable. Since there was no law on the Flats — save for what a man carried on his hip — brawls were looked upon as sporting pastime. Violence, random or otherwise, was taken for granted among men who prided themselves on being rough and tough and ornery. More often than not, it was bull-of-the-woods squared off against cock-of-the-walk, and blood flowed by the bucketful.

The first thing Dixon noticed as they came down the hill was the trading post. A crowd of cowhands in front of the nearest saloon paused to stare curiously in his direction, but he paid them no attention. He signaled the wagons to a halt, then reined his gelding in at the hitchrack. When he dismounted, the Texans eyed his mule-ear boots and slouch hat with knowing smirks. One of them, decked out in a fancy concho belt and spurs big as a teacup, looked him over with a wiseacre grin and nodded at the roan.

"Say, mister, where'd you get that goat you're ridin'?"

Dixon smiled crookedly. "Why, sonny, that ain't no goat. That's a sheep. Won him off a busted-down cow puncher shootin' marbles."

There was a moment of dead silence. Then somebody started snickering and most of the cowhands broke out laughing. The loud-mouth, his features red as an apple, started forward and suddenly stopped. Something in the plainsman's eyes told him to leave it alone.

Dixon nodded good-naturedly and walked on back to the wagons. Cabel Pryor, his head skinner, and older by a decade, was waiting for him with a sour look. "Billy, I'll swear to Christ. What was you gonna do, fight 'em all?"

"Don't you know when a feller's just funnin'? Take the boys in there and buy 'em a drink. I'm gonna have a talk with whoever runs that store."

Dixon walked off and left Pryor standing there. After a moment, the skinner motioned to the others and led them toward the saloon. Over the door was a sign — THE BEE HIVE — painted in bold blue letters. He glanced back in time to see Dixon enter the trading post on the opposite side of the street.

. . .

DARKNESS HAD FALLEN OVER THE FLATS WHEN DIXON CAME OUT of the store and crossed to the Bee Hive. The crowd inside was a mixed bag of tricks. Teamsters, slick-haired tinhorns, the usual assortment of cowhands and edgy-looking badmen—and just enough saloon girls to make it interesting. The saloon itself wasn't much to write home about. Log walls, a plank bar supported by barrels, and hardly enough tables to seat a Sunday school class. Off to one side, at the end of the bar, was a faro layout flanked by a monte spread and a poker table.

Shouldering in at the bar, he cleared out a place beside Pryor. The old grave robber was already about half pickled, clearly not feeling any pain. Dixon nudged him in the ribs. "You buying?"

"Well, looka here!" Pryor crowed, rearing back to get a better focus. "Got business all tended to, have you?"

Dixon signaled the barkeep for a glass. "Matter of fact, things worked out pretty good." The glass arrived and he paused to pour himself a drink. When he downed it, the whiskey hit bottom and bounced with a molten jolt. He shuddered and shook himself like a wet dog.

Pryor let go with a wheezy chuckle. "Takes a little gettin' used to, don't it? Barkeep calls it Taos lemonade. Grain alcohol, branch water, tabacca juice, and strychnine. Says that last is to keep yer heart beatin'."

"Well, I reckon I've had worse." Dixon studied the bottle a second, then shrugged and poured another shot. "Anyway, what I started to tell you. That feller across the road—name's Clark—tells me he opened up last year and business is boomin'. Says there's already some hunters operatin' around here, and he's got himself appointed agent for Lobenstein. He'll take all the hides we can deliver."

This was significant news. W. C. Lobenstein, operating out of Leavenworth, was the largest hide buyer in the west. Perhaps of even greater import, it meant that Dixon wasn't the only one who had his eye on the buffalo grounds of West Texas.

The old skinner snorted testily. "I knowed all that 'fore I'd been in here five minutes." He jerked his head sideways, pointed with his chin. "See that feller standin' next to you? Name's Frank Walsh. Buffalo man. If yer sniffer'd been workin' when you come in here you'd of knowed it right off."

Walsh turned at the sound of his name. "What'd you say, you old billygoat? I better not catch you bad-mouthin' me again."

"Mister, I done said all to you I got to say." Pryor slewed his eyes around and gave the man a corrosive glare. "But just so's you won't die out o' curiosity, I was tellin' my friend here that some dimdot name of Walsh is goin' around callin' hisself a buffalo man."

Dixon eased around to find himself faced by a barrel-gutted giant of a man. What Walsh lacked in height he made up in girth, built something on the order of a brick church. His face was pebbled with deep pockmarks, and his flat muddy eyes were fixed on Pryor. Dixon could pretty well guess what had happened.

Somehow the viper-tongued old devil had riled Walsh, most likely ragging the man's skills as a hunter. Although he had a glass jaw and the wallop of a cream puff, Pryor fancied himself a barroom brawler when he had a snootful. Curiously, since he generally ended up flat on his back, he never seemed to tire of the game.

"Old man," Walsh growled, "you'd better put that rooster to crowin' elsewheres, less'n you want your neck wrung."

Before Pryor could answer, Dixon shifted away from the bar. "Friend, why don't you just write it off to whiskey talkin' and let it go at that?"

Walsh glowered back at him with an owlish frown. "Well, first off, we ain't friends, and lastly, it ain't none of your goddamn business. Just step out o' the way 'fore I have to walk over you."

Dixon's eyes hooded. "If I was you, I'd back off."

Walsh shook his head ruefully. "Well now, looka here, there ain't no call for you to get your hackles up. The plain fact of the matter is, he done insulted me and my crew. Said up beside your outfit we was nothin' but—"

Dixon was listening attentively, trying to get the drift of the trouble, when Walsh hit him. The blow came without warning, with amazing speed for such a big man. Dixon went down like a poled ox and the whole right side of his head turned numb. Every tooth in his mouth felt loose as goose-butter, and blood leaked down over his chin. He had been hurt worse, but not by much.

Walsh moved toward him with uncommon agility, lifting his foot as he came. Clearly the big man was a barroom scrapper of considerable experience, and he meant to end the fight with a good stomping. Dixon rolled away, scattering tables and people in every direction as he slithered across the floor. The tactic worked, carrying him well past the reach of Walsh's boots. Even as he spun in the last roll, he came to his feet, slinging chairs, bottles, and saloon girls aside.

Walsh advanced like a human cannonball, snarling an oath as he lumbered forward. His first mistake was in letting the younger man gain his feet. Dixon generally minded his own business and tended to give the other fellow the benefit of the doubt. Until crossed. Or angered. Then something came unhinged back in the dark, brutish regions of his brain, and he turned wild as a mad bull in a spiderweb. Fists cocked, he waited, coldly inviting the big man to make his move.

Walsh took the bait. All his weight behind the blow, he threw a haymaker that would have demolished a stone wall. But it never came close.

Dixon ducked under the blow, and sunk his fist into the Texan's blubbery paunch. Walsh's mouth popped open in the roaring whoosh, sort of like letting the wind out of a church organ. He doubled over, clutching his gut in agony, and the plainsman exploded two splintering punches on his chin. Dazed, Walsh shook his head, sucking great gasps of air into his starved lungs.

But he didn't fall.

Just for a moment there, Dixon couldn't rightly believe it. Nobody had even taken those punches and kept their feet. Not in all the years he'd been busting heads. Still, he smelled blood—sensed the kill—and his wonderment was only a fleeting thing.

The plainsman kicked Walsh square in the kneecap. There was a loud crack, and the Texan let go a whimpering cry of pain. When he grabbed at his knee, Dixon clouted him dead center between the eyes. Walsh reeled backward, his crippled knee collapsing under him, and rocketed through the plank bar. Barrels, boards, and whiskey bottles went flying like a stick of dynamite had been set off. When the debris settled, Walsh was flat on his back, his nose ballooned like a rotten apple.

But still, he wasn't done for. He shook his head groggily, trying to clear the pinwheeling lights from his head. The shooting stars and swirling dots slacked off just a bit, and he came up on one elbow.

Dixon had seen men take punishment in his time, but never like this. Holding off now, though, was out of the question. More than one man had gotten his brains scrambled by backing away before the fight was finished.

Stepping over the clutter, he methodically kicked Walsh in the head.

The blow nearly tore the Texan's jaw off. Then a shudder went through his massive frame and his eyes rolled up in his head like glazed stones. A heartbeat later, he settled back in the sawdust.

He was out colder than a wedge.

Dixon steadied himself against the counter, breathing hard but still full of fight. His glare raked across the men in Walsh's crew.

"Any of you boys want a taste?"

The three men looked everywhere but at Dixon. Whether they held no great love for their boss or they just didn't want any part of this young buzzsaw hardly seemed to matter. They plainly had no intention of taking up the fight.

Everyone in the room commenced breathing again, and a ripple of nervous laughter swept over the crowd. Rough-and-tumble brawls, even knife fights and shootings, were no novelty to the Bee Hive. The place was a regular bucket of gore, and nightly donnybrooks took star billing as the chief form of entertainment. But as the excitement mounted, everyone started telling everyone else about what they had just seen with their own eyes.

They swarmed over Dixon, clapping him on the back and calling his name, shouting for drinks. Goddammit! Give this boy a drink! Glory be to Christ, did you see the way he hauled old Walsh's ashes? God save us, that last punch would've felled a full-growed steer. Weren't never a man hit like that and lived. Holy jumpin' Jesus!

Suddenly Cable Pryor started shoving men right and left, cackling hoarsely at the top of his lungs. "Give him room, you peckerheads. Whooiiee!! Fightin' him is like pokin' hot butter in a wildcat's ear. Move aside, consarn it. Set 'em up, barkeep! Let's have some more of that panther juice."

Dixon smiled gamely and accepted all the backslapping without comment. The way Pryor was carrying on, there wasn't much room left for talk, anyhow. Somebody shoved a water glass of Taos lemonade in his hand and he took a fiery gulp to the delighted shout of the crowd. Out of the corner of his eye he saw Walsh being dragged off by the heels, and a warm tingle of satisfaction passed over him.

Maybe he hadn't lost his punch after all.

The plainsman raised his glass to the crowd and flashed a wide grin. Then, just like that, one of his molars fell out.

Laughing wildly, he spit it out in his hand and held it up for everyone to see. The men pointed at it and doubled up in fits of laughter, roaring so hard their eyes welled over with tears.

Goddamn! There wouldn't never be another fight like this. Not ever!

DIXON CAME OUT OF THE ARROYO AND STARTED UP A LOW HILL. Moments before, he had heard the enraged bellowing of bulls squaring off for a fight. His gelding was tied back down the gully and the wind was in his favor. He knew beyond certainty that a herd lay just over the rise.

The grassy knoll was barely two miles from camp. Dixon had ridden out about nine, allowing himself a good hour to get into position. Finding buffalo was no problem—the shaggy brutes encircled the camp like a vast brown sea, the largest gathering he had seen since those early days on the Smoky Hill. Yet, though he still found it hard to believe, this great herd was less than two days' ride west of Fort Griffin. That they were found so effortlessly somehow boggled his mind. It was almost too easy.

The pattern Dixon followed this sunny morning was one established years back, when he was a greenhorn still learning his trade. Be in position by ten, shoot till the sun was straight overhead, and never kill more than the skinners could handle in an afternoon. Everything had its purpose, and if a man followed the rules he was most times assured of getting a stand.

Never hunt early in the day. The shaggies were restless and easy to spook until they had finished their morning graze. Afterward, with a full belly and a moist cud to chew on, they settled down for a little siesta. That was the time for a man to sneak up on them. If he moved slow and kept to cover, he might work his way to within a hundred yards of the dumb beasts. The other rule was just as practical. Maybe more so.

Never overkill.

It was a waste of time, powder, and hides. Anything the skinners couldn't get fleshed out by sundown was as good as lost. The wolves were sure to get at the carcasses overnight and spoil the hides. Even if they didn't, the skinners would botch it up come morning. Cold meat was hard to skin.

Overkill, though, had never been much of a problem in Smoky Hill country. Not last year, leastways. The herds had thinned out so bad, a man did well just to find a stand. Never mind worrying about downing too many. Thinking back on it, as he went into a crouch halfway up the knoll, Dixon was again filled with wonder at what he'd found in the land west of Fort Griffin.

They had rolled out of the Flats three days back, moving westerly along the Clear Fork. Nearing its headwaters, they had swung north, and within hours began sighting buffalo. At first it was just scattered bunches, but growing thicker the farther they went, and every man in the crew began to get that prickly feeling. The feeling that comes over a man when he holds aces full.

The sharp, savory taste of a winner.

Late that afternoon they had topped a rise and come to a slack-jawed halt. Stretched out before them was the greatest single concentration of buffalo they had ever seen. The high ground afforded them a view ten to fifteen miles in every direction, and as far as the eye could see, the earth was blanketed with a heaving mass of furry brown. Dixon estimated that it would take close to a week for the herd to pass any given point, and near as he could judge, its center was better than twenty miles wide. Any thought of numbers was too staggering to contemplate. Four million. Ten million. Perhaps somewhere in between. Certainly more than a man could count in the span of his days on earth. More than all but a handful of plainsmen had ever seen in a single moment of time.

It was the great Texas herd. Feeding into the wind in its ageless migration across the plains.

Backtracking, they had set up camp on a rocky creek shaded by tall cottonwoods. That night, while the skinners whetted their knives and spoke in awe of what they had seen, Dixon went over his equipment piece by piece.

His rifle came first. The big Sharps was a .50–90, throwing a slug nearly a half-inch in diameter. With its strong breech, the gun could handle just about any powder charge that suited the man, and Dixon loaded it with 110 grains. The heavy octagonal barrel made it a weighty piece, and it packed the kick of a young mule, but it was deadly accurate up to ranges of six hundred yards. The wallop of the big fifty slug was fearsome to behold, many times knocking a full-grown bull clean off his pins. A man needed a shoulder hard as nails to keep from flinching when he fired the Sharps steady for a couple of hours at a stretch.

Dixon fondled the Sharps, removing every fleck and speck with the utmost care. Next he looked to the shells, sorting an even two hundred into a tanned bull-hide pouch. Then he filled an oversized canteen from the creek, checked to see that he had plenty of swabs, and tested the forked sticks that would support the gun's heavy barrel once he started firing.

Looking it over one last time, he nodded with satisfaction. Everything was ready. Tomorrow he would start the kill. After a pipe, he rolled himself in a blanket and slept sound as a dollar.

That morning, when he rode out of camp, the sun had already burned the damp-earth smell off the land. Shards of light filtered through the cottonwoods overhead in soft golden streamers, and he thought it was a good time of day. Maybe even the best. When a man was fresh, full of vim and vigor, raring to lock horns with life. With the hunt before him, the broiling afternoon sun still hours away, and a land not yet filled with the stench of death.

It was as much as a man could ask for. More than most men ever found.

CLOUDS OF ORANGE AND WHITE BUTTERFLIES FLOATED LAZILY ON a gentle breeze, and the fragrance of chokecherry blossoms filled the air. Dixon scrambled out of an arroyo, where he'd left his horse, and cautiously worked his way up the grassy knoll. Crawling the last few feet on his hands and knees, he stretched out flat, hugging the earth, and slowly eased his head over the crest of the hill. He lay motionless, scanning the distant prairie as a wisp of wind brought with it the pungent buffalo smell. He filled his lungs with it, savoring the moist gaminess, full of fresh droppings and sweaty fur. But he waited, as a great cat would wait, unhurried and calm, absorbing everything about him before he began the stalk.

As he always did, he felt himself the intruder here, looking upon something no mortal was meant to see. About these still, windswept plains there was an awesome quality, almost as though some brutally magnificent force had taken earth and solitude and fashioned it into something visible, yet beyond the ken of man. A vast expanse of emptiness, raging with dust devils and blizzards, where man must forever walk as an alien. A hostile land that mocked his passage, waiting with eternal patience to claim the bones of those who violated its harsh serenity.

And however long he roamed these plains, he was still the intruder, an outsider with no sense of kinship for the forces which mocked him. As though—should he wander here forever—he would merely come full circle. Alone, a creature in a land of creatures, yet somehow apart. Which left nothing but the moment, and the predatory instinct that had brought him here. The kill.

Before him the plains were spotted with scattered herds of buffalo. At a distance it appeared to be a shaggy carpet of muddy brown stretching to the horizon. But up close the herds took form, and from the hilltop, individual buffalo assumed shape, even character.

A hundred yards beyond the hill, two ponderous bulls were holding a staring contest. Their bloodshot eyes rolled furiously as they tossed great chunks of earth over their backs, and their guttural roar signaled the onset of a bloody duel. Suddenly their heads lowered and they thundered toward one another, narrow flanks heaving, legs churning. The impact as they butted heads shook the earth and drove both antagonists to their knees. Stunned, yet all the more enraged, they lunged erect in an instant, locking horns as their massive shoulders bunched with power. The muscles on their flanks swelled like veined ropes; sharp hooves strained and dug for footing; froth hung from their mouths in long glutinous strings; and their tongues lolled out as the brutal struggle sapped their lungs. Then, with a savage heave, one bull flung his adversary aside and ripped a bloody gash across his shoulder. The gored bull gave ground, retreating slowly at first, then broke into headlong flight as his opponent speared him in the rump.

The victor pawed the dusty earth, bellowing a triumphant roar, and like some stately lord on parade, struck a grand pose for the cows. He had fought and won, and while he might fight dozens of such battles during the rutting season, for the moment he stood unchallenged.

Dixon eased over the top of the knoll while the herd was still distracted by the struggle. Slithering down the forward slope on his belly, he took cover behind a soapweed as the vanquished bull disappeared across the prairie. The bush made a perfect blind; after unstrapping his shell pouch, he set a ramrod and a canteen on the ground close at hand. Then he set up the shooting sticks and laid his Sharps over the fork. He was ready.

Alert, but in no great hurry, he began a painstaking search for the leader. Every herd had a leader, generally an old cow. Shrewder than the bulls—perhaps more suspicious—they made the best sentries. What he sought was a cow that seemed unusually watchful, on guard, testing the wind for signs of danger. Until a man dropped the leader, his chances of getting a stand were practically nil. After a long, careful scrutiny, he finally spotted her. And what a cunning old bitch! Hidden back in the middle of the herd, holding herself still and vigilant, and peering straight at him, trying to raise a scent.

Grunting softly, he eared back the hammer and laid the sights behind her shoulder, centered on the lungs. The Sharps roared and a steamy gout of blood spurted from the cow's nose. She wobbled unsteadily under the wallop of the big fifty slug, then lurched backward and keeled over. A nearby cow spooked, sniffing the fallen leader, and bawled nervously as she wheeled away. Cursing, he yanked the trigger guard down, clawed out the spent shell, and rammed in a fresh load. As he snapped the lever shut, the cow was gathering speed, ready to break into a terrified run. Thumbing the hammer back, he swung the barrel in a smooth arc, leading her with the sights. When the rifle cracked the cow simply collapsed in midstride, plowing a deep furrow in the earth with her nose. Alarmed now, several cows gathered around, and their calves began to bawl. The old bull wandered over, snorting at the scent of blood, and started pawing the ground.

But the herd didn't run. Bewildered, hooking at one another with their horns, they simply milled around in confusion for a while. Some of them pawed the dirt and butted the warm carcasses, trying to goad the dead cows onto their feet. Yet slowly, without apparent concern, the others went back to chewing their cuds or cropping grass.

He had his stand.

Loading and firing in a steady rhythm, working smoothly now, he began killing the skittish ones. Carcasses dotted the feeding ground, as each new report of the Sharps brought another crashing thud on the prairie below. Still the herd didn't stampede—looking on with the detached calm of spectators at a shooting match—seemingly undisturbed by the thrashing bodies and the sickly-sweet stench of blood. It was a drama of pathos and tragedy he had seen unfold a hundred times over in his time on the plains. Insensible to the slaughter around them, the dimwitted beasts had concern for nothing save the patch of graze directly under their noses. Eerie as it seemed, the instinct for survival had been blunted by the more immediate need deep within their bellies.

After every fifth shot he sloshed water down the rifle barrel to keep it from overheating. Then he swabbed it out, hurriedly reloaded, and returned to the killing. Yet he was steady and deliberate, somehow methodical, placing every shot with precise care. This was something he did well—took pride in—managed swiftly and cleanly, without waste or undue suffering. A craftsman no less than a predator, skilled at his trade.

A master of death and dying, and staying alive.

The Square Reporter

RICHARD S. WHEELER

An Ohioan of Quaker ancestry, William Wright (1829–1898), best known by his penname Dan DeQuille, *was* a square reporter, and among the best newspapermen of the nineteenth-century West—an elite brotherhood that included Bret Harte, Ambrose Bierce, and Mark Twain. The latter, still known as *Sam Clemens*, took his newspaper apprenticeship under Wright in Virginia City.

Wright became a reporter for the Virginia City *Territorial Enterprise* in 1862 and stayed on for thirty-one years (minus the several occasions when he was suspended to sober up), becoming an authority on Western mining and writing the definitive book on the Comstock, *History of the Big Bonanza*, in 1876. He is remembered as a gregarious, fun-loving character, and inventor of the "hoax story"—the outrageous, concocted newspaper feature—his hoaxes written so solemnly and authoritatively they were invariably reprinted in Eastern newspapers as straight news.

No writer can approach Montana's Richard S. Wheeler in writing of Western mining and mining boomtowns. Among his forty Western historical novels, *Sun Mountain, Goldfield, Cashbox, Second Lives,* and *Sierra* are all mining stories. He is a four-time winner of the Spur Award from Western Writers of America, and in 2001 was recipient of WWA's Owen Wister Award for lifetime contributions to Western literature.

puffery. They all do. There's not a mine operator in Virginia City who couldn't use some publicity when he wants to jack up the price of the shares. That's when they come to me.

He knew where to scout me. My crystal-chandeliered editorial offices are at the Old Magnolia, hard by *The Territorial Enterprise*. I am rarely in the newspaper plant itself. It is the privilege of seniority to issue my copy from my own venue.

I am William Wright, and I scribble the mining news in between various feature items and obituaries, so the mining magnates seek me out, along with my colleagues at rival sheets. We mining reporters are a privileged lot. Nowhere else on earth do millionaires and nabobs come, hat in hand, looking for a favor. They especially come to me because I accept no bribes, unlike certain fellows at other papers, so my services are cheap.

It's a game we play: They want to use us for nefarious purposes, and we reporters like to lounge around with flat pilsner in hand and tell each other how virtuous and broke we are, and how we value the loftier things in life and scorn the filthy lucre, except of course whenever we can get our mitts on some. But it is true that I own no mining stocks, and the world knows it.

After much contemplation, I have concluded that my success is due to my disparate parts. I am half Quaker and half cynic. By design I live a bachelor life in this liveliest and loosest metropolis of the West, while sending greenbacks now and then, mostly then, to my dear wife Caroline and five sprouts in West Liberty, Iowa.

They sought years ago to join me here, but I resisted. This is no town for innocents. If I, a true devotee of the Society of Friends, occasionally fall into a saloon brawl and joyously bloody my knuckles, against all my instincts and spiritual inclination, what hope is there for my stainless boys? So, to spare them temptation and a world of vices, I keep them in Iowa.

Now everyone agrees that it is impossible for a cynic and a Quaker to coexist inside the same skull, but I manage to reconcile the two at the mahogany bar of Old Magnolia. I begin my reconciliation about ten every morning, and by mid-afternoon I am fully reconciled and at peace with the world.

Jim Fair knew exactly when to catch me properly reconciled, and therefore arrived at two-thirty, bought me additional reconciliation to demonstrate his bona fides, allowed me one of his spastic crocodile smiles, which employ unaccustomed muscles, and turned at once to business.

"Old friend, we're turning up some pretty good silver sulphides, and I thought you might want to do a little story," he said.

Old friend indeed. Jim Fair has no old friends and few new ones. But this was progress. Fair and his shamrock partners, Mackay, Flood, and O'Brien, had kept a tight lid on their diggings and anyone snooping around was likely to get smacked with a shillelagh. They had found some decent silver ore, that was clear enough. I heard they were buying up neighboring mines, especially the California and Ophir, but it had been tough to pin down.

"I might," I allowed, edging my empty tumbler outward, but Fair didn't bite.

"You go in there, old friend, take all the samples you want, no one will job you. We're at the twelve-hundred-foot level and ore's getting richer the deeper we go. Get your samples assayed and write her up."

I allowed as I would, and nudged my forlorn glass another inch Fair-ward, but he ignored me, studying the fat nude over the back-bar. When it comes to drinks, there is nothing worse than an Irish Protestant.

I knew what this was all about. Mine supervisors actually mine the shareholders better than they mine ore, a fact little understood outside of certain gaudy circles on the Comstock, and this was a managerial attempt to jack up the stock. At any rate, I would be the first reporter down the Con Virginia shaft since the Irish scooped up the place, and that was story enough.

I collected my pick hammer, a tape measure, and a samples bag, and headed for the Consolidated Virginia shaft, where a double-decker cage dropped me from bright afternoon into the hot, dark, foul-aired confines of their works. They were sure busy down there, drifting into promising ore and running crosscuts to see the width of the lode.

I'm an old hand in mines, unlike some of the gross cowards who report the mining news from up on grass, like that kid Clemens who used to hang around this sinful burg. So I was looking not just for ore, but for country rock, diabase, porphyry, the stuff not worth a nickel that had to be hauled out too, the stuff that wipes out profits.

I peered about, my carbide lamp throwing livid light on the glistening black silver ore, took the measurement of the drift, some two hundred feet in all, and the width of the crosscuts, thirty to forty feet, which were impressive. Then I chipped off six samples I considered typical, while all about me sweating miners mucked and timbered and laid rail. No one jobbed me; no one steered me away from any area. I took my finds to an independent assayer I could bribe with *Enterprise* expense money, and just for good measure went back the next day and took two more samples and gave them to another assayer.

The results raised my brows. The four Irishmen had found a large body of good ore, not the highest grade by any means, but enough to put lace doilies on their armchairs. The first six samples averaged $379 to the ton, and the other two samples averaged $443.

I thought they were on to something. The *Enterprise* headlines said it all:

CONSOLIDATED VIRGINIA-

A LOOK THROUGH THE LONG FORBIDDEN LOWER LEVELS-

THE ORE BODIES AND BREASTS, WINZES AND DRIFTS-

RICH DEVELOPMENTS

I suppose Jim Fair thought that would inflate his Con Virginia stock, but I got the last laugh. The shares rose all right, from a flat fifty dollars to fifty and a quarter, and there they hovered weeks on end. The speculators had already priced his bonanza and yawned at my news.

Beetle-browed Rollin Daggett, editor of the *Enterprise,* chuckled along with me. When the mood was upon him, he shifted his editorial office to the Old Magnolia and edited the paper with a carafe of Steamboat Gin ever before him, sipping and scribbling, lipping Havanas and bellowing for a copy boy.

"They'll be back," Daggett said. "Soon as they figure out a new way to con their investors, they'll try again."

We drank to that. I intended to ask him for a five-a-month raise, but needed a good peg to hang it on. The moment had not arrived, but I kept waiting for an opening. He knew I was going to ask, so we circled each other like sumo wrestlers.

I turned to my other occupation, which was writing outrage. The world mostly knows me as Dan DeQuille, because that's the byline I use. The object of the game we scribes all play in Virginia City is to spin a whopper, and do so with such sobriety and earnestness that we sucker the whole subscriber list, most of California, and half the exchange papers on the other side of the globe into believing every word. It's a modest talent of mine, but not one that gets me raises.

I had in mind a little spoof, and set out to write the sad story of one inventor named Jonathan Newhouse, who contrived a suit of solar armor with which to cross Death Valley in the hellish heat of day. Within the armor, Newhouse wore a thick layer of sponge, and he artfully arranged that this sponge could be refreshed with water now and then from a portable reservoir strapped to his back. The water evaporating from the sponge would cool down Newhouse. So Newhouse set forth, confident that he was proof against the terrors of Death Valley, and so it seemed. But alas, water evaporated so fast in Death Valley that poor Newhouse froze to death. He was discovered sitting upright, a block of ice, the victim of his own genius.

I published that assay into science and technology and sat back, and ere long the London *Daily Telegraph* solemnly reported in its news columns the strange case of an inventor in far-off Nevada who had developed a suit of solar armor and had frozen to death inside of it.

Oh, we had fun with that. Daggett even bought me a bottle of rye, a thing unheard of in the long and sordid history of Daggettry. It was only later, when the rye was gone, that I sadly realized that he had craftily derailed my request for a raise.

I had a rival at this racket for a while, an edgy redhead named Sam Clemens, who tried his hand at the hoax business, didn't do badly, but lacked my touch. His literary efforts always seemed to have a target or two in mind because he was a mean customer.

After Clemens had hovered around the *Enterprise* for a couple of years, he wrote an item that managed to offend all seven virtuous women in Virginia City, was promptly challenged to a duel, and was advised by the city's impeccable authorities to make himself scarce within twenty-four hours or face the nasty consequences. He vamoosed for San Francisco, hung around there for a while, and then headed for other and warmer climates, unsatisfied with life as it is lived in the Far West, which is hard on the sensitive and neurasthenic.

Since then I've had no contender in the hoax department, and I rather yearn for a rival just to keep myself fit. Most people would suppose it is the cynic in me that produces these inventive stories, and the Quaker part of me that yields the fair-and-square mining news. But that would just be wrong. Only a true Friend, filled with Inner Light and an innocent spirit, could pen a piece that required absolute solemnity and earnestness. No, the cynic in me covers the mining news, for only a cynic could cope with the machinations and absquatulations of the stock jobbers and mine salters and bonanza manufacturers who populate every street corner of Virginia City.

Meanwhile, the four lucky Irishmen had not been idle. Sitting atop a modest fortune inspires one to purchase the neighboring lots, so they expanded their holdings in all directions, especially the Ophir next door, even while burrowing ever deeper into the hot wet stone of the Comstock. I kept abreast of this, mostly by nefarious means known to all reporters, namely bribing the miners for information and smuggled ore samples, and paying stockbrokers for tips. For the Con Virginia was once again sealed off from inquiring eyes, and that flint-lipped manager, Jim Fair, was death on the press.

What an odd lot those four sons of Erin were: Fair, squinty and suspicious, the type who cuts wages and blames the cut on his partners. John Mackay, gymnast and boxer, affable and generous, an empire builder. James Flood, who ran the San Francisco end of the operation, shrewdly buying and selling the company's stock. And William O'Brien, the most exalted of the lot, a former resort keeper, company errand boy, inclined to buy drinks for cronies and lose money at poker.

They were the best thing Virginia City had going, since most of the other great mines like the Gould and Curry were playing out, working low-grade ore and losing money.

One thing I knew for sure: the Irish were digging deeper than anyone else on the Comstock, and the deeper into that hot rock they pierced, the better the ore, and the wider the lode. So I published my small mining items in the *Enterprise,* sent a little pay back to West Liberty with admonitions to enjoy the wholesome climate and steady life of Iowa, and roved the resorts of the Comstock with such reprobates as I could collect for an evening's entertainment.

The day came, however, when I was summoned once again into the august presence of Jim Fair, who if anything had gotten craftier and meaner in the succeeding months.

"Go on in there and write her up again, DeQuille. No one will job you. Go where you want. Tell the whole bloomin' world what you see. You got sharp eyes. You're the one reporter what can do the job right."

That was the first compliment ever known to issue from Fair's lips, and it took me an hour to get over the shock and paralysis of it. I knew he wanted something in return, but it was still a watershed. In two years he had bought me three drinks in all, accompanied by six requests for one story or another, which came to half a drink per pleading. I knew him for the most successful mine manager on the Comstock, and his ways were plain: buy cheap, sell dear. I had been bought with a compliment.

I took note of the stock prices in San Francisco before descending that January of 1875. Fair and his cronies had managed to jack the price of Con Virginia and California and Ophir to record heights by gulling poor Philipp Deidesheimer, legendary mining engineer and *authority,* into announcing right out in public that the bonanza was worth a billion and a half simoleons. I wondered what Fair had poured into that bewildered man's lager.

In any case, the market value of the shares of the three bonanza mines exceeded the value of all the real estate in San Francisco, which says a thing about wily Jim Fair and his cronies. I supposed that the Irish were going for broke, and might soon own California unless they were planning to buy Ireland, which is why they summoned me, a lowly Quaker in Virginia City, to deliver the coup de grâce.

So down I went in my felt hat and jumper, this time riding the first three-decker cage on the Comstock, into the black bowels of the bonanza, and stepped off at the fifteen-hundred-foot level. Sample bag and pick hammer in hand, I edged into a fairyland, a long gallery supported by timbers and dotted by twinkling lights in every direction where hundreds of sweating and bare-chested men hacked at the ore. I was assaulted by a roar, as man and machine scooped and chipped and smashed rock with a mad frenzy.

Here was the bonanza. These miners weren't drifting along a six-inch seam; they were entirely *inside* the seam. Crosscuts every hundred feet showed that the ore ran far to either side. There was a fair amount of porphyry mixed in; this wasn't solid silver and gold ore, but there was more of the black stuff than these eyes had beheld in one glance ever before; more than I ever imagined I would see again, more than the whole world had ever seen in one place. What's more, shafts and winzes revealed ore from the twelve-hundred-foot level down to the sixteen-fifty.

Here was a body of ore that staggered the mind, turned pastry chefs and chambermaids into Midases, threatened to swamp the monetary system. I wandered about in a daze, my mind refusing to accept what my senses reported. I chipped samples out of the gallery at various levels, more from each of the crosscuts. My hands trembled so much I banged my thumb, and my fingers refused to guide my pencil. Then I took out my tape measure to put some footage into my calculations. I thought to myself, I could walk out of here with a thousand dollars in my pockets.

Shaken, I ascended to grass in the battered cage, gathered my wits, put an assayer to work on my samples, and began my calculation. I finally concluded, after ruining half a pad of newsprint, that the ore in sight down there, which ranged from nine hundred dollars a ton down to eighty, was worth over one hundred sixteen million dollars, and that was just what I saw with my own eyes. I published my findings on January 5, 1875, and the result was entertaining to watch.

San Francisco went crazy. People emptied their bank accounts and bought any Comstock shares, at any price. Even the four Irishmen went mad and bought their own stock, which begat even more madness. Brokers couldn't keep up. Banks shuttered their windows for lack of funds. People gathered in the streets to exchange tips and rumors. Some lucky stiffs whumped up fortunes overnight, getting filthy rich with one buy-and-sell. San Francisco sprouted multimillionaires as if they were cabbages. People did dizzy waltzes and jigs on the street, and tipped bellboys with silver dollars.

It didn't last. The smarter pencil-pushers studied my story, soon realized the mines had been overbought, so they began selling. Then it all came rumbling down. Brokers called in the margin accounts. Millionaires joined breadlines and banks quaked on their foundations. A few hundred million paper dollars vanished in hours. Actually, the bonanza mines didn't fare badly; the lucky Irish came out fine. But every shop girl in San Francisco along with the rest of the nation had been had.

I watched all this with a certain Quakerish delight. My bonanza story had gotten a better play than any of my hoaxes. And virtue had triumphed. Fair had wanted me to jack up stock prices that were already grotesque, and I had pulled the plug instead. Old Virginia City was the same as ever; it was California that had been wrung out and hung up to dry.

I took to writing sketches for the *Enterprise,* and dabbling with literary masterpieces, and no erstwhile millionaire ever wandered into the Magnolia and threatened to put me six feet under.

One fine spring eve Daggett lumbered into the Old Magnolia and arrayed himself at his accustomed spot at the rear. A carafe of Steamboat appeared, along with the appurtenances, which he handled with all the ritual and reverence of a priest, sipping and aahhing. In time, he summoned me with a nod of his shaggy head.

"Well, you did it," he said. "Because of you, nations wobble, millionaires are washing dishes, and Bible-thumpers are smug."

"It's a strange thing," I said. "I walked into that hole at the Con Virginia and before my eyes was the biggest pot of silver and gold in all recorded history, more than most men can even imagine, more than their wildest dreams. But it wasn't enough. Their greed had already ballooned it ten times over, and when they absorbed the truth, their dreams died. They never even understood the wonder of it."

"You have regrets?" he asked, one eyebrow cocked.

"For what?"

"You could have made a killing. You could have five butlers and a masseuse. Own the *Enterprise*. You could bathe in gin."

"Oh, that. No, Rollin, I did my duty. I'm a square reporter, right down to the garters. I own not one mining share, I'm influenced by no man, write nothing but the facts, and buy and sell nothing but words . . . It was a good story."

He nodded and sipped the Steamboat, whistled sonorously through his crooked teeth. "Yes, we newsmen have other and loftier pursuits," he said, eyeing me. "We are a noble lot. Morally superior."

"Without a doubt. For me, a good true story, a scoop, a light thrown on darkness, is worth more than all the millions those greedy rascals ever heaped up. It's not filthy lucre that motivates a man like me."

"I'm glad to hear it, Dan," he said. "Now I won't have to give you a raise."

Betrayal

LINDA SANDIFER

Myra Maybelle Shirley Reed (1846–1889) was a child of the Civil War in the Midwest. Born in Carthage, Missouri, Belle, as she was called, had a brother, said to be her twin, who served as an officer under William Clarke Quantrill, and Belle herself became a courier for Confederate guerillas in the early months of the war. She was captured on February 3, 1862 (her sixteenth birthday), by Union troops near Newtonia, Missouri, but was released and rode to Carthage to warn her brother of the enemy nearby. Ed Shirley escaped but was killed by Union soldiers shortly thereafter.

There's a story in being the wife of an outlaw, a bigger story when the wife of an outlaw becomes an outlaw herself. Such was the case with Myra Maybelle Shirley. She married James Reed in Texas in 1866 and . . . well, "Betrayal" tells the rest of her story.

Linda Sandifer is an Idaho writer whose novels of the Old West have devoted fans around the world where her stories have been translated into numerous languages. Of her twelve novels the most recent are *The Daughters of Luke McCall* and *Raveled Ends of Sky*.

SHE DID NOT CRY WHEN SHE
heard the news. Myra Maybelle Reed left her children in her mother's care, saddled her horse, and rode into the woods, winding along game trails until darkness forced her retreat. By the time she arrived back at her parents' farm, she had allowed the anger and the pain to grow and feed on itself until it became a self-sustaining, silent rage.

Her parents studied her stoic face with sympathy in their eyes. Her small children, Pearl and Eddie, sat at the table eating the evening meal and following the adults' movements in a wary way. They seemed relieved when their mother took her usual place at the table between them.

Curiosity got the best of six-year-old Pearl, however. After a few minutes, she said, "Mama, you look sad. Is Daddy in trouble again?"

Myra had tried to keep their father's line of work a secret from the children, but Pearl was in school now and her classmates seemed to delight in singling her out as the "outlaw's daughter," a term Myra was sure they had heard from their gossiping parents. James C. Reed, with a sizable price on his head, had become one of the most sought-after outlaws in Texas. His infamous activities frequently made the front page of the *Dallas Commercial*, along with a few other Texas newspapers including the *San Antonio Express* and the *Dallas Herald*. Now Myra was sure his death would make front page news as well.

Having no appetite, she lifted Eddie from his high chair and held out her other arm for Pearl. With a child on each knee, she pulled them close. Their precious innocence helped to ease the crushing weight settling onto her shoulders. Not only was Jim dead, but he had left her destitute. She did not know how she would support her children. At that moment, she made a vow to herself that she would never be at the mercy of another man, and she would teach Pearl that she, too, should grow up making her own living so she would never have to depend on anyone.

Little Eddie placed his soft cheek against Myra's breast. She kissed the top of his head, inhaling the fresh scent of his fine black hair. Then she kissed Pearl in the same fashion, knowing this would be hardest on her. On those rare occasions when Jim had been home, Pearl had reveled in any attention he had given her. She had felt particularly special when he called her his "little golden-haired girl" and sat with her in his favorite chair. Eddie, on the other hand, saw his father as a frightening stranger and refused to go to him until he'd been home for several days, only to have him leave again for weeks on end.

Pearl, for all the attention she paid to her father when he was home, was much closer to her mother. She had always been adept at reading Myra's moods and behaving accordingly. Myra saw a reflection of her own mental state in the child's eyes now. When Pearl had been a baby, they had moved to Missouri to live with Jim's mother. While Jim was off at the racetrack in Fort Smith, gambling, Myra had nearly always stayed home with Pearl. She had doted over the baby and dressed her in fine clothes. She had taken her to church every Sunday with the Reeds to show her off to the community. Myra always rode sidesaddle and held baby Pearl in her arms. They both enjoyed the attention as they rode down the main street of Rich Hill. Myra's parents had been one of the wealthiest and most prominent families in Carthage, and she wanted people to believe that the war had not reduced her position in life.

"Mama, you didn't answer my question. Is Daddy in trouble again?"

Myra struggled for the right words to explain the situation to her daughter. Very gently, she said, "Your daddy won't be coming home ever again, Pearl. A man who posed as a friend betrayed him for reward money." Myra lifted the child's hand to her lips, realizing she probably didn't understand words like "betrayal" and "reward money," but she understood the implication nonetheless.

"Did he go and get himself killed, Mama?"

How many times had Pearl heard her tell Jim that if he wasn't careful, he would get himself killed? The child was only repeating what she had heard. Myra released a long sigh. "Yes, baby. Your daddy is gone from us forever."

They sat in silence for several minutes, the children sensing from their mother that the moment called for remorse. Then Myra hugged them one more time and set them from her lap. Taking their hands, she rose. "It's time for bed now. Time for you to dream pleasant dreams and not worry your little heads. We will stay here with your grandparents for a while and everything will be all right." But she said the words as much for her own peace of mind as for theirs.

"Tell us a toe-ree, Mama." Three-year-old Eddie looked up at her with eyes so brown they were nearly black.

"Not tonight, sweetheart. I have a very bad headache and I need to lie down. But I'll tell you what. You can both sleep with me if you promise to be very good."

Eddie spoke around the thumb in his mouth, "Okay, Mama."

By early morning lamplight, the rage rose closer to the surface again, supplying Myra with the strength to do what had to be done. She spread the newspaper articles across the table in chronological order even though she knew the headlines and the stories by heart. Her mother had collected them over the past eight years, from the beginning of Myra's marriage, documenting Jim's downward spiral into crime, his spree of gambling, robbing, killing, and his final and ultimate betrayal: a love affair with another woman.

Next to the articles, Myra placed the photographs taken of herself and Jim at the time of their marriage, remembering him as a dashing young guerrilla, and the son of respected and prosperous parents. A man who had been a hero in the eyes of his confederates and who had ridden with Quantrill for the Southern cause, along with some of the best men in Missouri, including Cole Younger and Frank and Jesse James. She traced a finger along his face in the photograph, recalling how his skin had felt in the night when they had made love in those early years. Then she pulled away, envisioning him in the arms of his young lover, Rosa McCommas, and thinking that it was a good thing he was dead because she would have been tempted to kill him herself.

A floorboard creaked in the hall, and Myra turned to see her father, John Shirley. He came into the room, saying nothing, just placing his aged hand on her shoulder in a comforting gesture. Then he pulled out a chair and sat with her at the table.

"Did you get any sleep, Myra?"

She rubbed her eyes. They burned as if she'd been crying for hours, but she had yet to shed a tear. Then suddenly, as if all her strength drained away in one instant, she dropped her head to her hands. "How could he do this to me, Papa? I'll never be able to hold my head up in Dallas again. Even now I can barely walk down the street without people whispering behind my back, calling me that 'poor Mrs. Reed.' They all know about that McCommas woman. She was even posing as his wife. There are people who think I was in on those robberies, even the killings, when *she* was the one riding with him. He's made me a laughingstock, not to mention leaving me destitute. All that money he stole, and he barely gave me enough to put food on the table. He gambled it away and spent it on her."

John Shirley placed his hand over hers. "There was nothing you could do to stop him. You did the right thing by leaving him after that Grayson robbery."

"I knew he was going to rob Grayson. I should have tried to stop him, but I needed the money. When he came back to the river where I was camped, he counted it out and divided it up among the others. There must have been thirty thousand dollars. But all he gave me was a few hundred. He took the rest and rode away. Said he had gambling debts. All I ever wanted was a life like you and Mama have had where I could be respected and hold up my head." Her eyes turned cold and hard. "Now that no-good John Morris will collect the reward money. He's just waiting for me to identify the body. How could he double-cross Jim that way, him being a distant relative?"

"Jim did some bad things, Myra. Not just robbing, but cold-blooded murder. It was bound to come to this, especially with a reward on his head. You knew it. We all knew it. I'm just glad you haven't been implicated in any of his doings."

She met her father's sad eyes. "How can a person love someone yet hate the things he does? It's as if Jim was two different people."

"We all have another side, Myra." John Shirley rose to his feet and blew out the lamp. The first light of dawn had found the window and streaked across the newspaper articles on the table. "I'll go with you to McKinney."

Myra gathered the articles and returned them to their box. She appreciated her father's offer to go with her, but he was nearly eighty years old. She wouldn't expect him to make a thirty-mile journey in one day on horseback. "No, Papa. It would be too hard on you. I would rather you stay here with Mama and the children. I can go alone."

Dressed in a black riding habit, she now covered her hair with a matching, plumed hat. She tied a white silk scarf at her throat, pinning it in place with a brooch. Since she had been a spy for the Confederacy over ten years before, she had never ridden into the countryside alone without protection so it was perfectly natural for her to strap her holster into place just off her waist and check the load in the familiar pistol.

"I've been thinking about something," her father said, watching her prepare for her ride. "By identifying the body you are only giving Morris what he wants. He can't collect the reward without a positive identification, and according to the sheriff, there is no one in McKinney who can identify him, other than Morris. Besides, if you claim the body, you'll be forced to pay all the interment fees."

She hadn't thought about those things but couldn't be swayed. "I need to see Jimmie one last time, Papa. To lay him to rest in my own mind. It is possible that the man they have may not be him at all." She kissed her father's cheek and pulled on her black riding gloves. "Don't worry. John Morris will not get the best of me."

As Myra rode her horse north through Dallas, the words in the newspaper articles roiled through her mind. She found some comfort that her name had not been slandered. When she had been mentioned, it had always been in glowing terms and with sympathy for her situation. The *Dallas Commercial* had called her "highly educated" and an "accomplished lady." She kept these positive words flowing in her mind, giving her the mental strength she needed to complete the task ahead.

In McKinney, she went directly to the sheriff's office and introduced herself. The lawman came to his feet, giving her a once-over. "I'm glad you could come so quickly, Mrs. Reed. We'll get this matter taken care of right away." He motioned for her to lead the way outside. As they walked down the boardwalk, he told her, "Morris arrived not thirty minutes ago with the body, but I must warn you, it is badly decomposing in this heat and will have to be buried as soon as possible."

"Tell me what happened, Sheriff."

"From what Morris says, your husband had been going to the home of an old friend named Russell who, at Reed's request, went to Collin County to get—"

The sheriff suddenly looked uncomfortable in the August heat and avoided her knowing eyes. He ran a finger under his collar and removed his hat to wipe away a trickle of sweat that had crawled down the side of his face to his ear. Finally he continued. "I'm real sorry, Mrs. Reed, but Russell brought Rosa McCommas to Paris so your husband could be with her. Morris was also there. Rosa stayed behind as the men headed for Arkansas to conduct a robbery they had planned. Morris, who has been working undercover, had no intention of going through with the robbery but was setting Jim up to be arrested. When Morris felt the moment was right, over dinner at Mr. S. M. Harvey's house, he asked Jim to surrender. Jim said he would, then suddenly threw the table up between them. Using it as a shield, he tried to make his getaway. Gunplay ensued and Jim was killed."

They arrived at the house where the body had been taken. A crowd loitered around the door but moved aside to let them pass. Inside, several more men stood around smoking and listening to Morris brag about Jim Reed's capture and death. Upon seeing Myra, he cut the story off in mid-sentence, having the decency to look embarrassed. She wondered to what extent he had embellished the truth to make himself look less the duplicitous money-grubber, and more the courageous man who had brought down one of the state's most notorious outlaws.

She would have liked nothing better than to sit down and rest, but she wiped all emotion from her face and proceeded with her head held high. She was determined not to let anyone, especially John Morris, see the agony that rent her heart.

She had witnessed so much death during the war, her own beloved brother included. Her parents had buried another son since then—one who, like Jim, had stepped outside the law. She forced herself to remember Jim's breach of faith. She forced herself not to think of the early days of their courtship and the pleasures they had known, the love they had shared. She locked the memories into that other world, into that other life that now seemed so long ago it could have been a dream.

The sheriff and Morris and several others gathered around the shrouded form on the table, but they watched her closely as if they expected her to crumble. And she wondered why Jim's lover had not come to weep over his body.

The group moved away from the table, allowing her to step closer. The sheriff was right. Even with the windows open, the body had been in the heat too long. But she refused to show weakness by putting a handkerchief to her nose. It was not the first time she had smelled death.

The sheriff placed a hand on the sheet, hesitating as he glanced up at her face. "Are you ready, Mrs. Reed?"

The others waited, their eyes bright with the anticipation of how she would react and what she would say. Stiff-backed, she nodded. The covering was drawn back.

For a moment she forgot to breathe, but she gave no outward indication of the pain knifing through her heart. The face before her was indeed Jimmie's, and yet it wasn't. The bullet had gone into the side of his face between his nose and right eye, and the decomposition in that area made her stomach lurch. His light brown hair was awry and dirty, and thinner and longer than she remembered. Flies buzzed close to the sheet and the soiled clothing that covered his bloating body. He didn't look like the man she had married, the man she had loved as a teenaged girl. No, he was not that man. He was the man who had betrayed her trust and her love with another woman, and she must remember that. She must never forget it.

She turned away; the sheriff pulled the sheet up. She went outside, clearing the smell of rotting flesh from her nose. The lawman was right behind her, followed by John Morris, the latter eagerly awaiting her response. Despite the myriad emotions tumbling inside her, she held on to her composure.

"Well, Mrs. Reed. Can you identify that man as your husband?"

Myra lifted her eyes to the sheriff, who had asked the question, then to Morris. She allowed her gaze to travel over the bystanders as well, until several shifted uncomfortably from her scrutiny. When she spoke there was no weakness in her voice, no doubt. "I cannot help you, gentlemen. The decomposition is every bit as bad as you warned. But whoever that poor man is, I suggest you bury him post-haste."

Appreciating the fury mounting in John Morris's eyes, and deriving satisfaction that duplicity had many faces, she curbed a satisfied smile as she left the gaping onlookers. No one tried to stop her.

By the time evening began to darken the land, Myra was several miles from McKinney. She reined her horse off the road into a grove of trees where a stream dissected a meadow, making it a good place to camp. She could have taken a hotel room, but she preferred to be away from prying eyes and nosy questions.

Only when her horse was staked and brushed did she spread her bedroll and remove her hat and silk scarf. Feeling much older than her twenty-six years, she lay back on her blankets, more than aware of the hard earth pressing into her spine and shoulder blades. But as exhaustion claimed her, the rage seeped from her body like blood from a wound.

Feeling numb now, she watched the darkness swallow the forest bit by bit. Her ears were keen to the distant melancholy sound of the mourning dove's *coo-ah, coo, coo, coo,* and to the closer chirping and humming of the insects and cicadas in the tall grass. She had no appetite for the hardtack and jerky she had brought—water from her canteen was enough for now—so she ignored the rumblings in her belly.

She tried to remember Jimmie's face in life but saw only the disturbing image of the unpleasant face she'd seen in death. She visualized him in the arms of his lover and wondered if there had been other women as well. She considered what, if anything, she would someday tell Eddie and Pearl. She tried not to think of the course her life would now take. And she wondered why women loved men like James C. Reed.

In the end, she cried. But she did not know if it was for Jimmie, or for herself.

Thirty Rangers

COTTON SMITH

In its 167-year history, the Texas Rangers have produced so many extraordinary leaders-of-men it is impossible to single out the greatest Ranger hero. Names like Ben McCulloch, William Alexander "Big Foot" Wallace, John Coffee "Jack" Hays, John Salmon "Rip" Ford, John B. Jones, John B. Armstrong—and Leander H. McNelly—loom large in Texas history.

McNelly, a Virginian and Civil War veteran, has a special niche: he served in the Rangers only three years but all three years were the stuff of legend. Cotton Smith's story is both a tribute to this heroic and tragic figure and a lively recounting, as only a great fiction writer can create, of one of McNelly's exploits.

Leander McNelly died of tuberculosis on his farm in Washington County, Texas, on September 4, 1877, at age thirty-three.

Cotton Smith of Kansas has been a successful writer of fiction, history, and marketing strategy, and is also an accomplished artist and horseman. His novels, all critically acclaimed for their historical accuracy and memorable characters, include *Dark Trail to Dodge, Pray for Texas, Behold a Red Horse, Brothers of the Gun,* and *Spirit Rider.*

A TIMID MOON SEARCHED FOR courage in the blackened clouds. Nervous shadows watched a tall man ride toward the Texas Ranger camp. It was just past midnight, November 19, 1875. His silhouette took shape out of the darkness and thirty well-armed Rangers were instantly alert.

At their backs was the surly Rio Grande, warning the lawmen not to come farther. Sixty miles of hard riding lay barely behind them in a vain attempt to stop two hundred stolen Texas cattle from crossing into Mexico. That opportunity had vanished like the ripples from the last steer in the dark river. General Flores and his gang had struck again.

No one had ever gone after them. But this time the Rangers expected to join the U.S. Cavalry in a surprise charge into Mexico. A border-crossing attack had been agreed upon as necessary to stop the flood of stolen cattle disappearing across the Rio Grande.

The Rangers expected this quiet man to lead them. As always. He looked like a minister and had a soft, reassuring voice that tended toward shy. His appearance was that of a man no one would expect to see in this dangerous part of Texas, especially at night. The thirty Rangers knew differently. His voice might be gentle as a grandfather's, but his deeds were as forceful as a Gatling gun and his leadership, daring as a wolf. These Rangers would follow him anywhere. Anytime.

This time, they would be attacking a Mexican outlaw stronghold ten times their number, headquarters of the organized rustling. They would also be violating international law. Invading a foreign country, no less. An act of war. But they wouldn't be going alone. A hundred U.S. troops from Captain Randlett's cavalry, camped nearby, would be riding with them. That would even things somewhat. Expectations about the attack had been the main topic of discussion while the Rangers ate, along with the usual: guns, horses, and women.

Battle-savvy, this band of Rangers had cleaned up lawless Dewitt County, and, after eight months of fighting, had returned order to the Nueces Strip between Corpus Christi and the Rio Grande. Along the way, they fought wild Indians and wilder bandits savaging the border with pillage, rape, and murder.

They were the Special Force of Rangers and their fearsome reputation was justified. And he was their leader, Captain Leander H. McNelly. Some said their methods were too harsh. Most, though, liked their style of immediate justice. When one of their own was killed, McNelly's men responded by catching twelve rustlers, shooting them, and laying their bodies side by side in the Brownsville square.

With a well-developed spy system, they had killed rustlers on the Palo Alto prairie and intercepted stolen herds before they could be rushed across the border. Still, with cattle priced at $18 a head, the rustling continued, even with the higher risks. In private, authorities had agreed there was only one way to end it for good: crush the source in the sanctuary of Mexico. Let the thieves know they wouldn't be safe wherever they might ride.

Comfortable in the darkness, the rider sought each man with his gentle eyes and knew what he would see: courage and commitment, to him, and to Texas. Probably in that order. This time, McNelly was carrying bad news. He had been turned down for the second time today. No troops would support his venture into Mexico, even though there were plenty stationed along the border. Shadows had already heard the sour turn of events and whispered ideas to him as he returned to his men.

To make it worse, on the day before, Captain Randlett's cavalry had been close enough to capture the rustled herd at the river, but he decided against it. Reinforcements arrived during the night but Randlett was advised by his superiors that he still didn't have sufficient manpower to pursue farther. There was further concern, just surfacing, over "acting in bad faith" by crossing into a sovereign country.

None of McNelly's Rangers knew the military had passed up the chance to stop the rustlers. None knew the army had changed its mind either. Not yet anyway. They had been told that Major A. J. Alexander, senior cavalry commander of this border region, was all for the attack. So were other army leaders. But, earlier today, Alexander told McNelly the Mexican government had been assured of nonintervention on their side of the border. When McNelly asked about their earlier agreement, Alexander denied having done so. The Ranger Captain knew he shouldn't have trusted Alexander; he was too needful of pleasing Washington, regardless of what it cost Texas.

While his men ate a supper of mutton, McNelly had left for one last attempt to get the once-promised troopers assigned to him for the task. The Rangers assumed this meeting was to coordinate the attack. He went to his friend Captain Randlett, with his reinforced cavalry force bivouacked beyond the ridge. The meeting was short. Randlett's words burned in McNelly's brain as he returned.

Randlett's trembling mouth struggled with words that didn't want to surface. "M-my orders are c-clear, McNelly. I—I can't go— and I can't give you any men."

McNelly looked around the camp. The sight of readied troops with two Gatling guns was too much to take. He took a deep breath and said quietly, "I thought you boys wanted to stop this rustling."

"We promised the Mexican government." Randlett couldn't look the Ranger in the eyes.

"What about your promise to me?"

"Come on, man. There's too many of them. We'll get 'em next time—before they cross." Randlett's bearded face tightened. A face that had seen too much Texas sun and too many bureaucratic restrictions.

"No, my boys are going to get them *this* time."

Randlett chuckled self-consciously. "Well, I guess I can cross if you're about to be massacred." He paused and clarified, "But only then."

"That's mighty reassuring." McNelly turned and left, leaving a sheepish Randlett continuing to explain the army's reasoning.

Bitterness rode with McNelly until he reached the edge of the Ranger camp. Then angry frustration dissolved into an odd sense of understanding. He had been an officer in both the Confederacy and the Davis state police following the War of Northern Aggression. He knew the ways of governments and their armies. He pitied Alexander and Randlett, but would never tell them so. They were afraid to do the right thing, regardless of the consequences.

Was he? Quitting now meant more Texas herds would be lost. But what could thirty Rangers do against three hundred outlaws? Shadows whispered the soldiers would have to come to the aid of his men if they were trapped in Mexico. They would have to. Randlett had said as much.

McNelly smiled to himself. That was it. He must lay the lives of himself and his men on the line. No soldier could sit by and watch the Rangers destroyed by an overwhelmingly larger force of Mexican bandits. The threat would be enough to cut through all the red tape. Shadows smiled their agreement.

Only a month ago, McNelly had been forced to return home, so sick with chills and fever that he could barely see, much less ride. But this was far worse, having to tell his few Rangers what they were going to face. Swinging down from his horse, McNelly wrapped the reins around the makeshift remuda string, touched the rifle butt extending from its saddle sheath, and walked to the struggling campfire without speaking.

He stood there, reaffirming their advance alone in his mind. Flames painted his face with gold and red streaks like a Comanche warrior. Tiny reflections from a five-point badge made it the focal point of his thin frame. Ironically, the star, like the other Ranger badges, was made from a Mexican silver dollar.

A thick goatee added years to an angular face. McNelly pushed back his wide-brimmed hat to let wavy brown hair breathe the cool night air. Flickers of reflected firelight danced from the holstered revolver and knife on the bullet belt at his waist. Eager shadows tiptoed closer to listen.

Bringing his men together, McNelly told them what he had decided. They would cross without military support. The army would join them if needed, but they wouldn't go with them initially. Clearly, he was counting on the cavalry coming when they saw his men in danger of being wiped out, regardless of any border.

He folded his arms and concluded, "Boys, you have followed me as far as I can ask you—unless you are willing to go farther." Pausing, he scuffed the ground with his right boot and cocked his head to the side. "Some of us may get back. Maybe all of us will . . . but I don't want you to go unless you are willing to volunteer. You understand there is to be no surrender. We will ask no quarter nor give any. If you don't want to go, step aside."

When McNelly finished, the oldest Ranger, "Old Casuse," nodded his approval. No words. No questions. No hestitation. Short and stocky, the tough warrior may have been born in Mexico, but his heart was in Texas, and his loyalty, to McNelly. Casuse was the only name the other Rangers knew him by. He had led them on their race to this camp as he had many times before. He was the one who always knew the shortcuts and the younger men always turned to Casuse for reassurance.

The youngest Ranger, George Durham, studied the stoic Mexican, then glanced at Bill Callicott, another veteran lawman, for his reaction. Callicott stood with his high-booted legs apart and arms folded in a mirror response to McNelly.

Wearing a Mexican sombrero he'd taken from an outlaw, Ranger Callicott immediately agreed with Casuse's silent affirmation. "Captain, we will go."

The response from the rest was affirmative—and eager. Most of the men were young and they loved McNelly like a father. If he was worried about what might happen, he didn't show it.

"All right," McNelly said. "That's the way to talk. We will learn them a Texas lesson they've forgotten since the Mexican War. Get ready. I will take Casuse, Tom Sullivan, and myself first. We will take Casuse's horse."

The rest would cross in teams of three, taking turns in a small dugout canoe operated by a friendly Mexican. He would also act as their guide to the Las Cuevas Ranch on the other side. One horse would swim alongside the boat on each trip. The boat had a leak, but a Ranger in each group was assigned the task of bailing water. McNelly planned to swim the rest of the horses across in as many trips as necessary. He reminded them of the urgency to attack before daybreak.

McNelly left to make the final arrangements and the Rangers dispersed to get their weapons and pack leftover mutton for later eating. Callicott stood alone. Untying the bandana around his neck, he wiped his face. Suddenly it was very warm and he was sweating. He looked across the black water at what he couldn't see but knew was there. Waiting for them at Las Cuevas Ranch was General Juan Flores, Mexican outlaw king, and his bandit army.

Thousands of Texas cattle had been taken there over the years, before going on to other locations in Mexico. No one expected the Flores gang to hand over the livestock without a fight. Their previous engagements with Texans had been fierce with no thought of leaving survivors. Mexican officials had given promise after promise to solve the problem but nothing ever happened. Except the exchange of meaningless documents between governments.

Muttering to himself, Callicott retied his kerchief and yanked his watch from his pocket. The tiny belt chain jingled like the beginning of a song. It was 12:50. After replacing the watch, his hand went to the pistol butt at his waist, then to the cartridge belt across his chest. He looked again at the darkness and left to join the others.

By one o'clock, shadows crowded against the bank and watched McNelly's tiny force take on the dark river. The waters could be treacherous, even when calm. Wicked undercurrents, jagged rocks, and deep bogs waited. So did dead tree limbs lurking beneath the surface. McNelly's first boat made it without incident, but Casuse's horse nearly drowned and had to be pulled by a rope, slowing down travel considerably. The three men decided the animal was tired from the sixty-mile trip earlier.

Four more teams crossed and all had the same problem with their horses. Finally McNelly returned in the canoe to advise the rest of his men to forget bringing mounts. It would take too long to get them across. They would advance on foot.

"Bring nothing but your guns, cartridges, and grub." McNelly's voice was confident but urgent. "I want all of us over by half past three. We've got two or three miles to the ranch and it's going to take hard walking to make it on time."

By four A.M., thirty Rangers stood on Mexican soil with only the first five horses. McNelly barely noticed the problem as he outlined the rest of their mission. After marching down a narrow cow path, they would attack the ranch with the five mounted men going in first to attract attention. The rest would follow, killing any outlaws they saw. Their objective was to occupy a building and wait for the cavalry to join them. It was the first time they had heard that part of the plan but his confidence was contagious.

Enthusiastically, they entered a thicket separated by a meandering cow path. Fresh manure indicated the herd had passed this way only hours before. Thick chaparral, overgrown brush, and mangled trees on both sides of the cow trail cut off their being detected but also kept them from seeing what lay ahead. At false dawn they could barely see ten feet in front of them. Rifles moved in response to sudden movement in the thicket. A skinny jackrabbit scurried among them and was out of sight in two strides.

Enthusiasm gave way to weary tension. Were they really going to attack a three-hundred-man stronghold? Would the army really come to help—soon enough? How would they know when to come? Would anyone care if they died in Mexico? Only McNelly and Casuse seemed oblivious to any doubt.

As dawn unholstered itself from the horizon, McNelly walked up and down the line of tired men clustered at the ranch gate. "Boys, I like your looks all right—you are the palest of men I ever looked at. That is a sign you are going to do good fighting."

He put his arm on the shoulder of Casuse. The Mexican's face remained unreadable. "We'll let Casuse wake them up. Casuse hasn't had a chance to breathe Mexican air or give a yell in Mexico for over twenty years."

Without a word, the older Ranger swung back into the saddle and cocked his rifle as the gate was opened. With an eerie Comanche scream, Casuse rammed spurs into his horse and lit into the outlaw stronghold. His fearless charge triggered the rest. The tiny Ranger force hit the sleepy ranchyard like an artillery shell. Four Mexican bandits cutting wood for breakfast fires were shot down by deadly Ranger gunfire.

In minutes, no one was moving. Except Rangers. Something was wrong. Where were the hundreds of outlaws? As the sun took over the world, fading shadows chuckled at the situation. Within the sudden silence, the Mexican guide ran over to Captain McNelly standing in the middle of the ranch yard. Smoke from McNelly's rifle sought relief in the gray sky.

Eyes widened with fear, the Mexican yanked on McNelly's coat. "I have made the bad mistake, Capitán McNelly. This is Cachattus Ranch. Las Cuevas Ranch is half mile away. *Lo siento*. I am sorry, Capitán."

McNelly frowned and shoved new cartridges into his rifle. "Well, you have given my surprise away. Take me there as fast as you can."

After regrouping, the Rangers hurried toward their original target with McNelly in the lead. Their misdirected attack on the small outlaw hideout had a price. As they closed in on the main stronghold, a company of two hundred and fifty mounted Mexican soldiers roared into the ranch in support of the outlaws themselves. Mexican authorities had apparently been warned of the Ranger advance.

Without hesitation, the Rangers formed a line at the far edge of the vacant yard and opened fire. Only a few Mexican soldiers paused to shoot back; most scurried to hide in the closest buildings before firing in earnest. McNelly's plan — to occupy a house and hold it until the army took pity on his men — was impossible now.

Over the shooting, McNelly gave his orders. His voice was calm, like he was inviting them to a picnic. "Well, boys, our surprise is gone. It would be suicide to charge them with only thirty men — and do no good. We'll go back to the river."

In spite of overwhelming numerical superiority, the combined Mexican force of soldiers and outlaws hesitated to press their advantage as the Rangers slipped away. The tiny band of lawmen took on the steady persona of their leader. No one talked. Instead, their eyes sought and reassured each other. The objective was the same: get back the stolen cattle and arrest the thieves. Nothing had changed. Neither had the haunting question. Would U.S. troops come to their aid? After passing through the now-empty first ranch, they took up positions near the shoreline and waited for the assault they knew would come.

McNelly assumed their adversary would rush to the shore, expecting to pick off scared Rangers swimming back to Texas. Instead, the first assault came directly at them. Flashing a fancy, silver-and-gold-plated revolver, General Juan Flores led the charge himself, catching McNelly's pickets off guard and taking two of their horses, but injuring no Rangers.

As the firing enveloped his men, McNelly stood and turned toward the river. It was time to pull the cavalry into Mexico. Yet, separating them was more than water, it was the invisible wall of two nations. On the Texas side, soldiers watched along the bank. Two Gatling guns stood among them like ominous bystanders. Curious shadows shouldered their way between them for a closer look.

"Randlett, for God's sake, come over and help us," McNelly yelled.

Without waiting to see the result of his dramatic request, McNelly spun back to his men and ordered a counterattack. "Charge 'em, boys!"

Firing his rifle, he ran toward the Mexicans. Again, without pausing to see what effect his words would have. He knew what his Rangers would do. They responded like a flame from a match, rushing forward, shooting as they came.

The first casualty was General Flores. He spun from his saddle, the magnificent pistol still in his hand. Stunned by the sudden loss of their leader, his men bolted into the thickets beside the cow trail the Rangers had followed just hours before. McNelly pushed his slight advantage. Ordering his men into a firing line, they marched through the heavy growth, shooting into every possible hiding place.

They stopped when they reached the lifeless body of the general. While Rangers searched for Mexicans, McNelly picked up the pistol and shoved it into his waistband. With a quick view of the situation, he ordered a retreat to the river where their position would be better. They had stopped the initial advance but he knew it was just the beginning.

During the counterattack, Captain Randlett decided to cross, gradually bringing forty soldiers into Mexico using the same leaky boat McNelly had used. Later, he justified the action by referring to orders to cross if he thought "McNelly was about to be massacred." But he also stated, in his official report, that when the firing began, McNelly was on the Texas side, as if the Rangers were in hot pursuit crossing into Mexico. It was good cover for Randlett's reluctant decision to help a friend.

No sooner had the troopers arrived than McNelly asked Randlett to join him in attacking the Las Cuevas Ranch. Randlett was stunned. He thought he was coming to save a torn-up bunch of Rangers from certain death. It was the least he could do after the army originally promised to help. Instead, they wanted to attack an enemy more than ten times their size. Randlett declined. Such a move would require the approval of his superior officer and Major Alexander was not at the river yet.

A long, sultry day was spent repelling Mexican charges with the troopers fighting alongside the Rangers. But Randlett learned an additional two hundred Mexican soldiers had joined the assault and decided to return to Texas with his men. McNelly tried to change his mind when reports of a truce were shouted from the front. It was five o'clock. Both men stopped arguing to receive the Mexican flag-of-truce bearer.

With the wide-eyed envoy came a note addressed to the "Officer Commanding the Forces invading Mexico." It was from the chief justice of the state of Tamaulipas. McNelly had no intention of accepting something that said he invaded Mexico. Randlett received the document without that concern. The note demanded they leave Mexico at once but promised to consider the Texas complaint of lost cattle and rustlers afterward. Randlett thought the terms were reasonable and quickly agreed. Anything to let him return with some dignity.

McNelly frowned. He'd heard that song too many times before. A white-faced Randlett listened as McNelly folded his arms and spoke to the nervous envoy. The envoy's eyes glimpsed General Flores's gun in McNelly's belt and swallowed bile.

"Tell your boys I want the stolen cattle and the men responsible delivered to us now — or we'll attack." McNelly motioned toward the river and the troops watching on the far side. They were powerless to help but he was counting on the Mexicans' not knowing.

The envoy left and returned with a request that hostilities be suspended for the night. McNelly was advised that they could not deliver the cattle immediately because most weren't near. Some of the rustlers were dead; the others had fled. McNelly agreed not to attack during the night if his two captured horses were returned. He further agreed to give an hour's notice before starting active operations again.

Randlett couldn't believe what he was hearing. It was a daring statement at the very least. Thirty Rangers would give an hour's advance warning to an armed force now numbering over five hundred!

On the Texas shore, Major Alexander arrived and sent orders for Randlett to return immediately. The order wasn't necessary; Randlett was already leaving. McNelly sent his horses with the departing troopers. By six o'clock, the Rangers were alone again. Only this time their adversaries were not only ready, their numbers were increasing. Even the shadows were strange and menacing, crowding close to the band of Texas warriors.

Somewhere, a mountain lion screamed its impatience at not finding supper. The youngest Ranger, George Durham, glanced over at Casuse, then at Callicott, for reassurance. Neither man paid any attention to the growing night sounds. Both knew danger came only with silence. That would mean the enemy was advancing and wildlife had quieted for their own safety.

Callicott hitched up his gunbelt out of habit as McNelly came to the gathered Rangers and searched their faces for the determination he knew he would see.

"Boys, it's just us," McNelly pronounced. "The army won't let me have any men. Major Jones's Rangers are too far away to get here in time. But we're staying."

As if describing plans for Sunday school, he explained that their position—at the edge of the Rio Grande—would keep them from being surrounded or cut off from forage and water. They would also have a steady supply of mutton, bread, and coffee, through arrangements with the Mexican guide.

No Ranger offered the idea that the guide might be shot or captured. Or worse, that the huge Mexican force would simply overrun their position, if they decided to do so. As they ate leftover mutton and McNelly's newly acquired bread, he explained what their strategy would be. During the night, they would dig a deep trench behind the upper bank as their last line of defense.

"Boys, when the Mexicans charge us again, they will come in big numbers. We will fight them from the thicket to the bank; and if we can't stand them off at the bank, we will fall back to this trench and fight them to a death finish. I am willing to die with you boys and I expect as much from you."

They rotated three fresh men every hour until the trench was finished. Several commented that they were digging their own graves but none when McNelly could hear them. Bright starlight found the rest waiting. Waiting. A few slept. Most checked and rechecked their weapons, knowing what the morning would bring. Others stared into the dark land, half hoping to see movement because it would relieve the awful tension. Even Bill Callicott was edgy, almost firing at a stray cow that meandered into the bullrushes close to his sentry position.

McNelly stood alone. So far, he had failed. Escape for his men was impossible. In his heart, he knew no troops would come now. All he could do was bluff with their presence on the Texas side. Hopefully, the Mexicans wouldn't realize the troops had no intention of crossing.

"Shoot, boys! Here they are, boys, shoot!" George Durham jumped up, pistol in his hand. He was asleep and having one of his frequent nightmares. Rangers whirled their rifles toward the blackness. Nothing. Realizing what had happened, McNelly walked over, took the gun from Durham's hand, and eased him back to the ground. No one said anything.

Morning came, but without the expected Mexican charge. As the day grew stronger, Mexican forces increased but didn't attack. One Ranger prayed loudly but the rest watched and waited. McNelly expected to see Mexican artillery moved into place. Across the river, some of the army men turned away, not wanting to see what they knew was going to happen.

Washington, D.C., was dictating the moves today. General E.O.C. Ord at San Antonio was ordered to inform Mexican authorities that U.S. troops were under orders not to cross. Major Alexander received a telegram defining his next action:

> *Advise Capt McNelly to return at once to this side of the river. Inform him that you are directed not to support him in any way while he remains on the Mexican territory. If McNelly is attacked by Mexican forces on Mexican soil do not render him any assistance.*

Of course, the State Department was involved now too. They wanted the Texans out of Mexico, even if it meant their surrender. In mid-afternoon, U.S. Commercial Agent Lucius Avery, stationed at nearby Camargo, came to the Ranger entrenchment. A Mexican envoy accompanied him. Avery advised McNelly to surrender to the Mexican federal authorities. The directive was from Washington. Avery assured McNelly that he would personally go along to make sure they remained safe.

The Ranger captain's silent stare made Avery uncomfortable.

Surely McNelly appreciated what the State Department was doing for his men.

When Avery was finished, McNelly pulled on the brim of his hat. "I can't see it. Tell your boys 'no thanks.' "

Behind him thirty Rangers already knew what he was going to do. McNelly immediately turned to the Mexican envoy. "I promised to warn you an hour before we attacked. Count it so—or meet my demands."

Both envoy and agent scurried away. The Rangers readied themselves for a final assault. After consultation, the Mexicans agreed to deliver the stock they had recaptured, and as many of the thieves as they could catch, to Texas at ten o'clock the following day. With that declaration, McNelly withdrew his Rangers, announcing that he would return if they didn't comply. McNelly hadn't lost a man in the so-called Las Cuevas War, bringing an end to the massive border rustling.

On the following day, Rangers helped seventy-five cattle onto a ferry. That's all that remained from the herd. The number wasn't important; the action was. It was the first time Texas cattle had been returned from Mexico. No rustlers had been caught, but McNelly was again reminded his men had killed many outlaws, including General Flores. McNelly had to remind Mexican officials of their promise to deliver the livestock—with a masterful bluff that the commander of U.S. forces was nearby, waiting for their compliance. Of course, waiting was all he was doing.

In his reports, Major Alexander not only assumed credit for the return of McNelly and his men, but also for the return of the cattle. However, Texans knew the truth. Cattleman Richard King admiringly noted McNelly was the first man ever to get stolen cattle out of Mexico. With thirty men—and most on foot, no less. In honor of that feat, King cut off each right horn of his returned thirty-five animals. He turned them out on the range, where they would be a lifelong symbol of McNelly's daring. It is said shadows forever watched over them, smiling.

Across the border, a fifteen-foot-tall monument was erected in Las Cuevas to honor General Flores.

The Whispering

JANET E. GRAEBNER

July, 1876: The nation's centennial is celebrated at an international exposition at Fairmount Park in Philadelphia when news arrives of an Indian battle in faraway Montana Territory. Actually there were two battles: one on Rosebud Creek on June 17, and another, above the Little Bighorn River, on the twenty-fifth. The first had resulted in a rout of troopers commanded by General George Crook; the second resulted in the annihilation of five companies — 270 men — of the Seventh U.S. Cavalry, including their commanding officer, George Armstrong Custer.

Not mentioned in the fevered dispatches from the battlefields was the name of an Oglala warrior-mystic who led his people in both fights, and in many others against white interlopers before 1876: Tašunka Witko — Crazy Horse.

The great novel of Crazy Horse is Win Blevins's *Stone Song* (1995); the great story of Crazy Horse is Janet Graebner's "The Whispering."

Janet E. Graebner, a native Minnesotan with university degrees in economics and French, is a freelance writer in Colorado who studies the Sanskrit and Lakhóta (Sioux) languages. She writes essays and short fiction and is the author of two nonfiction books.

"ATÉ, FATHER! MORE RAISINS!" his daughter shouted, pulling at the bag he held.

He opened the skin sack wider and the children greedily grabbed the small wrinkled fruit, stuffing the sweet brown pieces into their mouths, their dark eyes alight with pleasure.

Crazy Horse clutched the red bundle closer, as though to press into it some of his own breath. His mind's eye saw her pale face and sandy hair, combed in two stubby braids, like little tails on her neck.

He recalled his own first taste of raisins, as a child living with old Smoke's band along the flat-water river, called the North Platte by whites. Grandfather Smoke had brought two bags of them from a raid near Fort Laramie, and Curly—called so because of his wavy light brown hair—had wondered how something from the whites could taste so good.

The burial scaffold creaked under his weight as he sat up, still holding close the small red bundle. The half-moon outlined his daughter's cradleboard and the toys left to ease her journey along *wanagi tacanku,* the ghost road. He reached out and pushed the rattle of strung deer hooves that he had made for her, the bony clicking ticking across the prairie like a *wicahuhu,* walking skeleton. Then silence folded over him again.

How could he have known that a *wicincala,* little girl, would give him so much joy? And so much pain. "I'm sorry," Black Shawl had said, returning from the birthing lodge three winters before, walking slowly and slightly bent as she entered the lodge. "It is a daughter." Her words fell quietly before him. "Every man wants a warrior son."

But he took the bundle she handed him, and as he looked down a small finger reached out and two old-person's eyes met his and focused steadily, the bond between father and daughter pledged forever.

"Hau, waśte," he said, the Lakota welcome sound soft and sin-

cere. "Then she is a new daughter for the Oglalas. She will grow up to be a great mother to her people and they will marvel at her sacred ways. The sinew of the old forms will thread her thoughts and guide her actions. We will call her They Are Afraid of Her."

How had he chosen that name? Black Shawl didn't want to break the solemn moment by asking. She knew that her strange man, as the Oglalas were wont to call her husband, would have his reasons, and she was content that he had accepted their first child so readily.

Click, click. Click. The rattle moved gently in the wind. *"Hun-hunhe!"* The sound of grief emptied itself into the night. "Another of the white man's 'gifts,' " he shouted, jabbing a fist at the sky. The small scaffold wobbled, threatening to plunge them both to the ground.

Riding into camp three days ago, he met women with bloodied arms and cutoff hair. They lowered their eyes as he rode by, and he knew.

His father, Worm, was waiting for him. "Son, be strong. Your daughter . . . It was the running-face. The whites call it smallpox. *Mitákoja,* my grandchild, got sick after you left to fight the big-beaked bird people."

Worm's tone was apologetic. "The long-chin trader brought blankets. We should not have taken them. We should have known that from what others told us. But *waniyetu,* winter, was coming hard on the fall whistle of the mating *hehaka,* elk."

"Hunhunhe!" Crazy Horse's slight frame shook with the sorrow sound that exploded from deep within him. How could he blame his father? He, Tašunka Witko, should have been here, not away fighting Crows, or hunting hairy mouths who broke apart *maka,* mother earth, for the sun-colored rock.

"Wašicuns!" Crazy Horse said, spitting out the word for whites that meant "takes-the-fat." "They take everything! They cross our land where they are forbidden by the marked paper! They bring death to our people!" His gray eyes—like his sandy hair and light skin, the resented leavings of a white man—were two ashy coals of hatred.

Worm reached out to touch his son. Crazy Horse pulled away. "Your daughter lies at little-beaver creek," Worm said, "near the old sundance ground. I will go with you."

"Lila pilamaya, até. Many thanks, my father, but I prefer to go alone. First, I must see my daughter's mother."

Their lodge was cold and dark, the fire allowed to die out so his daughter's spirit would not seek its welcoming light and be held in this world instead of following the road of the departed.

Black Shawl was huddled in the back, next to an empty space where her child's sleeping robes used to be. Her sobs caught Crazy Horse's heart. This dignified woman had come to him when blackness had filled him completely: the death of his carefree young brother, Little Hawk, and that of his brother-friend, Hump, both killed by the Snakes; the bad business with a youthful love, Black Buffalo Woman, when she left her husband, No Water, to be with him; then Little Big Man grabbing his arm when he drew a knife against No Water, who shot him in the face, which left a black powder scar that made him look even more white; finally, the stripping of the shirt, the honor that had demanded the hard duty of always placing others above self, the ultimate protector of the people.

After all this, Black Shawl—a woman near his own age of twenty-eight winters, late for marriage among their people—had come to his lodge as wife after he sent his mother to speak for him. "And you must tell her," he said, "how I am, never speaking much or singing and dancing as other Lakota men do. You must tell her there will be little joy in a life with me."

But Black Shawl, too, was a quiet one, and as their days together passed from season to season, she gently encouraged him to dissolve the darkness that lay within him. Now he must return to her the generosity she had shown him by sharing his lodge and giving him the daughter whose name would never again be spoken.

"Wife, Black Shawl." He walked clockwise around the fire pit and squatted, noting her face streaked with ashes and her hair raggedly cut around her face. Taking her hand, he said, "Do you remember how she would shout '*Sunghula!* Pony! Pony!' when I'd carry her around camp on my shoulders? She seemed so small and frail."

Até, *father, the end is written in the beginning.*

Unbidden words rose in his throat. "Black Shawl, perhaps our daughter's reason for coming so late to us and leaving so early is yet to be known."

She jerked her hand away and turned to face him, eyes horror-stricken. *"Yun!* What—what rea—" A cry choked her words. *"Yun!"* Her exclamation of pain hurt his ears.

Aaiii! Strange territory, this. Another blackness laid upon his heart. His face crumpled with dismay, which sharpened his thin nose and gave him the beaked appearance of a bird of prey. He was of no help here.

"I will send my mother to stay with you," he said, reaching over and touching her knee. Only a sob acknowledged his departure.

He crossed the camp to the lodge of his old friend and spiritual mentor, Horn Chips, the stone dreamer, who had given him the smooth white stone that he wore tucked under his left arm. Its power was great; many horses had been killed under him, but he had never been wounded by an Oglala enemy.

At Chips's lodge, Crazy Horse scratched the door flap to announce his arrival. "I know it is you!" a brusque voice called out.

Throwing back the flap, Crazy Horse stooped and entered the shadowy tipi; only a two-stick fire burned. It was smaller than most and crowded with the belongings of one used to living alone and hoarding all possessions.

"Sit," Chips said, without so much as a *hau* of greeting.

Crazy Horse squatted at the dreamer's right and waited. He was used to his mentor's rude behavior and dour attitude.

Finally, the dreamer opened his eyes, the pupils large in the dim light and still, fixed beyond the perimeter of the lodge as though not yet finished seeing what lay beyond.

Then he turned and transferred his distant gaze to the man beside him and said, "As long as a warrior has love for all things alive and all things dead, he will live twice but die only once."

Mute, Crazy Horse waited.

"You have lost three close to you. This last one holds more of your heart than you ever imagined. To grieve is natural, but the People live and require your attention now. Those who walk the shadow road ahead of us understand that. You must carry them in your heart, but your strength must be devoted to the People left behind. Revenge kills man's spirit."

Crazy Horse raised a hand requesting to speak. Chips shook his head. "Life is a circle," he said. "It begins in one place, flows for a time like a river touching many banks, then leaves, only to return again when and where it is needed, just as the water runs from the mountains, fills the streams, vanishes into the air, renews itself, and falls again from the sky."

Até, *there are hard decisions ahead.*

"You will know what is to come," Chips said. "It will be told to you." He reached into a small pouch at his side and held out his hand. "And this is to remind you of your duty."

Crazy Horse took the smooth *canśin,* pine-sap stone. He held it to the firelight and gazed at the lifeless insects trapped inside, then slipped the deerskin thong over his neck.

"You must see with the *cante iśta,* the eye of the heart," Chips said. "Now I will tell you what I have seen. The Lakota and Sahiyela, Cheyenne, will rise to greatness in two fights during *wipazuka waśte wi,* the moon-of-ripe-berries, the whites' month of June. Then your last fight, during *wiotehika,* when old-man-of-the-north is most bitter, you will face a severe test and must decide whether to resist for selfish reasons, or to act for the good of the People. What I have seen is this . . ."

WHEN THE WOLVES RACED INTO CAMP AND REPORTED THAT THE valley at *onjinjintka wakpala,* rosebud creek, was thick with soldiers, and that the one called Three Stars Crook led them, the Lakota knew they were in for a hard fight.

On hearing this news, allies from the agencies and far-flung camps gathered to counsel, and they looked to Crazy Horse to lead them. Speaking for all, He Dog said it was much that they asked of him, to take on what amounted to a death sentence. "It is a new kind of chief we want, one not tied to the petty jealousies between families, or of power brought to a lodge in exchange for a few ponies. This new duty is for life and cannot be thrown away this side of a red robe resting on a scaffold."

Crazy Horse's heart swelled with the honor laid on him, and so great was his hatred for the whites that he accepted. "We refuse to walk on our knees for the *waśicuns!*" he said. "Those who used to lead—Red Cloud, Spotted Tail, Man Afraid, and others—have sold themselves, just as they are now being asked by the Great Father in

Washington to sell the *he sapa,* the sacred black mountain. We are not for sale as long as we have breath! Trying to always remake people in their own image is a white man's disease."

"Hopo!" The young men began to heat the moment with their shouts. "We are ready! Let's go!"

"Hau! We'll go!" Crazy Horse assured them. "But think well before you ride away, for we must make a different kind of war, a final war so we can live in peace in our own country."

"Haiye! Haiye!" Cheers of joy and women's trilling filled the air.

A GENTLE RAIN HAD SOAKED THE DRY VALLEY. CRAZY HORSE breathed deeply, the damp fragrance of sage and wild roses a tonic for his weary body. It had been a long ride through the night, over the *heśka,* big-horn mountains, and away from the village on ash creek, which emptied into the river the People called little horn or greasy grass.

Since early light they had been fighting the bluecoats. The sun was now overhead. The dust rose like smoke and mingled with the scent of sage and rose petals crushed beneath boots and moccasins and hundreds of horses' hooves.

Crazy Horse and He Dog were resting their ponies atop a ridge. The two Oglalas could see that one army unit, cut off from reinforcements, was especially hard-pressed fighting the Sahiyela.

The Indians had surprised the soldiers at dawn, near the bend of the sluggish creek, which flowed toward the morning sun, then back-bended slightly and headed straight up to empty into the river-of-many-elk, called the Yellowstone by whites.

The valley ground was rough and strewn with rocks and brush. It was cut by a long ravine that ran in the direction of *wicahpi owanjila,* the star-that-stays-in-one-place. Bluffs crouched on either side like sentries. The Indians called it *mnikaośkokpa wayapepi,* ambush canyon.

The hours of charge and countercharge had taken a toll on warriors and soldiers alike, but the army was outnumbered and its lines had been badly split.

Lance and arrow met bullet and sword. War club clashed with tomahawk. Crook's Crow and Snake scouts fought with a vengeance against their ancient enemies, and raw recruits were forced to defend themselves hand to hand.

Crazy Horse shivered with nervous excitement as he watched the fighting below, his hand toying with the new stone.

"*Hé táku he?*" He Dog pointed at the yellow-brown stone. "What's that ? A new *wotawe*, war charm?"

"A reminder from Chips, just before we left. He said that a man is ensnared by his reckless actions, like the insects trapped inside this stone. They are fixed in a time not of their making, he said. But man, unlike our small buzzing relatives, can break free if he learns that real power lies in knowing himself."

"You are truly *witko*, Tasunka, crazy." They both laughed. It was an old joke between them, from a more carefree time when the boy Curly was only fifteen winters. Hump had led a party against the *mahpiyato*, Arapaho. Curly had counted many coups and killed the enemy without being hit himself. It was seen by all as proof that his vision medicine was powerful. Afterward, his father, Tasunka Witko, held a celebration to give his son his family name, and he took for himself the name Worm.

Embarrassed, Crazy Horse let go of the charm. "*Ho!* Enough foolishness, you he dog of a she dog! Our horses are ready and anxious. *Hokahe!*" His heels pounded the sides of his pony and he flew downhill as though carried by the wind. "A warrior hawk am I. Aiii! A warrior for my people."

A bluecoat charged in front of him and Crazy Horse let go of the reins and nocked an arrow as he raised his bow. He pulled the bow string and its release twanged in his right ear. He nocked another arrow and set it free before the first hit its target. Sweeping past the second rider, he thrust out his bow and knocked the soldier off his horse. "Aiii!"

Smoke, dust, and gunfire filled the valley. A rattle of shots and distant war whoops echoed from the hills. Across the creek, soldiers were up against two strong charges launched by Sahiyela on one side and Lakota on the other. Unable to hold the ridge, the soldiers moved downslope where-the-sun-sleeps to join another group.

Crazy Horse could see that a new spirit had indeed gripped the warriors. They fought together for a common cause: drive out the white intruders once and for all. Ignore the old way of fighting individually for scalps and coups and horses, he had entreated. Work together. He knew it was a hard thing he had asked of them. But today he was proud as he watched Sahiyela and Lakota battle with uncommon unity, charging Three Stars' soldiers and breaking their lines time and time again. It was a major change from hit-and-run fighting, and Crazy Horse could see that the troops were confused by it.

Shading his eyes, he saw that the sun had passed half its day's journey. Wild shouting drifted up and he turned his attention downstream. Bluecoats were trying to enter the canyon! But why? "Does Three Stars think our village is there?" he wondered out loud. "Perhaps he thinks he can attack us from the rear. Ha! The joke's on him!"

Até, *end this now.*

"*Wašte,*" said Little Big Man, pointing to the canyon and the advancing troops. "That's good." He pulled up next to Crazy Horse, drawing close enough that their knees touched in the manner of old friends. Crazy Horse nudged his pony to move away.

Little Big Man shrugged and said, "We have not lost too many warriors, and Three Stars' soldiers are scattered."

"*Hecetu yelo,*" Crazy Horse said, shifting his glance between the action in the valley and the cavalrymen entering the canyon. "That is true, but we must end this now, for good, the old way."

"Your old trick?" said He Dog, riding up in time to hear his friend's last words. "The bluecoats don't know what to do when we break their lines. They scamper like rabbits. Your plan is to trap them in the canyon?"

The Oglala war chief nodded. "We will pretend to quit. Ride into the canyon. The soldiers will follow to pick off a few more of us."

He Dog's horse pushed his way between Crazy Horse and Little Big Man. "Good. The canyon narrows and is clogged with rocks and fallen timbers that have been left by rains. The soldiers cannot easily turn their horses around."

Crazy Horse raised his eagle wing-bone whistle to his lips. A high-pitched sound floated across the valley. Twice more he blew the signal for his warriors to leave the field. Two shorter blasts told them to head for the narrow end of the canyon. He knew the Sahiyela on the other side would make their own decisions.

Soft laughter rose in He Dog's throat. "The soldiers have never understood our whistled signals," he said. "But we have learned many of their shiny-horn calls. They are good to know in a fight." His grin broadened as he turned to his companions.

A look of sadness moved across Crazy Horse's face, like water rippled in a light breeze. "No one really wins," he said. "But on a good day, when men know their families are in danger, they will fight like a cornered *hoka,* badger. Today is a good day."

Slowly he pulled his Winchester from its case alongside his horse's right shoulder, and just as slowly placed his bow inside. Then he raised his Winchester high in the timeless gesture of a victor and turned his horse downslope to where the deadly canyon lay.

As expected, mounted troops followed the departing warriors. The Lakota began to peel off as they neared the far end of the canyon, concealing themselves in the tangled brush and timber. Crazy Horse and a few men brought up the rear, looking back occasionally to check the enemy's progress.

Crazy Horse slid from his pony when the soldiers reached the dam of rocks and trees. His habit of jumping from his horse to shoot amused his friends. "I want to be sure of hitting what I aim at," he'd say to their teasing.

As he raised his rifle, he saw a rider rush forward and pull his horse up short at the front of the column. Holding his breath, the Oglala watched in amazement as the halted column struggled to turn its horses around and mount the slope to the sundown side. Firing could be heard from there. Then silence.

"Tóka he?" He Dog's horse skidded to a stop. "What's the matter? Where are they going?"

Crazy Horse cast a sidelong glance at his friend. *"Le wana henala.* Now it is done. That is good, for if the soldiers had come this far many more would have died."

Atéwaye kin, *my father, it is not done.*

THE DAYBREAK STAR STILL LINGERED AS THE TIRED WARRIORS RE-turned to camp on ash creek, bringing with them the wounded and those who would fight no more. Three Stars, the People were told, had turned his dust around and was headed back to his camp at big-goose creek.

Everyone seemed content to think the trouble with the whites was over. But Crazy Horse thought otherwise. Hadn't the whispering said it wasn't done yet? And there was still Sitting Bull's vision to consider, of soldiers falling into camp. No, it was not done.

The next day the People moved down to the fat-grass waters, sometimes called the greasy grass. It was rich with game and good browse for the horse herd. The People feasted and danced and exulted in their victory, activities that could not be indulged earlier in the village of death on ash creek.

Crazy Horse was repeatedly singled out. "Come dance! Come tell about the ambush that didn't happen! Come eat buffalo hump!" the People shouted. But he never took part in the dances or telling of exploits. His quiet manner and lack of ostentation were well known, but considered strange among a people whose customs indulged loud and wild displays of emotion at times of victory and mourning. He turned their invitations aside with a smile and sought the solitude of his lodge, where he crept to his sleeping couch and pulled a buffalo robe over his head to shut out the sounds of celebration. He knew soldiers would come again.

By way of distraction the next day, he decided to go to rosebud creek to gather scattered ammunition. "Who wants to ride with me?" he called to a clutch of Oglala boys.

By mid-afternoon they had combed the field carefully and filled several hide pouches with unused bullets and spent shells that could be refilled. Crazy Horse had them pry the horseshoes from dead army mounts, and even insisted that the boys pick up arrow tips. "Iron is scarce," he said. "Nothing must be forgotten."

"Guns are better," one boy said impatiently.

Crazy Horse recognized him as the son of a family that spent winters at the Red Cloud agency. Loafers, they were called, who came out to be with the northern bands during the summer. The Oglala warrior quietly said, "Guns, like arrows, are only as good as the eyes and heart behind them," and he turned away and spoke no more.

On their return, the camp was abuzz with news that soldiers were marching up the Yellowstone. More people had come from the agencies on hearing about the coup against Three Stars Crook. The victory had raised everyone's spirits, and they came with tales of the army's plans for increased activity in the north country.

And, of course, Sitting Bull's vision of soldiers falling into camp like locusts still awaited its time and place. Was this it? The valley of the *pejislawakpa,* the greasy grass?

Black Shawl was serving her husband wild turnip soup when shouts of "Soldiers! Many soldiers here!" rang out and running feet pounded past their lodge. The door flap was flung aside and He Dog thrust his head in. "Tašunka, I have your yellow horse here. Sitting Bull's vision is true! Soldiers in camp! *Hiyú wo!* Come on!"

"*Ho!*" But anxiety pinched his heart as he picked up his warbag and rifle. A brief moment holding Black Shawl to him and he was gone.

Até, *Father, the dust will rise like smoke. The earth will drink red.*

A small boy riding his fleeing mother's back shouted "*Hokahe!*" as Crazy Horse galloped past. "*Hokahe!*" he shouted, raising his rifle in salute to the child. The woman trilled the warrior-courage send-off.

Crazy Horse felt a fluttering of pride, strong and light, as though floating above ground, like the horse and rider in his youthful vision that had given him his life's guidance. The gopher dust that he had tossed on his horse allowed them to ride unseen before the enemy. No bullet could touch him.

As he rode, Lakota and Sahiyela fell in behind him; Crazy Horse riding the point of a great arrow that spread wider and longer and flew straight at the enemy. "Remember our families!" But the warriors needed no reminder.

MANY DIED AT THE GREASY GRASS, AND AT DAY'S END THE EARTH did run red.

Afterward, the People moved quickly toward the setting sun, camping deep in the *heška,* big-horn mountains. Stories reached them from the agencies about how they had killed the one called Long

Hair, Custer, and all his men, more than twice the soldiers killed ten winters ago in the hundred-in-the-hands fight, which the whites called the Fetterman Massacre.

"It will never be done," he told Black Shawl. "We are called savages, hostiles, simply for wanting to live our own way."

His heart was heavy, too, because it was known that some of their own people were leaving the north country to walk the white man's road, and some had agreed to help the army bring in the resisters, especially Crazy Horse and Sitting Bull, Dull Knife and Two Moons. "It is not good to have our own people against us," he said. "If that is so, then surely we are lost. Of what need the whites if Lakota are willing to kill Lakota?"

Até, *you must prepare yourself for something hard.*

SKIRMISHES WITH SOLDIERS CONTINUED FROM THE MOON-OF-ripening-cherries, June, to the moon-of-the-popping-trees, December.

The icy wind drove through threadbare clothes like needles as Crazy Horse led his band *itokagata,* southward, along the buffalo-tongue river, the shaggy beasts for which it was named long gone.

The army officer that the Indians called Bear Coat, Nelson A. Miles, had tracked them for days, the soldiers plaguing them like magpies after a scabby-backed horse, forcing them to move through deep snow, their meager supplies of food and shelter abandoned along the way.

The People called it *wiotehika,* the hard moon. It was indeed a time more difficult than they had ever known. The familiar warmth of the lodge and the laughter that used to fill the long cold wait between old-man-frost's appearance and the sweet-smelling, soft breath of *wetu,* spring, was no longer. "We hunker like camp dogs before a wolverine!" Crazy Horse said.

"*Hou!*" agreed He Dog. "Maybe . . . maybe, *mitakola,* my friend, for the good of our people . . ." He Dog raised the subject carefully, knowing Crazy Horse's desire to die free rather than surrender to the whites.

"*Hunhunhe!*" The sound of regret fell from Crazy Horse's lips with such depth of feeling that He Dog looked away to let his friend save face.

Até, it will take a very great man to save the People now. Many will hate him, and many will try to kill him.

Early the next morning, the Lakota and Sahiyela were forced into a half-day fight against Bear Coat's troops at a butte called Wolf Mountain, on the Tongue River. What began in a snowstorm ended in a blizzard; one could not distinguish friend from foe.

Finally, in the afternoon's winter darkness, the warriors retreated farther up the river with their women and children. *"Hokahe!"* Crazy Horse called into the swirling snow, the challenge a last war cry for all that had been.

The date was January 8, 1877.

DURING THE MOON-OF-SHEDDING-PONIES, MAY, CRAZY HORSE led eight hundred eighty-nine people and a large horse herd to Fort Robinson on the White River in northwestern Nebraska, a processional stretching for two miles. They came with raised heads and a firm step, some sitting their ponies like proud warriors, and all chanting the Lakota peace song.

"By God!" blustered Three Stars Crook. "This is a triumphal march, not a surrender!"

Along the way a small girl broke from the throng and ran to the side of Crazy Horse's pony. She held out her hand, filled with dried berries. He thought of his own daughter, wrapped in a red blanket and lying on a scaffold not too far away. He reached for the child's offering.

Até, the end is written in the beginning.

Crazy Horse smiled, and on his tongue he tasted . . . raisins.

The Fevers

C. F. ECKHARDT

There were countless opportunities to die on the Western frontier in the nineteenth century—accident, Indian attack, prairie fire, drought, starvation, to name a few. Of them all, sickness, in particular that caused by the nameless fevers that periodically swept the land, topped the list. Having a doctor nearby helped but even a wise one had severe limitations. "I can't treat what's causing the fever," Doc Fleming says herein, "because I don't know what that is . . . So you just blunder along."

This story, told by the horse rancher Ben Fowler, takes place in the San Saba River country of central Texas, but fevers, as the malaria, or perhaps yellowjack, described here, knew no geography, struck and killed homesteaders without warning, and moved on as suddenly as they had arrived.

C. F. "Charley" Eckhardt is a native Texan who grew up on a ranch near Georgetown, north of Austin. After graduation from the University of Texas as a history major he

worked as a soldier and police officer, a news-
paper columnist, and freelance writer and ed-
itor. Among his books are *The Lost San Saba
Mines, Unsolved Texas Mysteries,* and *Tales of
Badmen, Bad Women, and Bad Places*—*Four
Centuries of Texas Outlawry.*

He lives in a historic home in Seguin with
his wife, Vicki, "and numerous critters."

I was pretty much minding my own business, I reckon, pulling some water, when I saw a buggy coming down my road. My place ain't too big—just a couple sections—but it's still most three mile from the Brady-to-Menardville road to the house, and I don't usually get visitors at just about a quarter past daybreak. I stepped back into the house and got my six-shooter and tucked it in my pants just in case the visitors wasn't friendly. Not ever'body is, and when a feller raises and trains the best horses in the San Saba River country—you need it, I got it, saddle-horse, harness-broke, or cowpony—he deals in hard money a lot. Hard money ain't real easy to come by, and some folks, they decide it's easier to come by with a gun than by working for it. When there's fellers like that around—and, sad to say, there's a bunch of them—a feller's smart if he greets folks he don't know with a shooter tucked in his pants till their intentions are clear.

I didn't recognize the rig, but I did recognize the horse. I raised that big strawberry roan gelding from a colt—best buggy horse I ever raised. He could trot a mile in just a hair over two minutes with a sulky behind, but he was big enough to pull a road-buggy. Got two hundred dollars, hard money, when I sold him to Dr. Andrew Fleming, the new sawbones. Doc Fleming needed the best buggy horse money could buy in our country, and I had him.

Trouble was, I couldn't figure out how come Doc Fleming would be coming down my lane. I wasn't sick, I didn't owe him any money, an' he didn't owe me none. When I saw how ol' Red was sorta dragging along, though, I figured maybe he'd been out all night an' wanted to fresh Red up 'fore he went back to town. It being just a quarter or so past sunup, I didn't figure it was a social call, and from what I'd heard, Doc wasn't the social-calling sort noway.

My place is a mile wide and two miles deep, and it runs east to west. My lane comes in off a lane that runs north off the main road,

311

so ol' Red was coming in from the east, the sun behind him, and he had to get right up on me 'fore I could see Doc in the buggy. When I saw him, all slumped over in the buggy seat like he was, the first thing that run through my mind was "Oh, my God, somebody's done shot the doctor!" That's when I knew what Red was doing at my place. No hand on the lines, naturally ol' Red come home. Doc had him four months. I had him four years. My place was home.

As soon as they got in the yard I grabbed Red's bit an' pulled him in. That's when I saw how plumb wore out that horse was—hell, he hadn't had that harness off in two, three days, an' I could see galls under the buckles as big as cartwheel dollars. I was just about flat ready to whip me a sawbones' butt right there. That ain't no way to treat a horse!

I tied ol' Red to my hitch—away from the water, 'cause as wore out as he was, he could founder himself if he drank his fill. Then I pulled the doc up. He hadn't been shot, and I figured for a minute he was just dead drunk, but I couldn't smell no likker on him. For a man to be as drunk as he 'peared to be he had to be drinking whiskey, an' regular ol' tarantula juice at that. A feller can't get *that* drunk just on beer.

I pulled Doc outa the buggy and he just sorta come apart on me. He was looser'n the drawstring on a whore's bloomers, but he didn't act or smell drunk. He acted plumb wore out—so tired I couldn't wake him up. I picked him up and packed him in the house and laid him out on my bed, and he just commenced to snore.

Me, I went out to take care of the horse. Horses I know 'bout. I don't know much about people. I got pore ol' Red outa that harness—he had upward of a dozen bloody galls on him—and let him have a drink, but not too much. Then I took him over to my dry pen, put out some wheat—I wasn't 'bout to give him oats, tired as he was—and got some rock-oil grease and smeared it on them galls so they wouldn't draw blowflies. Then I went in to see about Doc.

I don't reckon I'd ever seen a feller so tuckered out as Doc was in my whole life. My daddy was in the war, and he used to tell me about fellers so tuckered out they fell asleep marching and just kept marching anyway, but I 'bout half didn't believe that. I believed it now—I couldn't wake Doc up.

I already had the coffee on, so I got me a cup, fried up some sowbelly and a couple eggs, and heated up some cold pone. After I eat breakfast, I went out to tend to my horses. Shoot, a feller raises, breaks, an' trains horses for his living, he has work to do. You gotta work green-broke horses every day. You let a green-broke horse go three, four days without a saddle on, you might near got to start over with him.

I'd been down to the pens maybe an hour, working a little *grulla* mare—I called her Button on account of she wasn't but about thirteen hands high, but she could pitch for fair—and I'd got the pitching out of her system and was working on reining. That's when I saw Doc come sorta staggering out of the house. I slid down off Button, tied her to the fence, and went over to see about Doc.

"Where the hell's my horse?" he said.

"In my dry pen to keep him from foundering, and he ain't going back in harness for a week, maybe more," I said. "He's got galls on his hide. You damn near killed a mighty good horse, and from the looks of you, you ain't much better off. What the hell you been drinkin'? I don't smell nothing on you."

He had a kinda wild look in his eye. "Where am I?" he said. "I know you. You're Ben Fowler. I bought my horse from you. Where am I?"

"My place," I said. "Six miles west a town. Red brought you home. I thought you was drunk, but it looks like you been lost for three, four days."

He took out his watch and looked at it, then kinda shook it. "Stopped. God, I don't remember the last time I had time to wind it. What time is it?"

"Four hours past sunup. Maybeso a quarter after nine. Almanac says sunup was a quarter past five today."

"What day?"

"Friday. Tomorrer's town day."

"My God," he said, "I was supposed to be at Paul Evans's place four hours ago."

"How come?"

"Fever. Got eleven cases, all east of town. Maybe more by now. I left Rob Phelan's place about a quarter of three, headed for Evanses'. Rob's down with it. So are the Evans girls."

"Mary Evans got the fevers?" I said. Mary was the prettiest thing north of San Antone. She had hair like a double eagle and eyes like a summer sky. She'd just turned sixteen—just getting to marrying age—an' me, at twenty-six and doing all right in the horse business, I'd been figuring on speaking to Paul Evans about calling on Mary as soon as I could.

"And Sally. And the Mercer boy—Lewis. Four others last night. God only knows how many by now. Get my horse hitched. Jesus Christ, it's ten miles back over there. Those girls could be dead by now. So could a half-dozen others."

"Doc," I said, "you go back in the house. Wash your face and shave—my razor's in there, and there's hot water on the stove. Hot coffee too. There's sowbelly and some eggs, and some cold pone. You get cleaned up, get something in your belly. I'm gonna slap some grease on your hubs—you had a wheel squealing when you come in—and then I'll turn them horses out and hitch up Brownie. She ain't as big as Red but she's a high-stepper for fair—a pacing horse. Then I'll drive you. You ain't in no shape to drive a rig. You're liable to go to sleep an' end up back here again."

"What about my horse?" he said.

"He ain't in no better shape to pull than you are to drive," I said. "I'll turn him out with the rest and we'll hope he don't founder himself in the creek. Now git. I'll handle what needs handling out here."

He went back in my house an' I set to it. I knew I'd have my hands full when I got back—nine green-broke horses and God only knew when I'd get a saddle on them again. I pulled the saddle and bridle off Button and turned her out, and then I got Doc's hubs greased—the off rear was might near bone dry, a feller oughta take better care of his rig than that—and was backing Brownie in the shafts when Doc come out. He still looked like a walking dead man, but he didn't stagger.

"How long's it been since you been to bed?" I asked, popping Brownie with the lines so she'd hit her pace.

"Three days. Mart Glover come down with it first. Jane sent their oldest boy for me, but it was too late when I got there. He was already gone. Then the Stovers' place. Both their boys got it. They'll make it, I think. You know where we can get a jug of shine?"

"Doc," I said, "this ain't no time to get drunk."

"Don't need it for drinking. I need the alcohol. Use to help break the fever. I ran out of medical alcohol at the Phelans'.""

"Luke Bonner at the saloon," I said. "We gotta go right by it."

"I don't have any money on me."

"I'll talk to Luke," I said. "We can owe him for it till you get the fevers took care of."

By the time we got to the saloon Doc was asleep again, so I went in. When I told Luke what I wanted and why, he said "Hell, you don't need good whiskey for that, all you need is something with a lot of alcohol in it. I got a whole keg of pure-dee rotgut. Keep it around for the ol' drunks. I'll run you off a couple gallons in a jug."

"What'll I owe you for it?"

"Nothing. Hell, I get the stuff for about six bits a gallon. Dollar and a half ain't gonna break me. Yawl just get out there an' help them folks. Good thing—worst whiskey in the world, and it might help keep some folks alive."

It was might near noon when we finally got to the Evanses'. "Where are they?" was all Doc said when Paul came out.

"In the house. Where you been?"

"He damn near died, that's where he's been," I said, "but he's here now. That's what counts."

In a minute Doc stuck his head out the door and bawled, "Bring that damn jug, Ben, and be quick. Paul, you come too."

We went in—I had the jug—and Miz Evans said, "What's in that?"

"Bad whiskey," I said.

"Doctor," she hollered, "we're Baptists. We don't 'low whiskey in our house."

"It's not to drink," he said. "We'll mix it with the water. The alcohol evaporates faster and maybe we can break the fever quicker. Ben, you and Paul come in here. Miz Evans, you get the pans of water like I told you."

"But Doctor," she hollered again, "you can't take them men in there—'specially not Ben Fowler. You done stripped my girls plumb nekkid."

"You want your girls to live?" he asked.

"Yes, but . . ."

"But nothing. It's gonna take all four of us to save them—if we can save them. Now go get the water—big pans or bowls. Paul, you get all the clean rags you can find, and get something to fan with—church fans if you got them. One for you and one for Ben. Hurry!"

Me an' Doc, we went into the bedroom. The window was open an' he'd jerked the covers plumb off the beds, and it looked like he'd just ripped their nightgowns off. Mary was a-laying there—pretty as a picture, like she always was—but her eyes was shut, she was all red like she was blushing 'cause she was nekkid and I was looking at her, and her breath was coming short and like it was hard to get it. Little Sally wasn't but ten, but she had the same blond hair and pale skin Mary did. I reckon every feller in a hundred miles woulda give a year's pay to see Mary Evans nekkid—but not like this. Sweat was pouring off her and her hair looked all wet and frazzled, and she looked as sick as she was. Ever now and again she'd catch her breath and sorta choke, and then she'd start breathing hard again.

Miz Evans came in with two dishpans and Doc poured most a third of that jug of whiskey in them. Then he grabbed a handful of rag, dipped it in the water, and commenced to sop it on Mary. "Fan her, Ben," he said. "Paul, you and Miz Evans do the same with Sally. Don't quit. If we run outa water, get some more."

Lord, I don't know how long I stood there, fanning that girl. I fanned with my right hand till it felt like it was gonna fall off, and then I fanned with my left hand till *it* felt like it was gonna fall off, an' then I fanned with my right hand some more. Doc just kept sopping that water and whiskey on her, and that bedroom smelt worse'n the worst saloon I'd ever been in in my life.

It was way late in the afternoon when that flush finally faded and Mary commenced to breathing soft and regular. "All right," he said, "now put some covers over them."

"Are my girls gonna live?" Miz Evans asked.

"We'll know in six to eight hours."

"What'll happen then?" Paul asked.

"Either they'll wake up—or they won't."

"You got anything you can give them, Doc?" Paul asked. "We got laudanum an' calomel—"

"You give those girls laudanum, you'll bury them tomorrow," Doc said. "Calomel'll take a little longer to kill them. Nothin' you can give them will help at this stage, and most of it'll hurt them.

What they need is sleep. It heals better than anything else right now. Natural sleep, not opium sleep. If they're strong enough, in six to eight hours they'll wake up. They'll be weak as kittens. Feed them thin soup—broth, not gruel. That, and give them all the water they can drink. Boil that water first, then cool it before you give it to them. We don't know but whatever caused this is in the water.

"When they wake up they won't be able to stand alone. Don't let them out of the bed except for the needs, and then make sure they use the chamber pot. They'll be too weak to make it to the privy. I've got six other cases—maybe more—to tend to."

We went out and got in the buggy, and I looked at Doc. He looked as tuckered as he did when he come staggering out of my house. "Where?" I said.

"Stover's. We'll have to see if there are any more cases."

"Doc, is Mary gonna live?"

He sorta shut his eyes. "Maybe so," he said.

"How maybe so?"

"Betting on it? Fifty-fifty. If she's strong enough, she'll live now that the fever's broke. If she's not . . ." An' he didn't say any more. I knew what that meant.

"How 'bout Sally?"

"I wouldn't even give odds on her," he said.

"You know they lost two kids. Their boy an' a baby girl."

"Ben," he said, "I doubt the little girl will still be alive when we get back. She came down with it first. Both girls were still conscious when their folks came to the Phelans' to find me. I told them to put the girls on the beds naked, open the windows, bathe them in cool water, and fan them. When I got there the window was shut, the girls were in outing nightgowns, and they were covered to their chins with blankets—worst thing you can do for a fever like that."

"You feel mighty cold when you got a fever," I said.

"Yes. You're hotter than the surrounding air, that's what it is. Normal human body temperature is between ninety-eight and ninety-nine degrees. As long as the air temperature's twenty to thirty degrees cooler than our bodies—between sixty-eight and seventy-eight degrees—we're usually pretty comfortable. Above seventy-eight degrees we feel a little warm—but when you elevate the body's temperature, like in a fever of 104 or 105 degrees like those girls had, even ninety-degree weather feels cold. People wrap up when they have a fever, and as long as the fever's just a small one—one to two degrees above normal—that's not going to hurt them. When it's as high as this fever's getting, it can kill them. The fever has to be broken, and it won't break as long as the body remains hot. That's why we bathed them in a mixture of cool water and alcohol and fanned them. Alcohol evaporates faster than water—it cools quicker. You know how you cool off in a breeze if you're wet. If you've ever spilled whiskey on you, you know how much colder that was, and how much quicker it got cold. By mixing the two, we could cool their bodies fast, but not too fast. Once we got the body cool on the outside, the fever broke inside."

"Is Mary gonna be all right, then?" I asked.

"I think she's going to live, if that's what you mean. Whether or not she'll be 'all right' depends on how long that fever lasted, how high it got, and what damage it did. A real bad fever can cause a lot of problems later. I've seen patients who had a really high fever who lost all their hair and it never did grow back. I had a woman patient once, before I came here, who was as slick as a cueball—not a hair on her from the top of her head to the tips of her toes. Fever did it—killed all the hair follicles. I remember a little boy, when I was in medical school, who had a high fever that lasted six days. He really didn't have a mind left afterward. No telling what a fever will do."

"You mean—Mary might not have a mind left?"

"Oh, I don't think hers was that high, or lasted that long. Are you sweet on that girl, Ben?"

"Gonna be trying to get that way," I said. " 'Bout time I found me a wife. I been studying on going to talk to Paul 'bout me calling on Mary."

"Well," he said, "I'd say the odds are fair you can talk to him about that in about four or five weeks. She should be back on her feet by then. The little girl—well, I just don't know. That's the worst part about being a doctor—we're supposed to know everything, and we really know damned little. Take this fever—I'm just treating the fever, but I can't treat what's causing the fever because I don't know what that is. It's like trying to find your way on a moonless night. There are indications of where to go—you can see the stars and there's some very dim light from them, but not enough to show you anything. So you just blunder along, hoping you don't fall in a hole or run into a tree."

When we got to the Stovers', the news was good. Both boys were awake and eating soup—broth, like Doc said. "Have they been drinking a lot of water?" he asked.

"Purty good," Oscar Stover said. "They acting like they're mighty thirsty."

"Give them all they want and then some," Doc said, "but you make damn sure it's been boiled first, then cooled. I don't know what's causing this fever, but it might be in the water."

"What you reckon could be in the water?" Oscar asked.

"A microbe. A little thing so tiny you can't even see it with a burning glass. Water can look clean and taste sweet an' still be crawling with those things. Once I get the fevers broken, I'll get water samples everywhere I can and look at them under a microscope. I might see something in them. Or for that matter, it might be like malaria—just carried in the air, and it blew past."

"How come me and my wife didn't get it?" Oscar said.

"Maybe you had it when you were little and you're immune to it. Maybe you ate something or drank something that kept it off. Oscar, I don't know. All I know is I've lost Mart Glover to it and there are at least two more in real danger. I've got to look in on them."

We hit the Mercers' next and the news there was good. Little Lewis was wanting to sit up in bed, but he was too weak. The news at the Phelans' wasn't good. Rob died during the night—he just never woke up. The Burnses' place had good and bad—Tommy woke up, but Sam didn't. Lizzie Johnson was coming out of it, and so was Barbara Moore. No more cases were reported. That left the Evanses' place, and we got there just after daybreak.

"Well," I said as we pulled up, "at least nobody's digging a grave."

"That's something," Doc agreed. "Let's go in and see what we see."

What we saw was good. Mary was looking more like herself—pretty as a picture. Sally was asleep, but she'd been awake and had some broth and lots of water. Miz Evans was asleep, but Paul was up—though he looked as bad as Doc did.

Mary looked up at me. "Pappa tells me you were in here when I was so sick," she said.

"I fanned you," I said. "Doc sopped water and bad whiskey on you and I fanned you."

"Lord," she said, "this place smells like a sour pigsty from that stuff. Is it true I didn't have any clothes on?"

"I reckon it is," I said, "but I wasn't looking on you lustful or nothing. I was just trying to keep you alive."

"Ben, you won't never tell nobody you seen me without my clothes on, will you?"

" 'Tain't nobody's business 'bout that," I said. "Take a powerful bad feller to go talking 'bout that."

"How old are you?"

"Twenty-six. An' you're sixteen," I said.

"You go to church?"

"Not much," I admitted. "I got too many horses to work. Working green horses is a full-time job, an' you gotta do it every day. Green horses don't pay no 'tention to Sundays."

"We have a box social at our church once a month," she said. "You know—the kind where the single girls pack a dinner in a box and the single men bid on the boxes without knowing who made them, an' then they get to eat dinner with the girl who packed the box?"

"Heard of them," I said. "Never been to one."

"We had one last month, but I was still fifteen then and Mamma wouldn't let me pack a box for it. She said I could when I turned sixteen. The next one's next week, but I don't reckon I'll be up and around for that one. Even if I am, I won't go. They're always on the third Sunday, after church. Would you come to the one in October?"

"How would I know I'd find the box you packed?" I asked.

"Well, you're not supposed to know," she said, "but I like to put a big blue ribbon round the box I'm gonna pack. Look for a big blue ribbon, and bid on that box."

"I reckon I will," I said. "I'm gonna speak to your daddy—'bout calling on you. If he says I can, will you be to home?"

"I reckon I'll be to home," she said. "Might near any time you call, I'll be to home—if my daddy says it's all right."

When we got back in the buggy Doc said, "Well—I got fooled. Twice."

"Twice?"

"I wasn't expecting the Mercer boy—or Sally Evans—to live. I like to get fooled that way. This came out pretty well, all things considered—eleven cases of a fever, I don't even know what it is for sure, and I only lost three patients to it. Mort Glover I expected to lose—he was dying when I left to go to the Stovers'. The little Burns boy I didn't expect to lose—he looked strong when I left. Rob Phelan I didn't expect. He was strong as a horse. Lewis Mercer and Sally Evans I expected to return to find dead, and I didn't. I count myself lucky, Ben," he said. "Usually, from something like this, a doctor can figure on losing half the patients if he's lucky, all of them if he's not."

"There wasn't nothing you could do more than you done," I said.

"When you don't know what causes something—and I have no idea what caused this—all you can do is treat the symptoms. The symptom in this case—high fever. I treated fever, not what was wrong with the patients. It worked seventy percent of the time—this time. Next time it may work ten percent of the time—or not at all.

"Now—could you put me up for a couple of days? I need some sleep—and so do you—and after this I feel like getting real drunk, and I don't want the folks in town to see me that way."

"What'll we use for whiskey?" I asked.

"Well, we've got the rest of that jug."

"Doc," I said, "I wouldn't give that stuff to one of E. J. Davis's police. Let's go get some *real* whiskey."

Well, Doc and me, we got drunk—and we slept the clock around and then some—and I let him have the loan of Brownie until Red's galls healed up. I went to the October box social at First Baptist and bought the box with the big blue ribbon around it—it cost me five dollars, hard money, 'cause there was a bunch of fellers bidding on it. I wanted it bad, though, and when it come to hard money I had them cowboys and town boys both beat, on account of I never sold a trained horse for nothing but hard money. The bidding started at four bits and it was up to three dollars and six bits when I bid five dollars, gold. When I reached in my pocket and laid that half-eagle up there, the bidding was all over.

It was Mary's box, all right, and we eat cold fried chicken and biscuits together. I got to take her home in my gig, but her mamma and daddy was right behind us in their buggy. I ain't never had a top for the gig, so they could see us clear all the way. All we got to do was hold hands.

I talked to Paul about calling on Mary and he said it was all right. I bought me a suit of clothes and a boiling shirt—hadn't never had neither one before—on account of a feller, he's gonna call on a lady, he ought not do it in brown duckins.

Up and bought me a buggy too—isinglass lights, side curtains, leather forecurtain and all. Even has two coal-oil lamps on the dashboard for lighting your way home in the dark. A lady ought not have to ride in a gig with no top on it, 'specially when the weather gets chilly. 'Sides, it's kinda hard to see through that leather back curtain, and if a feller wants to kiss his gal, he really don't want her mamma an' daddy and baby sister right behind them in another buggy a-looking on. After six months I asked her daddy for her hand and he said yes and so did she.

If I'da known it was gonna be so much trouble marrying a Baptist, I mighta thought it over more. I ain't been baptized—I just got sorta sprinkled on—so I gotta let that preacher try to drown me in the creek. I done warned Mary—if I get water up my nose, I'm coming up on the fight.

My house ain't good 'nough, I reckon. Mary's mamma says I'm gonna have to close in the dogtrot and put a shed room front and back, and then buy a cast-iron stove so she can have a kitchen in the back shed and a parlor where the kitchen is. When the babies start coming I'm gonna have to raise up the roof so I can put a long loft in where the boys can sleep at one end and the gals at the other, with a curtain atwixt them so there won't be no peeking.

I won't have to give up drinking altogether, though, s'long's I don't go getting drunk, but there's gonna be a power of Baptist ladies praying I get the strength to give it plumb up. I won't have to give up chawin' 'cept in the house but she won't never kiss me if I've got a chaw. I'll have to commence going to church at least ever' other Sunday too. I tried to tell her them green-broke horses ain't gonna understand Sunday, but women, they got funny ideas thataway.

I Killed King Fisher

RILEY FROH

John W. "King" Fisher (1854–1884) grew up in South Texas, a handsome, rough-and-tumble lad who after burglarizing a house did a stint at Huntsville Prison at age sixteen. He did not reform. While still in his teens he was a hired gunman for stockmen in Demmitt County, leader of a gang of toughs in the town of Eagle Pass, and by age twenty-three was said to have "killed seven men, not counting Mexicans." Like many another outlaw (Henry Plummer, John Selman, "Mysterious Dave" Mather, and English-born Ben Thompson come to mind) Fisher switched sides and wore the badge until his past caught up with him.

Who did kill King Fisher? It's a lingering mystery of the Old West and Riley Froh provides an answer—and a good one, too, with America's most reviled assassin playing a bit part.

Riley Froh grew up on a hundred-acre spread outside the tiny central Texas settlement of Luling, descended from the town's founders.

With a Ph.D. from Texas A&M University, Froh taught Texas and U.S. history and British literature from 1969 to 1997 at San Jacinto College in Pasadena, Texas.

He is the author of two nonfiction books, periodical and scholarly journal works, and many stories, and is at work on a history of rodeo calf roping.

THE PROPER IDENTITY OF THE
killer of King Fisher has remained a mystery over the several decades
since that fateful night of March 11, 1884, when the smoke finally
cleared in the Vaudeville Theater at 401 West Commerce Street, to
reveal sprawled and crumpled on the floor not only Fisher but the
notorious Ben Thompson as well. Both were shot to pieces. Joe Foster limped off from the bloody scene carrying a bullet in his leg.

Theories abound to this day about who killed whom: some main-
tain that the two Texas gunmen shot each other; others give the
credit to Jacobo Coy, the house bouncer; Joe Foster, who died of
his own wound shortly thereafter, is suspect; still others finger Ed
McLaughlin, the bartender, or Canada Bill, a gambler, or Harry Tre-
main, a variety actor. Finally, the dandy Billy Simms is even mentioned as the person responsible for the two deaths. But the name
of the real triggerman never surfaces even remotely in the various
perusings. The only thing certain is the location of the celebrated
event. Baedeker accurately refers to the spot as "The Fatal Corner."

Oh, you can read the misinformation on who supposedly did it,
from the hacks in their dime novels to the dilettante historians and
on down to the work by the academicians, who aren't nearly as good
as the aforementioned pulp and grassroots boys, but I'm here to tell
you how it really was. And the reason that I know is that I, Percy
Hicks, killed King Fisher!

I single-handedly eliminated that feared Texas gunman with the
many notches on his gun, that friend of the undertaker who never
grieved over even one of his bloody deeds. But unlike the cruel and
warped cretin I dispatched, I had good reason for my actions.

The "official" record does not mention me, of course. The legal
document itself, which is a matter of public domain, gathers dust in
the Bexar County Courthouse. Yellowed with age, the fragile paper
still bears the India ink pen scratches: "We the jury for the coroner

in and for the County of Bexar in the State of Texas do find that
Ben Thompson and J. K. Fisher came to their deaths on the eleventh
day of March, 1884, from pistols held in and fired from the hands
of J. C. Foster and Jacobo Coy. And we further find that the said
killing was justifiable and done in self-defense and the immediate
danger of life."

And so two of the deadliest gunmen ever known wind up with
this badly phrased summation of their final moments on this planet.
They had lived fast, killed indiscriminately, died middle-aged, and
left a checkered memory.

Much about King Fisher has already been recorded in history or
is generally well-known, for he was certainly flamboyant. He in-
truded arrogantly into peaceful lives, scattering to the winds the few
rules of civilization of that time just for his own misguided pleasures.
Then he would swagger on to further mischief, unrepentant of any
consequences of his actions. His wicked sky-blue eyes mocked the
very families whose lives he wantonly destroyed. The costume he
sported — ornamented Mexican sombrero, purple sash, embroidered
buckskin vest, and linen shirt — was more like a hootchy-kootchy
dancer's than a man's, though no one would dare to tell him so.

While he was maintaining his vast cattle-rustling operation in
South Texas, he actually placed the sign THIS IS KING FISHER'S
ROAD; TAKE THE OTHER at a fork in the road. This was a public
thoroughfare, mind you, and not a private lane. And yet this degen-
erate blackguard would presume to tell honest men where to travel!
And all this in the home of the free and the land of the brave. But,
of course, he could get away with it. What few local officials he
hadn't scared, he'd bought.

At least the Rangers weren't afraid of him. In May of 1877,
famed Captain Leander McNelly clapped Fisher and his whole band
of brigands in irons, forced the trembling grand jury to indict, and
hung around to see the entire bunch sprung by a judge and jury of
little backbone. Once again, evil triumphed over the courts and the
very institutions of the government of the great state of Texas. But
King Fisher still felt the heat, realized the Rangers would circumvent
the courts next time, and knew in his black heart that he would be
"shot while trying to escape" in future.

So he pulled the switch that desperadoes frequently turned in

Texas and flip-flopped into a law-enforcement job. That way he could still carry a gun and shoot people with impunity. He even became respectable as sheriff in Uvalde, where he made a surprisingly good marriage. At the time of his death, he stood unopposed for reelection.

My own reason for killing the scoundrel dated back to his outlaw days. Various accounts of western annals mention in passing that King Fisher nonchalantly shot a whiskey drummer in Cotulla on a bet that he could glance a .44 slug off the drummer's bald pate. Of course he spread the man's brains all over the bar. It is a true tale, but where such bloody foolishness establishes Fisher as a memorable character, the victim is all but forgotten by the public.

That poor, sweet, honest soul that Fisher callously destroyed is remembered, though, by those of us who loved him. That man was my uncle and the primary economic support for his sister, my widowed mother, as well as his own wife and their large brood. King Fisher just laughed at the time of the senseless murder. Modern readers chuckle at the historical record today, and I guess it is amusing if you weren't involved and don't give the casualty and the sufferers a thought. I wept then; I planned revenge, and I got it.

I had nothing against Ben Thompson, who got caught in my crossfire, but he was just as big a homicidal thug as Fisher. Their murderous careers even bear a marked similarity.

Ben got started a little earlier than King, having attempted his first killing at age thirteen. Deadliness increased with age and his dedicated drinking habits. The lawlessness rampant during the late War Between the States gave him reason in his own mind to take every opportunity to rid the world of several gamblers who didn't appreciate the way he beat them at draw poker. After a brief stint as a paid goon for the railroad interests, he drifted into civic law enforcement for the city of Austin, a convenient position for one of cutthroat tendencies. He had returned to full-time card sharking as a livelihood when he stumbled in the way of one of my bullets.

My own background contrasts sharply with the two gunfighters I dispatched. My whole tribe descends from clerks, counter-jumpers, and drummers, a class of drones necessary to progress but considered of little worth by the general public and of no value to the likes of King Fisher, who removed what little economic security we had with the shot that stilled the kindly heart of my salesman uncle. Curiously, I didn't even feel inadequate when I vowed revenge against such a monster, although I had never even held a gun. I just knew that someday I would destroy him out of sheer desire if nothing else.

As a youth, I learned the general mercantile business, working my way up from general flunky to clerk. At night I studied math and accounting, since poverty had driven me from the one-room school-house I loved. I read any book I could get my hands on to continue the education I desired.

After I found a fair position in the Alamo General Store in San Antonio, I got into theater work after hours by offering what skills I possessed as a general step-and-fetch-it, and here I found my niche in life. I treasured the essence of mixing with the great and near great. These were real celebrities with whom I mingled, actual theater people. I never even noticed the long hours and, because of my willingness to run errands, Adah Isaacs Menken, Sarah Bernhardt, and Lillie Langtry addressed me with familiarity. Even Edwin Forrest called me by my first name. "Percy!" they would cry, and I was at their beck and call. I was in heaven.

My experience was not limited to the legitimate theater; I also worked for cheap vaudeville and even found employment in the smelly halls of bawdy burlesque, which was just a step above the smutty peep shows. The lowest thing I ever had anything to do with was to fill in as curtain puller for a fake Egyptian "princess" who performed a lurid dance with a snake.

If I own any other claim to fame, it is that I had the greatest good fortune to meet one of the true giants of the world's stage, both public and private, namely John Wilkes Booth. I actually made his acquaintance nearly two decades after he supposedly died from his wounds outside that flaming barn near Bowling Green, Virginia. I heard the facts of this phenomenon from the man himself.

The patriotic assassin of the vile and evil Abraham Lincoln, acting under the stage name of Irving Edgecomb, thrilled audiences with his Shakespearean roles in *Hamlet* and *King Lear,* although his portrayals of any character won great success. A preeminent tragedian, he was the second generation to tread the boards as the best of his time. To be around him was to stand in the presence of greatness, whether he was acting or merely conversing. I never understood why people avoided him. Perhaps it was his open acknowledgment that he was in truth Booth. I think people actually feared him. He was like a lion in a zoo one wants to touch but hesitates to do so, instinctively fearful to reach through the bars.

We became fast friends, sharing many late-night drinks together in the Buckhorn Saloon, and although he was never interested in listening to my life story, I never tired of hearing his, a fascinating tale that helped me pull off my own perfect crime—if you can call eliminating two members of the scum of the earth from society criminal.

John Wilkes Booth would have been even more famous in the profession than his brother Edwin had he not become fascinated with Confederate politics. He was actually present at the hanging of the fanatic John Brown in 1859, and when he filled every seat in the cozy Montgomery Theater in that city in Alabama in December 1860, he read as a curtain call the historic words of "Dixie Land," which he also later scrawled on the backstage wall of the theater itself. Then he retired to a gourmet restaurant to give one of the early toasts to the Southern Confederacy in that pleasing, melodic voice of his.

But he performed his greatest role in Ford's Theater on the night of April 14, 1865. A play, he said, was the perfect setting for assassination because all eyes but the shooter's are on the stage. Then, when the gunman merges with the action, he becomes the greater drama, dwarfs the scheduled presentation with his play within a play and achieves perfect synthesis. His leap upon the stage shouting, "Thus dies tyranny," completed his immortal performance in Washington.

To hear these poetic words from the lips of the man who actually slew the Illinois bumpkin masquerading as the president of the United States was histrionic art itself. The tragedy, of course, was not the death of "Dishonest Abe" but the flaw whereby Booth broke his leg and barely escaped.

Avoiding capture during the largest manhunt in American history required all the skills my hero could muster, and in this episode his consummate acting ability stood him in good stead. On the simple pretext of carrying out a practical joke, Booth paid a tramp to exchange clothes with him. Little did this poor vagabond realize that by accepting the payment to stand in for one the great pivotal figures in history he had sealed his own doom. Booth had always maintained handsome understudies on the stage, and ironically this wastrel bore a striking physical resemblance to him. So it was an unknown transient who looked enough like John Wilkes Booth to be his twin that was shot and killed in the burning barn.

For five years after his "death" Booth traveled incognito, sometimes alone, sometimes in medicine shows, always apprehensive that Secretary Stanton and other Yankees who had conspired with him to rid the land of Lincoln would find him out and silence permanently his role in their conspiracy. Oh, the plot was widespread, mind you, including cabinet officials, radical Republican congressmen, and high-ranking army officers, all fearful of the President who would assimilate the South too quickly and rob them of the fruits of an extended victory through a harsh Reconstruction policy.

In time Booth ceased to fear. The gullible public had bought the myth of a single Southern assassin with a few dimwitted henchmen to such an extent that the truth had died with Booth's stand-in. The folklore had become fact. Most of the Yankee conspirators had died off or lost their power. Only the mighty John Wilkes Booth remained. And what a man he was! I can picture him now, sitting across from me at our regular table in the Buckhorn, his eyes deep pools of mystery, his pale skin reflecting the portrait of a Romantic, a Byronic hero—and the genius who gave me the idea of how to kill King Fisher and get away with it.

The play's the thing to catch the Fisher of a King!

The actor's trail from Virginia to San Antonio made many entrances and exits. Quite logically, Booth took refuge in Texas, a locale with frontier enough to lose oneself and the handy availability of a convenient escape across an international boundary to Mexico if necessary. He began to give readings in saloons, stilling even the most rowdy crowd with recitations as meaningful and significant as the heroic act which drove him from the legitimate stage. At last he gravitated to the bartender's trade, continuing to entertain customers with that marvelously winning presence he had even as he served them, remaining a stand-out personage in whatever capacity life placed him.

Settling as a saloon keeper in Granbury, Texas, in 1870, he introduced himself as John St. Helen. Very soon, the Lady Gay Saloon, with its educated and sophisticated manager, became the cultural center of the entire county. Booth advised the local thespians to the point that their amateur productions took on the character of professional theater.

The great typhoid epidemic of 1871 brought him to the point of death, so weakening his indomitable spirit that he revealed his past to his attorney. This was not, you understand, out of any feeling of guilt but rather to set the historical record straight and possibly expose those few remaining Yankee leaders who had sold him out after conspiring with him to rid the land of the obscene hack who became President. Booth even parted with the prized derringer with which he had drilled the bloody tyrant in Washington's Ford Theater.

But the grim reaper passed him by, and my hero moved south in the dead of night, only to lose himself by sinking to employment at Rowdy Joe Lowe's seedy and sordid bar in Luling, Texas, an establishment that was more dance hall and brothel than public house. Luling, a tough little cowtown on a main branch of the Chisholm Trail lying only fifty miles east of our Alamo City, is no place for a gentleman.

It was in this state of disgrace that Booth conceived the brilliant idea to hide from the authorities by becoming overly conspicuous himself. He based the ploy on Edgar Allan Poe's "The Purloined Letter," in which the stolen letter is "hidden" in plain sight and the police overlook the obvious in their frantic search for the document. Ironically, Booth even resembled Poe, with his white forehead, black locks, and flashing eye. Both men entertained proper Southern sympathies.

So my friend returned to the real stage in our fair city, freely acknowledging that he was indeed John Wilkes Booth to anybody who asked, thereby allaying all suspicions. In this happy state, he gave me the inspiration for the eradication of King Fisher, not as low a man as the meddling Abraham Lincoln, of course, but certainly a creature almost as odious.

Fisher, as well as Ben Thompson, frequented the varied places of entertainment in San Antonio, establishments that attracted all classes of citizens, including the gunfighter, cowboy, soldier, gambler, lawman, and a smattering of decent residents out on the town. So, the degree of amusements represented bathos itself, running from the bouquet of fine wines and the wafting strains of Beethoven in the Turner Theater on down to the aroma of Jack Harris's place, where you could smell the beer in the air, and the street vendors laced their tamales with dog meat. Even on Sunday in the ancient City of the Spanish Missions the saloons are all open and the variety theaters run matinees. In each of these places, I went about my duties, blending ever more silently into the theater landscape, all the while watching for a chance to play the role of assassin.

People became used to my presence, including my ever-present toolbox with its false bottom containing my Winchester '73, with its tight, levering mechanism that threw another .32 cartridge from magazine to chamber with the reassuring and permanent metallic click of the closing of a coffin lid. My brace of pistols gleamed against the black felt. Each time I beheld these beauties I saw in my mind's eye the hated face of King Fisher.

I knew his modus operandi when it came to a night on the town. First he took in a civilized performance at the Turner. It was then that he retired to more fleshly scenes at Harris's Vaudeville Theater. The key was to know when he was to be in town, not really a difficult task since the city authorities kept tabs, for trouble followed him as sure as a fly will find an outhouse or a freshly baked pie. My police contacts were numerous. Both on- and off-duty officers frequented our establishments and were encouraged to do so by the management as a means of beefing up free security.

Curiously, on the night of March 10, 1884, word flashed from Austin that Fisher and Ben Thompson were headed by rail from the capital, both fueled by alcohol and planning to continue their celebration in a different locale. I sensed that their trails would lead inevitably into my gunsights, for Thompson loved to return to the scene of one of his more successful murders, the killing of Jack Harris, former owner of the Vaudeville. Thompson's perverse nature enjoyed rubbing things in, and he probably planned to notch another slot on his pistol grip by showing up around the deceased's old cronies. But he kept a rendezvous of a different sort. I notched him instead.

Ben Thompson's killing of Jack Harris follows the pattern of so many of his homicides, for he frequently shot someone in retaliation for the very same offense that he regularly inflicted on others. In this case the bad blood originated in Thompson's welshing on a gambling debt honestly acquired in Harris's establishment.

One-armed Jack Harris had noised it about that the next time Thompson staggered into the theater looking for trouble, he'd catch a load of buckshot in the midsection. Quite naturally, given the temper of the times, on July 11, 1882, Thompson, full of whiskey and vengeance, calmly strode into the dive and drilled Harris through the Venetian blind screen behind which he lurked, hitting him solidly with the first shot, catching him fatally on the way down with his second try, and missing the newly made corpse completely with the third and unnecessary round.

Of course Thompson was indicted by a Bexar County grand jury and of course he was acquitted since Major Walton, the "gunman's attorney," so ably defended him. Walton pointed out that under the rules of evidence Harris was waiting to gun Ben down and covered up the obvious fact that Thompson was going to kill Harris no matter what. I digress into this matter merely to point out that when I riddled Thompson in my efforts to slay his drinking companion, Ben got what he deserved no less than the bully and braggart King Fisher.

These were men of reeking halitosis rather than the fire-breathers legend has made them out to be. My homicides were excusable, justifiable, and praiseworthy.

Arriving in San Antonio at eight in the evening, the two miscreants repaired to the corner of Houston and St. Mary's, entered Turner Hall, and took in the drama *East Lynne*. From here they stumbled through at least one saloon on their way to the Vaudeville, where I, cleverly, on one pretext or another, was "working" on the curtain track on the walkway high above.

I could sense Thompson's evil disposition even at a distance. He was out for blood. But neither he nor Fisher was going to start anything until the show was over, for the entertainer was the remarkable Fanny Peale, whose fan dance was the talk of Texas. A true artiste, she somehow combined lewdness and grace in her performance as she flashed in and out of her feathered coverings, provocatively turning the sordid sublime.

The real game of management was an old one. Just as the free salted peanuts caused customers to spend more on drinks, Fanny

Peale aroused the inebriated to the need for a quick assignation with one of the courtesans available in-house. For that reason, my two unsuspecting targets were surrounded by the well-used Madame Blanche Deerwoode, Madame Carrie Anderson, and Waco Ida. They camped conveniently at nearby tables sipping fake champagne and revealing teasingly whatever blandishments they could muster.

And once the show started, I, like my intended victims, could not tear my gaze from Fanny Peale's broad-stepping, curve-shaking number. For that reason, I was barely conscious of the men who joined the new arrivals. Billy Simms, executor of the Harris estate and now comanager of the Vaudeville, strolled up with his house bouncer, Jacobo Coy. They joined King and Ben.

I had a splendid angle on the hated Fisher. His broad chest in its gaudy vest presented a perfect target. But I had missed my opportunity to fire, having become captivated by the false allure of the prancing female below me.

Meanwhile, Fanny, wheezing heavily from her unnatural exertions, retired to her backstage dressing room, from which I noticed a shaft of light cutting through a crack in her ceiling. Temptation overcame me, and I edged to a spot where I could take a peek.

The behind-the-scenes truth was shocking. What everyone thought was nudity was actually Fanny's oversized torso stuffed into a casing like a sausage. Puffing mightily, she was undoing the catches of her confining, skin-colored costume. Suddenly, the real Fanny burst forth, ponderous breasts and buttocks counterbalancing a pouching belly surged outward, seeking natural freedom. On the stage she twirled an hourglass figure. Alone and unwrapped, she sported a shape where the sand had drastically shifted.

Blowing a sigh, she grabbed a bottle of rotgut, swigged a draft, and followed it with another double gulp and gurgle for good measure. She lit a thin cigar for a chaser and plopped noisily and unceremoniously down on her thundermug to read the *Police Gazette*.

But my major business was elsewhere, and just in time I glanced back down into the theater to see Joe Foster, Simms's partner, approaching the party of doomed men. The Greeks knew what they were doing when they built their tiered amphitheaters. Since sound travels upward, I could hear perfectly all that was said below me. And what a drama that unfolded! Unwilling actors played their natural parts to my stage marks and stepped to my direction while I stood poised to yell "cut" with the bark of my firearms. Their spoken lines were classics of low drama.

"Hey, Foster!" Ben ordered. "Get yourself over here."

"Easy now, Ben," cautioned Simms beside him.

"Why not join us," Waco Ida invited.

"Maybe later," King Fisher muttered.

"Any time," wheezed Madame Blanche.

"We're always handy," Madame Carrie giggled.

How degraded the dregs of society! And all at their own peril. I can't count the times I have heard the great John Wilkes Booth—speaking as the actor Irving Edgecomb, of course—intone the speech of Hamlet bemoaning the fact that Claudius slew his father "full of bread" rather than fully prepared to journey to the other side of the grave. And how firmly Booth's Hamlet spoke the lines of hopefully eliminating his stepfather uncle while Claudius was enjoying the "incestuous pleasures of his sheets" in order to gain the full measure of revenge. These profound lines rang in my head as I prepared to send King Fisher through the Gates of Hell.

The drama was now reaching its climax, for Foster truculently strode up to the table of fools.

"Watch who you're ordering around, especially in this place, Thompson," Foster said harshly.

"I'm in charge wherever I'm at," Ben spoke back. "And now I'm telling you to have a drink with me by way of apology."

"Some other time," said Foster.

Almost too quick to see, Ben slapped Foster with his left hand while he reached for his pistol with his right. Coy grabbed Ben's arm immediately as Thompson squeezed off several shots, one of them striking Foster in the leg. All five men merged as the group locked in a desperate struggle. The women screamed their lungs out.

By this time I was delivering lead, aiming as best I could at my sworn enemy King Fisher and remarkably hitting only one other of the party, namely Ben Thompson. When my rifle clicked empty, my brace of pistols spoke fervently until they too were spent. Somewhere in the melee Foster, Coy, Simms, and even King Fisher got off shots, firing wildly, I suppose, but Thompson was hit nine times, whereas Fisher caught thirteen rounds, so possibly other shooters found their marks. But I know that I got in the most licks, for I saw the rascals jerk when I fired my weapons.

I could see through the veil of smoke that Simms had vanished unscathed. Coy, who had been dragged down by Thompson, arose unhurt to help Foster limp from the battlefield with the slug that proved fatal lodged deep in his leg. The three soiled doves were crawling down a hallway, advertising their best sides as they scurried off. In my own rushed state, I didn't have the presence of mind to check Fanny Peale. What a scene of shimmy and shake I must have missed by not glancing down again through that peephole.

I had learned from my hero Booth not to leap into fame. Instead, I quietly faded stage left, carrying the truth of an unsolved mystery to this day.

No, I never killed again, ending my brief career as a Texas gunman with two of the finest notches in Western history carved in my memory. In one short scene I had slain a pair of the deadliest badmen in Lone Star annals. Then I simply went back to my usual duties as jack-of-all-trades theater worker, enjoying as a fringe benefit free passes to every and all entertainment from ballet to burlesque, from Shakespeare to Ned Buntline. A man may hold all sorts of posts if he'll only hold his tongue.

I carried myself with a new sense of accomplishment, and when acquaintances remarked on my newfound confidence, I laughed and said that it came with a growing maturity and the perfection of my job skills. I said I was simply more comfortable with my position. I could hardly tell my secret, but every time I peer into a mirror, to my great delight I behold the face of Percy Hicks, the man who really killed King Fisher.

Noah

EMERY L. MEHOK

Kid Russell, the friend of the narrator of this story, doesn't often show up in Western fiction, maybe because, as the most beloved of Western artists, he is thought to be a sedentary figure, cooped up behind his easel in some comfortable studio in San Francisco or, worse yet, back East.

Not Charles Marion "Charlie" Russell (1864–1926). Born in St. Louis and related to the Bent family of Bent's Fort fame, Russell went out to Montana in 1880 and roamed the wilderness for two years, then went to work as a nighthawk for the 12 Z&V Ranch in the Judith Basin. He rose to full-time cowboy and for over a decade drifted as cowboy, hunter, keen observer, and artist in watercolors and clay. Late in the 1880s, *Harper's Weekly* and *Frank Leslie's Illustrated Newspaper* began using his drawings and by 1896 he had married and moved to Great Falls where he set up a studio and worked the rest of his life, producing an estimated 2,600 works and several illustrated books.

Emery Mehok is an Indiana teacher who over the past six years has hit his stride as a freelance writer. His forty stories and articles have appeared in such magazines as *Cowboy Magazine, Cowboys & Indians, Western Digest,* and *Frontier Trails.* In 2001 he was presented the Remuda Award for best Western-themed fiction in *Literally Horses* magazine.

rather quickly when, as a yonker, I took a fall on one of R. W. Clifford's colts near Ubet, Montana. I broke both legs and one never quite healed correctly. Even now, well into my sixties, I still walk with a limp.

I moved into Utica, which was the site of the biggest cattle roundup in that country in those days. I could ride, but I couldn't tolerate the long hours in the saddle necessary to keep a cowboy's job. I had some experience and talent in leatherwork and Mr. Clifford was kind enough to bankroll my start in the saddle business. I got to doing leather repair and making equipment while I was recuperating. My hope was to parlay that skill into a moneymaking job. I was certainly in the place for it. The Judith Basin was almost a cattleman's paradise. Cattlemen needed horses, and good horse equipment was vital to their success. I hoped to fill that need and earn a livelihood for myself.

In my spare time I wrote stories. It was an outlet for me, a pleasure that my departed parents had fostered in me. I even sold some articles to the *Helena Weekly Herald* and the *Helena Independent*. One day that desire to write would lead me to pen stories for the fledgling motion picture industry.

In those early days a good friend of mine was Kid Russell. We were alike in some ways. Our ages were similar and we even physically resembled one another. While I worked on leather goods, Russell toiled as a wrangler for John Cabler and spent his spare time drawing and painting for fun. I have written about him and his success several times. What a storyteller he was! How entertaining he could be! His art will live forever as an accurate representation of the West of our youth.

But I don't mean to mislead you. This story is not about Charlie Russell, although he is in it. This story is about Noah Toobers.

His real name was Noah Two Bears. Somehow, over the years it got altered, and I doubt if he cared. Maybe it helped him. Some people might've shied away from a half-breed. There were still a lot of Indians in our part of the country then, and the Indian wars were recent history. It had been not quite ten years earlier that Custer and his command had been wiped out at the Little Big Horn.

Noah didn't look like an Indian except for his skin, which had a reddish-brown tint. There was some talk that he might've had some Negro blood in him. I don't know. No one had the courage to inquire — certainly not me.

I believe he was the most dangerous man I've ever known. His appearance, though, was fairly common. He was short and stocky, not very imposing or frightening. He wore a hat with a Montana Peak crown atop short-cropped, raven-black hair, a faded shirt, a leather vest, and cotton duck trousers with deerskin sewn on the seat and inner thighs. These pants were tucked into stovepipe boots. Silver-mounted spurs with jinglebobs hung on his bootheels, so that every step he took made a little music.

The deadly aspect of him was due to the gunbelt strapped over the red sash at his waist. He carried two handguns, a short-barreled revolver on his right hip and a longer Colt in a crossdraw holster on his left. In addition, nestled in a scabbard sewn to the back of his vest was a wicked-looking bowie knife. The talk was that he could use all those weapons effectively along with the Spencer carbine he carried across his saddle.

Kid Russell and I were sitting in Cray's Saloon when we saw Toobers ride up.

"Is that Toobers?" Russell asked.

"It is," I said. "Ain't you never seen him before?"

"No," said Russell. "What a pony he's riding!"

Toobers tied his palouse stallion to the hitch rail. The animal was a beauty, well muscled and a solid sorrel from head through chest. A white blanket generously splashed with spots of all sizes covered the stud's rump and hindquarters. The horse was adorned with a rawhide braided headstall, reins, and romal. A finely tooled, center fire-rigged saddle with eagle beak tapaderos sat on his back.

Kid Russell and I both had something to admire. Charlie fairly loved horses and immediately took a pencil from his vest pocket and began to sketch on a piece of brown wrapping paper. I, of course, admired Toober's rig, wondering if I could ever produce something as beautiful.

It was the end of fall works and Cray's was crowded. Whiskey was consumed as conversation ebbed and flowed. When Toobers entered the room, there was a noticeable drop in the volume and amount of talking.

He strode forward, approaching the bar where several cowboys stood drinking. I saw Lucky Red Donovan lean aside, shielding himself from Noah's gaze.

"Red Donovan," Toobers called out, his deep voice exceptionally loud in a room that had fallen silent. "You are a horse-thieving son of a bitch, and I've finally caught up to you. Now you'll join your friend Stringer Jack in hell, and I can retire."

One by one men began to move away from the bar. Russell whispered to me, "What's he talking about?"

"Stringer Jack and ten other horse thieves were caught by a posse last July below the mouth of the Musselshell," I said. "Three escaped. Two were later caught and hanged. One got away. Granville Stuart led that posse, and he wanted a full sack. You know yourself he's a cattleman who hates to be disappointed."

"You can't prove nothing on me," stammered Red Donovan unconvincingly. He looked like a trapped animal. His hands remained on the bar, not making any move toward the gun on his hip.

"I can and will," said Noah. "You just step out in the street here. This saloon is crowded. I wouldn't want innocent people hurt. Mark my words now. You either surrender or die."

That was it. Toobers stated the situation so matter-of-factly that it seemed there was no other possibility than what he had set forth.

Noah backed through the batwing doors then. As he turned to step into the street, I saw Red Donovan frantically reach for his handgun. I guess he felt it was his only chance at staying alive.

"Toobers!" I screamed, and then Kid Russell and I hit the floor. Handguns were notoriously inaccurate, and I was scared of becoming a casualty of a stray bullet.

Donovan's shot splintered the saloon doors. A split second later another shot sounded. This bullet did not shatter the doors because it was fired through the open space beneath. Toobers must've dropped down to make himself a smaller target and so was able to aim directly at Donovan.

Lucky Red's luck ran out as he was slammed back against the bar. A second shot struck him as he slid to the floor, his eyes already wearing a deathly glaze.

Toobers walked in again, his Colt still in his hand. He approached the body, checked it for any signs of life, and then holstered his weapon.

He turned to our table as people began to rise from the floor. "Who yelled?" he said.

Rather sheepishly, I replied, "I did."

"Much obliged," he said. "I owe you."

He then grabbed Red Donovan's legs and dragged the body out, Red's head bouncing down the steps to the street.

I never regretted what I did. After all, Donovan meant to shoot Toobers in the back. People had long suspected Red of wrongdoing but just hadn't been able to prove it.

Noah was true to his word. About a year later a beautiful palouse colt was delivered to me in Utica with this note: "Thanks. I owed you one. N. Toobers."

I heard later he had moved all the way to Washington State and was raising palouse horses there.

I had the drawing by Charlie Russell of Toober's stallion framed. It now hangs on the wall in my study. Since Kid Russell has passed away, it means more to me than just a priceless piece of art. It is also a priceless memory.

My guess is that Noah Toobers has also met his maker. I still have descendants of his colt on my place—another priceless memory.

I may just have to make old Noah a character in an upcoming screenplay. Audiences will think it is all make-believe, but I'll know the truth.

The Big Die-Up

TROY D. SMITH

The killing winter of 1886–1887 cut a swath of bitter cold (temperatures of minus forty-five degrees in places) and relentless blizzards from the Dakotas to Texas. The year before had been a drought year in the west and northwest, with barely measureable rain in the spring and none in the summer. Everybody watched the sky, cattlemen especially attuned to signs of a bad winter to come: geese and ducks winging south earlier than usual; beavers and muskrats building thicker lodges.

The winter was worse than any could have predicted, a November-to-February catastrophe in which even the biggest cattle operations lost two-thirds of their stock.

Here, in Troy Smith's grimly real story, a man with a thousand head of longhorns faces what cowmen called "The Big Die-Up."

Troy Smith has been a minister, a furniture mover, truck unloader, floor cleaner, creative writing teacher, and volunteer worker with Haitian immigrants in New York City.

He is author of the novels *Bound for the Promised Land* and *Caleb's Price,* and over forty short stories and articles in a wide variety of periodicals.

JACKSON VICK BREATHED DEEP, clutching the reins of his black horse so tightly that his knuckles showed white. The sun was shining brightly on the melting snow. It glistened and twinkled, mocking him. He wished it were a human enemy so that he could smash a fist into its smug face, so that he could stare insolently into its eyes.

But it was not a human enemy. It was a blanket of melting slush, all that remained of the biggest snowstorm in living memory. The Great Blizzard of 'Eighty-six, they were already calling it. Underneath that blanket lay Vick's livelihood, all the gambles he had taken to build a future for his family, all the years he had slaved for a few dollars a month herding someone else's animals. All of his dreams. He rode over the snowy range, looking for some evidence of them — a hoof, a horn, uncovered by the tardy sun and offering some proof that he had indeed been a cattleman.

Billy Seabolt rode beside him, and Vint Knight. They worked for Richard Luden over at the Rocking-L. Seabolt was foreman there. Together, now, they inspected the damage wrought by nature upon their respective ranches. Vick had less to lose, where numbers were concerned. He had only owned a thousand head. Luden had ten times as many. But in effect their fates were intertwined, for each man had sunk all he owned into his spread. Their fates were intertwined literally, in fact, for their herds had mixed together beneath the fury of the storm.

Vick was exhausted near the point of collapse, but that had been true for so long that it almost seemed natural. How many eighteen-, twenty-hour days would this one make? He could not remember. How many desperate trips had he made to outlying ranches, pelted by snow and sleet, looking for hay where there was none? At least he still had all his fingers — almost a third of the cowboys he knew had lost at least one digit to frostbite.

There had been no reason to anticipate such an event. The winters had been mild every year since the railroads had brought the cattle business into prominence in the West, only twenty years before. The snow had been light enough that the cattle could find the grass underneath it. It was not like back East, where fences were erected and barns were put up and filled with hay. Out here everything roamed free. A whole way of life had grown up around that philosophy—men found their freedom of spirit reflected in their barely domesticated longhorns. There was no reason to believe it would not continue unchanged forever.

Vick had discerned almost immediately that this snowfall would be different. He had packed up Ruby and the kids and headed for the Rocking-L, where he had once been foreman, knowing that they would have to work together to weather the catastrophe. The same thing happened all over, as friendly rivals forgot their differences and tried to save their stock.

Those first few days at the Rocking-L were difficult, and very frustrating. The snow fell so fast that the hands had to lash themselves together to get from the bunkhouse to the kitchen. It was almost a week before anyone was able to ride more than a few yards away to look for strays.

Vick was the first to find some. Three cows, frozen stiff, almost covered with snow. Upon examining the unfortunate creatures, Vick came to the frightening conclusion that the wind had driven sleet up their nostrils, suffocating them. It was a pitiful sight, to be repeated many times in the days which followed. Frozen cows, their backs to the wind in futile instinctive hope, huddled together like children.

He wondered if their simple minds had been able to conceive of rescue. He hoped not. He felt bad enough as it was. There had been nothing he could do, save venture out a short distance from the ranch house in hopes of finding a stray. It was a hope that was fulfilled all too rarely.

Even those forays were limited due to the storm. Most of the time the men had sat around playing cards. There was no laughter of fellowship, no crowing from winners, no grumbling from losers. They were simply occupying their time as best they could while their jobs wandered blindly and froze to death.

And still it snowed. It snowed, and the harsh wind blew the

powder across the plains. The awful white crystals spread and flowed until they found some obstruction—a fence, a building. Then it stopped, piling higher and higher, until the drifts were sometimes ten or twelve feet tall.

When it let up enough that a person could see for more than a few feet, the cowboys mounted up and waded into it. They were growing desperate, for they knew their cows would be drifting with the storm. This would take them farther and farther from home. The men turned them and herded them back in the right direction—a difficult task, for every instinct told the cows to keep away from the biting wind, and especially not to head into it.

Then the snow stopped and the temperature began to rise.

The crisis seemed to have passed. A few head were lost, of course, but nothing crippling. The mercury rose above fifty, and hundreds of ranchers breathed a sigh of relief. Most of the snow melted. Vick prepared to count up his losses.

But winter had not finished its cruel game. Overnight, temperatures had fallen from fifty to twenty below zero. The recently melted snow froze solid, a thick sheet capping the ground. An arctic wind blew in, the worst in history, and suddenly it was forty-five below. For five days it snowed in clumps—sixteen inches outside the bunkhouse. Entire houses and stables were covered. Vick had to take a shovel just to reach his stabled horse when it was time to feed him.

The cowboys were forced into the same routine as before but with the knowledge that conditions had considerably worsened. For one thing, the cows were now starving; the icy shell on the ground kept them from reaching the grass. It seemed like all the winters since time had begun had been saved up and dumped on unsuspecting ranches all at once.

Now it was finally over. Nothing remained except to round up what survivors there might be. Vick and Luden had calculated that they would each lose ninety percent of their stock. This would be about average compared with the ranchers they knew. An unfortunate few lost everything. Bill Tilghman was one of these; Vint Knight had brought the news that Tilghman was completely wiped out. A knot tightened in Vick's stomach at the information. If fate had not spared the famous marshal of Dodge City, what hope could he have?

There had still been no sign of cattle, alive or dead. The eerie silence continued unbroken, for the cowboys had no words; they felt as empty inside as the land around them.

They found a large portion of the missing herds near line-shack number two. They were piled up so neatly they might almost have been stacked by a diligent butcher. Did they wander here by coincidence, Vick mused, walking blindly until some object stopped them, as the snow had? Or did they associate the little building with their human guardians, and come there seeking aid?

The latter was a silly thought, he knew. The longhorns were too free-spirited to come humbly to a human keeper. The fact was, the cattle probably viewed man as a different sort of animal, if they viewed them at all. Vick's conscience was forcing such foolish questions. The helpless experience of sitting by a warm fire while one's herd freezes can sour a man.

"Good Lord," he said aloud. "There's hundreds of 'em." *And more than a few with my brand.*

Seabolt shook his head, clearly choked up. "This is the sorriest sight I have ever seen," he said.

Vick dismounted and picked through the frosted corpses, dully searching for his brand. He stopped abruptly near the body of a steer.

"It's Old Dan," he said. Seabolt made a consoling sound. Old Dan had been one of those smarter-than-average steers that took it upon himself to keep the herd in line. He led them on the drive to the railway station each year. He had made the trip almost as many times as Vick had.

Vick's fists clenched. He could no longer rely on Old Dan to help lead his herd, but then he no longer had much of a herd anyway. One bad winter had ended it all. Anger and grief welled up from deep within him, the fire in his belly made the cold disappear.

"You stupid animal." he shouted, kicking Old Dan's stiff side. "Stupid stupid stupid!" He launched kick after kick at the steer, tears streaming down his reddened face. Knight looked away, embarrassed, and Seabolt nudged his mare closer.

"Take it easy, Vick."

"Stupid . . ."

"It ain't that bad," Knight said.

Vick whirled around. "Ain't that bad? What do you know about bad? Do you know how many years it took me to be my own man?"

"You can do it again," Seabolt said gently.

"You don't understand, do you. Neither of you understands. You think that even if the Rocking-L is finished, you can drift someplace else. This ain't just the end of me and Luden, it's the end of all of us. Somethin' like this could happen next year, or any year—we know that now. No rancher is gonna run the risk. He's gonna put up fences, and cut hay, and cut back on his herds. There won't be any more open ranges. There won't be any more freedom, for the cows or us either.

"It's all over."

The other two cowboys were bewildered. "You're just frazzled, Vick," Seabolt said. His eyes spoke as well: *Don't worry, I won't tell nobody about this scene,* they seemed to say.

Vick smiled bitterly. "You're prob'ly right, Billy," he said. "You're prob'ly right."

He bent down beside Old Dan. He blinked the tears away. "Stupid animal," he said softly, stroking the weathered forehead.

He turned and walked slowly back to his horse.

Do the Dark Dance

ARTHUR WINFIELD KNIGHT

A Georgian by birth, a dentist by profession, a tubercular from his youth, John Henry Holliday (1851–1887) spent fifteen of his thirty-six years gambling and roaming the West—Dallas, Denver, Cheyenne, Deadwood, Dodge City, Las Vegas, New Mexico, Tombstone, Tucson, and finally Glenwood Springs, Colorado—most often a few steps ahead of the law. He was a high-profile friend of Wyatt Earp's and a participant in the O.K. Corral gun battle in Tombstone, Arizona Territory, in 1881 and, together with Jesse James, Billy the Kid, Wyatt Earp, and Bat Masterson, is a name from the Wild American West recognized around the world.

Doc Holliday dying: a fabled tableau, perhaps best depicted in film by Val Kilmer in *Tombstone* (1993); most memorably in print, here, by Art Knight.

Born in San Francisco, Arthur Winfield Knight has been a public school teacher and university professor, and is a playwright, poet, novelist, editor, and an authority on Jack Kerouac and the Beat generation writers of San Francisco. His novels include *Blue Skies Falling*, *Johnnie D.* (on John Dillinger), *The Cruelest Month* (short stories), *Outlaw Voices* (poems), and *The Secret Life of Jesse James*. His wife, Kit, is a poet and critic.

He leaned over the bed. It was hot in the room, humid, and Wyatt remembered why he had never liked the deep South although his best friend had come from there, the best friend who was now dying on the small bed next to the corner window with its smudged panes weeping in the heat.

"How are you, Doc?"

Holliday had always been gaunt but he seemed to have shriveled, like a carrot left out in the sun. Probably he didn't weigh a hundred pounds now and his face seemed gray in the bleak light that shone through the dirty window.

"Dying's a dirty business," Doc said, as if reading Wyatt's thoughts, "and I've been at it a long time. I'm tired." He coughed and spat blood into a handkerchief that used to be white. Wyatt had seen him cough and spit a thousand times, but he'd never seen him so wracked and bent—and old.

"You'll be all right," Wyatt said.

"I made a pretty good living playing cards because I could read people," Doc said. "I studied them, made them my business. I know you, Wyatt. That's why you could never beat me at cards." He coughed again. "We've never lied to each other, so don't start now just because I'm dying. Leave the bullshit at the door, all right?"

"All right," Wyatt said, stepping to the window. He watched the steam rising from a huge swimming pool heated by hot springs. The water was supposed to be medicinal.

Doc propped himself up with two pillows and wheezed from the exertion. He picked up a bell from the small table next to his bed and rang it. When no one came to the door, he rang again. He tried to yell but his voice was raspy. "Goddamnit, what do I have to do to get some service around here? I need a bottle of whiskey. Wyatt, get me one, will you?"

· · ·

DOC DAYDREAMED. HE SAW HIMSELF STANDING IN A GARDEN BE-
hind his parents' house in Valdosta. The moon shimmered in the
heat and he could hear the cicadas in the tall grass. He wove a gardenia into his cousin's hair, his hands shaking. He said, "Mattie, I
can't marry you now. I can't marry anyone."

"Why?"

"My doctor told me I have consumption."

"I don't care," Mattie said. "Maybe it can be cured. I'll pray for
a miracle."

"Might as well pray for rain," Doc said. It was muggy. Heat
lightning cracked the sky. "I was told a drier climate might help. If
it does, I'll send for you, wherever I am. Meantime, I'll have to do
the dark dance alone."

Mattie dabbed at her face with a white handkerchief that looked
like a moth fluttering in the moonlight.

A BELLHOP WEARING A RED SUIT AND A MATCHING RED HAT, LIKE
a fez without a tassel, pushed Doc's chair to the vapor caves. Doc
thought the man looked like an organ grinder's monkey.

"You shouldn't let people make a monkey out of you," he said,
trying to smile. The bellhop was probably fifty, but people called him
boy. I'd rather be dying of consumption than dress like that, Doc
thought, as the man helped him onto a bench in the cave.

Naked except for a towel around his middle, Doc breathed
deeply, sucking steam into his lungs. He began to cough. Sometimes
he thought the vapor aggravated his condition. He told the bellhop,
"I want you to get me a bottle of whiskey before I expire from
thirst."

"Sir, I don't think the doctors want you to drink."

"I'm not paying you to think," Doc said. "Drinking's the only
satisfaction I have left. It's as if there's a conspiracy against me." He
peered through the steam. "Are you a part of it?"

"No, sir, I'm not."

"Then I want you to get that bottle and run back as fast as you
can. If you make it in less than ten minutes, there'll be a five-dollar
gold piece waiting for you once we get out of this goddamn cave
and back to my room. Do you understand?"

"Yes, sir," the bellhop said.

. . .

HE STILL REMEMBERED KATE SAYING, "I CAN ONLY STAND SO much respectability, Doc."

They had been living in Dodge City, where he was practicing dentistry, for three months, but he missed the flash of the cards across the green felt tables and the smoky light at the Long Branch and the good tension that came as you waited to draw into a flush or a full house.

"I'm your woman," Kate said, "but I need to go back to work." She'd been a prostitute when they'd met and she missed her calling, too, no matter how improbable that seemed.

She called herself Mrs. Holliday that summer. They were two of a kind. Doc understood that, but he didn't like it. He sat across from her at the Dodge House, sipping crème de menthe over crushed ice. He said, "You don't need to work, Kate."

"I'm gonna go crazy sittin' around the house all day with you gone. A woman can only do so much shoppin'."

He watched her wipe the sweat from her breasts that filled the low-cut blouse she wore. It was ten at night, a hundred and ten degrees. He remembered how hard it was to breathe.

"I can't allow it, Kate."

"I'm not askin' your permission," she said. "You can like it or lump it."

He leaned back, swirling the green liquid in his glass. "Then I guess I'll have to lump it."

"I'VE BROUGHT JOSIE, DOC."

The light in the room seemed hazy and for a moment he thought he must be back at the Oriental Saloon or the Birdcage Theater in Tombstone. "Mattie," he said. "Mattie."

"No, it's Josie," Wyatt said. "My wife."

He remembered. She was a thin Jewish girl who'd come to Tombstone with a theater company from San Francisco. She had been Sheriff Behan's mistress, but had left him for Wyatt. She had long black hair and firm breasts and he liked her because she'd been good for Wyatt.

When Josie took his hand, he said, "I'm sorry I can't get up out of this bed to greet you properly but I've been indisposed recently."

"Wyatt told me," Josie said. She almost seemed to sing when she spoke, trilling her words, and Doc remembered seeing her in a light opera the night they met.

"However, indisposed as I may be, I believe I can offer the two of you a drink. Would you prefer whiskey or whiskey?" he asked and he tried to laugh. "I'm afraid you'll have to take it straight and all I have are water glasses. I've complained on numerous occasions, but the room service here remains terrible."

"I'll take the whiskey," Josie said.

EVEN AS HE FLOATED IN AND OUT OF CONSCIOUSNESS, DOC remembered: It was the last Wednesday in October. He was finishing a breakfast of ham and eggs at a time when most people had already eaten lunch. He sat on one of the high stools along the bar at the Alhambra Saloon, drinking orange juice with a liberal amount of dark rum. He called it dirty orange juice and it was what he drank each afternoon when he began his day.

Doc pushed his way through the swinging doors to the saloon. He saw Wyatt and his two brothers coming down Fremont Street. Doc was wearing a long gray coat, a red brocade vest, and gray pants. He leaned on a fancy cane he'd purchased in Denver. He watched the group come toward him until they were less than ten feet away. "Where're you going, Wyatt?" It was a rhetorical question. Doc would follow them whether they were going for a drink at one of the saloons down the street or departing for Paris, France.

"We've got some business with the Clantons and McLaurys," Wyatt said. "They've been shooting off their filthy mouths, telling everyone what they're going to do to us, and we're tired of it."

"It's about time," Doc said. "I'm glad I'm up early or I wouldn't be able to get in on the fun."

"You saved my life once," Wyatt said. "You don't have to do it again. It might get you killed this time."

"I've been dying for years," he said.

"Take this," Virgil said. He was a United States Marshal. He handed Doc a sawed-off shotgun in exchange for his cane. The four of them continued along Fremont under a sullen sky. Doc could see snow on the peaks of the Dragoon Mountains in the distance as they headed toward a vacant lot next to the O.K. Corral. They walked slowly, their boots kicking up the red sand from the street.

Sheriff Behan ran out to meet them as they passed Bauer's Butcher Shop. Behan raised his right hand and said, "I don't want any trouble. I told the Clantons and McLaurys that and they've promised to give me their weapons."

"In a pig's ass," Doc said as he and the others pushed their way past Behan. Everyone knew he was in league with the outlaw element.

"I'm telling you not to go any farther," Behan yelled. "I'm the law in this county," but nobody answered.

They approached the lot next to the O.K. Corral, its gate flapping and banging in the wind. Five men were waiting for them. Doc liked the odds, liked a good fight. Last night, when he was in the Alhambra, Ike Clanton had threatened Wyatt and his brothers and he had slapped Ike's face and told him, "Go for your gun," but Ike had said he didn't have one. Well, he'd better have one now.

Wyatt said, "You sons of bitches have been looking for a fight so we'll give you one right here."

Someone yelled, "Let 'em have it," then a gun banged—then another and another, then everyone was firing. Doc watched Frank McLaury double over, his eyes wide, as Wyatt's bullet hit him in the stomach.

Tom McLaury shot at Doc and yelled, "I've got you now, you bastard," but the bullet ricocheted off Doc's holster. He shot McLaury in the chest with the sawed-off shotgun and said, "Not yet, you don't."

McLaury was lifted off his feet by the heavy double charge of buckshot. For a moment his body seemed to levitate against the blue Dragoons in the distance, then he landed on his back in a pile of tin cans and garbage.

When the shooting stopped, after less than a minute, two of the five outlaws were dead and another—a boy—was dying. He lay on his back, staring at the sun, groping for a pistol he couldn't reach.

The boy said, "Pull off my boots. I promised my mother I'd never die with my boots on."

Wyatt looked at his brothers and at Doc, grinning, his face smudged. Virgil and Morgan were wounded, but they were still standing. People yelled to each other as they ran down Fremont Street. Doc's ears were ringing. Unlike the boy, he wanted to die with his boots on.

I always knew you'd come back, Mattie says.

It has been fifteen years since they've seen each other, but she has not aged. Her skin is still pale, there are no lines around her eyes, and her body seems evanescent as she walks across the garden toward him in the warm summer rain.

I can't believe it's you, Doc says. He'd heard she had grown tired of waiting for him and had become a Sister of Charity. He's glad it's not true. The gardenia he wove into her hair still shimmers in the moonlight.

I told you I'd pray for a miracle, Mattie says, told you your cough would go away and that we'd be able to get married and have children.

I never believed it, Doc says, but I'm glad it will turn out that way.

Wyatt and Josie held hands, their heads bowed, as the Reverend Rudolph delivered the eulogy. He said, "John A. Holliday died yesterday at ten A.M. but his spirit now resides with the Lord."

Wyatt whispered, "At least he could have gotten Doc's middle initial right."

Josie said, "It doesn't matter, Wyatt. He's gone now. All that matters is that we remember him."

They could see the Roaring Fork and Colorado rivers from where they were standing on the bluff in the Linwood Cemetery. It was late afternoon and the sky was purple over the Crystal Valley. Rain clouds hovered over the dark mountains.

The reverend said, "Doctor Holliday came to Glenwood Springs last May and by his quiet and gentlemanly demeanor during his short stay, and the fortitude and patience he displayed in his last two months of life, he made many friends. That he had his faults none will attempt to deny; but who among us has not, and who shall be the judge of these things?

"Let us pray for his soul."

"Amen," Wyatt said.

Letters to the Stove

ELAINE LONG

I have been greedy for the facts of my own Western heritage," Elaine Long wrote in an eloquent letter accompanying this story. "My relatives spread out on ranches throughout Colorado, Wyoming, and Montana. Whenever I visited or worked there, I always met the women who stayed on the ranches and helped make them profitable . . . The women worked terribly hard (and still do), and they yearned for culture and beauty.

"I have come to believe, after knowing these women and hearing of their mothers and grandmothers, that, while the West was won by men, it was *held* by the women who stayed."

Elaine Long of Colorado is a novelist and a writer of short stories and songs, member of the Author's Guild and Western Writers of America, and founding member of Women Writing the West. Her books include *Canyon Wings, Bear Ridge, Tunnel Vision,* and *Jenny's Mountain,* which won the Medicine Pipe Bearer's Award from WWA.

The research she has conducted for her novels about contemporary women of the West has taken her from seventy feet down a mine shaft to 13,500 feet above sea level (as pilot of a Cessna 172), and from the lambing sheds of Montana to the bear dens of Utah.

NORA O'NEAL RELUCTANTLY
crossed out October 31 on the wall calendar by the table. Standing
for a moment, pencil in hand, she looked out into the drab dawn.
Clouds massed in the west beyond the river, bare cottonwoods in
front, gray on gray.

She built up the fire and set the teakettle over the open stove
hole. There wouldn't be any coffee until John got back, but she could
drink hot water and warm herself against the day.

November first. John was overdue. It looked like snow. She
hated November.

She sat at the table, waiting on the kettle. Her writing paper and
pencil lay there as always. "Dear Mama, I am alone." She crossed
that out and started again. "Dear Mama, John has gone on his annual
fall ramble. He calls it a roundup, a necessary trip to get the cattle
to market. So few of our cattle, Mama, so many days to drive them
somewhere — anywhere — for a buyer. He's always gone too long. His
uncle Walter always finds him more cowboying to do . . ."

She thought of the early October day John had left. He'd come
to the door and stepped down from the saddle for the lunch she had
packed. The dog and Davy, the boy he had hired, waited behind the
steers, seventeen of them. Davy was riding her horse. John stowed
the lunch in his saddle bag.

"I hate to leave you alone. Don't forget that shotgun."

She leaned against him, her head as high as his shoulder. "I
won't." She heard the tense, tight sound in her voice, as they stood
looking toward the dust and noise of the small herd.

He said, "I wouldn't go if I didn't have to."

She looked up at him then. "Yes you would." She saw his jaw
tighten, but didn't care. "Nine years since we claimed our home-
steads, four years since you bought this place, and every year you've
said the same thing. 'I wouldn't go if I didn't have to.' But if we had

371

ten hired men, you'd still go. You'll *never* be done cowboyin'.'"

John's weathered face deepened a shade, and the blue in his eyes cooled to an icy gray, but all he said was, "I'll get the things on your list."

He put a foot in the stirrup, swung the other leg over the saddle, and wheeled away.

"We didn't part well, Mama. I was shrewish in my fear."

What if I never see his blue eyes again? She looked out the window—the dreary view outside the precious window. She bit the pencil. "I insisted on going with him once, Mama. That was a mistake. When he's cowboyin', he drinks. Not like Papa, but it changes him. His eyes go gray and cold."

Nora tossed the pencil on the table and rose. She tore the sheet in half, lifted the teakettle, and dropped the pieces into the fire. She couldn't write a letter like that to her mother. It wasn't fair to worry her mother. It wasn't right to criticize her husband.

The teakettle began to rumble. She poured a cup of hot water and sat down again at the table, holding the hot cup to her cheek. She looked out the window at the dried, dead pastures, gray as the sky. They needed snow, any moisture, but, dear God, not until John got home.

"Dear Mama, Today I was thinking about the fringed scarf on your piano—the velveteen one with all the colors—the rose and mauve and violet and magenta and gold and green and blue. Blue, deeper and bluer than John's eyes. John's eyes are the only color around here all winter."

Suddenly, the Irish in her rose . . . a great flood of pent-up tears washed against her breastbone, stealing her breath, pushing up into her throat. *I will not cry.* The German in her set her jaw, and she clamped her teeth until the tide began to ebb. The silence moved in around her, the fire in the stove licking softly at the wood.

She pushed her cup aside, rose, and reached for her coat, hat, and gloves. Any company would be better than her own—the cow, the chickens, that aggravating pig.

"If you can, keep that pig in the pen and get him as fat as possible," John had said. "We'll butcher when I get back."

She wrinkled her nose. Butchering a fat hog was a greasy, messy business. But the lard was good. She used it all year long. She salted the meat and layered it in the crock, alternating pork and lard and pork and lard. But now, last year's pork was gone, the lard too.

She stepped through the back door into the shed, grateful again to the unknown builder of this house. John would never have built her a lean-to for hanging laundry on cold days, for a cool pantry for butter and cream, for washing up on the way in from the barn. John would not improve a house until the barns and corrals were adequate, and that was never going to be.

He saw no reason for the back door either. "Just another place to let in cold air," he said. "Ought to board it up." But she protested and he didn't mention it again.

Nor had he wanted the window. But four years ago, at another roundup season when he had left her to go cowboyin' for Uncle Walter, he'd promised to bring her whatever she wanted. When she said, "Window glass," he had tried to talk her out of it.

"Wouldn't you rather have some pretty cloth — a rocking chair — a mirror?"

"I know what I look like," she had said. "I don't want to see me. I want to see through these walls."

She picked up the milk bucket now and stepped outside. Bending her head against the wind which tugged at her hair and whipped her skirts around her, she walked to the barn, a sturdy log building with layers of sod around the bottom to add strength and warmth.

The cow swayed and bumped her way into the stall from the corral in a familiar ritual. Nora fastened the stanchion, dumped a can of oats into the manger, then placed the milking stool beneath her, and sat. Bending her head against Bess's side, she brushed the tough, hairy bag and began to milk.

Bess ate the oats, then humped her back and raised her tail to pee. Nora stepped away until the cow had finished the steaming spray. She wiped the bag again with her glove to be sure the teats were clean and finished milking. She stripped the teats, rose, and hung the milk stool on its nails on the barn wall, and set the pail of foaming milk on the oat bin while she released Bess from the stall and put her into the corral. She opened the gate to the pasture. She hoped the cow would stay around. It would be a cold walk this evening. "I hate it when John takes my horse," she said aloud to Bess. "You stay close."

She opened the chicken house and scattered feed for her laying hens, the tough old rooster, and the three old hens that were destined for the dumpling pot.

She took a hammer and nail can to the pigpen. The pig grunted and rustled among the husks on the ground until she tossed in some ears of dried corn. He was an ugly beast—gray-white, ill-tempered. Last year's pig had been a pretty black-and-white belted Hampshire; this one came rumbling to the fence where she gave him another helping of corn to keep him busy while she renailed the boards they had put across the hole where he had escaped before.

"Now stay put. Make lots of lard. That Hampshire didn't last."

She stood in the cold, looking at the animal she was going to help kill in a week or two. Glancing at the barren land beyond the barn, she thought suddenly again of the colorful piano scarf and then of the piano itself. In the nine years that she had been married to John, she had never touched a piano. She had had her hands on a lot of things: the garden shovel, fencing tools, calf hooves and afterbirth, the rope on the well bucket, the branding iron, the raw lye soap she used for her wash, corn for this pig. But never once, not once in nine years, had she touched a piano.

A fierce gust of wind rattled the pigpen gate. She turned back to the barn for the milk, set the bucket on the table in the lean-to, and went back out into the wind for a bucket of water from the well. She strained the milk through a cloth into a crock, then rinsed the cloth and hung it over the rope clothesline John had strung inside the shed. The milk cloth was as gray as her dish towels and the sheets and her faded everyday dress. She was almost out of blueing, not that she could see that it did much good in the rinse water.

She decided to bring in enough water to wash the sheets and brought in more wood to build up the fire. She set the tub on the stove and filled it, but only halfway because John was not there to help her lift it from the stove.

She stripped the bed in the corner of the room opposite the table, pulling the quilt back over it. In nine years of everyday use, her wedding quilt had faded too. She glanced out of the window, hoping for a sliver of blue sky, but the clouds seemed heavier than they had at dawn.

While waiting for the wash water to heat, she sliced a piece of bread and covered it with butter and some of the wild plum jam she'd made in early fall. She never felt like cooking big meals when John was away.

She eased the tub from the stove onto the two kitchen chairs, put the washboard in it, pushed the sheets down into the hot water and then scrubbed each of them on the board, using the square bar of lye soap she had made last fall.

The sheets were heavy and scalding hot. She wrung them quickly, draping the twisted rope of muslin over her shoulder. Her hands had turned bright red. She dipped out the wash water with the bucket until she could handle the tub.

She rinsed the sheets in cold water in the shed and looked at her hands—large, capable, bony. *A description of me,* she thought as she draped the sheets over the clothesline in the corner of the shed. As she'd told John, she didn't need a mirror to see the combination of her Scotch-Irish mother and her Pennsylvania Dutch father. She was glad of the German in her makeup. If she cried at everything the way her mother did, she'd never have lasted out here—doing the required work to get the deed on the homestead she had claimed before their marriage and then helping to build the shack on John's claim as well. Her mother cried for sad, cried for happy, her red face turning redder, her curly red hair ever a bush, her faded blue eyes teared and watery. Nora had inherited the wild hair and the sensitive skin, but her eyes were like her father's, that indiscriminate color called hazel.

She had also inherited her mother's tendency to weep, but never gave in to it. When her father drank and roared, and her mother wailed and cowered, Nora looked her father in the eye, squared her German jaw, and left home as soon as she could find a job.

Such thoughts were gray as November.

It was nearly noon when she took the mending basket to the table, pushed her writing materials back, and sat down in John's chair, which gave her a better view out of the window. She glanced toward the river. Six months at least before the cottonwoods might show a hint of green.

She slipped her darning egg into one of John's socks and began the tedious job of interweaving the threads to make a smooth repair of the hole at the heel. The light was poor, but the coal oil was low, and she needed the lamp for the early dark. She glanced at the shelf above the bed, at the Bible, the Almanac, and the two Scott novels her mother had sent. The evenings would be endless if she didn't have a light for reading.

With her chair closer to the window, she thought she saw some kind of movement about halfway across the near pasture. She scanned the colorless field, but nothing moved except the windblown dry grass.

She bent to her darning, lifting her eyes from time to time to rest them. She glanced at her writing materials, the next-to-last sheet of paper. *How many of those letters did I actually mail?* One had been sent to her mother when they had proved up on their claims, another after John had bought this place and they had moved here. She'd written when she was first pregnant, but that had been winter, and by the time someone rode through who could have taken the letter, she had already miscarried. That one had gone in the stove. Only once had she mailed a letter about Uncle Walter. The German had risen sharply in her when John had come back with less money than their own cows had brought, even though he'd also gone to cowboy for Uncle Walter for three weeks. Her mother's reply, suggesting that John needed to stand up to his uncle, had not set well with John. She never mailed another of her money-worry letters. And this time, she hadn't even told *John* yet that she was pregnant. After being so long barren, what were her chances of carrying this baby full-term?

She had almost finished darning a third sock when her chickens began a terrified cackling. She dropped the mending into the basket, strode across the shed, and reached for the shotgun by the back door. *That was probably a coyote I saw earlier in the grass.*

She stepped out and stopped abruptly. A small, bearded, dirty man in gray clothes had just wrung the neck of her best laying hen. She was about to raise the gun when the man turned toward her.

He was gaunt—the cheekbones and the bones over his eyes prominent, his cheeks themselves sunken. The creature was starving, and caught in the act of killing her chicken, he simply stood and gazed at her with yellowy-green eyes, somewhat like those of a coyote's. Except that the man did not look crafty or defiant like a coyote. The yellow eyes were desperate.

Nora set the shotgun on its stock against the wall of the lean-to. "Well, since you've killed my best laying hen, you'd better pick it and clean it so I can cook it."

The man stepped forward, then stopped and looked down at his hands. He still clutched the bled-out chicken by its leathery feet. "Ma'am, I'm too dirty to touch food. Do you suppose I could wash first?"

She was amazed. He was starving, but wanted to wash. "Come into the shed. I'll get the teakettle."

The man put the hen into the milk bucket she gave him, and Nora poured water into the gray enamel wash pan. The little man dived greedily into the wash pan and despite the icy air in the shed took time to wash his face, ears, neck, hands, and wrists, and to dry vigorously with the rough, gray towel from the nail above the washstand. Nora poured the rest of the boiling water over the chicken, scalding it thoroughly.

The man replaced the towel and, leaving his sleeves turned back from his scrawny wrists, began to tear away the sodden gray-white feathers with quick, practiced strokes.

Watching the agile hands, Nora said, "You've done that before."

The man tossed her a quick glance. "I used to help my mother," and then, his face coloring, he added wryly, "I've picked a few hens lately." He grinned at her, startling her with the sweet humor that leapt into his eyes. "But I haven't picked a *scalded* hen for quite a while."

"While you finish there, I'll stir up some dumplings," Nora said.

The man asked for a knife, and she gave him her best one. *John would be appalled. Not only had she set the gun aside, she had handed this stranger—this chicken thief—a sharp knife.*

While they waited for the chicken to cook, the man warmed himself at the stove and then, after wolfing down the bread and jam she gave him, said, "I'm sorry I killed your best laying hen."

Nora laughed (and was aware how long it had been since she had heard herself or anyone laugh). "It's probably a good thing you did. If you'd killed one of those tough old hens I was heading toward the stewpot, it would be morning before it was tender enough to chew."

When the chicken was nearly ready, she dropped the dumplings into the greasy broth. "Sit," she said, nodding toward John's chair. She set the table with her plain heavy white crockery plates instead of the tin ones she and John used most of the time. The man glanced at her letter. She felt it would be rude to snatch it up, and so she simply served the chicken and dumplings.

The man was obviously starving, yet he ate with manners; after his first helping, even taking time to make conversation.

"Is this your homestead?" he asked.

"It's a homestead, but it wasn't originally ours," she said. "After we got the deeds to our own places, John mortgaged his to buy this place."

"But not your claim?" The man grinned at her.

She felt herself blush. "I wouldn't let him mortgage my claim. It's got a good spring and good meadow grass. We could go back there if we lost the other two."

"Did you know the people you bought this from?"

"No. John got it from the bank. The man just left after his wife died." Nora nodded toward the back of the house. "She's buried a ways out behind the barn." She looked out the window. "John hopes someday to buy river-bottom land. We can't afford it now. We'd do a lot better with river-bottom."

She enjoyed watching the man's face—his name was Luther, he'd said—as he filled his plate once more and ate. After refusing a third helping, he turned to her with that quick smile that had brightened his face before. Now that he didn't look like a small, starving boy, she was aware that he was a man, a strange man, but a man. She smiled too.

"You're wrong, you know," the man said. For a moment she thought he'd been reading her mind, but he gestured toward her letter. "There are many colors here, even if John's blue eyes are gone." He studied her. "There's that beautiful strawberry-red hair that sparkles in the firelight when you open the stove. And when you stood in the door with that shotgun, your face was a wondrous rosy red. And just now, as you start to disapprove of my words, your eyes are gray and rust-speckled and glowing with a greenish light. I wish I could paint you."

Nora could not speak. Her eyes filled, but she blinked the tears away.

He said softly again, "I wish I could paint you."

His words gave her an odd fluttery feeling in the pit of her stomach. She swallowed and finally managed to speak. "Don't," she said hoarsely. Her breath caught because the man's golden eyes never left her face. "Please don't," she whispered.

Luther looked out the window. The wood crackled in the stove, but before the silence became uncomfortable, he turned to her and smiled again. He reached for her last clean sheet of paper. "There are all kinds of colors here." He looked out the window once more, then asked, "Do you have some lard?"

"No, we're out of lard, but I have butter," Nora said, puzzled.

Luther rose, and picking up one of the white plates, said, "I'll be right back." He hurried through the lean-to and out the back door.

She took a deep breath. Her mother would be shocked that she had let a man speak to her that way. John would be furious that she had let the man in at all. But the day was so much lighter, and Nora was filled with a glittering curiosity.

He came gracefully through the door carrying her plate and a handful of chicken feathers. When he set the plate on the table, she could see that he had made three separate heaps on it—one of ashes, one of the reddish-tan dirt found near her garden, and one of the black dirt from around the chicken house.

"It was a real shock to lose my kit, my gear, and all my paints in the river," he said. "I never knew it would get that deep." He took the other empty plate and said, "May I use some butter?"

"Won't the butter just make a greasy mess?"

"That's a possibility." His eyes sparkled. "But I wasn't planning to hang this picture in the Louvre." He used a knife as a scoop and a mixing tool. He put butter on the empty plate, added a heap of ashes, and mixed them into a gray paste, which he then spread evenly over the paper.

He lifted the stove lid and ran a chicken feather around the edge of the hole until the feather was black with soot. With a few deft strokes, he sketched the trees and the line of the riverbank about three-quarters of the way up the page. Before Nora could remark on the grayish tinge, he had mixed more butter, this time with the red dirt, and dipping another feather into the mix, he began to re-create the grasses of the pasture that stretched almost from her window to the river.

As he put in tawny vertical strokes on the gray background, she could see that he was actually painting what was there. She had not really seen that pasture. The colors were subtle shades of ochre, orange, and tan, and suddenly a plummy red. Without asking, the artist had spooned a little wild plum jam onto the plate and was adding a deeper shadow to several clumps of taller grass.

He sketched swiftly, and Nora stood silently, filled with an odd sort of joy as Luther mixed the darker dirt and began to create shadows among the trees he had sketched along the river. Now the old cottonwoods were no longer gray on gray, but a rich, textured mix of brown and gray and creamy tan. The trees became a grove, deep and mysterious, with all sorts of shadows.

"I need some blue," he said.

"Blue? There's no blue in that sky."

"If I had some blue, I'd show you."

She moved into the shed and retrieved her blueing bottle which had a few drops in the bottom.

"Ahh!" He took the bottle and carefully, using another clean chicken feather, touched the sky above the riverline very lightly and then wiped away most of the color, leaving a faint wash of blue which brightened the whole scene. And when she looked from the picture to the river, Nora could see the faint bluish tinge there that kept the sky from being totally gray.

"It's wonderful," she said. "I never saw those colors before."

"I just wish I had some green," he said, and suddenly Nora was laughing again.

"You *can't* convince me there's any green out there on the first day of November."

Luther laughed with her. Nora said, "Wait. I do think I know where there's some green. There's a small frozen tomato on a vine near the front step. I don't know how a tomato planted itself there. It's all frozen now. I've been meaning to toss it into the pigpen."

She opened the front door and started out, but turned back immediately, shutting the door behind her. "The sheriff is coming up our lane," she said.

Luther's face paled, and he suddenly looked gaunt and hungry again—and frightened.

"Quick," Nora said, "come into the lean-to." Leading the way into the shed, she pulled aside the wet sheets which hung nearly to the floor. "Go back here, clear into the corner. Stay quiet." The artist stepped into the cramped space. She heard the sheriff call, "Hello, the house," as she dropped the sheet, tugging it a little so that it touched the floor.

Nora went to the front door and stepped out. "Well, hello, Barton. What brings you here?" Her heart jumped as she asked, "It's not John?"

The sheriff had stepped from his horse. "No, no, Nora. Nothing like that. It's really just a small thing."

She released her breath and said, "Well, come in. It's cold out here." The sheriff followed her into the cabin. "I can't offer you coffee," she said, "I'm out, but how about a hot dish of chicken and dumplings?"

The sheriff grinned and put his hat on John's chair. "I'd like that, Nora. I know your chicken and dumplings. But I'll have to eat on the run. I've got a few more places to go today."

She dished up some of the hot food. "Are you stumping for reelection way out here?"

He took the plate and spoon she offered and scooped up a big bite. "No, actually I'm trying to warn folks. It seems we've got a thief in the area. He's hit several henhouses on his way through, and someone thought they saw him head up the river your way."

"Well," she said, "it's quiet around here." It was the truth. There wasn't a sound from the shed.

The sheriff downed the rest of the chicken and dumplings, handed her the plate, and glanced through the lean-to door. "I see you've got your shotgun handy. That's good. Might be a good idea to take it with you when you do chores."

He picked up his hat and stood for a moment looking at the unfinished picture which lay amid the odd clutter of saucers and feathers, the paper a bit crumpled from the moisture in the butter and jam. He glanced from the picture to the view out the window and said, "You've done a lot with that dead grass."

"I'm trying to see more color out there," she said. That was true now too. "Sometimes, November gets me down."

"Well, I reckon John will be home one of these days. Ain't nobody movin' cattle this late."

"He let his hired hand ride my horse," Nora said. "I haven't been able to check on our cattle. They're on the grass on my claim, and they're probably okay. The stream never freezes completely because of that spring. If you go by there, would you give 'em a look?"

"Glad to," said the sheriff. "I better get going. It's late, and it gets dark pretty early now." She walked with him to the door. "Thanks for the food," he said. "Keep that shotgun handy."

She shut the door and stood on the front step until the sheriff's hat was all she could see far down the lane

In the lean-to, she pulled the sheet aside. "He's gone."

Luther came into her kitchen. "I'd better go too."

"You can't leave yet. They're looking for you. Someone might see you." She smiled at him. "Besides, you haven't shown me the green in that picture." She retrieved the green tomato outside the door.

He squashed a small amount of the pulp on a saucer and, with a few light strokes, made a faint green undershadow around some of the clumps of grass. Then he added a whisper of green to the horizon line along the river. And that green was actually there, although in the fading daylight, it was dim.

"Green. The color of hope," Nora said.

"I'd better go," he said.

"You'll freeze to death out there in the dark. Why don't you stay in the barn and leave in the morning?"

The eyes that turned to her now were golden and warm again. "I can't stay. It would never do for someone to see me leaving your place, especially leaving in the morning."

He left by the back door and disappeared toward the river in the dusky light.

She went back to the table and picked up the dishes, scraped off the paint and washed and dried them and placed them on the shelf.

She held the picture in her hand for a long time. The butter would turn rancid, the jam and tomato would spoil. John knew she had never painted a picture in her life. She stepped to the stove, lifted the lid, and dropped the picture into the flames, which crackled greedily all about the butter-soaked paper. When the picture was no more than a curl of black, she turned back to the table and picked up her unfinished letter, dropped it into the fire, and replaced the stove lid.

East Breeze

DAN AADLAND

Here, a short-story master works with a deceptively simple concept: a Norwegian rancher named Knute surveys his lands and finds a Crow Indian burial scaffold up in a pine tree. That sacred place and its occupant makes Knute think, and thereby makes us think.

Although not stated in the story, the locale of this poetic tale is somewhere in south-central Montana, probably near the town of Absarokee, a short distance west of the Crow Indian Reservation and Agency and the Little Bighorn battlefield.

Dan Aadland is a cattle rancher, manager of a Tennessee Walking Horse breeding and training facility, and a writer. He is a Marine Corps veteran of Vietnam, a Ph.D. (in American studies at the University of Utah), and a teacher of English, drama, and social studies, with twenty-two years' experience in Montana. His books include *Sketches from the Ranch: A Montana Memoir, Women and*

Warriors of the Plains, Horseback Adventures, and his periodical work has appeared in *Equus, Western Horseman, Montana Outdoors,* and many other publications.

He rode across the just-completed wooden bridge, grunted "Good" at the solid sound of hooves on rough-cut cottonwood planks, crossed the spring-high creek, and headed east toward the hill pasture. From a distance the hills were April green, but he needed a closer look to see if the grass was tall enough to carry the hungry herd cooped in barn and corral, now devouring the last forkfuls of hay from the loft.

From a post to his right a meadowlark sang. New grass, wet with dew, scented with sage, tugged at him. The pony single-footed along, snorted, warmed with the pull of the slope. Yes, it was good, *svaert gud*. It was his and it was good. The Indians were gone, moved east, and so was the government, the fort and the agency just ruins now. He'd bought one of the outbuildings left at the agency and skidded it behind his work team, Per and Peder, the half-mile to his homestead to sit by the new log barn and someday be a chicken house.

He was not sure when he first smelled it. The pony knew too, his measured gait slackening, his ears going up. It did not belong there, mingled with the good smells in the breeze that eased toward him down the slope. Maybe just a deer, dead since winter, ripening now in the April sun. And then it was stronger, and the pony balked, and then both of them saw it, the platform in the gnarled pine, cross poles spanning low branches, a blanket hung with trinkets spread on the poles, an object of weight inside.

For a moment he froze, staring at the mouth of the coulee looking upward toward the burial. "Heathens, goddamn heathens." He kicked the pony forward, clawing for the lariat, tearing it from its niche by the saddle horn. And then he stopped. On the crest of the hill, on the skyline just to the side of the morning sun, on a painted pony and leading another, was an Indian, motionless. Across two hundred yards of sage and sandstone their eyes met and held. Vapor rose from the nostrils of the ponies, and the sun filtered through the vapor. Slowly the Indian raised his right hand, and, still watching, lowered it, turned, and was gone. Knute still stared. Then he carefully replaced his rope.

The burial would stay, at least for now. He would not like it, riding widely around, his pony spooking at the smell whenever they came close. He would not like avoiding a spot on a ranch that was his. But the chiseled image of the Crow spoke somehow of prior claim, and for a reason Knute himself did not understand it was a claim he would honor. He would tell his hired man to leave it alone. It would stay.

A WEEK LATER THE GRASS WAS GREEN BUT STILL SHORT. HE CIR-cled the range on his pony, circled it gingerly, glad when the pony stepped on quiet earth instead of noisy rocks. He talked to himself and the horse in soft Norwegian. There was something in the air begging not to be disturbed, something he honored grudgingly. It was there in the air when the wind was just right, but there in other ways too. So he rode carefully, starting his circle of the full-section, mile-square range clockwise. The range was still unfenced, but he knew the locations of his stakes so well he could ride from one to the next in a path as straight as a taut string, except when a big juniper or sandstone outcropping made him detour.

Ready or not, the grass would have to stand the cattle. The hay was gone. He would release them tomorrow after branding the calves, let them make their first frantic feed up the side hills, desperate for half-mouthfuls of something green. Then, riding daily circuits to keep them near home, he'd begin his barbed-wire fence.

Knute found the northeast stake and stopped to fill his pipe. Crocuses bloomed purple around the stake. It was pleasant here. He did not hurry. He found a likely spot for a gate in the eventual fence, dismounted and made a small pile of stones where each of the gate-posts would go. When his herd was larger he would join the asso-ciation of ranchers using the open range farther east, the range without nice creeks along which to homestead, the shared range.

On his way south Knute detoured back toward the center of his section onto the tracks of the road once called the Bozeman Trail.

He slowed the pony, eyeing the wagon tracks, which were bare of vegetation. Soon he saw them, saw where they crossed the road, confirming with tangible marks on the ground the existence of the ghostlike mounted Indian he'd seen last week. The tracks of two ponies pointed west toward the timbered coulee, two drag marks of travois poles flanking the tracks made by one of the ponies. A hundred yards farther south he struck the return tracks, the eastbound ones, the travois marks now gone. "He would have dumped the poles, or maybe used them to build it," Knute said aloud.

By the time he got to the southeast stake his hands were clutching the reins more tightly than needed. Turning west, the pony livened up, anxious for home, spooking at a jackrabbit that streaked out from a juniper. Knute cussed the horse more sternly than necessary, the Norwegian words rough. Then came the descent into the pine-studded coulee and the scent less terrible than expected. He could see it now, this time from above, the angle making the old tree seem smaller. On the platform through the blanket he could clearly see the shape of a body. He imagined his cattle working their way up the coulee. They would rub on the tree. They would bed under it, perhaps loosen the poles, maybe even . . .

"They had no need to be dumping it on me," he said to the pony. "There's plenty of room on Pryor Mountain." The pony stopped, eyeing suspiciously the stirrings of the platform and its contents, touched softly by the east breeze.

He circled upwind and tied the pony, which was oddly sedated now, to another tree, then faced the burial and made the sign of the cross as best he could remember the preacher doing it at the ancient Lutheran church on the fjord of his boyhood. He walked toward the tree from the uphill side and took the one long step needed to stand on a low branch and bring his head even with the shrouded one on the platform.

Old tales of grave robbers stirred and pinched him—it seemed an evil thing to do. But then, under his breath, "It's my ranch, damn it, I have a right to know. What am I to tell someday if I've never known?" So his hand went out gingerly and worked at the fold of the blanket, worked back the leather thong that wrapped it (the smell immediately worse, but bearable), and then peeled the blanket back. It was old and it was female, those things he could tell immediately, and it meant him no harm—that he could feel. It had come to be here for reasons he would never know, but which must have been awfully important to it, for there truly was much room on Pryor Mountain (which he had been able a few minutes ago to study, still snow-capped to the east). It was already decaying, but slowly, leathery, not putrid or green or maggot-ridden. The skin on the face was nearly black, the lips pulled back slightly revealing soiled teeth. The eyelids, closed after death, were now partly lifted, the whites of the eyes inside cast over with a green, puckered layer. A fly landed on her cheekbone. Knute hastily brushed it away, inadvertently touching the skin as he did so. He shuddered. Then, after a pause, he reached out and lightly touched her cheek again before replacing the blanket and securing it tightly under the thong.

The next day he returned. Before releasing the cattle he built a crude but strong, three-pole fence around the gnarled pine.

Big Tim Magoon and the Wild West

LOREN D. ESTLEMAN

J ust as it is impossible to think of the modern Western story without crediting Loren Estleman for his enormous contributions to it, it is impossible to think of the Old West without considering William Frederick "Buffalo Bill" Cody (1846–1917). His spectacular career defies capsulizing: Iowan, miner, trapper, Pony Express rider, Indian fighter, Kansas Jayhawker in the Civil War, scout, dispatch rider, stagecoach jehu, buffalo hunter, Indian agent, and the greatest showman of the nineteenth century (not excepting P. T. Barnum).

Cody's "Wild West" captivated audiences from 1882 until his death and any hint that Buffalo Bill was in the vicinity was enough to put a town's politicos in a tizzy, as is the case with Big Tim Magoon of Paris City . . .

A four-time Spur Award winner, Loren D. Estleman's first novel appeared in 1976 and in the twenty-six years since he has averaged two books a year (generally alternating between detective and Western novels) plus many stories, articles, and reviews.

Among his recent Western novels are *Black Powder, White Smoke; The Master Executioner, Billy Gashade, Journey of the Dead,* and the ongoing series of novels featuring Page Murdock, frontier marshal.

He is married to novelist Deborah Morgan.

prosperous county seat in the state for as long as most of its citizens could remember, and for as long as most of its citizens could remember, Big Tim Magoon had been its mayor.

Paris City was not named for Paris, France, and predated Paris, Texas. It was the largest producer of plaster of Paris products west of Chicago.

Every child who passed through Paris City's schools knew Big Tim's story: how he'd come over the Wahaxie Mountains at age nineteen looking for gold, and after riddling the foothills for three years had been about to give it up as a bad job and head back East when he discovered a vein of gypsum as wide as the Little Wahaxie River (which was actually bigger than the Big Wahaxie River, but by the time the mistake on the surveyors' map became known, it was too late to change). In the forty years that followed, a city of 40,000 had grown up around the Constance O'Faolin Magoon Plaster of Paris Works, named for Big Tim's deceased mother. Its founder's girth had grown as steadily, so that the gaunt pioneer of '52 whose framed lithograph appeared in banks and the post office next to President Harrison's required the assistance of a whalebone cane and an aide at each elbow to alight from his ivory-paneled, iron-reinforced phaeton before the Paris City Gentlemen's Club.

Despite this inconvenience, Big Tim was in ruddy good health for a man of sixty-two and three hundred thirty-nine pounds stripped. His huge muttonchopped face was sunburned from his famous marathon speeches upon the platform in Constance O'Faolin Magoon Park on Founder's Day, the Fourth of July, and every other holiday of spring and summer, and he was a skilled croquet player in matches conducted every Saturday afternoon on the front lawn of City Hall. His suits—sober black broadcloth in winter, dazzling white gabardine from May through August—were cut youthfully, and once upright and moving in a forward direction, he had a spring to his step, swinging his cane like a boulevardier.

Big Tim signed all official papers in his corner office overlooking the principal intersection of Stucco and Calcine streets and had his photograph taken there, shaking hands with John L. Sullivan and presenting checks to members of the board of governors of the Constance O'Faolin Magoon Memorial Hospital. However, anyone who wished to conduct business with the mayor was obliged to present himself in the foyer of the Paris City Gentlemen's Club and await an invitation to the game room, where Big Tim played whist, made free with the club's private stock of aged Irish whiskey, and either extended or withheld his blessing regarding city contracts, usually on the basis of hard cash or exchange of services.

It was in that room nearing the end of Big Tim's eighth term in office that the chairman of the state Democratic Party invited Big Tim to run for governor. The incumbent had announced his retirement, and so far only Olaf Krueger, an assemblyman residing in Craterville, the state's second most prosperous city, had announced his candidacy for the office on the Republican ticket. Big Tim deliberated only half a glass before accepting the call. Life in Paris City had begun to stagnate, and he hated Assemblyman Krueger—to whom he was pleased to refer during ceremonial occasions as "Oaf Krueger, the squareheadedest squarehead in Squareheadville"—with the kind of hatred that transcended all bounds, political and ethnic. The race was begun for November 1892.

On an unseasonably hot day in May of that year, a quiet man in his middle thirties removed his dove-gray bowler in the club foyer and inquired of the ancient steward if the Honorable Timothy Magoon was engaged at present. The steward looked at the fellow, at his neatly trimmed beard and unobtrusive lightweight charcoal worsted, and asked who was interested. The stranger handed him a business card, engraved in rich brown ink on good white stock:

BUFFALO BILL'S WILD WEST
Nate Salsbury, General Manager

The steward carried the card into another room. Moments later, he returned and asked Mr. Salsbury to follow him.

At that hour the game room had but one occupant, which is not to say that it was in any wise near empty. By dint of physical presence and personality, Big Tim appeared to fill the twenty-by-thirty-foot space from his leather and horsehair chair on the opposite side of the mahogany players' table. A game of Patience lay on the table's inlaid top. The business card in his broad manicured hand with its bulbous gold Knights of Columbus ring appeared scarcely larger than one of the beauty patches currently fashionable among the ladies of quality of Paris City. When the great man rose to shake his visitor's hand—a gesture afforded to very few, owing to the amount of engineering involved—the room shrank further. Mr. Salsbury, who was not himself a small man, might have been compared to a supplicant standing before a cathedral.

"Do I understand correctly that you represent Buffalo Bill?" inquired the mayor, after unwrapping his fingers and palm from the other's.

"I do, although he prefers to be addressed as Colonel Cody. He is a modest man."

"One would not know it from his advertising. The last time I came through Denver, his posters were plastered on every barn and telegraph pole for miles around."

Mr. Salsbury smiled faintly. "The Wild West is another matter. He comes close to boasting about that. As a matter of fact, it is the Wild West that I have come to discuss with you. One hears of Timothy Magoon everywhere in this state, and with nary a poster to bring it about. Colonel Cody decided, and I concurred, that you would be the man to approach about bringing our little exhibition to Paris City."

A tiny lurch of recognized opportunity—which Big Tim disguised as a belch—stirred his insides. "Your modesty outdistances your employer's. Your 'little exhibition' has appeared before the Queen of England, the Pope of Rome, and the President of the United States. Please have a seat, Mr. Salsbury. May I offer you a libation?"

"I am a man of temperance. I would not decline a glass of lemonade."

This proved a difficult order to fill in the Paris City Gentlemen's Club, but eventually a waiter appeared bearing a tray, by which time the two men were deep in discourse on opposite sides of the table.

"I shouldn't think the addition of a discreet banner would compromise the aesthetics of your posters," Big Tim said, his sly negotiator's smile firmly in place. " 'Timothy Magoon Presents Buffalo Bill's Wild West.' "

Mr. Salsbury's brow furrowed. "I doubt the colonel would concede the point. He is suspicious of outside sponsorship. Last year he turned down a princely investment offer from P. T. Barnum over the prospect of adding a freak show."

"I would not dream of interfering with the exhibition. I would sooner rearrange the Stars and Stripes. Leith Corcoran, the proprietor of the Emerald Isle Arena, is a personal friend and political supporter. I'm certain he will reduce his rental in response to my endorsement."

"The proprietor of the New Athens in Craterville has offered to waive his fee altogether, in return for a percentage of the concessions."

This was a blow to Big Tim's heart, Craterville being the base of operations of the despised Olaf Krueger. "Corcoran's a prudent businessman. I doubt he would refuse a similar arrangement." He fiddled with his untouched glass; lemonade had not been his drink of choice for half a century. "Purely as a matter of curiosity—"

"Five hundred dollars per performance is the average, from refreshments, programs, autographed pictures, and copies of Colonel Cody's biography. Twenty percent was suggested in Craterville, for six performances conducted during three days."

The mayor of Paris City carried an abacus in his head. Six hundred dollars would flood half the cities in the state with leaflets. Big Tim owned the Emerald Isle. Leith Corcoran's name appeared in the county records to hold down the property taxes. "I will speak to him," Big Tim said.

"We've put off answering the Craterville offer because the New Athens insists we put up a surety bond against liability. We had an unfortunate episode with a runaway buffalo last year in St. Louis," Salsbury added hastily. "A thousand dollars was the amount."

"Against property damage?"

"A man was killed in St. Louis. A regrettable accident, and unavoidable under the circumstances. The judge didn't see it that way.

The award to the family bankrupted the arena." The general manager of the Wild West show fidgeted uncomfortably.

"Forgive me for being blunt, Mr. Salsbury. Is Colonel Cody strapped for cash?"

"I find the phrase loathsome but, unhappily, accurate. The European tour, while a grand success, turned out to be more expensive than anticipated. The quarantine fees alone ran three times the cost of travel. That is why we're extending the homecoming excursion to include your state."

Big Tim heard music. "I have no doubt we can reach accord. Where can I get in touch with you?"

"The colonel and I are staying at the Hotel Olympus in Big Neck."

"Big Neck! That's only twenty miles away. How is it word didn't reach me of such an illustrious visitor?"

"As I said, the colonel is a modest man. He's traveling under the name of Horace Thorpe. The press, although a friend, is sometimes cumbersome."

"You and Colonel Cody must join me at my home tomorrow evening for dinner. Wire me what train you'll be arriving on and I'll send my phaeton to the station."

They shook hands.

"A THOUSAND DOLLARS!" LEITH CORCORAN'S LONG BLACK-IRISH face, usually as gray as a Killarney noon, flushed an unhealthy liver color.

Big Tim filled his glass from the siphon. The putative owner of the Emerald Isle Arena occupied the seat that had been vacated by Nate Salsbury an hour earlier. "Smooth your bristles, Leith. You won't have to pay it."

"It ain't the bond, it's what it represents. A man kilt! I'd be on hook for it. It ain't your name in the books."

"It's safe as houses. This year the odds against a buffalo running amuck are bigger than ever. The law of averages is on our side."

W. B. Halloran, chairman of the state Democratic Party (described by the opposition press, not without accuracy, as a "dyspeptic leprechaun"), stopped pacing and popped a fresh peppermint into his mouth. "I don't see why the party should have to put up the amount. Buffalo Bill's the one running the risk."

"If we don't put it up, the Republicans will, and Oaf Krueger will be our next governor. What he stands for don't matter. All the voters will remember is he brought the Wild West to Craterville."

"Corcoran could waive the bond requirement."

Corcoran shook his head sadly. "Tom Duncan was running the New Athens when all of us was in knickerbockers. If he won't take the risk, I sure won't."

"A thousand's precisely what we planned to spend on advertising at the capital," Halloran said.

"We'll get back three times the amount in contributions following the extravaganza." Big Tim drank. "Incidentally, the thousand ain't the end of it. Salsbury says adding a banner to the posters'll run another five hundred."

Halloran stuck a finger at him. "That comes out of your pocket, boyo. That amount's already budgeted for bands and bunting."

"I'll stand for the five hundred if the party will stand for the thousand."

The party chief chewed another peppermint and produced a checkbook from his inside breast pocket. Big Tim dipped a pen.

THE MAGOON HOUSE WAS A BRICK QUEEN ANNE, SPIRED, TUR-reted, and separated from its neighbors on North Sulphate Street by a wrought-iron fence painted the green of the Irish flag. Big Tim's phaeton rumbled through the open gate and a tall specimen of well-conditioned manhood stepped down behind Nate Salsbury. Buffalo Bill Cody flicked a limestone pebble off the white sleeve of his fringed doeskin jacket, removed his whiter Stetson, and ran strong slender fingers through his famous shoulder-length mane of chestnut curls. Big Tim found the Great Scout's grip to be as strong as his own. He admired Cody's white teeth and the barbering of his Vandyke beard.

"A signal honor, Colonel Cody. I've greeted John L. Sullivan and Chester Arthur upon this very portico, but this is its finest moment."

"You are too kind, Mr. Magoon. Your generosity lives up to its reputation." Cody's theater-trained baritone rang in the evening air.

"Your home is magnificent," said Salsbury, shaking Big Tim's hand.

"The voters of Paris City have been gracious." He waved his visitors inside.

After an excellent dinner of roast crackling duck, prepared by Big Tim's excellent cook, Greta, and served by Reginald, former valet to a prince of India, the three men retired to the study and sipped cognac while Colonel Cody regaled his listeners with the details of his historic fight with Yellow Hand, chief of the Cheyenne Nation. Cody had told the story many times, and now embellished it by standing and acting out both roles, finishing with a final bowie thrust that stained the hearth rug liberally with twenty-year-old Napoleon. After Reginald carried away the rug for cleaning, Big Tim with a solemn flourish thrust out a check in the amount of $1,500 before Cody, who held up a palm and tipped it toward Salsbury. That gentleman accepted the check graciously and placed it in an inside pocket without looking at the amount.

The hour was late. When Salsbury put away his watch and announced that he and his companion had just time to catch the last train to Big Neck, Big Tim insisted upon placing the presidential suite at the Koh-i-Noor Hotel at their disposal. When Salsbury demurred, the mayor tut-tutted him into silence and added that they must charge all their expenses to the hotel. He did not add that the Koh-i-Noor was another Magoon enterprise, not so registered in the county ledgers.

Cody shook his hand with enthusiasm, declaring that Big Tim must agree to ride in the famed Deadwood Stage when it was attacked by Indians employed by the Wild West. "His Highness, the Prince of Wales, was so pleased as to request a second turn," he explained.

For a time after his visitors left in Big Tim's phaeton, Paris City's most prominent citizen prowled the rooms of his mansion, thumbs hooked inside the armholes of his vest and practicing his pet political phrases for the speech he would give upon alighting from the Deadwood Stage in the Emerald Isle Arena. "And that for you, Oaf Krueger," he finished, transferring one thumb to the end of his nose.

. . .

The bill at the Koh-i-Noor Hotel came to a surprising five hundred dollars and change, including liquor, barbering and manicures in the shop on the ground floor, a torn dress belonging to a female guest accosted by an inebriated and impassioned Cody in an upstairs hallway, and the cigar stand's entire stock of top-quality Havanas. Big Tim pursed his lips when he saw the bill, then shrugged and decided to absorb the expense personally, without going to the Democratic Party. Two thousand dollars was more than he had ever spent upon a political campaign, with the election still six months off; but it was for the governorship, after all, with the promise of humiliating Olaf Krueger into the bargain.

He did not mention the bill the next morning, when he posed for photographs in his office, shaking hands with Salsbury and the Great Scout and passing a pen back and forth to put the official stamp on their arrangement. While the photographer busied himself exchanging glass plates, the general manager of the Wild West beckoned Big Tim into a corner.

"We have a problem," Salsbury murmured. "The Cheyennes are threatening to desert the exhibition if their living conditions don't improve. The Sioux are in sympathy. Arizona John Burke, who looks after the company while the colonel and I are away, sent this last night."

Big Tim accepted the furtively offered telegram. It confirmed the information. "What does it mean?"

"It means the Indians will refuse to perform if their demands are not met."

"Can they be replaced? The reservations are filled with idle savages."

"There isn't time to rehearse. It took us two years to train the crew we have. Ordinarily, I'd say we could get along with counterfeit braves until the situation is resolved, but I fear the result to your reputation should someone's plaited wig fall off during the attack upon the Deadwood Stage."

Big Tim felt the full horror of this description. A politician could recover from any disaster save public humiliation.

"What is the cost?" he asked.

The photographer's magnesium powder flared, capturing a solitary pose of Cody standing before a framed plat map of Paris City. Salsbury's voice dropped to a whisper. "The last time this came up, fifteen hundred was the estimate, to feed and shelter squaws and children. We put them off then, but Indians have long memories."

"Fifteen hundred! Mother of God!"

"I rather think twelve would do it. I wouldn't try cutting any additional corners. It would be a loan, of course," he added. "You will be repaid out of the Paris City profits."

Big Tim chewed his mustache, but once again the pair clasped hands.

IN A MAGNANIMOUS SHOW OF CIVIC SUPPORT, BIG TIM RETURNED half his salary to the city treasury, accepting in return his roof and board and such gifts of haberdashery as were offered by the merchants who supported his administration. His liquid assets were therefore limited, and he applied to Silas Gast, the loan officer at the First Pioneers Bank of Paris City, for an advance against his agreement with the Wild West. Gast applied a powerful lens to the ornate document bearing the signatures of Big Tim, Nathan Salsbury, and William Frederick Cody, muttered something about irregularities, and issued a draft in the amount of $1,200 on a promissory note charging a full percent above market interest, which Big Tim signed with a full percent above his usual flourish.

He had hesitated before doing so, but by the time he endorsed and handed the draft to Salsbury at the railroad station, he had already begun to calculate the gain to his campaign chest from so sound an investment. He waved at the departing cars with the energy he normally reserved for Independence Day, and as he left he flamboyantly clanked a silver dollar into the tin cup of the legless veteran of Chancellorsville who worked the platform.

LATER THAT AFTERNOON IN BIG NECK, TWO MEN PACKED THEIR clothes in the room they shared at the Railway Arms. Among the items that went into the seriously dilapidated trunk were the fabulous doeskin jacket and whiter-than-white Stetson. The man who had worn these things then removed his shoulder-length wig and folded it carefully into its compartment.

"We ought to invest some of the fat baboon's money in some new grips," he announced. "It's a sin to store good props in this old horror."

His companion peeled off his beard. His chin looked considerably weaker without the adornment. "In Craterville, maybe. We might even get Krueger to stand the cost."

"Do you think Craterville's a good idea? Magoon won't waste any time noising this about."

"All the more reason to catch the next train."

The other admired his Vandyke in the mirror above the washbasin. This beard was genuine, although the chestnut color was not. He was still known as Baltimore Blackie in certain Eastern towns he considered it unwise to revisit.

"I could get used to this Great Scout business," he said. "Did you see how that pretty teller looked at me when we cashed the check? She didn't even glance at the identification. That was a waste of money."

"Better to have it and not need it than to need it and not have it. You can't always count on getting a woman."

"Buffalo Bill could."

Baltimore Blackie's friend changed out of Nate Salsbury's quiet gray coat into his own loud check. He smiled. "Don't settle in. Remember, we agreed I get to be Buffalo Bill next time."

The True Facts About the Death of Wes Hardin

JOHN SELMAN
EDITED BY BILL CRIDER

Arkansan John Selman (1839–1896) had one of the most versatile careers of all Old West gunmen. After moving to Texas as a youngster, he deserted twice from Confederate forces, became a vigilante, expert bushwhacker, gang leader, cattle rustler, and killer. He enjoyed notoriety as John Wesley Hardin's assassin for less than eight months.

George A. Scarborough (1859–1900) was a sheriff in Jones County, Texas, before becoming a deputy U.S. Marshal in El Paso. He died following a shootout with rustlers in the Chiricahua Mountains of Arizona.

When he was fifteen, John Wesley Hardin (1853–1895), son of a Methodist preacher, killed a black man; by the time of his own death by gunfire, he may have killed forty others (he listed a modest twenty-seven in his autobiography).

Bill Crider writes mystery, private eye, horror, suspense, and Western novels, books for young readers, and a lot of short fiction. He is author of the Sheriff Dan Rhodes series (latest of which is *A Ghost of a Chance*), the Truman Smith series (*Gator Kill, Murder Takes a Break*), and other series novels. His Westerns include *Texas Vigilante, Outrage at Blanco, Medicine Show,* and others. Another of WWA's Ph.D.s, Crider chairs a department at the Alvin, Texas, Community College.

I BOUGHT THE FOLLOWING manuscript from a dealer in an on-line auction. When I asked about the document's authenticity, she told me that she had purchased it at an estate sale in a lot that contained, in addition to the manuscript, a doorstop, ten old books, a battered Zippo lighter, and a couple of rusty horseshoes. She wanted only the doorstop, and she hoped I'd bid on the other items, which she was also offering for sale at auction. I declined.

The manuscript itself appears to be quite old. The paper is yellowed, and the pages heavily creased and stained with water. Or liquor, tears, or sweat. The staining, along with the execrable handwriting and worse spelling, has rendered the text even harder to read than it would normally be, and sometimes it has blurred the ink so much that words are virtually indecipherable. I have corrected the spelling and attempted to translate the blurred words into something readable. In cases where I could not, I have so indicated in the text. As for authenticity, readers must judge for themselves.

Bill Crider
Alvin, Texas

I, John Selman, sometimes called Old John Selman because my [indeciperable] son is fixed up with the same first name, being of sound mind, though pretty much shot all to hell, do hereby set down this account of a few things I figure ought to be put straight in case I cross over to the other side sometime soon, which is mighty damn likely considering the number of bullets in me. The doc says there is one of the bullets lodged against my spine, which explains why I can not feel a damn thing down there, much less move my legs, and he is going to dig it out first thing tomorrow, and then I will be just fine. Either that, or he will kill me, which if I was a betting man, and I am, I would pick for the actual outcome, much as I hate to say it. You start digging around on a man's spine, and there is not much room for a slip of the hand, and the doc has not been real steady since he took to drinking. Which given the way he looks was about fifty years ago, if I am any judge, and I guess I am.

The things I want to set straight are how I got myself all shot to shit today, and what really happened the day I killed Wes Hardin. There has been plenty of false tales spread around about that last one, like the story saying I shot Wes in the back, which is a bald-faced [indecipherable] lie, and the trial they put me through came out with a hung jury because nobody could prove it was anything except self-defense, which it was, as you will see.

It all got started when Martin Morose, as bad an apple as ever spoiled a barrel, rounded up a few cattle that did not happen to be his over in New Mexico, sold them, and kept the money for himself. The folks that claimed to be the real owners did not take kindly to that kind of business dealings, as Morose should have known when he rustled the cows in the first place, and the owners were planning to have a little necktie party for him. He said he didn't look good in a necktie and took off across the border, where he hid out in Juarez, waiting for things to blow over, and his mistake was to leave his wife behind in El Paso. Her name was Beulah, and she took up with Wes because she hired him as her lawyer, which is the trade he had learned while serving his time in the state's prison for one of his many kill-ings.

After a while, though, Wes and Beulah started having the kind of relationship that some people accuse most lawyers of having with all their clients. That is, to put it in plain talk, he was screwing her pretty regular. I could never figure out just why since she had a plain rough face like a potato only with less eyes. She was a fightatious woman, too, who liked her drink and was always causing trouble just about anywhere she went. And besides that, she was so big that when she tried to get herself fixed up, she looked like a bale of cotton dressed up to go to church.

No matter how she looked, though, Wes liked her a lot, and so did her husband, so she must have had some kind of skills that were not real clear from just looking at her. There are women like that, all right, and I have met a few of them, but they would not be any good to me right now, what with me not having any feeling below the belt and being afraid to move around too much or do much jiggling, what with that bullet just about touching my spine.

Anyway, whatever skills she had in the jiggling line, her husband liked her plenty, too, or maybe he was just worried that she was spending all the money he got from those rustled cattle, but for some reason he decided he was coming back across the border to kill Wes. It must have occurred to him that he would be arrested and hung if he did, though, so what he did instead was send word that if Wes ever came to Juarez, he was a dead man.

That kind of thing would not bother Wes, you might think, him being a well-known shootist and all, with thirty notches on the butt of his pistol so they say, but it did. Which is why he came to me to ask me to kill Martin Morose for him.

I did not want anything to do with it, so I told him, "Wes, you know I can not do that. I am a lawman, and my job is to uphold the law, not go around killing people just because somebody wants me to."

Wes had a bushy mustache that he was mighty proud of, and he stroked it now and then. He said, "You talk mighty big for a man who has been known to rustle cattle for a living."

"I never did that," I told him. "And you know it. The jury let me off because there was no evidence of any such thing. I am an upstanding citizen who used to sell John Deere farm equipment for a living, not rustle cattle. Now I am a constable, a keeper of the peace, and you should not talk to me any such way."

"I will talk any way I please," Wes said. "If you are a lawman, you should be able to take care of Morose without any trouble at all, it being your duty more or less, whereas I could get sent back to the pen, which I don't want to do. And this is a way you could make a little money on the side."

"I would not ever think of taking any money on the side," I told him, "for I am as honest as the day is long. So you will have to find somebody else to do that job if you can not do it for yourself."

And that was what he did, hiring another lawman named George Scarborough to do the work. That was where George came into things, and it was too bad that he did, but I did not know that at the time.

Scarborough did not do it himself, of course, him not being much on tackling a man like Morose, or anybody else for that matter.

What he did was to get Morose to walk into an ambush where he was shot down and killed by a couple of other fellas. I do not know how my name kept coming into the story later on, since I turned Wes down flat and was never even brought to trial the way George was, but that is the way people are. They got to have something to talk about, I guess, and I am glad I got the record set straight by writing it down here. This being something in the way of a dying man's declaration, assuming I am dying, which I do, I know it will be believed by any that happen to read it, but that is not the main thing I needed to tell about.

If it was not for my [indecipherable] son, I might not ever have got in trouble with Wes, seeing as how he did not care much that I never killed Morose since somebody else did it anyway. He would have left me alone after that if my son had not arrested Beulah Morose for being drunk and disorderly, which she was, running all around town waving a pistol and threatening to kill any man that messed with her. That did not bother John none at all, him taking after his daddy and not being afraid of anybody, much less a woman, even if she was about the size of a grizzly bear and packing a pistol. So he arrested her, and that did not set well with Wes, who went and called John any number of things, some of them not reflecting well on his ancestry, or mine, for that matter.

Wes did not go for his gun, though, so John did not either, taking after his daddy again and not being the type to pull first. All Wes did was cuss him out good, and then come looking for me, figuring that cussing the son was not enough so he might as well cuss the daddy too.

It was one of those hot August days like we get in El Paso when you can not even find a tumblebug in the horse droppings because they are all under a porch or a well housing in whatever shade they can find for themselves, not that it is all that much cooler there. Wes found me out on the street, doing my job, which should not have come as any surprise to him since I always do my job no matter what the weather.

He walked right up to me. "You are a son of a bitch," was the first words out of his mouth, which is not the best way to start a calm discussion to my way of thinking.

So I said, "You are another one, and if you do not step aside, I will have to run you in for disturbing the peace and hindering an officer in the performance of his rightful duties."

"Your son has already run somebody in, and that is the trouble," Wes said. "He has arrested Beulah Morose, who never done a thing and would not harm a hair on a man's head even if she said she would."

Now that was a lie, as anybody listening would know, and there was plenty of them listening, Wes being a loud kind of a fella when he got all wound up like he was then. Beulah would go out of her way to step on a spider or kick a dog, and there are some who said she whopped Martin a time or two besides. But there was no point in telling that to Wes, who knew it as well as anybody if he had thought about it.

So I just said, "Wes, you were [indecipherable] another man's wife, you paid to have the man killed, and now you are saying that my son ought not to have arrested the woman in back of all that trouble. If you ask me, you have brought it on yourself, and I am telling you again to step aside or pay the consequences."

Just about everybody who was listening in had run for cover by that time, as I know they expected the bullets to start flying any second, and so did I, but Wes fooled me. He said, "John Selman, you are a crippled old liar, and the truth is not in you. You will rue this day as long as you live."

And then he stepped around me and went on his way. I knew he meant what he said, though, for despite him being the son of a preacher and being named after a famous one, that idea about forgiving and forgetting had never taken a hold in his head the way it ought to have. Besides that, he was wrong in calling me a liar, as everybody knows that I am a truthful man, and always have been. Lying might come easy to some, but not to me, for I have ever been a truthful man. I am also not a cripple, though I do use a cane, having been shot twice in the leg by Bass Outlaw who was drunk and disorderly and had killed another man just before shooting me. I shot Bass, but not in the leg, and he will not be shooting anybody else unless they issue sidearms in hell.

Unlike Wes, I am a man who knows how to forgive and forget, and I had pretty much forgotten what he had called me when I went to the Acme Saloon later that same evening. Wes was there already, and not being the forgetting kind, he started right in on me.

"You have a hell of a lot of nerve to come in here while I am drinking," he said, smoothing that mustache of his. "That tapping of your cane on the floor bothers me, and I am going to have to do something about you, I guess."

"You can try," I told him. "But I do not think you will come out the top dog."

You could hear chairs scraping the floor all over the saloon then, as people started to find themselves whatever cover they could, as they were sure that the bullets were about to fly. Poor old Henry Brown, who was a fat grocer and probably didn't even own a pistol, was standing at the bar with Wes, and his knees were shaking so hard that you could have tied him to a churn and made butter.

"I do not want anyone in here to be hurt," Wes said, which was probably a big relief to all of them. "If you will go out into the street, I will meet you there, but I am telling you that when I come, I will come with my pistol smoking."

I was not one to be scared by that kind of talk, which he should have known, so I told him that I would be glad to meet him in the street, but he should give me a few minutes to get it cleared.

"I will do that," he said, reaching for the dice cup that sat on the bar.

I went out into the street, where it was getting a little cooler as evening came on and the shadows spread out. There was a couple of dogs sleeping close by, and I sent them on their way, along with a few men who were thinking of going into the saloon. They spread the word about what was going to happen, and the street pretty well cleared off. I was standing easy and ready for Wes to come out smoking, as he put it, but he did nothing of the kind.

After about fifteen minutes I figured that he was playing me for a fool, which is one thing I will not stand for, so I went back inside the Acme Saloon, where Wes was standing at the bar. He had just rolled for the drinks with Brown, and he called out, "Four sixes is what you have to beat, Henry."

Then he heard my cane on the wooden floor and saw me in the mirror behind the bar, and he knew what was on my mind, all right, for he turned around quick as a rattlesnake, his hand going for the gun that he wore in a shoulder holster.

Now I never pulled first on a man in my life, but if a fella draws on me then I am ready to trade lead with him, as I have never backed down from a fight in my life.

The truth of the matter is that Wes was by no means as quick as he once was, not to mention that he was a little slowed down by having had more than a few drinks with Henry Brown, besides which the pistol grip caught on the lapel of his coat, and all of that resulted in me having my gun out and ready before Wes could get his pulled.

I never said I would not shoot first if the chance presented itself, which it did in this case. My bullet hit Wes in the side of the head, and that must have hurt him plenty, but he was game and kept trying to claw out that pistol even while he was sinking to the floor, so I was forced to shoot him again. I hit him in the arm, and he forgot all about that gun in the shoulder holster, but that was only a part of his arsenal.

He was carrying pistols in both his back pockets, and he tried to drag out one of those, looking at me all the time with his hot black eyes, though by now he had sunk to his knees. He started to say something, probably to call me a liar or a cripple or a son of a bitch again, but whatever it was, he couldn't get it out. He fell over on his face, and I went over to finish him off. I have known too many good men who have got themselves killed by a man who by all rights should have been dead, and I like to make sure of things. I shoved his pistol aside with my cane and it bounced off the bar before I put another bullet in the back of his head, which is the one that some professional prevaricators have said was where I shot him first. But that is not the truth as you can tell from having read this account, which has got all the facts lined up right, as told by the one man who was there for every second of it and who is writing this on what is most likely his deathbed and not about to tell a lie, considering that he might be meeting his Maker fairly soon.

Now that the shooting of Wes Hardin is all laid out plain and truthful for all to see, there is only one thing remaining for me to tell, and that is how I find myself in this pitiful condition, shot all to [indecipherable] with a bullet lodged right up against my spine. Since this is Easter Sunday, you might say a little resurrection would be mighty appreciated should I go on across the river, but in my case I believe it would be too much to expect. The whole scrape might be comical if it was somebody else who was in this kind of shape, but since it is me, I do not seem to be able to laugh much about it.

I doubt that George Scarborough will be doing much laughing, either, because he is the one who will take the blame for shooting me if I do not tell anyone different. If I live, I will set things straight for George, and if I die, this document, which is my true sworn word, will do the same.

I was in another saloon today, not that it is my habit to go into saloons, especially on a Sunday, but I was there because of my work, and George Scarborough came in. He was nervous and his face was red as a turkey's snout, so I thought he must have been drunk, but that was not the case. He came up to me and said, "John, I hear you have been spreading lies about how I took money off Martin Morose after he was shot and that I split the take with Wes Hardin."

I moved out from the bar, for I like to be ready if a man tries something on me, and said, "That is a lie, George. I have never said any such of a thing, and you should know it."

"Well," he said, "that is what I heard, and I think we should get it settled right now."

People started to scatter then, just the way they had when Wes Hardin and I had words, so I told George, "If that is the way you feel, we can get it done. But we should go outside so as not to hurt anybody but ourselves."

"That suits me," George said. "You can go first."

I did not think I wanted to turn my back on George, so I offered him the honor.

"We will have to go out together," he said. "For I do not want to be shot in the back like Wes Hardin."

That got my dander raised, and I said, "Wes Hardin was shot in the face, and you will get the same."

"We will see about that," George said. "Now are we going out, or are we going to stand here jawing?"

We walked out side by side, me leaning a little on my cane for support, which was not because I had drunk too much but because the leg with Bass Outlaw's bullets in it was paining me a little. It is not paining me now, however. It has been cured by gunshot.

The street was not crowded, but George said, "I think we should go into the alley so as not to kill anybody but ourselves."

I had not ever known George to be so concerned with the public safety before, but there is always a first time, so I went into the alley with him, ready to pull my gun at the first sign he was going to shoot.

But I never got a chance because somebody stepped out of an open door behind us. I turned my head and saw Beulah Morose standing there, and she lifted George's pistol from his holster and fired four shots before I could do an [indecipherable] thing. I fell to the dirt, and I knew that I was hit, for there had been a sudden sharp pain, but now there was nothing at all, at least not down below the belt where the blood was leaking out of me.

"Goddamn," George said. "You have shot him all to Hell, but he is still alive."

I looked up and saw what seemed like a bale of cotton on legs looming above me, and Beulah Morose said, "It is just as well, for he is the wrong man. I meant for you to get that [indecipherable] son of his back here. He is the one who started all the trouble, and he is the one I wanted to teach a lesson to, not this one. You are as worthless a man as ever I met, George Scarborough."

With that she thrust George's pistol back into his holster and stepped back through the door. I heard it slam, and about that time there were people all around us, most of them talking loud and asking George if he had killed me.

"Boys, you know I am not afraid of John Selman or any man, but I swear to you I never pulled my gun."

Nobody believed either of those statements, and they had good reason not to since George's reputation was known to all, and his gun had been fired four times. George, being a kind of a gentleman in his own way, couldn't see blaming what had happened on a woman, I guess, or maybe he was ashamed that he had let a woman do his work for him. At any rate, he did not admit to what happened. Maybe he will do it later, but I doubt that anyone will take his word for it.

I did not feel like speaking up for him myself because I thought at the time that he was a scoundrel who deserved whatever he got. Now that I have thought it over, I have decided to redeem him, it being Easter, after all, so I have written this true account for all to read.

But on second thought, I do not really care what happens to George, and it would be an embarrassment to me if people learned I had been shot in the back by a woman, at least if I lived to face it. If I am not alive, it will not matter much, so I will stick this account, the true sworn word of a dying man, under the mattress I am lying on. If I live through getting that bullet off my spine, I can one day walk back here and get these papers, whereas if I go to meet my Maker, or, more likely, in the other direction, somebody will find them someday and George will no longer be thought ill of. I do not hold it against Beulah for shooting me, though she meant to do it to my [indecipherable] son, who I hope will bring his old daddy a drink sometime soon now because by God I could surely use one. Written and signed by his own hand: John Selman, Constable

El Paso, Texas
April 5, 1896

John Selman died on April 6 when the doctor attempted to remove the bullet that rested on his spine. Whether he went to meet his Maker or in the other direction I won't venture to say. I hope he got that drink, though. — Editor

The Darkness of the Deep

ROD MILLER

Underground mining was big business in the Old West beginning at mid-century when California argonauts dug "coyote holes" with pick and shovel to find new gold deposits and Nevada miners stumbled upon the fabulous Comstock silver lode.

Here, on the eve of the Great War in Europe, at a time when Utah miners were turning mountains inside out and creating the largest open-pit copper mine in the world, one renegade miner holds a town hostage, and the mine that created the town.

The story is factual.

In a poem on López, Miller writes:

> *A life, in the end, a total loss,*
> *his epitaph:*
> *Rafael López: Dross*

In his college days, Rod Miller of Sandy, Utah, spent his summers working in an underground hard-rock lead and galena mine to finance his tuition. "That gave me an interest in and appreciation for mining," he says, "and perhaps some understanding of what López and the men searching for him may have experienced. It's damn dark down there when the lights go out."

Miller's poetry appears regularly in such magazines as *American Cowboy, Range,* and *Western Horseman,* his short fiction in several anthologies.

I FEAR DARKNESS. AT TIMES IT wrings sweat and squeezes the breath out of me as I lie abed wishing for the illumination of dreams. It has not always been so. I can trace the origin of my fright to a precise time and place: twenty-three years, seven months, thirteen days ago; the Alta Incline in the Minnie Mine. I shall relate how I came to be at that place at that time.

The year was 1913. The "Wild West" was but a faded memory in most locales, but the narrow defile of Bingham Canyon was as raucous and rowdy as ever was any town at the end of the trail or the end of the rails. As you might have surmised, Bingham Canyon was mining country, a mountain filled with treasure but trapped in ore so low in grade that only large mining syndicates could afford the machinery and manpower required to extract paying quantities of metal. The mines needed men, so the town was awash in men. A regular stewpot, it was — Cousin Jacks, Chinks, Micks, Bohunks, Canucks, Greasers, Scandahoovians — every kind of man you can think of. Too many men, and too few women. Therein lies the beginning of this tale.

Rafael López, they say, was at the end of his one day off in the week. A day spent swilling what passed for liquor in the town's saloons. He stumbled and staggered through stupor and snowstorm uphill to the shack where his "sweetheart" lived and met a friend making his exit through the door López planned to enter. They argued. They fought. López pulled a pistol from his pocket and shot the man dead.

Now comes Police Chief J. W. Grant. Dub he was called. By the time he arrived at the crime scene, López was long gone. But there was no shortage of witnesses to the fact that the killer, sobered by his deed, had gone to his own quarters, loaded up with firearms and ammunition, and hightailed it out of town afoot.

Standing in fresh-fallen snow at the edge of town, Dub shivered as he eyed the trail.

"Well. He ain't likely to get too far too fast," he said. "I suppose mornin's soon enough to start after him. Sorenson!"

"Yeah, Dub," answered Jules Sorenson, deputy sheriff assigned by the county to the canyon.

"Gather up Otto Witbeck and Nels Jensen and meet me here at first light."

Dub and the deputies followed the clear trail across the divide into Utah Valley, surprised as the sun climbed higher how much of the country López had covered. Crowding the western shore of Utah Lake, the Mexican led them all the way south into Goshen Valley. After spotting from his saddle some fresh footprints, Dub, keeping Sorenson at his side, sent two of the deputies on a small circle to attempt to corner the fugitive. He warned all to stay alert.

Too late. Rifle shots rang out from the willows.

"Dub, I'm a dead man!" Sorenson said. He looked surprised as he slid from the saddle.

The other riders, still but a short distance away, spurred up to ride to the defense of the police chief, whose horse was pitching and milling in the hail of bullets. Otto took a bullet just under the hat brim and rolled backward off his mount. Another shot hit Nels in the shirt pocket. With half his force shot out of the saddle and half of what was left mortally wounded, Dub controlled his horse, grasped the reins of the horse Nels was clinging to, and fled the field with appropriate haste.

Now begins my part in the hunt for Rafael López.

By the following morning, Dub had gathered a considerably larger posse for the pursuit. I was a member, one of twenty or so down from Bingham Canyon. While sincere in my intention to aid in the capture of the desperado, I confess a secondary ambition—to capture the excitement of the event for the readers of the *Canyon Chronicle,* for which I was employed as a reporter and typesetter. In spite of the mostly indoor nature of my vocation, I was not unfamiliar with the outdoor life, the squeak of saddle leather, or the use of arms. As the fourth son of the third wife of a polygamous Mormon father, my prospects of maintaining a livelihood in my family's livestock operations were nil. Being bookish by nature, I opted for a college education and the literary life. The education, at least, had panned out. Authorial success beyond the newspaper page was yet some distance into the future.

But I digress. Our posse was joined that morning by another dozen men from the nearby burg of Lehi, with small groups from elsewhere swelling our ranks as the day passed. We found nothing of López, despite scouring the shores of the lake in ever-growing circles radiating from the scene of the fugitive's ambush of Dub and the deputies. The snow had somewhat melted away and drifted so no trail was apparent. An uneventful day, all told. The next day started the same, save that there were now in excess of a hundred men in our camp, the perceived excitement of the chase having spread from village to town.

"Men, this Raphael López we're after is a bad hombre," Dub announced to the assembled mass. "He knows how to shoot and he's not afeared to pull the trigger. Most of you know by now that he's killed three good lawmen and a no-account Mick miner already. So be sharp. Don't do nothin' stupid. We don't need no dead heroes."

We rode out in contingents of twenty riders, directed by Dub to various parts of the lakeside mountains as if on a gather. Late in the afternoon, shooting broke out somewhere north of our location. We hastened over the intervening ridges until reaching the dry canyon whence the shooting originated.

López had ensconced himself in a jumble of boulders at the top of a steep draw that offered no access from any direction save below, due to surrounding cliffs and shale-covered slopes. From his eagle's nest, he could hold off an army, which is exactly what he was doing when we arrived. After the initial flurry, the noise of which had attracted virtually the entire posse to the area, those in pursuit realized they could not get a clear shot at the pursued, who, with a few well-placed shots, kept us at bay until nightfall.

Morning brought renewed attempts on our part to infiltrate the Mexican's lair. It soon was apparent that the site was undefended, our quarry having disappeared into thin air. Shell casings revealed that López had expended all available ammunition for his discarded rifle, and his use of pistols the evening before had been of necessity rather than choice. Finding no clue as to his current whereabouts despite hours of casting about for a sign, the posse disbanded. Those of us from Bingham Canyon turned our mounts north.

"Dub, where do you suppose he's gone to?" one of our party asked the police chief.

"Well, I reckon he's on the way to California. There's a whole lot of nothin' between here and there but if anyone can make it, and plenty have, that pepper belly can sure do it."

"So you're not going after him?"

"Nope. Not unless someone reports seein' him somewheres. Like I said, there's a whole lot of nothin' out there."

"But Dub," I chimed in, "what can I tell readers of the *Chronicle* about the disposition of the case?"

"Hell, I don't know. You're the newspaperman, not me. But I guess you can say we got rid of López. Maybe it's not all neat and tidy like a trial and a hangin' but he's gone all the same."

Life in the canyon had settled back into its routine of changing shifts, clanging hoist bells, the felt but not heard thump of blasting deep underground, and the ring of ore car wheels rolling on steel tracks when word reached the police that Rafael López was back in town.

"Bullshit!" Dub sprayed into the pale face of the store clerk standing before him. "You're nuts!"

"N-n-no sir," the clerk managed to force through rattling jaws. "It was h-him. He's carried an account at the company store since I been there. I've waited on L-López a dozen times at least."

"Well, what the hell did he want this time?"

"B-b-bullets. He wanted bullets for a rifle and two kinds of pistols. And s-some food. You know, canned stuff. Stuff that would keep."

"And you gave it to him?" Dub asked.

"No, sir. I didn't give it to him. I sold it to him on account. Like I s-said, he's on the books."

"Damn. A cold-blooded killer and known fugitive waltzes into the store pretty as you please for supplies and gets them, just like that. Lemme guess what happens next—he invited you up to his shack for supper in appreciation of your cooperation."

"No, D-Dub—Ch-chief—sir. He didn't. He didn't go home. He went into the Minnie," the clerk said.

An interesting turn of events, I thought. I overheard the greater part of the conversation after beating a quick trail to the police station upon getting the news from a street urchin we pay to keep us informed of events.

So here we have Rafael López on the lam in a vast network of drifts, stopes, shafts, winzes, and inclines deep in the dark bowels of the earth. Knowing the Minnie mine well from his employ there, he would likely be able to elude capture for quite some time—or at least as long as provisions allowed. Dub, seeing no other course, opted to wait him out. Guards were posted at every point of egress from the Minnie, with simple instructions to be especially vigilant during shift changes, and to arrest López when he surfaced to replenish his supplies.

But he never resurfaced. Plenty of miners reported encountering him in the depths of the mine. Some claimed he robbed them of lunch buckets at gunpoint. Others reported food and water pilfered from places they had stowed it while working. As time passed, Dub was convinced the Mexican had accomplices—willingly or under threat—carrying supplies into the mine.

Finally giving up on his ineffectual siege strategy, Dub decided to smoke out the fugitive. Literally. He as much as ordered the mining syndicate to shut down operations for a shift at tremendous expense. Engineers closed off certain ventilation shafts to control airflow through the mine and Dub had huge bonfires built at all the intake vents. Additional guards were posted at every point of escape from the mine. Then piles of wet straw, moldy hay, and green juniper boughs were heaped on the fires. Clouds of greasy, acrid smoke poured into the mine and eventually found the outlets. Dub ordered the crews to keep the fires smoking and the sentries to keep a sharp eye. But, in the end, smoke was the only thing that came out of the mine.

"Well, hell. There's no way he's still in there," Dub opined. "If he ever was."

"But there have been eyewitness reports. Besides," I asked, "if López isn't in the Minnie where is he?"

"You ever been in a mine, copy cub?"

"No. I've never had occasion."

"Well, let me tell you somethin'. It's dark down there. Real dark. So dark it can make you see things that ain't there. And you hear things. Hell, I don't have any idea what them witnesses thought they saw."

"But what about the stolen dinner buckets?"

"That's easy enough explained. Come the day after payday, a lot of them miners down that hole ain't got two nickels to rub together. I don't suppose chowin' down on somebody else's lunch would weigh too heavy on their minds. As for your other question, I can't even guess where López is—but I don't intend to lay awake nights worryin' about it. There's plenty enough misbehavior out in plain sight in this canyon to keep me busy."

So, once again, the routine of changing shifts, clanging hoist bells, the thump of blasting deep underground, and the ring of ore car wheels on steel rails held sway. But not for long. One day a visibly shaken miner rushed into the police station. By happenstance, I was there checking arrest records for anything that might prove newsworthy.

"I have a message for the police chief," the miner said.

"And who might you be?" Dub said.

"My name is Gustav Mueller. They call me Dutchy. I am a timberman at the Minnie."

Dub perked up at the mention of the mine. "What's the message and who's it from?"

"The man, he said his name is Rafael López. He said to ask about the deputy he met by the lakeshore—if the deputy has a bad headache."

Dub mulled that one over, realizing that while it was no secret that Otto Witbeck had been shot and killed, not many knew or cared that his death resulted from a bullet placed dead center in his forehead. The chief's interest heightened.

"What else?"

"This López, he seems very angry. He said he wishes to meet Dub Grant at the Alta Incline in the Minnie between shifts tonight. He said he will kill Dub Grant."

"He says that, does he," Dub said. "Well, here's what we'll do, Mr. Dutchy. You're goin' to keep my appointment with Rafael López."

"Oh no, sir! I do not care to see this man ever again."

"But you'll do it, Dutchy, or you'll find yourself behind bars for aidin' and abettin' a fugitive or whatever other reasons I can come up with to put you there. And by the time I decide to let you out on account of the whole thing being a big mistake, your sorry life will have passed you by. Now pay attention, and tell López this—tell him that that headache ain't botherin' that deputy no more, but that it's still likely to cause him—López—plenty of pain and sufferin'."

The reluctant miner attempted to deliver the message, he claimed, but the Mexican failed to show at the appointed time and place. Despite the futility of the previous attempt to smoke the renegade out, Dub considered another try to be a smarter approach than sending men into the Minnie to poke their noses into all the dark corners to see if López would shoot them off. So the miners showing up for morning shift were sent home and the fires were kindled again. Again, the result was a disappointment. As the final wisps of smoke vacated the mine, Dub decided to comb the Minnie despite the difficulty and danger.

Dub lined up a reluctant posse, recruiting as many miners familiar with the Minnie as possible to serve either as guides or deputies or both. At each of the mine's several levels, teams trooped outward from the shafts, breaking into ever smaller groups, following branching drifts toward working faces and raises that led to overhead stopes. I obtained permission to accompany Dub. Guided by Dutchy, we hiked directly to the place of the miner's reported encounter with López.

The Alta Incline is, in the jargon of the mining trade, a winze—a tunnel that angles upward from the 825-foot level to the 700 level. Dutchy led our parade upward by the light of a miner's torch he carried; our only light, as Dub and I had our hands full of armament. We had proceeded maybe a third of the way up the incline when a rifle roared, effectively deafening us with its initial report as well as its echoes in that confined space. Dutchy pitched face downward and the lantern shattered, plunging us into instant and complete darkness save for the bright spots burned behind my eyes by the muzzle flash.

I could see nothing. I could barely sense my own presence in the pitch-black let alone that of Dub, Dutchy, or our attacker. And while the feeling of isolation was frightening, the fact that I knew I was not alone was even more disconcerting. I did not know what had become of Dub. Perhaps the shot that downed Dutchy had taken the police chief out of action as well. I dared not speak, fearing my voice would betray my location and provide an effective, if unseen, target for the assassin. So I waited.

The blackness was so overwhelming that my very senses failed. Although I hugged a rock wall, I had no sensation of being upright. For all I knew, I might have been lying down or even upside down. I know not how long I sat in fear and silence. It seemed an eternity, but might have been mere moments—my ability to sense the passage of time no longer functional. There were sounds. Small sounds, strange and unfamiliar; their source or location indecipherable. And the occasional rattle of pebbles falling, or rolling.

"You there, scribbler?"

Had I known up from down I would have jumped a foot in the air. The voice of Dub Grant boomed out of the silence, although he spoke barely above a whisper.

"I am here. Are you wounded?"

"Nah, I'm fine. You?"

"I have not been shot. But I am not fine."

"I know what you mean," Dub said. "This is a strange fix I find myself in."

"At least you can find yourself. I am not even sure I am me."

Dub did not respond. The darkness that had seemed to lift with our conversation once again weighed on me.

"Dub?"

"Yeah?"

"Do you think he's still here? López?"

"Can't say for sure, but I don't think so," he said. "I've been listenin' and I can only hear the two of us breathin'."

"I guess that means Dutchy is dead."

"I fear so. The last thing I saw was the back of his head turnin' inside out."

Having no response, I allowed silence to descend. I heard nothing except my own breathing, unable even to detect the sound of Dub's, though he could mine, he had claimed. After an interval that seemed interminable came the sound of pebbles dribbling down.

"What does that noise mean, Dub?" I asked.

"Beats the hell out of me. Rats, maybe. Might just be the ground